The Curse of the Cole Women

Also available by Marielle Thompson

The Last Witch in Edinburgh

Where Ivy Dares to Grow

The Curse of the Cole Women

☾ *A Novel* ☽

Marielle Thompson

Books should be disposed of and recycled according to local requirements. All paper materials used are FSC compliant.

This is a work of fiction. All of the names, characters, organizations, places, and events portrayed in this novel are either products of the author's imagination or are used fictitiously. Any resemblance to real or actual events, locales, or persons, living or dead, is entirely coincidental.

Published in the United States by Alcove Press, an imprint of The Quick Brown Fox & Company LLC.

Alcove Press and its logo are trademarks of The Quick Brown Fox & Company LLC.

Library of Congress Catalog-in-Publication data available upon request.

ISBN (hardcover): 979-8-89242-379-3
ISBN (paperback): 979-8-89242-380-9
ISBN (ebook): 979-8-89242-381-6

Cover design by Michel Vrana

Printed in the United States.

www.alcovepress.com

Alcove Press
34 West 27th St., 10th Floor
New York, NY 10001

First Edition: December 2025

The authorized representative in the EU for product safety and compliance is eucomply OÜPärnu mnt 139b-14, 11317 Tallinn, Estonia, hello@eucompliancepartner.com, +33757690241

10 9 8 7 6 5 4 3 2 1

For my nana
For my grandma
For my mother,
and every piece of you I discover in myself.

Nobody hears of anybody dying of homesickness for New York, or Albany, or Maine, or California, or any place on the broad continent; but to the wild and lonely spots like these isles humanity clings with an intense and abiding affection. No other place is able to furnish the inhabitants of the Shoals with sufficient air for their capricious lungs; there is never scope enough elsewhere, there is no horizon; they must have sea-room.

—Celia Thaxter, *Among the Isles of Shoals*

Prologue

October 24, 1680

Hampton, New Hampshire

Goody Cole had hardly been dead an hour before they drove a stake through her heart.

That's what was done to witches, after all. A stake through the heart of a corpse was the only way to keep the old woman—"*the witch, the witch*"—from rising from the dead and seeking vengeance against the townspeople. They might not have killed her—age took care of that for them—but Goody Cole certainly had reason to seek revenge.

Three times they had sent her in and out of prison. She was too outspoken. She wanted to own the land in her dead husband's name. She was angry. She was independent. She stood up to the man next door who abused her—and who else could have cursed his cattle but a too-loud woman? She tried to lure a young girl from town to her farm, of course to steal her beauty, for that is what old hags do, is it not?

Everything that Goody Cole was was too much. Was proof of witching ways. Perhaps, to her, it was defiant enough to die of old age in her own home, rather than being burned at the stake or hung from the gallows, much as the distrusting people of Hampton might have tried. But they feared that she would want more, even in death. Too-loud women always want more. Best to stop that in its tracks. Best to drive a stake through their unbeating hearts.

History often forgets the lonely women from the lonely towns.

For centuries, no one knew what happened to Goody Cole and that stake in her heart. She became the witch of folklore, haunting the seacoast. Some said the townsfolk buried her in an unmarked grave on the far side of town, forgotten, a school eventually built over her. Some said she was thrown in a ditch by what would come to be the highway out of town. Men wrote poems of her, immortalized her as a witch who lurked, ugly and alone, cursing her neighbors.

History often keeps secrets. But some of the people of Hampton did not.

On that October evening in 1680, Bradbury and Fuller—the same men who had testified time and again that Cole was a witch—acting on behalf of the entire town, took her corpse, stake and all, and loaded it into a small boat. They paddled hard through the angry Atlantic waves, toward the small collection of islands off their shore, straddling coasts. The truth is Fuller and Bradbury took the boat to the island right near what would be White and Seavey, not too far from Star. They pulled the tiny boat up to the shore of the island that would come to be called Juniper, which was empty and desolate but for a small hut used briefly by passing fishermen. The truth is they took Goody Cole's body to the rocky cliff's edge of Juniper Island and threw her into the ocean, watching as she sank and was swallowed into the darkness.

The truth is they so feared the woman that they punished her one last time even in death.

The ocean was the only thing angry enough to trap the corpse of an angry woman.

History remembered Goody Cole as a witch and not a woman, so it often forgot that Goody Cole was not alone. That she had a daughter and that the villagers took her too, and her newborn daughter held in her arms, onto the boat. That they thrust her into the small shack on Juniper Island and left her alone as they paddled back to the mainland. They left one dead Cole woman in the ocean and left another for dead on the shore.

And there, on the country's tiniest sliver of coast on mainland Hampton, people moved on. But not too much later, some came to live on Juniper Island. And when they came, the living Cole woman and her daughter were there waiting for them, having survived against the odds. The island provided for the woman and her child, as though it wanted to keep her. The island gave her fresh water from its depths and sustained her on the sweet-bitter juniper berries that would come to give the island its name, purple-blue bulbs thriving despite the wet, sandy soil.

The new arrivals from Hampton built the island up and created a community and did their best to survive in the presence of a witch's daughter. The mainland might have moved on, but secrets and gossip were taken as history by those on Juniper Island.

As far as they were concerned, the woman and her young daughter's very survival was a sign of witching ways inherited in their blood.

The islanders tolerated the woman, and her ancestors, and the lighthouse the Cole women built for themselves on the rocky shore come the nineteenth century—perhaps because such a beacon aided the community as a whole. Perhaps out of fear. But fear doesn't only make people stagnant; it makes them cruel.

The islanders knew of what had been done to Goody Cole and her daughter, and the tales grew as they passed from mouth to mouth. It wasn't long before every person on Juniper Island knew that the Cole women, dead and living, had not only been abandoned on the island. It was said that they were cursed, their dying ancestor's last words used to doom her lineage, witch that she was and evil as a witch ought to be.

But the truth was, Goody Cole was not the one who had created a curse of hatred and vitriol. It was Bradbury and Fuller, in their gloating anger, who spoke words on the edge of Juniper:

"May there never be more than two Cole women living, and the world will be better off."

"May every Cole woman die and rot in these seas."

Anger is its own kind of magic, and those words echoed across the white waves; the men's spittle seeped into the earth of Juniper.

And so it was.

From the very beginning, the island knew the power of angry men with a secret to keep and vengeance and fear both rotting in their hearts.

Though the people of Juniper Island misremembered the origin of the curse, they believed it true, and they taught their children and their children's children. And as the Cole women had their daughters and all of them, without fail, ended up dead in the ocean before ever becoming grandmothers themselves—well, who could deny the truth of a curse indeed?

The Cole women were cursed to perish in the sea, to be trapped there in death as Goody Cole was. But with their many eyes in the sea, they looked out for their descendants. Each time a living Cole woman lit the lighthouse beam and that light swept across the dark sea, the dead Cole women within knew that their descendant was alive, that she was well. For now. The curse, the deaths, always lingered.

But if the beam did not come, if the ghosts of those Cole women within the water were not assured of their descendants' well-being . . . it was said that they would become angry.

If Goody Cole's body was going to be abandoned to the sea, then she—and all those descendants of hers who had been cursed to die in it too—would become the sea's teeth. With every cursed Cole woman who walked to her death in the sea, the stronger their presence there became. They became the sea. And if they did not see that beam, if there was no Cole woman in the lighthouse, alive and well, then those spirits within the deep would rage. Angry waves, in the murky depths a terror so true that all living beings around the island's shore would suffer. Those dead Cole women would take a life, take lives, if they did not see proof of their own.

At least, that's what the stories said.

The Cole women were cursed, yes. But if they had to be, then they would *be* a curse too.

It is not only men's anger that is powerful.

As long as people have stepped foot on the soil of Juniper Island, they have whispered of the curse of the Cole women.

The people do not forget. The earth does not forget.

The ocean does not forget.

In 1938, the people on the mainland of Hampton, New Hampshire, officially pardoned Goody Eunice Cole against accusations of witchcraft.

The people of Juniper Island did not.

One
Simone

January 4, 1998
New York, New York

"Your mother is dead."

The hum of Eighty-First Street buzzed against the window, but Simone Cole could hardly hear it. All she could hear were those words, tinny through the receiver she held to her ear. For a long moment she couldn't say anything.

Not because she was surprised. She wasn't.

From the time Simone was old enough to turn on the beam of the lighthouse on her own, she had known to grieve her mother. She'd never loved her mother, Rebecca, and her mother had never loved her, but Simone still knew to grieve the loss of her. She knew she would spend most of her life without a mother, just as her own mother had, and her mother before her.

On the island they called it the curse of the Cole women.

Simone knew it wasn't a curse, though. That made it sound like something fantastical. And there wasn't anything fantastical about it.

Simone didn't ask how her mother died—that too she knew—but Jimmy Allan answered as if she had. "It, well, it seems she, well, she went into the ocean. One of her shoes was found lodged up in the rocks last night, and I went to check the lighthouse and she was nowhere to be found."

Simone closed her eyes, breathing deeply through her nose. She tried to steady herself, the way her therapist had taught her.

She had known it was coming and she wasn't surprised. But she *was* surprised by just how much her chest ached still.

She knew the exact shoe they must have found, the beat-up old brown Birkenstock clogs her mother always wore, no matter the weather or the chill in the lighthouse. Rebecca Cole was a creature of habit, and not even the New England weather could keep her from being herself.

"Are you okay? What's going on?" Ezra asked, suddenly appearing at Simone's side, having crossed their apartment silently. He laid a gentle hand on her lower back, his warm, dark eyes flitting from the receiver to her face like a morbid tennis match.

At the same time Jimmy's distant voice asked, "Are you there, Simone?"

She nodded distractedly to her husband, not even bothering to cover the mouthpiece as she said, deadpan, "My mother is dead."

My mother is dead. My mother is dead.

"Is no one investigating her death?" Simone asked, back into the phone. She could practically picture Jimmy wincing at the sharp edges of her tone.

There were no police on the island, but surely the feds from the mainland would come. But, of course, none of the islanders would have called them. Because they did not suspect foul play.

"Well, no," Jimmy said, frazzled. "None of us thought it necessary. It seems clear enough what happened. Considering, you know . . ."

The goddamned curse.

Every generation of Cole women had thrown themselves to the sea, to their death, allegedly following the fate of their witchy ancestor.

Simone didn't believe in witches. And she didn't believe in some bullshit curse.

She had already made enough decisions in her life to know there was not some centuries-old magic curse that determined her fate. She did.

". . . care for the lighthouse." Jimmy's voice sliced through Simone's thoughts.

"What?"

Ezra stayed close to her side, rubbing soothing circles along her back, his dark brows crumpled with concern. It was only his presence, his touch, the sound of traffic through the window and not the crash of waves, that kept her grounded.

"With your mother gone, the lighthouse belongs to you now," Jimmy answered. "It's yours."

"I don't want it," Simone responded immediately, panic slicing through the center of her chest like a line of fire. The Cole women had been on the island for a long time. Some long-ago ancestor had built the lighthouse on the rocky cliff-side coast, and ever since it had been passed down to their daughters, for daughters it always was. Daughters and dying mothers and, somehow, never a father to be found. Cole women were left and Cole women died. It was what they did.

It would not be what Simone did. "This is me officially gifting it to the town. It's yours. *I don't want it.*"

Jimmy sputtered down the line. Most of the people on the island were, in Simone's opinion, superstitious, close-minded assholes. As far as she was concerned, they could keep their curse and their lighthouse. She wanted none of it. All things considered, though, Jimmy Allan, the sole lawyer for all concerns on the island, was marginally nicer than most.

So Simone almost felt bad for snapping at him. Almost, but not quite.

"But we need . . . if one of you doesn't, well . . ." Jimmy's voice trailed off, his anxiety clearly at an all-time high. Simone knew what he was floundering at. She knew what he was trying not to say.

She knew how superstitious they all were. With her mother gone, there was no Cole woman in the lighthouse. There was no Cole woman to "keep the sea at bay." And, naturally, that meant all the fish would dry up and the islanders would lose their lives to rough waters. More bullshit.

It felt so, so good for Simone to say, "That's not real, Jimmy. And it's not my problem."

But Jimmy wouldn't be deterred. Everyone knew Simone didn't believe in the curse, any of those dumb rumors, but she did listen to sound logic.

"It's full of your mother's things. And your grandmother's too, I'd imagine," Jimmy said nervously. "Maybe even further back . . ."

"Okay. Throw it all away. I don't care." She pressed the heel of her hand against the center of her chest until the ache on the surface overrode the one deep within.

"I, well, it's just, we can't, no one would . . ."

Jimmy couldn't seem to finish, but Simone didn't need him to. She knew what he meant; no one on the island would ever dare touch anything belonging to the Cole women. Who knew if their belongings, too, were cursed.

The island wasn't too far from the others that made up the Isles of Shoals, nor too far from the mainland. But she imagined the ferry was still sparsely run and, moreover, the islanders would be suspicious of all visitors, even if it was just a moving crew Simone hired to clear the lighthouse out. The islanders liked to keep their secrets.

It seemed she had no choice. If she wanted to be free of Juniper and the lighthouse, she would need to return to it first.

She had left a decade ago, a young woman who would not be trapped. She had gone to Yale, moved to New York, met a good man, gotten married. She had *escaped.*

She would return to the lighthouse only long enough to clear it out. Then she'd be gone again, that place firmly and permanently in her rearview. And if the islanders thought that left them to die at the hands of the sea—and the Cole women within it—well, maybe that's what they deserved.

It was almost enough to make Simone wish she believed in curses.

Simone *didn't* believe in the curse of the Cole women. Still, it seemed, Juniper Island would not let her go quite yet.

The lighthouse always called its girls home.

Two
Mabel

March 27, 1951

Juniper Island, Isles of Shoals, New Hampshire

Mabel paused just outside the lighthouse, the brine on the air tickling at her raw throat. She had never even thought to lock the main door to the lighthouse, but she contemplated it now. She wasn't even sure the rusty screws would turn, they were so disused.

But for once there was no one waiting within the lighthouse when Mabel left.

Her mother had been dead nearly three weeks. Nineteen days, seventeen hours.

The lighthouse was the only refuge the Cole women got on Juniper Island. Now that refuge was Mabel's alone, as the last of them, and it felt like anything but.

Mabel continued on, the lighthouse at her back. Let someone try to break in if they so pleased. She knew none would dare. Besides, Mabel was already in the midst of her darkest time, grief a choking hazard burrowed in her throat. What could be worse?

Mabel could walk from her tip of Juniper to the center of town with her eyes closed, on touch alone. She was the soil, the worn rocks, the unending expanse of raging sea that hugged them. This island was all she had ever known, the limits of its rocky coast the limits of her life. Mabel was used to the endless indigo of the island, the perpetual in-between of its twilight, which was the same today as it always was.

It seemed something, everything, should have changed now. Everything was different, wasn't it, now that Mabel was alone, the last of the Cole women? Yet everything was the very same.

She pulled her coat tighter across her chest as a gust blew up from the sea, even as Mabel walked inland. The seasons were in flux, spring on the calendar but winter still in the air.

Few trees occupied Juniper, making the view of the sea buoying them visible all around. In the near distance Mabel spotted the town center, where buildings leaning against one another began to pop up; everyone else on this island huddled together while the Coles and their lighthouse were left to bear the cold and the brute weather alone on the very edge, here but apart.

Cole, singular. Just Mabel now.

She paused in the space between hers and theirs, turned to look out at the endless sea. It stretched forever, water a deep-blue watercolor as twilight sank above them. Blue, blue everywhere she looked and everywhere she was. The mainland was just barely visible, a needle laid on its side. The other isles bulged from the water surrounding Juniper like beached whales, still too distant to lend companionship.

Mabel had never longed for anything more than Juniper, than this. She was this land and it was her and hers. But for the first time she looked out at the distant mainland and searched for a peek of her future.

Because Mabel had been raised on Juniper, she knew the curse as well as she knew her own skin and the sound of the waves slapping the lighthouse. There could only ever be two living Coles on this land. And with her mother gone, well, Mabel knew what that meant. Her mother had not walked herself into the sea, drifted into death, for nothing. She did it because it was the role the Cole women played, the siren song they heard from the whitecaps when it was time. If her mother had heard that tune, had gone the way of the curse, it was because, soon, another Cole woman would be coming.

Mabel had never touched or been touched. She knew that the people of this island could never look at her without fearing a witch, no matter how she had spent her twenty-seven years living in their image, being polite and docile and helpful. She would always be a Cole first and foremost in their eyes, and to be a Cole was to be a witch.

But for the Cole women, each death was birth, each end heralded a beginning. A child was coming. Her child. It must be, or her mother would not have been called to give her life to the sea.

Mabel did not think a new life, a child, would be brought to her within the island. Which meant it would come from there, that far speck of another world.

The distant chatter of the islanders broke her reverie. She pressed on until the sea fell away, blockaded by the walls of buildings on either side of Juniper's main—and only—street.

The door of the Fuller house sat propped open, a swirl of voices spilling out into the evening. The interior of the house glowed golden, warm and beckoning. Mabel cast one final glance at the sliver of black sea visible between homes before stepping inside.

Faces turned to her, some glances hardening with unease. But there were a few smiles among the small, gathered crowd. Mabel had worked hard for those smiles, and she returned them. No matter that she had attended every town meeting for the past eleven years, Mabel still felt like a visitor. She suspected that was what the islanders wanted—what they had always wanted. For the Cole women to remember that their existence on Juniper was a grudgingly given gift that could be revoked at any moment. Even if they all knew it wasn't true.

The kitchen was warm from the gathering of bodies within and the whistling kettle on the stove. A cluster of mismatched chairs occupied the room, making the large space feel intimate. Most seats were occupied, but Mabel found an old, upholstered dining chair in the back of the room. She tucked herself into it, nestled into the shadows along the wall. Dotty Allan and her husband, Chet, were beside her, and they turned to give Mabel a smile as she settled in. Their expressions were tight but almost welcoming.

"Hi there, Mabel. Would you like some tea?" Mabel looked up to find Evelyn Fuller standing at her shoulder, an outstretched tray holding a teapot and cups in her hands. She was a vision of the perfect hostess.

Evelyn had been two years ahead of Mabel in school, but the tiny one-room schoolhouse meant that all the children of Juniper had been pushed together. Often to young Mabel's teasing detriment.

But they were girls no longer, and Mabel knew little of Evelyn Fuller beyond the shy schoolgirl she had once been, back when she was still Evelyn Bradbury, of the island's most esteemed family.

Evelyn wore a flowing skirt and a fitted sweater that Mabel thought must be considered stylish on the mainland, prim and colorful and sweet as candy. She had the trademark Bradbury crown of golden hair, styled now in perfect roller waves that fell to her collarbone. No matter how much Mabel slept on a bumpy bed of rollers—much to her mother's eye rolls and sharp, judging breaths—she never awoke like that.

"Thank you," Mabel said, polite, as she took a cup. She wouldn't drink it, but turning it down was impossible.

Before the women could exchange any further niceties, a gravelly throat was cleared, calling the room to attention. Evelyn disappeared to her seat toward the front of her kitchen as a hush fell over the room.

All eyes turned to the stove, where the hulking figure of Dean Fuller leaned. Mabel suspected it was the only time the patriarch of the house had ever touched the appliance.

Dean loomed large before them all, his thick flannel straining across his biceps as he crossed his arms. Mabel had never found the man handsome, with his sharp blue eyes and blond buzzed head, but she suspected that had more to do with the unease his very presence caused in her. He had never been outwardly cruel to Mabel or the Coles—no more than any of the other islanders, at least—but something in those icy-blue eyes screamed distrust to Mabel. Dean Fuller, since childhood, had seemed a man with something to prove. Mabel knew how dangerous that could be.

She was glad to be in the back of the room, nearly out of sight, as he stood up front beside his brother-in-law, Jay Bradbury.

Evelyn and Dean's little boy, Richie, darted between the chairs with exuberant energy. But one sharp look from his father had the boy dropping into a seat beside his mother. Evelyn ran a gentle hand over the boy's head, placing a kiss on his brow as the meeting commenced.

"We've got a few things on the bill for tonight," Jay began, his voice deeper than Dean's but somehow seeming more soft-spoken.

Jay was a Bradbury and he had power inherently, as much as he had inherited the island's most lucrative fishing boat that kept their little economy afloat. Dean, on the other hand, still needed to stronghold his power.

Dean cleared his throat. "First order of business is sorting out the Smith cottage. We need someone willing to take it on."

A few heads nodded, eager to tackle the topic. The old Smith place was a single-room fishing cottage that had been left to its own devices since Bert Smith died about six months back. Bert was the last of the Smith line on Juniper; the cottage had nowhere to go, so it had fallen to the town. It seemed it had become a burden that the town—which is to say Dean Fuller and Jay Bradbury—no longer wanted to bear.

The Smith cottage, like most buildings on Juniper, was a few centuries old, the wood worn by the weather and the structure cobbled together like a Frankenstein's monster over the years to better bear the brunt of the raging, salty air. It sat just on the edge of the island's center cluster, the opposing endpoint to the Cole lighthouse. Maybe, as such, Mabel felt a kindred connection to it—almost accepted but not quite. Perhaps, she thought, embracing the home herself and using it to serve the island's community would help her gain that acceptance she had so long worked for. Mabel was as surprised as the rest of the room to find her hand stretching over her head.

"Well now, Miss Cole, I imagine you've got enough on your plate what with tending the lighthouse," Jay Bradbury said in his gruff voice. "Especially with your mom gone now."

It was a blow, as Jay intended, and it was no concern for Mabel that kept the property from being passed to her care.

All heads turned to Mabel, and she struggled not to fidget under the weight of the attention.

"Exactly." Dean stepped in, his daunting presence seeming to fill the small room. "It ought to be used for something to serve the community."

She heard what Dean did not say: *Of which you are not a member.*

Despite the fact that her very presence on Juniper kept them all safe. And they all knew it. And hated it enough that it made them hate her. Despite so, so much trying.

But Mabel was not a quitter. She would try more, try harder.

"Well, I was thinking we ought to have a place for folks to get books," Mabel barreled on, daring herself to hold Dean's eye through the gaps of those sitting between them. "We could turn the cottage into a library—"

"Miss Cole, I just can't imagine you'd find the time on your own." Dean enunciated each word to make sure the woman would not miss the subtle threat beneath them. She didn't.

The room was silent with crackling tension. Mabel knew it best to back down, to not make waves, she was already—

"I'll help Mabel." It was Evelyn's small voice that broke the quiet. "I think a little library is just what Juniper needs."

Dean turned a hard eye to his wife. It was plain as day that he didn't like it, not one bit. But Evelyn had spoken before the town. And she was his wife; to disagree with her on this now would make it a family matter, and family matters were something everyone knew Dean Fuller kept behind closed doors.

A tic had formed in his rough-set jaw as he looked at his wife. Evelyn sat up straight, the buttons of her sky-blue sweater straining across her chest. She lifted her tiny chin, clearing her throat, looking right back at her husband.

"Don't you think that'd be nice, dear?" she said finally with a little pink-lipsticked smile, every bit the perfect wife.

Dean nodded his blond buzzed head, eyes falling to Mabel. The suspicion was still there. "All right, then."

No vote was needed. Dean Fuller's word was as good as law.

Within the golden glow of the kitchen, Dean and Jay led the town on to the next order of business. But Evelyn Fuller's blue eyes found Mabel across the room, and her little smile seemed to hold a bit more mirth than it did before. Mabel smiled right back.

Three
Rebecca

July 29, 1971

Juniper Island, Isles of Shoals, New Hampshire

Rebecca was lost at sea.

She always was when she swam—that's why she did it. She dove deeper into the deep blue, swimming out farther, far enough down that her body cut the water beneath the waves. It was her own world down here, her mind silent, the sounds of Juniper nonexistent. Just her and the blue and all the other sea creatures, sharing their home.

She dove deeper, deeper, farther, the world behind her closed lids burning black. She dove until her chest ached with the need for air. With that familiar pang of resentment, she pushed up, pumping her feet hard until her head broke the surface of the water with a gasp. And just like that, she was back in her own life. The sounds of Juniper at her back twisted their way to her on the sea breeze. She treaded water, letting the waves push her backward, looking out at the open sea, the islands White and Seavey in the near distance. One day she would be out there. Not the other isles. The mainland. So far that folks didn't even call it the mainland anymore. So far that the name Cole meant nothing to them. But, for now, she was here.

At least she was alone out here. No one dared step foot in the waves just behind the lighthouse; this part of the ocean was full of generations of dead Cole witches, after all.

Sometimes Rebecca swore that she could feel gentle hands ghosting across her skin when she was deep in the water, buoying her. That she could hear soft, indistinguishable sounds when the water pressed in against her eardrums. If there were dead Cole women in here, well, Rebecca felt differently about them than the islanders did. She was used to water and ghosts being her only companions.

She closed her eyes, drifting on her back, letting the water carry her. She trusted it. Time slipped away.

Rebecca's peace was cracked by high-pitched, layered laughter, the sound close enough to make her flounder upright. With a thankful breath Rebecca saw that she hadn't drifted far enough to be seen. But *she* could see. Rebecca pumped her legs, swimming closer to the island's edge, bobbing in and out of the salt water. When she reached the rocky coast where the island curved, she pulled her upper body to rest on one of the rocks. Her sharp chin rested on her folded arms, her stomach scraping pleasantly against the rock face as her legs drifted out in the water behind her, a half-moored mermaid. From here she could glimpse the rocky beach. Four girls sat on thick towels laid across sand made pearlescent by the sharp edges of mussel shells.

From this angle Rebecca could see them, though she was nestled well enough against the rocks that she doubted she would be visible, her long dark hair wetted to the same hue as the stones. She felt her hair tickle the small of her back as she floated, ears tuned to catch the girls' words over the sound of the water around her.

"Yup, Jimmy set off yesterday." Barbara Allan was the center of the group, just as she seemed to be the center of everything on Juniper. The other three girls sat around her like she was their queen, her fair blond hair catching all the sunlight, perfectly styled and prim as the girl herself. Her voice was haughty as she continued, "We're all so proud that he's the first one on the island to go serve our country."

On cue, the other girls cooed their agreement. Rebecca could hardly help rolling her eyes. For one, Rebecca's brother hadn't chosen to go fight overseas. He had been drafted, left without a choice. Forced to go fight in a war that was questionably immoral and violent, as far as Rebecca—not to mention many on the mainland—was concerned. But, of course, in the small conservative minds of Juniper, the war in Vietnam was necessary and serving one's country was an honor.

Rebecca had been happy enough to be rid of Barbara Allan in her daily life since finishing school, but the princess of Juniper wasn't so easy to escape. For everyone on the island around Rebecca's age, Barbara was the sun they moved around. Not that it mattered; Rebecca had never been in the orbit.

Pulling herself farther up on the rock to get a better view, Rebecca tuned back in to their conversations from where she was hidden beneath the shadow of the lighthouse. But she froze when she heard her own name. Then, on instinct, she flattened herself to the rock, heart pounding against the rough surface.

But no, they hadn't spotted her. She knew well that, on Juniper, Cole women were talked about but no one wanted to see them.

"I just don't like being so close to that creepy lighthouse." Donna shivered dramatically, quickly looking to catch

Barbara's reaction. They all did, these girls who were pretty enough but not as pretty as Barbara. Liked well enough, but not beloved like Barbara.

"Yeah, for all we know, Rebecca could be up top brewing some hex on us right now," Natalie said. "She might not look like a witch, but she is one, right?"

Muffled assents were given. Barbara seemed to be ignoring the other girls, looking straight out ahead at the water. But she snapped back to attention when Donna said, "Though she is sort of pretty. For a Jew, I mean."

Rebecca's stomach bottomed out, a hot, lashing feeling expanding in her chest. Shame, shock, anger. Her legs had long gone numb where they drifted in the water, but the icy cold suddenly felt too hot, not enough to cool and cleanse her.

No matter what she did, she wasn't good enough for them; she was too beautiful, or beautiful *for a Jew.*

"Don't be disgusting," Barbara snapped, turning her blue eyes on Donna. Her voice was a whip crack.

Rebecca wasn't sure what it was that disgusted Barbara—the hate and prejudice in Donna's statement or the idea that Rebecca's beauty was acknowledged at all. Sometimes, in this town, Rebecca felt inhuman, less than human. Not just other, but *wrong.*

Before Donna could apologize, which she surely would, Barbara's face bloomed into a smile as she stood. Rebecca had been so absorbed in observing the girls that she hadn't noticed the lobster boat drifting up to shore until it was docked just in front of the girls.

Usually, everything on the island happened on the other side. No ships or swimming children lingered on this end. It was just Rebecca and Mabel, her mom. Until now. It was a new addition, the Bradburys' lobster boat docking on this side of the island, just beside the lighthouse. Their fishing boats still went out on the other side, but the lobster contraption was big, needed more space. So, for the past few weeks, they'd been on her doorstep.

Not literally, of course. Rebecca had only ever seen the boat dock from within her Rapunzel's tower that was the lighthouse. This was the closest she had ever seen it.

She had a prime view as the handful of men deboarded, water sloshing around their movements. They wore heavy pants over their outfits, sturdy hats; a shadow of what the fishermen wore, but harder, more protective. Whatever they were doing out there was somehow more.

Rebecca had the perfect view as Cal Bradbury stepped onto the shore. He had already discarded his gear, standing strong and tall in a white T-shirt that glowed pristinely against the deep hue of his tan. The sleeves stretched over the swells of his arm muscles as he ran a hand through his sandy-blond hair, pushing the wavy strands from his forehead. Time seemed to crawl as Rebecca looked at him, her breath, on instinct, held. He was only a year older than Rebecca, yet somehow just looking at him made her feel so young, like a child. He was so strong, every movement steady and confident, so sure that this island was his to occupy.

A smile split his beautiful face, and for Rebecca it felt like the sun coming out from the clouds. But the smile wasn't for her, of course, it was for Barbara. The blonde wrapped her arms around Cal's neck, standing on her toes to kiss him. A different kind of heat striped across Rebecca's chest, tightening it.

If Barbara Allan was the princess of Juniper, Cal Bradbury was the prince. Charming, handsome. Perfect.

The type of man who would shape and change Juniper. The type of man who, if he ever looked at Rebecca the way he was looking at Barbara now, could change everything for her.

But, of course, Cal Bradbury was not for her. It was a stupid thought.

As if he could hear that thought, Cal's head turned toward Rebecca, Barbara's arms still held around his neck. But Rebecca was already slipping away from the rocks, diving back down deep beneath the sea.

Four
Mabel

March 27, 1951

Juniper Island, Isles of Shoals, New Hampshire

Mabel quickened her steps, bracing herself against the bashing sea wind that picked up the closer she came to the island's rocky shore. Her fingertips were burning with cold, and she'd need to run them under the hot tap before she'd be any good to the oil, but there was nothing to be done for it. Twilight was falling quickly, the sky already fading into a deep-hued blue.

This was her job. Hers alone. The reason she lived and died on this island.

The lighthouse loomed in the distance, growing closer with each step she took. Even without its swinging light on yet, the hulking white figure was Mabel's beacon.

The world was quieter out here beyond the reach of the town's chatter. The sound of the water lashing the rocks was so familiar it lulled Mabel's mind into a trance as she made her quick way toward home.

She wasn't sure what had come over her back at the town meeting. More so, though, she wasn't sure what had come over Evelyn Fuller. It was likely a dangerous task, taking up with someone with as much sway as Evelyn, even if the woman didn't seem to realize the power she wielded on Juniper. But more than that worry, Mabel felt warmed in her chest by a sense of rightness. Like, for the first time in nineteen days, things were falling into place. Like the curse was set in stone but finally, that stone spelled something good for Mabel.

The only things left in the lighthouse were her and the books, and the books had always been her mother's first love. The only love a Cole woman was allowed to keep, after all, was inanimate.

Her mother had always struggled to come by books, orders from the mainland often taking months. The ferry from the mainland to the isles ran weekly in the spring and summer, but the winter waves made it too dangerous. Everyone went sparsely supplied, with monthly mainland deliveries, if they were lucky, weather permitting. Mabel had seen the way the cold months, the long nights, wore at her mother. How having access to some new books when she needed them most could've changed everything. How it would've allowed her to get lost in worlds in which she wasn't cursed by her lineage, her whole life a ticking clock until she was as worn down as the rocks that lined the island's coast. Even the veritable mass of paperbacks she had gathered over the years had hardly sated her appetite. A library would have changed her life.

Mabel had never known her mother, had never allowed herself to get close enough to do so. Her mother was othered, her mother was a Cole. And, for so much of Mabel's life, she had thought that othering herself from her mother would somehow make the islanders see her as something other than a Cole.

It had never worked. All it meant was that Mabel didn't know her mother and didn't realize she wanted to until the older woman was in the sea.

But she knew the woman through her books. The romance novels that lined her shelves spoke of a softness beneath her icy exterior. The fantasy left dog-eared on the kitchen table hinted at a longing for worlds beyond the one they knew. And books were how Mabel's mother had gotten to know her daughter too, the only mutual language they could speak. It had become nearly an expectation for Mabel to find a book waiting for her on her bedspread each night, somehow always exactly what she most needed in that moment.

For nineteen days she had not touched paper and ink.

But now, to Mabel, it felt right to share that love. That language.

The town had never bothered getting to know her mother, had feared and resented her as they had all the others in the Coles' long line. But Mabel thought that if they held her mother's books, her heart, the islanders might just learn to love the Cole women back.

The darkest part of the island was always just beneath the lighthouse, standing in its hulking shadow, the one place the light could never reach. Even though night hadn't fully set in, Mabel already struggled to see as she pushed through the door, her tawny hair lashing against her cheeks. Thankfully, she knew the lighthouse as well as her own skin, and she made her way inside without a hitch, pressing the door against the wind until it rang closed. The echoing sound faded, and then it was just her and her breath.

Mabel didn't bother to flip on the kitchen light, crossing the small space in the darkness to the stairs. She began her trek up the narrow, twisting stone steps. She climbed above the kitchen, higher still as the steps passed between the narrow bit of hall between her room and her mother's. The latter sat with the door only just ajar, housing its ghosts within. Mabel's legs did not tire as she continued her ascent. This was what Cole women were made for.

At last she came to the point of the lighthouse, the light and its contraption taking up the bulk of the narrow space. Mabel had taken over the duty of keeper years ago; in the past decade or so, more often than not, her mother had been too lost in a book or her own mind to take on the task. That was okay. Mabel didn't mind. This ritual was hers.

She had heard that some lighthouses elsewhere were being modernized, electricity incorporated in. But Mabel was glad that hadn't happened to theirs, at least not yet. The calluses on her hands, the brown spattering of scars from hot oil—they were her proof of her job. Proof that she was good at this. That, even if she would never be thanked for it, this was her way of protecting the people of Juniper.

The light was something so great, a beacon, a rescue for the lost and endangered. Mabel thought it right that that came with some hardship, that something that great needed to take something in return. She had never minded giving to the lighthouse.

Everything was set as she had left it, just in its place. She moved the oil quickly, the dim space illuminating for a minute as she struck a match and lit it. Then, finally, with a tumbling whir, the light clicked on.

Though her fingertips and knees were still stiff from the cold of walking home just moments before, Mabel was a creature of habit. She pushed through the little door on the far side of the curved glass wall, stepping out onto the gallery. The air was lashing up here, brutal and sharp as knives. Mabel gathered her hair in a fist, tying it into a knot so she could look out over the edge of the world, the black ocean her domain, hers alone to protect.

She loved her many rituals, but she could feel things shifting.

The roll of the light across the black waves was the only thing Mabel knew for certain, the only thing she knew she would always have. That was her family. She loved it as such.

She would happily give her body and life to it one day, when the curse came for her, as she knew it would.

But for the first time, Mabel suspected she had a lot of life to live between now and then. For the first time, Mabel felt that she was at the beginning.

Five
Mabel

March 30, 1951

Juniper Island, Isles of Shoals, New Hampshire

The Smith fishing cottage was in worse condition than Mabel had expected.

The single room was spacious enough, but at the moment, unfortunately, that only meant spacious enough to see just how rough it was. Sunlight streamed in through the warped window, highlighting dust motes floating through the air, the worn threads and moth bites on the chair and couch that were the only furniture left behind in the space. An old net lay tangled in the corner, and Mabel swore she heard a rustle come from within. She feared to think what animal had made itself a home in the knots.

She shivered as a cold breeze swept down through the hole in the center of the roof, smack in the middle of the room. It was clear no one had bothered to patch up the cottage for winter snowfall and it had worn right through, broken wood gathered in a pile beneath the circle of blue sky visible above. The floorboards had been swollen from the cold, bulging underfoot like a restless beast, giving Mabel a distinct sense of seasickness that even an islander was unnerved by. Cobwebs crisscrossed the space, each fine strand dripping with morning dew.

She certainly had her work cut out for her before the structure was safe for occupants to enter, let alone insulated enough to keep books from molding within a fortnight.

But she wasn't alone.

Mabel stood in the center of the cottage's sole room, looking around her, awaiting Evelyn Fuller. A situation she certainly never expected to find herself in.

The other woman hadn't even arrived yet, and Mabel found herself inexplicably embarrassed at the sight of the rough, decaying space. It wasn't hers, and, in fact, it had been Evelyn's own husband who was meant to be caring for it the past few months—a job he had clearly neglected. But taking it over, transforming it, had been Mabel's suggestion. One that Evelyn had gone out on a limb to support, even if the woman's sweet tone and smiles might have looked like anything but a risk at the other night's town meeting. But Mabel saw it for what it was.

Mabel herself had spoken up, caused waves, and Evelyn had hitched her wagon to that—all without ever seeing the space. If Mabel had, she wasn't sure she would've done as she did. Her resolve was already weakening.

Mabel ran a flat hand over the single window, eroding some of the grime that had collected, though the weather still warped the pane in waves. Still, she could make out what sat on the other side. The day was bright and springlike, finally, the waves just kissing the rocks beyond, the Bradburys' big fishing boat a speck out on the water.

And right before the window were dozens of little crosses that marked the buried islanders long gone, Juniper's own little graveyard right there on the edge of the island. No headstones had been given; they weren't needed. Everyone knew everyone and everything, and any islander worth the salt in their veins could tell you every person buried in that plot for the past two centuries and change. Mabel looked out at the small field of crosses, their wood worn as the bodies buried beneath.

Dozens of bodies immortalized in Juniper's soil, and not one was a Cole.

The Cole women didn't go into the soil; the sea got them instead.

At least, in staying here on Juniper, Mabel was keeping those spirits in the sea at ease, keeping more crosses from springing up, empty coffins buried for bodies forever lost at sea. Still, it was an uneasy sight for her twice over.

The creak of the door pressing open startled Mabel from the window. Backlit by the rectangle of the blue sky through the open door, Evelyn Fuller glowed, even in the shadows of the barren cottage.

"Morning, Mabel." Evelyn nestled closer into the scarf wrapped around her elegant neck. Her white skin was made pearlescent by the offset of her perfect pink lipstick, her pale-blue sweater, her wide skirt covered in colorful flowers.

Mabel was very aware of the worn hems of her trousers, the fact that she wore trousers at all. The bulge of her sweater and heavy coat, the way her gloves were worn down so her right pointer finger peeked out. Even Mabel's fair brown hair clustered around her face, fallen from the bun she'd knotted it into. Somehow Evelyn's gold strands rested perfectly as if they were still set in their rollers, unaffected by the brine and beat of the sea air.

Evelyn looked out of place not only beside Mabel, but certainly within the crumbling shadows of the cottage. It was inherently, obviously wrong.

Mabel was used to working in the lighthouse; she dressed for rough work and warmth and the beating down of the elements. Evelyn kept a home and husband. Mabel kept a lighthouse; her husband was the ghost of ships that would never make port and the ghost of her ancestors buried in the deep blue.

Mabel scrambled to give Evelyn a way out before the other woman was forced to do it herself. She would rather burn herself than let anyone else do it for her.

"Sorry about this," she chuckled, gesturing to the structure around them, though the hole in the roof made Mabel feel like maybe *structure* was too generous. "I hadn't realized the shape it was in before I suggested we take it on."

Evelyn's dark brows rose, her mouth parting to speak, but Mabel barreled on. "Don't worry, I don't expect you to help clean up all of this; I know that's not what you signed up for. Just give me a few weeks to take care of cleanup, and then I'll let you know when it's all shipshape and you can come back and help sort out the books and whatnot, because of course you shouldn't—"

"No need." Evelyn stepped fully into the cottage, kicking the door closed behind her with a small foot. A little smile struck up on her lips, not the polite mask Mabel was used to seeing her in. One that was almost a smirk, playful, a smile that showed there was someone beneath the good name and manners. "I'm not afraid of a bit of hard work."

Then, to Mabel's shock, Evelyn Fuller quite literally rolled up the sleeves of her perfect little sweater and placed her hands on her hips. She strolled to the center of the room, looking up at the hole in the roof like a disapproving mother. "Let's get down to it, shall we?"

Mabel had thought she knew every inch of Juniper, every rock and juniper bush and person. But, she realized, maybe she didn't really know Evelyn Fuller. Not yet, at least.

Six
Rebecca

August 1, 1971

Juniper Island, Isles of Shoals, New Hampshire

Rebecca's head burst above water. She hauled herself up on the jagged rocks in the shadow of the lighthouse, twisting her body until she sat atop it with a squelch. She tugged at the front of her swimsuit, tenting it away from her chest and stomach before it snapped back into place. Wiping her heavy hair from her eyes and forehead, Rebecca looked over her shoulder, to the sandy port.

The lobster boat was already docked on the shore, empty. Silent. She had entirely missed it coming back in the time that she was dipping in and out of the water.

Not that she had slightly altered the time of her swim to correspond with the docking so that she'd have a chance to glimpse Cal Bradbury, close but still far enough away to be hidden. Of course not.

Still, her stomach hollowed with disappointment.

She shivered with the pleasant feeling of air meeting sea, her toes still dipping into the icy water, her skin everywhere else hit with the sharp, familiar pinpricks of a breeze on numb skin. She twisted, preparing to haul herself off the rocks and back into the lighthouse. But her motion froze as she saw a figure cresting the top of the rocks. Golden hair, wide shoulders, tan skin. And a gleaming smile when he saw her sitting there as though she'd been waiting for him.

Rebecca watched, unmoving, as Cal Bradbury made his way down the rocks toward her. He didn't step carefully on the wobbling, jagged edges. He was of the island. He hopped down the tilting rocks like he knew they would hold him.

He came to a stop looming over Rebecca, blocking out the sun at his back, casting him in a halo. Rebecca's breath caught.

"Hey," Cal said. Easy. As if this were normal. As if they were friends who had planned to meet here. As if they had ever spoken before.

"Hi," Rebecca breathed back. Her voice was a whisper over the sound of the waves. But Cal's smile pulled up at the edges.

He didn't ask if he could join her before he folded himself down onto the rock beside hers. Because of course he could.

He bent a leg, resting his arm across it lazily. His knee brushed against Rebecca's arm. Her numb skin seemed to be burning through on that very spot.

"I thought I spotted you over here the other day." He said it like it was an inside joke between the two of them. Rebecca's thoughts were a whir. "At first I thought maybe you were a mermaid or something." He laughed easily. Rebecca, haltingly, joined in. "I mean, it's not every day you peek a beautiful girl floating in the ocean."

Beautiful. Rebecca knew she was; she looked at her long, shining hair in the mirror, her full lips, her high cheeks, her deep-brown eyes with their own gravitational pull. But beauty had given her nothing on Juniper. Her name cast a shadow over it, so no one had ever called her beautiful before.

Rebecca had always assumed Cal was charming. When you looked like that, when you were born into that kind of power, charm was a given. He had proved her right.

"I swim out here most days." She shrugged, hyperaware of the way her wet suit clung to her skin, the bareness of her thighs so close to his, the deep V cut of her one-piece. She was too shy to look at him directly, instead staring out at the sea. She knew her silence often came across as arrogance or disinterest. But, truthfully, she just rarely found herself feeling the need to speak.

Thankfully, Cal was happy to fill the air.

He laughed again, the sound warming her body. It might just be Rebecca's new favorite sound. She wasn't sure why Cal was sitting beside her, if he'd sought her out or just happened to stumble across her. But he seemed so at ease, settled into the hidden nestle of rocks beside her. Just the two of them and the ocean, Juniper at their back.

"Don't worry, I don't have such a big head that I thought you were out here just to look at me. I'm sure you've got plenty of men following you around that you can look at."

Rebecca turned to look at him sharply. Was he mocking her? Was that why he had sat here beside her?

He had lived on Juniper all his life. He must know that no one—man or otherwise—ever dared get too close to her. She could count on her hands the number of times, over her nineteen years, that someone other than her mother had spoken to her unless it was out of necessity. The islanders preferred to fear and resent from a distance.

But Cal's face showed no mocking. He was looking at her openly, a little smile on his mouth. Rebecca couldn't help her eyes darting down to it. And then her heart was beating for a whole different reason. She had hoped the involuntary glance was quick enough for him to miss it, but the lift of his smile told her no such luck. Her cheeks flamed red, even as she shivered in the sea air.

Cal chuckled lightly, without menace. He reached out a hand toward her, and Rebecca's breath froze. Surely he wasn't going to touch her. Or—no, he wasn't going to kiss her. He couldn't be. He was Cal Bradbury.

He didn't kiss her. But his fingers did glide across her cheekbones before settling into her hair. Rebecca's dark eyes stayed locked on Cal's, the two of them unblinking in the extended moment.

Then Cal's hand withdrew, a small piece of seaweed resting on his fingers. He flicked it back out at sea easily. Rebecca thought about diving back beneath the waves where the world was muted enough that she could drown herself away from her embarrassment.

Of course Cal Bradbury wasn't going to kiss her.

But as he pushed himself to stand, he smiled down at her, her neck craning to look up at him. "I hope I see you around soon, mermaid."

She watched him leisurely make his way back up the rocks until he disappeared over the swell and back onto land. All the while, Rebecca's heart rattled in her chest like a winter storm.

Seven
Mabel

April 1, 1951

Juniper Island, Isles of Shoals, New Hampshire

Mabel nearly missed the knock on the door. It wasn't that it was so loud—only the same sounds that she had always known within the lighthouse: the creaking of the wood and metal settling, the waves beating on the exterior and rocks like the water's heartbeat that Mabel's own always matched.

It was simply that she could not remember the last time anyone had knocked on the lighthouse door. In fact, she was fairly certain no one ever had. The islanders tended to steer far clear of this tip of the island—who knew what witchery those Cole women got up to in there? Who knew the ways they conversed with those dead ancestors of theirs who haunted the sea? Best to steer far clear.

Of course, Mabel didn't talk to the Cole women that they said vengefully haunted the waters. Still, she couldn't deny that lighting the beam felt like its own sort of voice.

No matter what the truth was, it was a fact that the women of the lighthouse never received visitors.

She was just pulling the casserole dish out of the oven when the knock sounded again, faint and almost nervous. Mabel startled, nearly dropping the dish as she deposited it on the countertop, stripping off her mitts. She paused a moment to pat her hair into order before she pulled open the door, curiosity biting at her.

Mabel's first thought as she looked through the open doorway was that she had somehow fallen into one of her mother's novels. Those ones where dark, handsome strangers stood on cliffsides, black coats billowing in the wind, deep-hued hair spilling across their brows. Because on Juniper Island there was no such thing as strangers. No stranger—far as Mabel had been alive to see—had ever stepped foot on the isle for more than a few moments. Certainly none of them made it out to the lighthouse.

But the man on the other side of the door was just that.

In that unbelievable moment, Mabel knew that things were finally beginning.

When he looked up and saw Mabel, he nervously unwound the scarf from his neck, twisting it in his hands. His dark eyes were nearly black, large and round, and stayed down on his feet. Mabel found she desperately wanted him to look up at her.

"Hello. Are you the . . ." His fair cheeks stained pink in a sudden wash. He paused before correcting himself. "The woman who lives in this lighthouse?"

Mabel noticed he had an accent, faint but there still, something a bit rough around the edges.

"Yes, hello." She stuck her hand out. "I'm Mabel Cole."

Mabel was so unused to meeting any newcomers she hardly knew how to interact, but the man's shyness somehow bolstered her own confidence.

He reached out, gripping her small hand in his larger one. He looked at her, and Mabel was able to see the full depth of his dark eyes, the strong cut of his nose and jaw beneath thick, flattering brows. "Otto Weitz," he introduced himself, the sounds of his name throaty and deep.

Otto cleared his throat, returning his twisting grip to his scarf as he held it before him. Mabel noticed he had something on the back of his head, a dark circle of cloth sitting over his hair, kept in place by measures Mabel couldn't discern. "Miss Cole—"

"Mabel, please."

"Mabel." He nodded, a small smile on his face that somehow made him even more handsome. "I was coming to visit the island. I took the ferry over. I thought I would stay for the day, perhaps two. I did not realize until I was here, the ferry long gone, that the boat would not return until next Sunday."

Mabel's eyebrows rose. To her, it was second nature that the ferry ran only weekly at best, but she supposed to a newcomer that may be quite shocking indeed. She wondered just how different things were on the mainland, if the rumors were true and the world moved at a different, breakneck pace out there beyond.

"I'm sorry to hear that," she replied, trying for a chuckle as she said, "Not exactly convenient, is it? But Juniper is a great place to visit!"

She guessed; how could she know?

"I am certain it is, yes," the man replied. "But, of course, I'll need somewhere to stay if I am to be here the week."

"Oh! Of course!" Mabel perked up, finally understanding why the man was here. The ferry dropped off not too far from here, and likely he had chosen the wrong direction, come toward the lighthouse instead of heading to the town center. "You see, if you head on that way"—she pointed inland, where the cluster of buildings could be seen as a speck—"you'll find plenty of folks. We don't have an inn or anything; we don't get many visitors. But it's Sunday, so I'd reckon folks will be at the church. You could go there and explain, and I'm certain someone will be able to help you."

Mabel smiled, certain she had helped the man. So she was baffled when his face twisted further with discomfort.

"I'm afraid I did. Go to town for aid, I mean. They . . . no one was willing to give me a place to rest."

"No one?" Mabel was shocked. The islanders weren't warm, certainly; she knew that better than anyone. And they were definitely wary of outsiders. But she hadn't thought them *coldhearted* to those outside her family.

"No." Otto tilted his head, looked at her meaningfully, as if she should understand something that, clearly, she was missing. "But I was told that you recently had a spare room in your home."

He gestured to the looming lighthouse at her back, where she lingered in the doorway still. The breeze off the sea ruffled his hair, and Mabel's breath caught at the beauty of him. "I can pay for your hospitality, of course."

It was Mabel who was being asked to open her home, yet somehow it was Otto who seemed nervous. Mabel's heart lurched out to the man, left out in the cold on Juniper, a feeling she was all too familiar with. The islanders loved to shove their unwanteds to the very edge.

Though she could not fathom why they had done as much to Otto. If the rest of the island had refused this man, Mabel knew she was meant to too. This felt like a test, a reminder that she was not one of them, that to be so she had to act as they did, make others outsiders in order to be on the inside.

For the first time in her life, Mabel thought that if this was what it took to be one of them, she didn't want to be.

She opened the door wider and invited the man in.

* * *

Mabel stared at the man sitting at her kitchen table. A man, at her kitchen table. She had never seen another soul sit there besides her mother.

With a great deal of coaxing, Otto had hung his coat on the rack by the door, his small satchel placed beneath it. He still looked nervous as he watched her move about the kitchen, setting a plate and cutlery before him.

She was glad she had cooked the casserole, which was still warm from the oven. That she still hadn't managed to shake the habit of cooking for two.

She set the dish down in the center of the table, dropping into the seat across from her guest. *Her guest.*

"Would you like some?" The question was really just out of politeness; Mabel was already scooping a hearty portion onto his plate. But Otto held a hand up, pausing her.

"Is it—see, I do not . . ." He trailed away.

Suddenly, Mabel understood the tight knit of Otto's brows, his twitching fingers. He had been to the town center. Of course.

"I'm not what they say I am." Mabel couldn't help the defiance in her voice, the notes that covered up her hurt. "You don't need to be afraid of eating food from my table. I don't mean you any harm. It's . . . it's just things they say about my family on this island because we're, well, they say we're different than them. But I don't want to hurt you."

Her passionate words echoed in the small kitchen, bouncing against the stone walls. For a long moment there was no sound but the rhythmic beating of the waves beyond.

Finally, Otto shook his head. "I did not say because I did not want to offend. But yes, they told me to come here to find the witch who lived in the lighthouse."

A sudden, sharp pang split in Mabel's chest. All she'd done was be kind but not too suspiciously gentle. Be open but not share too much. Be small but not invisible. She had shunned her own mother for these people, and it hadn't distinguished her to them. It meant nothing. She would still, always, be just another witch in the lighthouse.

"But that is not why I hesitate, Mabel!" Otto continued, leaning forward. He reached a hand out toward hers that were resting on the table, her rough fingers at some point having become coiled into a fist. At the last moment Otto retracted his touch before it could land. Mabel was sorry for it. "I do not care about that. I don't believe it. I am used to being . . . apart. It is simply that there are some things I do not eat is all."

"Oh." Mabel felt her heart rate, her indignation, slow. "Well, this is just some vegetables and sauce. Potatoes. No meat or cheese or fish." She wasn't sure what it was that Otto abstained from, but her casserole was distinctly lacking. Money wasn't exactly ripe as of late.

For the first time Otto truly smiled, not shy and small but a blooming, opening expression. "In that case, I would be honored to share a meal with you, Mabel."

Mabel slid him his healthy portion, and the two ate in silence. Mabel did her best to ignore the inexplicable heat that rose to her cheeks each time she looked into his dark eyes.

Eight
Mabel

April 3, 1951

Juniper Island, Isles of Shoals, New Hampshire

Mabel couldn't quite settle this situation as reality. In the tiny, dimly lit Smith cottage, she was joined by the two most beautiful people she had ever seen outside of a television screen. To her left, Evelyn Fuller held a ladder steady while atop it Otto Weitz balanced, hammering a covering over the now-nonexistent hole in the roof. They joked casually as they worked, moving like a well-oiled, three-pronged machine.

But Evelyn had been deeply hesitant of the stranger at first, when Mabel had arrived at the cottage that morning with her houseguest in tow. By then Mabel had grown used to Otto's presence, was almost soothed by the sound of movement behind her mother's bedroom door, no longer haunted by the dark and silence within it. The lighthouse felt full of life again, simply with the presence of shy, respectful Otto Weitz.

Evelyn glanced down at her wristwatch, exclaiming, "Oh, time's flown! I've got to head off to meet Richie."

Mabel took over her role, her worn work pants gliding against Evelyn's somehow still-spotless dress and sweater.

With a quick word of goodbye, Evelyn left the cottage, heading the meager distance toward her own home. The school would be out any moment, Richie and the other children walking the mere feet from the school building to their homes, where each mother would wait, smiling in the doorway, a snack prepared in the kitchen within. Sometimes it still ached at Mabel to see the scene. She had never had that; her walks from school to the lighthouse had been marred by taunting from the other children until she spent the last leg alone, letting herself into the lighthouse, where, at best, her mother's cavernous greeting would echo down to her.

Mabel was so lost in her mind it took her a moment to realize Otto was climbing down the ladder. "That should hold," he said, smiling down at her, gesturing up to the perfectly repaired ceiling.

"More than. Thank you, Otto, truly!"

The man blushed a deep, flattering pink. "It is nothing, Mabel." Mabel had noticed that when he was nervous or embarrassed, his accent seemed stronger, looser. He had been staying with her nearly two days, and yet Mabel knew nothing about her houseguest or his history, why he found himself on Juniper at all.

"Why don't we call it a day, yeah?" Mabel suggested as Otto's boots hit the floor. "We can take a walk. I'd love to show you around the island a bit."

Otto's thick, dark brows rose in surprise before mellowing. "That sounds lovely."

The afternoon air was crisp and lashing as they stepped outside, but thankfully spring seemed to have gotten her roots into the island and the sun shone down, warming Mabel's stiff fingers. The island was never quite busy or lively, by any means, but they'd managed to set out at its most crowded hour.

Children crisscrossed their path as Otto and Mabel walked side by side through the center of town. As always, the forms of mothers filled the open doorways, calling for their children to pause their play and come in for a snack. Each doorway the two passed housed a familiar face, but the expressions turned to the pair were anything but welcoming. As Otto and Mabel strolled by, each woman cut them with glances ranging from suspicious to nervous to downright villainous.

Little Jackson Poole, cackling, chased Linda Richards with his arm outstretched, a crab shell in his hand as the girl squealed away. When Mabel and Otto had to suddenly step apart for the chase to pass between them, the kids seemed to notice how close they were to the adults; the chase stopped promptly and both children moved away, as if their mothers, watching from the doorways, had told them to steer clear.

Mabel twisted her fingers together within the deep burrows of her jacket pocket, hyperaware of Otto by her side and what the man must be thinking. It wasn't as though these looks were unfamiliar to Mabel. She was a Cole, after all. But they seemed particularly elevated today, soft eyes hardened and smiles dropping like anvils rather than the tight expressions and whispered words behind her back she had grown accustomed to in the past few years as she'd clawed her way into the islanders' . . . well, not *good* graces but nearly acceptable ones.

She laid a hand on Otto's arm, startling the man, who was walking with his eyes cast down. Clearly, he felt the weight of those gazes too. Mabel's shame and embarrassment crowded her throat. She led Otto onward, quickening their steps. They didn't say a word until they were through the dense line of buildings in the town center. Once the homes fell away and only the island's rocky shore and the distant form of the lighthouse loomed far ahead, Mabel finally felt as though she could breathe.

Without words she led them toward the left, to walk along the uneven edge of the island. Mabel looked out at the endless expanse of sea, the slight glimpse of Seavey in the near distance, as she gathered her courage around her shame. "I'm sorry about that. They're not usually so . . . open in their dislike of me anymore."

Otto turned to look at her, and even from her peripheral vision Mabel could see the confusion scratched across his face. She couldn't look at him. It was too much to have someone new, someone outside of this incestuous, gnawing island, see how even on the only home she'd ever known, she was never quite at home.

"I'm sure you're wishing you'd managed to find somewhere else to stay." She tried to laugh, but the sound came out simply awkward instead.

Otto laid a gentle hand on her arm, pausing her movements as they reached the very edge of the shore, the ground becoming uneven with jutting rocks. "I don't think it's you that they glare at, Mabel."

Her brow furrowed. She knew that they had all refused Otto housing, that they were wary of newcomers. But not as wary as they were of Coles, surely. The breeze was strong directly on the edge like this, waves flicking off the rocks to throw droplets across their shoes. Otto reached up to adjust the little circle of cloth he wore on the back of his head as the breeze ruffled his hair flatteringly.

"They are suspicious of *me*. Because I am Jewish. That is why they would not allow me any housing or refuge within the church." Otto said it like it should be obvious, as though he was surprised Mabel had not realized.

And once he said it, she supposed it was obvious. Mabel had never met anyone who was Jewish. And news might reach Juniper far behind the rest of the world, but she had still seen the heartbreaking photos and headlines of the horrors that had befallen the Jewish people across Europe. Her teenage years had been colored by memories of those stories, of the heartless violence and hatred that had occurred for years on far-off shores.

She had not realized that that hatred was global, that those suspicions and stereotypes were nestled in the hearts of the people of Juniper too. She supposed she shouldn't be surprised; she had seen the way they all settled themselves into church each Sunday, one place she never dared enter, somehow knowing it would be an offense, not a way to win them to her. She had noticed, distantly, the way that crosses decorated so much of the island, the way that Jesus's name was spoken in reverie. Those had never been her beliefs, another part of the *them* that was not *us*. She knew the way they all preached kindness, loving thy neighbor. And yet those words meant nothing when it came to her; she knew they were little more than that: words. A way for the people to think themselves holy like their witch-hunting ancestors while being anything but. On Juniper, religion was little more than another remnant of the past, another club that Mabel could not join.

She knew well how the people here loved to hate anyone who was not just like them.

Mabel sat down heavily on the large stone beneath her. She draped her feet over the edge, watching as the waves splashed over her shoes, the steadying beat of the water wearing down the earth. A juniper bush sat to their left, shielding them from view. The prickly branches poked Mabel through her coat as she leaned back on the rock.

"I'm sorry," she breathed quietly over the sound of the waves. "About them. They're assholes."

Otto startled out a laugh, dropping to sit on the stone beside her. His face was split by that easy, true smile again, and Mabel couldn't help but mirror it.

"A bit, yes." He adjusted, getting comfortable in the uncomfortable position. "But I have grown used to it, I'm afraid."

Mabel looked over at Otto, the sharp lines of his face in her periphery. She found him more handsome than ever, in the foreground of the endless navy sea and the swaying grass and stones of Juniper. He did not look like he had grown out of this soil or been washed ashore by the sea like the rest of them, and Mabel found his differences endlessly beautiful.

"How did you find yourself on Juniper after all?" she asked, stomach swooshing when he turned to look at her.

"I have been living in America for nearly ten years. In New York and then Boston. I am from Munich, but when . . ." he paused. Mabel had read the news. She knew what Germany had looked like a mere decade ago. "I was separated from my family. My parents were taken to a camp. They are gone now."

On instinct, Mabel reached out to lay her hand over his where it rested on his kneecap. She was even more surprised when he flipped his hand and allowed their fingers to lace together.

She had thought she knew hatred, knew loss. And while she could relate to those strains of hurt in Otto's voice, she could not even imagine what he had gone through, the depths of cruelty and grief he—his people—waded through.

"I did not know what became of my sister, two years my junior. I thought she, too, was gone. I got refuge to come to America in '40. I arrived in New York alone, twenty-three years old, with little English. I have made my way, on my own, since. It is . . . I grew up within my community. But here, I am too afraid to find my people. To find my beliefs again." Mabel looked at the deep, haunted expression in Otto's dark eyes. The war had been over for years, Mabel had thought. But looking at Otto, it was clear that it had not. That so much had been taken from him: home, family, beliefs, safety, community. That no matter how much time passed, for him and so many others, those horrors lingered.

She ran her thumb across his knuckles as he continued. "But two weeks ago I received a letter from my sister. She is alive, in London, with a husband and a daughter. She had thought I, too, was gone, and only now discovered my address."

Mabel could hear the joy in his voice at the thought of reunion, the fear that it was too good to be true. He released her hand to dig into his pockets and extract a photograph, weathered from being held so much, from perpetually resting within a pocket that sat over his heart.

In it a young woman with long, dark hair and Otto's same warm, round eyes smiled as she looked down at the little girl held in her arms. The girl smiled back at her mother, her curly hair dancing around her, a face of innocence. Looking at it through Otto's eyes, Mabel saw the photo for what it was. Reunion, yes, family too. But also resilience, the resilience of his people and their love and their survival.

"They're beautiful," she answered honestly.

Otto smiled at the photo once more before tucking it back in his pocket. It was so clear that despite all that had been done to him, he still had so much love to share. Mabel wished he had not come to expect cruelty and exclusion and that the people of Juniper had not shown him that he had been correct to do so.

Mabel wanted to take his hand again, but she didn't quite see how.

"I am moving there, to be with them," he said. For some reason, Mabel's stomach tightened at this. She didn't know why. She wanted Otto to be with his family, to be happy and safe. And she knew she would never get to keep him. "I wanted to see some of America first. I traveled up to see Vermont and New Hampshire, heard of the beautiful, isolated isles off the shore. I saw the ferry running and thought I would visit for the day." He smiled over at her, playful this time. "Clearly, that was not to be."

"That's beautiful, that you've gotten to see some more of the world than where you were born," Mabel replied. "Though I'm so sorry for the horrors that brought it on."

Otto nodded in agreement but did not allow the clouds of grief to overtake his face as he asked, "Have you traveled much yourself?"

Mabel couldn't help it—she laughed. "No, no. I have to stay on Juniper. I'm . . . trapped here. In a sense." She shrugged, used to it as she was. There was no "sense" of being bound to Juniper for life. She *was.* But she didn't bother to explain the curse to a mainlander who wouldn't understand.

Though listening to Otto speak of his sister, she couldn't help but think how much she longed for a reunion in her own family. How much that was impossible. There were no reunions for the Coles except in death in the sea. Generations of loneliness. Of early death. She would never want that for her descendants, and she couldn't help but think that Goody Cole must have felt the same. Goody knew her daughter, her granddaughter—why would she ever want to punish them when it was the rest of the town that wished them ill will? The islanders had always said that it was Goody, a witch, who set the curse. But dooming Cole women to loneliness and death? That felt more like the islanders and their historic animosity. Mabel had never questioned that the curse was real, but for the first time she questioned whether its origin was as she had been told.

"What traps you?" Otto asked, dark brows pulled together.

Mabel thought for a moment. "I guess we do. My family."

She thought of the Cole women in the sea that kept the living from leaving, that would punish all who remained if a Cole woman left Juniper. Even if her ancestors had loved their family in life, in that way they kept their descendants trapped. Mabel had always known that one day she'd walk into the sea—whether Goody Cole or someone else cursed her to do so—but she was finally realizing that she would become a part of that horde of phantoms in the sea that keeps her descendants trapped on the isle. The thought turned her stomach.

Otto opened his mouth, face clearly confused, but Mabel changed the topic before he could speak. "Never mind all that. I'm luckier than many."

It was obvious Otto had questions, but he merely nodded.

"I'm glad you'll get to be with your family so soon." Mabel steeled herself to speak a truth, the closeness of Otto's body thrumming through hers despite the whirlwind of her mind. "And, well, I'm glad too that you had to stay here"—*with me*—"for more than just the day."

That feeling she had—*that* she had no question about whether it was true. She looked into Otto's eyes and he looked back, and for once she felt there was something better to gaze at than the sea and its depths.

"As am I, I'm finding."

"Thank you for telling me your story," Mabel said softly. "The lighthouse is my sanctuary. If you'd like, it could be yours too."

Otto's dark eyes softened, and it was clear he understood how much Mabel was offering with those words. She looked at this man, this stranger becoming less of one, and found that she wanted to know more, know every piece of him she could while she still had time.

Nine
Rebecca

August 4, 1971

Juniper Island, Isles of Shoals, New Hampshire

Rebecca straightened the deep, hanging neckline of her dress. She shook the fabric out where it draped over her legs, ending at her ankles, being kissed by the waves each time they swelled up on the rock she sat on. The lobster boat had docked about ten minutes ago already. Rebecca had done her best not to look at it to see if Cal was stepping off; it wasn't like she was waiting for him.

She just wanted to be here on the rocks—their spot?—in case he happened to wander over. And if her heart flipped with a bit of guilty pleasure when she saw Barbara Allan and her friends weren't waiting on the shore? Well, so be it.

A few more minutes passed, Rebecca's gaze out at the open sea, her feet stinging with the pleasant licks of the icy Atlantic. Nervously, she twisted her hair over her shoulder, weaving it into a long braid that fell down to her waist. She watched as the summer clouds drifted above like puffs of smoke, lit peach by the falling sun.

This is stupid.

He called me beautiful. That doesn't mean he ever wanted to speak to me again.

He probably only talked to me so he could tell his friends he actually spoke to a witch and—

Cal Bradbury appeared at Rebecca's side like the embodiment of every daydream she'd ever dared to have. She looked up at him in the twilight, and her heart turned over twice.

"Hi," she breathed. Cal smiled that smile that knocked her breath from her lungs.

"Hey, Beck." Rebecca had never introduced herself to Cal; Juniper was small, and they had both grown from its roots. Everyone here knew everyone, and everyone especially knew the cursed Cole women. But it seemed that to Cal she wasn't Rebecca Cole: witch, Jew, cursed.

She was Beck. And she didn't know who Beck was, but God, she was excited for them to find out together.

Cal folded himself down to sit beside her, closer than he had been last time. His body pressed against hers from knee to shoulder and everything in between. Rebecca had never been so aware of her body before. She felt lit on fire, burning in the best way.

Gathering her courage, she turned to look at Cal, fingers nervously unbraiding her hair so it tumbled down across her chest. She watched his gaze follow the locks, lingering for just a moment on the triangle of tan skin visible above her neckline. She flushed all the way down.

With a small smile, Cal turned to look out at the sea. For a moment neither of them spoke, Rebecca's brain a chaotic whirl, desperately trying to find words to say that would make her sound mysterious, interesting, anything but how she felt. She counted her heartbeats in time with the waves. Cal leaned back, resting his weight on his hands, his biceps turning and swelling with the movement.

"This is a beautiful spot," he said softly. "It's so quiet on this side of the island. I wish I had known about it before." His blue eyes bored into her own.

Rebecca knew maybe it was just desperate hope talking, but it seemed like maybe what he meant was *I wish I had known about* you *before.*

"Yeah, not many people come over here." She paused. "Well, no one, really."

The reason why sat between them. Because no one else would dare to sit next to a Cole woman. This side of the island was theirs. But Rebecca was more than happy to give Cal a little piece of it. She'd give him as much of it as he wanted.

As if he could hear her thoughts, he said, "Well, they're missing out, then. I like it over here."

This time, as he looked at her, those lips pulling up at the corners, she knew what he meant for certain.

"Folks around here have got a lot of backwards ideas," he continued. "Sometimes I wish I could just get out of here for good. Go live somewhere on the mainland."

"*Yes*," she breathed, enthralled. So much so that a shiver coursed down her body, her bare arms rising in goose bumps.

Cal's eyes followed the swell across her skin.

"Here." He sat up, crossing his arms to pull the long-sleeved shirt over his head. As he did, Rebecca caught a flash of his stomach, faintly lined, ever so slightly lighter than his tan face and arms. He held the sweater out to her. Rebecca's heart flipped over and over and did not stop as she reached out, feeling the soft black fabric on her fingertips.

She didn't ask if he was sure. She tucked it over her head, the too-large garment enveloping her in the smell of musk and salt and the tartness of crushed juniper berries. She wanted to live in it forever.

Cal Bradbury sitting beside her, lending her his shirt. The prince of Juniper telling her that he, too, dreamed of getting out of this place. For so long all she had wanted was for the people here to accept her. She had thought that if someone like Cal did, maybe they'd follow suit. Now, though, she thought of a world where no one needed to be convinced to accept her, where she was a stranger in a strange land, with Cal Bradbury by her side. It was ridiculous, though, she knew. A few conversations didn't mean they'd run away together. Besides, Cal had Barbara.

Doing her best to hide the giddy storm of her thoughts, Rebecca kept her voice flat, almost disinterested, as she said, "I didn't think you would ever want to leave."

Cal's eyes glinted at her tone. Rebecca knew he was so used to everyone here singing his praises, bending themselves over backward for him. And here was Rebecca Cole, speaking to him like she could take his presence or leave it. She could see that he was intrigued, suddenly enraptured by her strategic response. She hoped he had no idea she was just as captivated as he suddenly was.

"Oh? Why not?"

Rebecca raised her eyebrows, painting her face in playful skepticism to cover the heady thrum of her heart. She watched Cal love every minute of it. It was a sense of power she had never felt before: being wanted. Being chased.

"Everyone here loves you. You have all that Bradbury acclaim and money and power. Besides," she quipped, "you've got your golden girl by your side."

She watched the way her words inflated his pride, his body subconsciously swelling with it. Until he paused, his dark brows pulling together.

"Who?" When Rebecca didn't answer, Cal continued, "Barbara?"

Rebecca raised her own brows, a silent affirmation. An unspoken *of course.*

Cal laughed. "Barbara and I aren't together anymore. Everyone just expected it, you know?"

No, Rebecca did not know what it was like to have expectations put on her besides centuries-old presumptions.

"We never were, not really. She wanted to be, but no, we're not." He turned to look at Rebecca directly as he spoke his next words. "She's not the one I want."

Rebecca felt her cheeks burn, the flush moving down her chest. Cal's eyes followed the heat down, up, landing finally on her lips. Her heart was thundering so loudly she couldn't even hear the waves as Cal leaned forward. He paused, his full lips ghosting across her own, her quick breaths tickling them. He was so close, but he waited. She could not.

Rebecca pressed forward, nervous, tentative, but unable to help herself.

Her first kiss was with Cal Bradbury.

Her first kiss was perfect.

His lips slotted against her own, soft and sure in a way hers were not. He led her through the motions, his tongue finding its way to hers, spreading a fire down through her entire body. He lifted a hand to rest on her jaw, his touch big and strong and so certain. Certain that what he wanted was her.

Her shaking hand rested along his wrist, almost holding it there, terrified he would pull back. But he did not. Their mouths explored each other for enough heartbeats that Rebecca lost count, her body floating away.

Finally, Cal did pull back. Just the slightest, his face still close to hers, his hair tickling her forehead, his eyes closed, lips smiling. Lips she'd just *kissed*.

Eventually, as though it pained him, Cal leaned away, his fingers trailing down her hair as he did. She shivered again and he smirked.

"I have to get home." Cal pressed to his feet.

Rebecca's heart sank. Had she done it wrong?

But then he bent down, tucking a finger under her chin to tilt it up to him. Holding her there, he kissed her one more time, feather light. Then he turned and disappeared back onto Juniper proper.

Every girl on this island wanted Cal Bradbury. And Rebecca was no different. But she thought maybe, just maybe, she might be the one he wanted back.

From then on, Rebecca would always think of her life as before and after this moment.

Ten
Mabel

April 6, 1951

Juniper Island, Isles of Shoals, New Hampshire

Mabel had been so unsure, almost embarrassed, when she had asked Otto if he would share himself with her. His beliefs, that is.

They felt so essential and integral to the way the man moved through and saw the world, and Mabel wanted to welcome that too. She had assured Otto he could say no, that she understood if it was private, if she could not partake or witness. She had been surprised when a smile broke his face and he told her he'd be happy to welcome her in his Friday night rituals he called Shabbat.

By daylight their Friday had been spent in the kitchen, Otto cooking chicken and vegetables, teaching Mabel how to lace the thick ropes of bread one over the other. And as nighttime swept closer above the waves, Mabel had shared her own lighting rituals with him, taking Otto to the top of the lighthouse to watch as she worked, to stand beside her to see the result of the reaching light swooping across the black water.

For once it was not only the phantom presence of her ancestors below that kept Mabel company up there.

Now, settled back in the kitchen, the warm, heady smell of roasted food permeated the small space. The light outside the window was not yet dark, but the purgatorial purple indicated that it would be soon enough. Mabel handed Otto the two white beeswax candles he'd asked for, ones made by Dotty Allan on the other side of the island. Their hands brushed as they passed the short, tapered sticks, and Mabel felt as if it was her own skin that was lit on fire.

Otto nestled the candles into the worn copper holders Mabel had provided, placing them equal distance in the center of the small round kitchen table. Mabel turned off the lights around them. The room was silent, split only by the staticky swipe of a match. Otto's large hand brought the match to each wick, the small orange flames dancing across the room, embracing them in a warm glow, as though nothing outside of the peace of this room existed. Nothing beyond the two of them.

Mabel watched, entranced, silent, as Otto closed his eyes and began to speak words in a language that Mabel did not recognize but sounded holy on the man's tongue. He finished, slowly opening his eyes, his gaze following the flicker of the flames with a kind of renewed reverence.

Mabel wanted to ask what he'd said, but she was aware that, even though it was her home they resided in, she was the guest this night. She did not want to interrupt the moment. Thankfully, Otto seemed as aware of Mabel as she was of him and readily explained, "It is a prayer for lighting the candles on Shabbat."

He looked out the window, where night was starting to nestle down on the island. "The candles must be lit before night falls and stay lit until they burn out. Then, for the next twenty-five hours, we devote ourselves to rest, to peace. A day free of work."

Otto had explained the boundaries of the day to her earlier; she knew that he could not cook during that twenty-five hour window, that he could not carry heavy bags or touch light switches or anything beyond rest. Mabel couldn't imagine as much. And though she had readily offered to assist him during that time, which he had gratefully accepted, she was thankful, too, that she got to partake in this day in any way she could. The beauty of it was not lost on her.

The food sat on the table already, and Otto and Mabel sat before it, the scent on the air making Mabel salivate. There was a browned roast chicken, a large bowl of vegetable soup, the heavy loaf of braided bread—challah—they'd spent the day twisting together.

In front of the food—and the wine they poured alongside it—Otto softly spoke more prayers in the language of his people. The words might have been unintelligible to Mabel, but she could clearly feel the emotion, the sentiment, behind them.

When he finished, he took another moment of silence, somber. Then a small smile pulled at his face as he began to serve the food to them both. They ate with only the sound of the sea and small chatter, the food so delicious it distracted Mabel's mind entirely. Their conversations were light, were peaceful, were simply companionship and safety within the octagonal space of the lighthouse.

The food was warm and comforting and tasted like memory and love, even to Mabel, but it was not enough to distract her from the heady sensation of Otto's closeness. The table was small enough that they had to sit close together, knees pressed against each other beneath the table. The room was thick with the flames of the candles and the scents of the food, but Mabel knew that was not why her body felt so flushed with warmth.

And every time Otto's dark eyes found hers, colored by softness and something like disbelief, she knew he felt it too.

As she took her last bites, Mabel felt comfortably full and warm, at peace, truly. "Was this . . . did you celebrate this night with your family?" she asked. Not from her own curiosity per se, but because she wanted Otto to know that as welcome as he was in her home, so too were the memories of his family that he carried with him.

"When I was a boy, my mother would say our Shabbat prayers, light the candles just before nightfall." Mabel could hear the longing and loss in his voice as clearly as it colored his face. Her heart lurched. For him, yes, but for her own mother too. For the memories they did not have together and the loss that Mabel weathered by herself, a loss that was cursed to doggedly follow the Cole women, motherless, *alone*.

"It must be nice for you to still have this," Mabel said, no longer so worried she was saying the wrong thing. It was clear that Otto was forgiving to her learning, that he was readily sharing this with her. "These routines and beliefs to remember her. Them all."

All of them. Because Otto had had a community, a people. Mabel had only ever had her mother, and even then, barely. All she had was a curse. A feeling of presence in the water that, honestly, she wasn't sure was anything more than internalizing the islanders' rhetoric. Mabel had seen so little of the world, had experienced nothing beyond the isle, and all she knew was what she had been told. The curse, those women in the water, they were never a belief; they had always just been fact. She couldn't imagine what it would be like to have a community, bound by blood and belief. She couldn't imagine what it would be like to so violently lose that.

"I was never so strict with my beliefs or practices back then, before," Otto said as he pushed his cleared plate forward so he could rest his arms on the table before him. "I did them, not out of obligation, but routine, I suppose. I did not give them much thought. Now, though, that I have had to fight for them, now I care for my practices. My beliefs are me. They are my tie to my family and my people and myself. Now every prayer I speak, every candle I light is a remembrance. A defiance. Proof that we survive."

Proof that we survive.

"That is . . ." Mabel swallowed a lump in her throat made of empathy, of pride in him, of gratefulness for his presence. "That is beautiful, Otto. Powerful."

Mabel did not have proof that her family survived beyond the words whispered and glances cut by the islanders. Sometimes, especially now that she was alone, she felt like she hardly had proof that she lived. But now, looking at Otto Weitz, Mabel Cole knew she was alive.

It was temporary. Mabel could not keep this man. He was never meant to be hers. But it seemed there was a reason he had found his way here, to her table. They both knew how fleeting and temporary life was, so they acted on life while they could.

Mabel leaned across the small gap of space between them tentatively, showing Otto what she wanted but letting him decide if she could have it, if he wanted it too. He hesitated only a moment before he too leaned forward and their lips met. Mabel had never kissed a soul before, had never been touched. She had thought of it before, of course, worried how it would feel, that she would fumble her way through.

But Otto was a teacher tonight, and he guided her patiently. Their kiss tasted of the earthy wine they had consumed and the peace on the air.

Mabel's hands found the smooth, sturdy skin of Otto's hand as it rested on her jawline, gentle and devoted, as though she, too, was a sacred thing on this night. For perhaps the first time ever, Mabel felt real.

She led Otto up the twisting staircase, pausing at the barrier between her bedroom and the one he had been occupying. Mabel no longer wanted to lie in bed and hold her breath so she could hear the sound of his rustling sheets and fanning breaths as he slept across the hall, as she had for the past few nights. She wanted to see it, hear it, feel him herself.

She twisted their fingers together as she led them into her room. Mabel's hands shook as they settled together on the bed she had spent her life in. Though they both knew Otto would be gone in two days' time, nothing seemed to matter beyond this moment.

There were fumbles, yes, and apologies. But also giggles and soft-spoken words and, eventually, sighs Mabel had never heard her mouth make before. They twined together as the light spun above them, the beam cutting through the port window and illuminating the room in turns. And each time it did, Otto's face and body and skin cast in soft white light, Mabel found something new to admire and long for. There, in the room she had always known, as a lonely child and a desperate teen and a sorrowful adult, Mabel finally felt that the beginning had, in fact, begun.

Eleven
Rebecca

August 6, 1971

Juniper Island, Isles of Shoals, New Hampshire

He kissed me.

Cal Bradbury kissed me.

The words couldn't stop bouncing around Rebecca's mind, the most beautiful echo.

She settled herself into the worn, overstuffed armchair in her room, tucked just beneath the large window that overlooked the endless blue sea. No matter what window she peeked through, just endless blue.

But maybe, maybe, not forever.

She knew, logically, that she was getting ahead of herself. Cal had mentioned he'd love to leave the island; that didn't mean he wanted to leave with *her*. Still, the thought latched on to something deep in Rebecca that she could not shake. That she didn't want to.

The small slip of paper rested on her bent knees. Its edges were worn down from being nestled between rocks, just out of reach of the stretching waves. Tucked there for her to find. In what she had long thought of as her spot but now, quickly, had repainted itself in her mind as *their* spot.

Beck—

Can't talk tonight
See you tomorrow

—C

She had read it a dozen times already, at least. But she curled up in her chair, rain beating down on the window, and read it again and again and again. Until each curling letter, each stroked line, was memorized in her mind's eye. She ran her pointer finger along each letter, feeling how Cal must have felt when he wrote it. The way the letters pressed together, the self-assured swoop of the *C*. The way he'd written her name. She traced that over and over until her fingertip felt numb, until she stopped because she was afraid she'd wear down the ink to nothing. Her name, there, in Cal Bradbury's hand. Rebecca wasn't sure she felt like Beck yet, but she *wanted* to be her. Cal and Beck. Beck and Cal. *Him and me. Me and him. Us.*

Rebecca Cole was a witch, a Jew, odd, other, cursed.

Beck Cole could be anybody. Maybe even Beck Bradbury.

Yes, Rebecca knew she was getting ahead of herself, but she didn't stop her thoughts. She didn't want to. For once, she liked having something to be excited about, something to look forward to. For once, she liked not being alone.

She heard her mother on the steps, heading down from lighting the beam. Hastily, Rebecca shoved the note into her desk drawer, just as her mother's head poked through the gap in the door.

"You want to come down and help me cook, baby?"

Rebecca immediately chafed at the nickname. She was not a baby. She was nineteen now. She had been *kissed*. She was a grown woman. A grown woman with her own future.

She couldn't help her irritable sigh. "Not right now, Mom. I'm busy."

Her mom's eyes cut around the room, still and empty, Rebecca seemingly just relaxing in her chair. Shrugging, she said, "All right. I'll call when food's ready, then."

"Okay." Rebecca's voice was short, anxious for her mother to leave so she could return to her note.

With a surprised flick of her brows upward, her mother took her leave, her soft footsteps retreating down into the kitchen. Before Rebecca could even reach for the note again, her mom's voice drifted back up. So she wouldn't have to hear it and be interrupted from the beauty of her reverie, Rebecca hopped out of her chair.

She went to the large bookshelf by the doorway. Only a handful of books sat on it, mostly old paperbacks that must have belonged to her mom. Most were romances, something Rebecca had always found odd from her lonely, isolated mother. Rebecca hadn't read any of them in years; she got enough time with books working in the library.

But still, the shelves were full to bursting. Because while Rebecca Cole might not be a bookworm, she was certainly a lover of music. That was her lifeblood. It was easy to pluck out the record she was in the mood for. She crossed the room, setting it on the player, lowering the needle. Promptly, the heady bass rang out around the room, overriding the sounds of her mother down in the kitchen. Rebecca settled back into her chair just as Robert Plant sang the opening of "Whole Lotta Love."

She reached over to her desk, grabbing the note along with her favorite, worn notebook and a pen. She read the note again and again, welcoming the rush of warmth that spread from her chest down to her toes, as real and thrilling as Cal's lips on hers.

It felt like Cal Bradbury had cracked her open, cracked open her world. Suddenly, everything seemed possible. She began to write a header on the blank notebook page, swirling a large, confident *R*. But then she paused. No. She easily turned the *R* into a *B*. The blast of rock music drowned out the scratch of pen on paper and the dreamy nature of her drifting thoughts, Cal's face always at the forefront of her mind.

As Rebecca wrote, she imagined herself and Cal walking down a cobblestone street, fingers intertwined. She imagined kissing his full lips in the shadow of the world's greatest monuments. She imagined them holding each other in the most beautiful places in the world, places where no one knew them and she didn't have to hate herself, places where she would never have to hear the sound of waves. More than anything, she imagined the two of them riding the subway, buried in the crowds of rock concerts, strolling the East Village; she imagined her and Cal, a life in New York, among the concrete and the lights.

By the time the sharp guitar of "Heartbreaker" bounced around the room, Rebecca had filled a whole page with her scratchings.

Beck's Travel Bucket List

- o *New York City*
- o *Boston*
- o *Paris*
- o *San Francisco*
- o *London*
- o *Vienna*
- o *Rio de Janeiro*
- o *Rome*

- o *Tokyo*
- o *Lisbon*
- o *Marrakesh*
- o *Amsterdam*
- o *Everywhere but Juniper*

She didn't care if the curse said that the lighthouse, that Juniper, would never let Cole women leave for long. She didn't care that the stories said that if she left, the people of Juniper would suffer, would die themselves at sea in the stead of a Cole woman.

None of that seemed real. Anything seemed possible with Cal by her side.

Instead of putting her notebook back in her desk, Rebecca brought it—and the note within—to her bed. She tucked them beneath the pillow, where they could soak in the scent of Cal's shirt that was already burrowed beneath. Soon enough, every bit of her home, everything she held dear, would take on his scent. She welcomed it eagerly.

Twelve
Mabel

May 18, 1951

Juniper Island, Isles of Shoals, New Hampshire

"Wow! This place is cleaning up nicely!" Judy Poole's round face peeked through the door to the Smith cottage.

It was clear the woman was speaking to Evelyn, beaming at her from the doorway. Even Judy's rolled hair and flared skirt seemed like a pale imitation questing for Evelyn's approval, but her brassy hair fell flat and her skirt slipped from her waist, not creating an hourglass figure. Meanwhile, Evelyn floated and made it look effortless.

Mabel was still a bit tender and frazzled from the dream she'd awoken from just an hour or two prior—but still, even with hazy images of her mother wandering on the beach bleaching Mabel's waking mind, she was certain she wasn't dreaming the way Judy never quite looked at her.

The woman's hazel eyes were locked on Evelyn as the blonde moved across the space, broom in motion. Judy's smile, too, was aimed at Evelyn; her gaze only occasionally flitted to

Mabel's bent-over form in the corner. Each time it did, that smile seemed to dim.

Mabel expected to feel that instinct to smile and be overly nice, to get Judy to like her. That instinct that had become second nature for the last decade of her life. But she remembered the way Judy had looked at Otto from her doorway, and Mabel couldn't find that desire for acceptance. She remained hunched over the strewn parts of the bookcase they needed to build, her lower back twanging with a deep ache.

Though Mabel couldn't deny Judy was right.

The Smith cottage was looking good. They'd made it look good, she and Evelyn. It finally was starting to come close to looking not like the Smith fishing cottage but the library it would be.

At the very least, it was equipped for the weather now.

The roof had been patched, the floorboards replaced so they no longer bulged. The window had been scrubbed and cleaned and repaired, and the stunning blue of sea and sky in spring could be seen beyond.

Back straining, Mabel lifted the longest slat of wood that would become a shelf, dropping it on the rough-hewn love seat that Evelyn was intending to repair as a seating area for patrons.

Mabel had been tuning out the polite chatter of Evelyn and Judy, but she noticed it stopped as Evelyn suddenly appeared at her side, plucking the wood board from her grasp.

"May, you ought to let me help you." Evelyn gave her a long, assessing look that passed from her head to her toes. Mabel couldn't read it, but she felt embarrassment or something like it flash through her. *May.* Mabel had never been close enough to anyone to get a nickname before.

Judy, clearly unhappy to lose Evelyn's attention, piped up from the doorway. She still didn't cross the threshold; after all, as far as Judy thought, there was a witch within. "Ladies, you ought to have your husbands build those shelves!"

The woman's eyes finally settled fully on Mabel. "Well, husband." Her smile twisted apologetically, but even Mabel could tell how false it rang.

Surprisingly, Evelyn seemed to as well. Her earlier politeness toward the woman slipped as she said, in a clipped voice, "No need. We ought to get back to work now, if you wouldn't mind."

Mabel just barely resisted gaping at the curt dismissal. Judy, on the other hand, couldn't help herself. Her round cheeks stained pink as she mumbled a goodbye and left, the door clattering closed behind her.

Evelyn kneeled, continuing to sort through the wooden slats on the ground. "Judy can be a real pain," she said.

Mabel swallowed a laugh. Never, in the weeks they'd spent together, had she heard Evelyn Fuller speak poorly of anyone on Juniper. Mabel hadn't thought she'd ever have any reason to; Juniper didn't have a monarchy, of course, but if it did, it was clear Evelyn would be the natural choice for its queen.

Comfortable enough around the other woman by now, Mabel opened her mouth to quip back a joke, but the words died on her tongue. As Evelyn reached forward, the sleeve of her sweater slid up her arm. Mabel had wondered how the other woman managed to still wear her pristine, thick sweaters even as the sun began to beat down on the island.

Now, stomach dropping through, Mabel realized why. As the sleeve road up Evelyn's arm, Mabel caught sight of four bright stripes of deep-purple bruising marring her pale skin. Four fingers gripping a thin wrist tight enough to leave a mark of anger, to do damage.

"Evelyn." The word fell heavy from Mabel's mouth, loaded.

Evelyn seemed to hear it all in that one word, for her large blue eyes darted down to her wrist. Seeing the black-purple bruises exposed, she quickly tugged down her sleeve. Evelyn turned her eyes from Mabel, steadfastly keeping her gaze on the splayed wood before her.

"*Evelyn,*" Mabel said again. She had so many thoughts, a storm of concerns, but couldn't quite find the words.

"Oh, that?" Evelyn tried for lightness and failed miserably. Still she did not look up. "Just a little accident in the kitchen, caught the edge of a hot pan. I can be so clumsy."

Mabel finally seemed to find her words, her torrent of thoughts settling into anger. She might not know much of the world, but she knew what a bruise like that meant. She didn't care if the world, if the island, thought Dean Fuller, as a husband, as a man, could do as he pleased. She wished she really were the witch they all believed her to be, so she could curse him through every level of Hell.

"Evelyn, that is no—"

"Let it be, Mabel." Evelyn's voice was quiet now, but steady. She looked up where Mabel stood above her. Her blue eyes were sad, but they were hard.

For once, it was not Evelyn deftly, smoothly, protecting Mabel from the people of this island. And Mabel found that her desire to protect Evelyn was not polite and smooth and underhanded. She raged. But Evelyn Fuller had become a friend, one she did not want to push away by pushing too far. Though Mabel felt a rock lodge itself in her throat, she nodded. She would let it be, for now, though every instinct told her not to.

But she knew, too, suspected at least, that this might just be the burden of being a wife. She wished she could save Evelyn from that too.

Clearing her throat, Evelyn stood, dusting invisible dirt from her skirt. The air was thick with discomfort, and it was clear the blonde was trying to smooth it over.

"I think we've earned a little break, don't you?" she said, rifling through the basket she'd brought that rested by the doorway. Evelyn nudged the door open with her hip. "I made us some juniper berry jam. Let's try it out."

She smiled that same controlled, polite expression Mabel knew now was a facade. Then she slipped outside. Mabel, still trembling, followed.

Evelyn had settled herself on the rocks behind the cottage, the contents of the basket spread out around her, the waves tickling at her toes. Mabel sat by her side, the hard surface of the rock twinging that pain in her back once more.

Evelyn's eyes fell to where Mabel's hand had come to sit on her lower back, as if she could push the pain back into her spine. Evelyn's dark brow crinkled, but she turned away, unpacking the goodies. The lapping of the waves was the only conversation as Evelyn twisted open a jar of deep-purple jam, the color of fresh bruises.

Mabel's stomach twisted.

But quickly she realized it was not just from the coloring. Her stomach continued to sour, mouth swelling with spit, her cheeks suddenly going numb. Mabel hardly had a moment to think before she leaned forward, spewing her morning's black coffee and breakfast onto the rocks by her feet. She couldn't even think to be embarrassed as her throat burned and her eyes stung, water slipping down her cheeks, and she retched. Finally, her stomach seemed to empty and the embarrassment set in.

Mabel swiped her cheeks dry as the water, blessedly, swept the sick out to sea, the scent of brine quickly covering the acidic smell.

"God, I don't know what came over me. I swear, it wasn't your jam." Mabel tried to chuckle. "I haven't been feeling quite myself lately. I think maybe—"

Evelyn's face was not surprised. Not uncomfortable. It was serious, dead set on Mabel.

"Mabel," the other woman said, the name once again weighted heavily with meaning. But this time, Mabel did not understand the weight.

"What? I'm sorry, that was—"

"Mabel, have you not noticed?" Evelyn's brows pinched together in sympathy now. "I've suspected for a few days now. The dreams you mentioned, the nausea, the . . . well . . ." Evelyn's eyes cut down to Mabel's chest, which strained against her shirt uncomfortably in a way it never had before.

Still Mabel did not understand. She did not want to understand. It couldn't be.

"I think you're pregnant, Mabel," Evelyn said gently. "I've been pregnant twice. I know what the early signs look like."

Mabel could hardly hear Evelyn's words or the beating of the waves. There was a sound in her ear, like an emergency wail, ringing and ringing in her skull.

Distantly she registered the wrong part of Evelyn's words, noticed that the woman cited two pregnancies though she only had little Richie. Mabel wanted to ask her friend, offer sympathy, but she couldn't hold on to any thoughts over the ringing.

"I don't mean to imply anything, of course," Evelyn continued, voice finding Mabel through a long, dark tunnel. "I mean, could it be?"

Mabel finally pulled her eyes from the sea to find Evelyn's.

Yes, yes, it could be.

In fact, Mabel realized, there was no *could*. It was. She should have realized sooner; she might know little of the world, but she knew much of the curse that poisoned her family line. She had thought of it only as a negative, something that leeched on the Cole women and stole their lives, beckoning them out to sea when it was their time.

But that was the thing—they were cursed for there to never be more than *two* Cole women on Juniper. Her mother, who had so recently walked into the inky-dark waves, was finally called. Because the curse knew what time did not, what humans did not. That soon there would be a new Cole woman on Juniper.

Mabel thoughtlessly placed a hand on her stomach. Still flat, but she knew it would swell soon.

It seemed the *soon* of a new Cole woman had arrived.

Thirteen
Mabel

May 20, 1951

Juniper Island, Isles of Shoals, New Hampshire

Mabel's first thought was *I need to tell Otto we're having a daughter.*

Mabel's second thought was *I can't tell Otto. I have no way to tell Otto.*

Because, of course, that was the way they had left things. On good terms, smiles and hugs, secretive looks—but good-byes nonetheless. Otto did not know what his phone number or address in London would be, and by now he was certainly settled abroad. Settled in with his sister and her daughter, with his family, and Mabel had no way to tell him that that family was growing. All she could hope was that maybe he would return to Juniper one day.

Of course, she knew he wouldn't. Because that was the curse, wasn't it? Only two Cole women, a line of fatherless daughters. History repeating itself to punish Goody Cole and all who came after her, like the waves always breaking against the rocks, receding, only to return again.

And that was Mabel's third thought, the one that nestled into her bones like a truth: *The curse is real.*

She didn't know who had cursed them—her ancestor Goody Cole, as the islanders believed, or someone or something else. But Mabel had always accepted the curse as their truth, just as her mother had taught her. But it had always seemed abstract, far off. Now she knew it was real and it was here. She was fated to have this daughter soon enough, and so the curse must have started whispering to her mother, calling to her from the sea, until she stepped into it for good. And then, just on time, Mabel conceived a child.

The curse of the Cole women.

But at that moment, as Mabel sat atop the lighthouse, legs swinging over the edge of the gallery's curving balcony, it seemed more like a gift than a curse. Yes, her mother had died quite young, but all Cole women did. At least Mabel would not be alone. She would be a mother herself.

She sat on the edge of the gallery, legs swinging into the open air, arms and chin resting on the low railing as she looked out. A few months ago Mabel would've been lighting the beam already, but spring had quickly bled into summer and the sun fell much later these days. It was hardly twilight, the sun only starting to fall in the sky at her back. Mabel looked out at the waves that crashed against the rocks beneath her, the warmer months painting the depths a lighter navy. The world seemed warmer, more welcoming. She was glad that this was the world her daughter would be born into, this world of the lighthouse. Watercolor stripes of pink and orange had started to paint the sky, sherbet to offset the endless blue sea. The air was hard as ever, tangling Mabel's hair to straw, stinging her nose with its scent that was the most familiar thing in the world.

She knew she should call on Chet Allan soon. The man was the island's best shot for a doctor; his wife, Dotty, was the island midwife. But Mabel knew she was pregnant. She knew. She didn't need a doctor to tell her just yet.

Besides, Mabel wasn't quite ready to face the shame that she knew was coming her way, that she could feel brewing like a storm over the waves. But for the first time in her life, the thought of the islanders' exclusion, their hard looks, made Mabel *angry*.

She didn't care if every last person on the island would hate her: a Cole, a witch, soon an unmarried mother to a baby conceived with a Jewish man. She didn't care what they thought of her, and she would raise her daughter to do the same. She wasn't even a mother herself yet, and already Mabel felt as though she understood her own mother better.

Mabel had been raised having no knowledge of her father. Her mother never spoke a word, and, frankly, Mabel had forgotten to ever ask. It was simply understood that fathers were not a thing Cole girls got. But Mabel's girl would know of her father, even if she could never meet him, even if he never knew of her. She would know that he was a kind man with a gentle smile and gentle hands. She would know the hardship he and his family had lived through, know that that was her family too now. Mabel would ensure her little girl knew of her father's heritage, his beliefs, that they would become the little girl's own heritage.

Mabel would make sure her daughter had the world and then some, and—despite the hostility of the land and its inhabitants—this island was the most beautiful corner of the world Mabel could think of. She would make sure her little girl knew Juniper was as much hers as it was any of the islanders', no matter what they said or did. Her girl would be as Mabel herself was: born of brine and soil and thorns and curses.

Fourteen
Rebecca

August 8, 1971

Juniper Island, Isles of Shoals, New Hampshire

the lobster boat port. midnight.

—C

The beach glowed, the washed-up mussel shells so pearlescent they seemed to reflect the moon back to it. Rebecca stood on the shore, dark hair billowing behind her like a shadow, salt brine and nerves on her tongue. She stood at the point where the waves kissed the pebbles and sand, looking out at the endless expanse of blackness that was the sea. She didn't want to face the island, didn't want to seem like she was waiting for Cal—though, of course, she was. She didn't want to have to see if Cal never came at all.

Sure, he might have invited her here, the note slipped between rocks in their spot. But still, Rebecca thought it just as likely he never came, that the note disintegrated into sand where it was nestled beneath her pillow. That she woke up to find this had all been some dream.

She was so tangled in her mind that she didn't realize Cal had arrived until his arms twisted around her middle, his warm body pressing to the back of hers. Rebecca was glad she was looking out at the sea so he couldn't see the sudden, splitting smile that she had to bite down.

She turned in his arms, finding them face-to-face. For a moment Rebecca was self-conscious, remembering how Barbara Allan had barely reached Cal's chest, yet here Rebecca was, only a few inches shorter than him. But then Cal's face grew into a smile so genuine, so singularly focused on her, that it nearly knocked the air from Rebecca's chest.

"You came." She felt the breath of his words tickle her skin, they were so close.

"I came." Rebecca smiled right back.

His arms pulled her tighter, her body pressing into every line of his. It felt like her skin was on fire. Hesitantly, nervously, Rebecca reached up, arms hooking around his neck. He leaned forward, his nose gliding across hers, their separate spaces becoming one. Rebecca held her breath.

"Seems only right that I'd find you here, wandering out of the water." He smirked and she felt the movement against her own face, all the little peach fuzz hairs there rising in anticipation.

Rebecca wished she had a clever retort, but her mind was whirring, nothing sticking. So rather than saying something that might not be smart, witty, mysterious, she kissed him.

Rebecca had only had her first kiss days ago, but already kissing Cal Bradbury was second nature, was what she knew. They came alive against each other's lips.

Rebecca wanted to ask him why he wanted to meet at midnight—why here? But it seemed words weren't their strong suit. Their bodies seemed to know each other in a way that Rebecca felt in her chest; solid, real, right.

Cal's hands fisted her dress at the small of her back, pulling her closer to him, close as possible but still, somehow, not close enough. Rebecca lost herself in the movement of his lips on hers, his golden hair running through her fingers, the warm, strong hold of his arms.

And then he pulled away with a startled laugh, looking down at the cresting wave that had just soaked through his shoes.

"Come here." Cal smiled, taking Rebecca's hand. She let him lead her away from the soft, wet sand, back toward the rocks on the island's edge. In one spot they jutted out, creating a little alcove, tucked away from the world. Cal pulled her down to settle on the sand beneath the rocky awning. He settled her against him close, his mouth immediately finding hers once more, as if he couldn't bear to part from her for a moment, as if he could not get her close enough. Rebecca understood. Her hands grabbed at his biceps, his hair, his jawline, getting as much of his body in her memory as she could. As their movements progressed from exploration to hunger, Rebecca thought there would never be close enough; she didn't just want Cal to want her, she wanted to become one, to breathe the same air, share the same skin. Rebecca desperately wanted—*needed*—Cal to want her the same way.

Gently, he guided her to lie on her back, his body stretching across hers. The cold sand seeped through the thin layer of her dress, causing her skin to shiver, but it tightened quickly at the warmth of Cal pressed along her front. His body was a delicious weight, grounding her, hovering over her, keeping her safe from the rest of Juniper. Here, it was just them. Here, he was just hers.

Cal's large hands found Rebecca's calf, trailing up her leg, bunching up her long dress as he went. She forgot how to breathe, all the air she knew coming from between his lips. The sound of the waves lapping was distant, the only true sounds their breathing, the slight hitch in her breath as Cal's hand found her thigh, squeezed. Rebecca's body felt too hot for even the floaty presence of her dress. The spot between her legs pulsed so heavily it was almost uncomfortable.

But then Cal's hands found their way there too. Self-consciousness held Rebecca close, but so did Cal, and soon any nerves slipped away beneath his touch. Rebecca didn't know what to do with her hands, how to touch Cal to return the feeling he was giving her. But Cal was an eager teacher, guiding her surely. Rebecca did her best to push out thoughts of how he knew this dance so well; if it was Barbara Allan he was used to having beneath him, if he wished Rebecca were smaller, blonder, more loved. But Cal was here with *her*. They were together, here. This was theirs.

Cal pulled back a moment, the pressure of his hands disappearing. He looked down at her, his blue eyes so earnest, boring into her own. Without thought she reached up, trailing a featherlight touch over his brow, feeling the bone beneath his skin. Feeling how real he was, no longer a figure of her daydreams but a real man, one who was choosing her. Cal smiled softly down at her, gold hair falling across his brow, tickling her fingers.

His hand found its way to Rebecca's jaw. On instinct she tilted her head, mouth reaching up for his. Before she could make contact, he whispered, "Do you want to?"

Rebecca had never. She suspected Cal knew that, but she certainly wasn't going to tell him when she was almost certain he had. But she knew what he meant, had read books, had heard songs, had never even dared to dream.

But yes, yes, she wanted to.

Looking up into Cal's earnest, open expression, Rebecca nodded, for she found that her tongue was too heavy with nervous anticipation to speak. That smile broke on Cal's face like sunrise and Rebecca's chest glowed, her decision affirmed.

Cal was gentle with his touches across her body, gathering her dress up around her waist, his body finding hers. It took a beat before it was comfortable, before the nerves holding her body taut could relax. But slowly, she did, Cal's heavy breath ghosting warm against her neck, where he nuzzled into her. Rebecca looked up at the star-dotted navy sky, welcoming her new beginning.

Fifteen
Mabel

June 21, 1951

Juniper Island, Isles of Shoals, New Hampshire

A river of sweat twisted along Mabel's spine as she leaned against the outside of the lighthouse. In the near distance, the form of Evelyn Fuller grew bigger and nearer, and with each step closer, Mabel's sweat bloomed a little bit more.

The air still carried a bit of a chill—they were on the Atlantic, after all—but summer had certainly settled atop Juniper Island. The lighthouse on her back burned through Mabel's sweater, heated by the late-afternoon sun. Of course, she would have loved to wear something lighter. But, of course, she could not. Not yet.

Mabel was twisting her fingers with unspent nervous energy as Evelyn finally came to a stop just before her, beneath the shadow of the looming lighthouse. It seemed so unnatural, Evelyn's golden beauty against the rough soil and rocks out here on the island's edge, where no one but Coles ever dared venture.

"Hi, May." Evelyn beamed at her, the wind lifting her fair hair in a somehow still-perfect whirl around her diamond-shaped face.

Mabel nodded. She couldn't quite find her voice.

She knew that Evelyn had volunteered to come over and help Mabel sort her mother's books, choose which ones to relocate to the library. But still, something deep seated and long ago planted in Mabel's mind whispered that it wasn't right for an islander to be in the lighthouse. That they would hate it, they would judge it, that this sanctuary was the Cole women's alone and no one else would understand. That to let in an islander would let in the islanders' hatred, into this one place it couldn't reach. And she knew the islanders believed this side of the island was particularly dangerous for them too, even if there was a living Cole woman present to keep the sea phantoms at bay.

But Evelyn, standing in front of the doorway, smiling softly and looking eagerly at the large structure—not with judgment, just with soft fascination—was different. By now, Mabel knew that. Maybe Evelyn was even safe.

The thought was absurd. Evelyn Fuller, Evelyn Bradbury, the island's golden girl. But she had never given Mabel anything but friendship.

"Come on in." Mabel stepped through the door into her home, holding her breath as Evelyn followed her.

Mabel expected Evelyn to be silent during the tour of the lighthouse, to be quietly remembering every detail of the *witches' home* so she could tell stories to the others. But she wasn't. She was still the Evelyn who Mabel was getting to know well. She smiled and chatted, picking up a naked-butted picture of a young Mabel with a smirk. Eyes wide with fascination as she inspected the light, complimenting Mabel on her ability to run it on her own, though to the other woman it had always been second nature. But Evelyn's eyes glittered the brightest as they stepped into the empty second bedroom.

Her mother's room. Otto's room. Soon enough, her daughter's room.

There were only two bedrooms in the lighthouse, but the curse demanded there never be more than two Cole women anyway, so more were never needed. Mabel kept the door to her own room firmly closed, and though she saw Evelyn's eyes flicker to the barred space, Mabel did not extend her tour there.

Her mother's room was a tangle of smells twisting around the large space, an eight-sided circle just as every room within the lighthouse was. Mabel had not changed the sheets since Otto had stayed; it was still too painful to be in this room alone. And the crumpled bedding still bore the indent of his head and the faint waft of his scent. But more overpowering even as it slipped further each day was the smell of Mabel's mother. Briny sea air, fresh-crushed juniper berries, old books, earthy soil, and something sweet and floral beneath it all. The smell of her mother was the smell of her island, somehow most concentrated in this room.

Mabel felt flayed raw to share it with Evelyn, but she did.

Evelyn flicked on a light switch, casting a golden glow over the room. Everything here was earth tones, just like her mother. Mable had hardly touched a thing: thick knit blanket still tossed over her cushiony reading chair, a tea-stained coffee mug on the bedside table, dog-ears still folded into the books.

Evelyn, somehow, seemed to see all these little pieces of Mabel's mother that she could not bear to upend. A woman Mabel had hardly known, hadn't even realized she had loved until it was too late. Instinctually, standing in the center of the room, Mabel placed a protective hand on her stomach.

Her daughter would know her mother. Her daughter would know she was loved.

"Did your mother paint these?" Evelyn asked, trailing a featherlight finger along the edge of a canvas pinned to the wall. On it a thousand shades of blue swirled together, the view of the ocean through the little porthole window on the far side of the room. Mabel stepped up beside Evelyn, nodding.

She could smell the scent of lavender braided through Evelyn's hair from this close.

"It's beautiful," the woman said. "I'm sorry I didn't know your mother better."

Evelyn's voice was so earnest. *No,* Mabel thought, *she is certainly not like the rest of them.*

"Me too." She knew that Evelyn misinterpreted her response, and she allowed her to.

Mabel cleared her throat. "So, as you can see, we've got a pretty good starting point for the library."

She gestured to the three floor-to-ceiling bookcases nestled into the room, books spilling out of all of them. The two women stepped up to the shelves, began pulling books, assessing their quality, Mabel determining if she was prepared to part with them.

With the exception of a copy of *Rebecca* so worn the cover was nearly falling off and the pages carried the oily stains of her mother's fingers, Mabel was happy to bring them all to the library. The way she saw it, she was not parting with them. The library would be as much her mother's creation as it was hers and Evelyn's.

By the time they had sorted through almost two of the bookcases, Mabel's lower back was aching. She gingerly stepped through the dozens of piles they'd created across the hardwood floor, making her way to chug a glass of water left on a small table also piled high with books.

"Your mom sure loved to read, huh?" Evelyn smiled from where she sat between stacks, her summer skirt around her like a watercolor puddle. She watched Mabel drink, a hand held to her lower back. "I remember what the first trimester is like. My back was constantly killing me. Unfortunately, it only gets worse."

When Mabel didn't answer, Evelyn continued, voice tentative, testing the water. "It's good we'll be clearing the room out a bit. For when the baby comes. This will be their nursery, won't it?"

Mabel stuttered through the lump that formed in her throat. "Yes, this'll be her room." She nodded shortly.

Feeling, for once, comfortable in someone else's presence, Mabel offered up the truth that had been sitting in the pit of her stomach for weeks. "I'm afraid," she breathed out, unable to look at Evelyn as she spoke. "Everyone in town . . . they already hate me. I know they'll hate me more than ever now. I don't have my mother. I don't have a husband. I don't know what I'm doing, how to raise a baby. I'm afraid to do this on my own."

She looked resolutely out the window at the sea wearing down the rocks, at the endless blue. All the women who had come before her—who could help her—were out there. Looking out for Mabel, sure, if the story was to be believed. But Mabel didn't need vengeance right now. She needed support.

Mabel heard the sound of Evelyn gracefully pushing to stand, crossing the room to pause at Mabel's back. She expected the other woman to perhaps lay a gentle, comforting hand on her elbow, if anything at all.

So she was shocked when Evelyn's soft, round cheek fell to Mabel's shoulder, the other woman standing close at her back. Evelyn threaded her fingers through Mabel's, where they crossed over the slight swell of her stomach.

"You're not alone, May," she said softly, her voice a hum beneath the sound of the ocean. The two women watched the water turn into stripes of silver with the passing beam of the light for three counts before Evelyn spoke again. "You have me now. You have me."

Mabel squeezed her friend's fingers, grateful for the warm feeling of another person's skin, for the fact that, for once, there was someone there to hold her up.

Sixteen
Rebecca

August 13, 1971

Juniper Island, Isles of Shoals, New Hampshire

Arms wrapped tightly around Rebecca's waist, pulling her backward, away from the bookshelf she was reorganizing. She jumped, her heart in an immediate panic. Then the scent of salt and juniper hit her nose. She relaxed, chuckling as she spun around, doing her best to cover her embarrassment at her initial reaction.

Cal grinned down at her, beautiful as ever. Her heart kept its quick pace for a whole different reason now. He quickly checked over his shoulder, looking around the empty library. Then he pressed a kiss to her mouth, the touch immediately alive and hungry, his hands grabbing at her. Rebecca giggled with his mouth against hers, hands finding his jaw as he pulled away.

"My mother is around here somewhere, you know?" she said lightly. But Cal's face immediately grew tense as he took a step away, taking her sinking heart with him. Rebecca pushed the feeling of loss aside, doing her best not to let it show on her face.

He was just private. This thing was still just theirs. That was okay. That was the way she wanted it too.

"I'm glad you came to visit me," Rebecca said softly. Cal smiled again, though it faltered after a moment. Sheepishly, he ran his hands through his gold hair.

"Of course. Also, uh, my aunt Evelyn sent me over. Said she forgot her favorite sweater, asked me to grab it for her on my way over."

"Oh. Okay." Rebecca walked around the desk, grabbing the soft blue sweater draped over the chair. It had been there when she and her mother arrived, the sight inexplicably freezing Mabel. Rebecca had dim memories of Evelyn from when she was young, but she could count on one hand the number of times she'd been in the same room as the other librarian in recent years.

Rebecca wondered if Evelyn and her mother had some sort of animosity; it wouldn't surprise Rebecca. Her mother was too stubborn to try to appeal to any of the islanders, after all.

Cal took the sweater from her hand. Rebecca stepped closer, looking up at him through her long eyelashes, thrilling in the way his gaze darkened, eyes passing down her body.

"Meet tonight on the beach?" she whispered, doing her best to sound seductive, though to her own ears it just sounded clunky. Not to Cal, it seemed, who swallowed heavily before shaking his head.

"Probably not. I'm actually headed over to my aunt's to help her clear out the house a bit." Cal stepped away, as though Rebecca were enchanting his mind and he needed a bit of distance. She wondered if he actually believed that, if he actually thought she was a witch. No, of course not; he cared for her. He knew her. More than anyone else on this island already. "Richie's new wife and her baby are going to move in with Evelyn. So I'm helping them sort out all the stuff in the house, move things up to storage, I guess."

Rebecca's chest lightened to hear Cal speak about babies. Her mind immediately was sent in a whirl of daydreaming that she had to stopper. "You're so sweet, helping them out." She smiled.

Cal preened, shrugging, shoulders pressed a bit farther back. A sound of whooping on the other side of the window startled Cal into stepping away toward the door. "I'll let you know if I can manage to get away tonight." With one more suggestive smile, he ducked out the door.

Rebecca stepped up to the window, watching Cal cross the island, receiving endless waves and greetings and shouted compliments. Everyone on Juniper loved Cal Bradbury. And Cal wanted *her*. Sometimes it still put Rebecca in awe, like a fairy-tale prince suddenly coming to life, like one of her favorite singers suddenly appearing before her in the flesh, real.

At that exact moment, Rebecca's mom came around the corner from the back of the library, a tall stack of books in her arms nearly obscuring her face. She set them down on the go-backs cart with a grunt, massaging her elbow. "Who was that?"

Rebecca spun away from the window, crossing her arms defensively. "No one," she snapped.

Mabel put her hands up. "Whoa, all right. You were talking to yourself, then?" Her brows pulled together in confusion, a small, baffled smile on her face.

"Yup," Rebecca said sharply, ignoring the way her mother's face flashed with hurt and further bafflement. This thing between her and Cal, it was theirs. He understood that. It wasn't secretive; it was private. Her mother, who didn't care if anyone on this island liked her, who was hardly a part of the island at all, would never understand. She would never get how much it meant that someone like Cal liked Rebecca, was choosing her; her mom didn't give a shit if anyone liked her. Well, Rebecca wasn't like her mother.

With one last searching, confounded glance over her daughter, Mabel turned away. She pushed the go-backs cart along the wall to be handled tomorrow.

"It's getting dark," she said to Rebecca. "We ought to head home to light the beam and start getting things in place for Shabbat."

Rebecca felt her stomach sink. She didn't want to spend another Friday night like an outcast at home with her mother. She didn't want to keep doing these rituals and routines of Jewishness when all her Judaism had ever given her was ostracization.

The two women closed up the library, stepping out into the summer evening. The sky was still blue, a sparrick circling overhead. Mabel kept her chin up as they made their way across the island toward the lighthouse. Plenty of folks were outdoors, embracing the lingering warmth of summer, but everyone avoided their eyes. Her mother didn't seem to care at all, if she even noticed. But Rebecca felt her chest cracking, shame and embarrassment spilling out into her bloodstream. They passed Evelyn's house, and Rebecca caught a glimpse of Cal through the kitchen window, with his broad chest and gleaming hair, so assured and confident wherever he stood on this island.

She turned to her mom. "I think, maybe . . . I'm going to skip Shabbat tonight."

Mabel's head whipped to her. "What? Rebecca, it's Friday night."

Rebecca resisted rolling her eyes. "I know."

But what if Cal did call on her after all and she was busy eating and praying over candlelight with her mother? He'd never understand that. And, at that moment, Cal's appreciation felt a lot more important to her than God's.

"Are you . . . do you have plans?" Her mother was so baffled, as though it was unbelievable that anyone would ever want to hang out with Rebecca. But she was wrong. Rebecca wasn't like her mother. People here wanted her. Well, *a* person. For now.

"I just . . ." Rebecca trailed off. They crested the slight hill, the lighthouse coming into view, Rebecca's stretching jailer. She knew there was no way to get out of tonight without telling her mother her actual plans. Or what she hoped her plans would be. "Nothing. Never mind."

They entered the lighthouse, the rest of the island cut off as the door closed behind them. But for once, Rebecca felt like she had a lifeline there, on the other side.

Seventeen
Mabel

August 2, 1951

Juniper Island, Isles of Shoals, New Hampshire

Mabel pulled the door of the library closed behind her, the books nestled on the shelves sliding out of view. From the outside, the old Smith cottage still didn't look like much, but from inside it was finally properly a library. And she and Evelyn were running it as such—not that business had been particularly booming. Of course not, now that the witch, the harlot, the soon-to-be mother of another witch—and a Jewish one at that—was working there.

She had gone to see Chet Allan, finally, at Evelyn's insistence. They both knew that once Chet knew, the whole island would, but her friend had convinced her that it was for her own health—and her daughter's—that she see a doctor.

So she had. And so now everyone knew.

She had heard enough whispers to know that they had put together that it was Otto who had fathered her child. The timing wasn't exactly subtle. Moreover, Mabel suspected this was the easiest answer for them all. Because if it wasn't Otto, that meant it was someone on the island—and that, she was sure they all thought, was unfathomable, uncomfortable. They all knew without words, had been taught in gestures and exclusions from their parents and grandparents, that Coles were not one of them, not to be touched, that they were witches in the lighthouse and the sea.

Mabel stepped into the bustle of town. The single street was dotted with locals, folks spilling out of their homes to take advantage of the good weather. Mabel kept her chin up as she twisted between people going about their business. When they shot their glares at her, she did not look back. When they tugged their children from her as if she were contagious, she did not flinch. She kept her chin up, her eyes forward, no longer hiding her growing bump beneath unseasonable sweaters and jackets. She wore a dress that did nothing to hide the swell of her stomach, because she would not hide herself or her daughter.

As she passed through the doorway of the Poole Market, she could not believe she had ever given one damn about what these people thought of her. That she had spent a decade shrinking herself—shunning her own mother!—in hopes that they would show her the barest acceptance. If they couldn't accept someone like Otto, if they couldn't accept the daughter growing inside her, then Mabel didn't give a damn if they accepted her either. For the first time in a decade, she felt lighter, free of the weight of expectation.

Still, Mabel moved through the tiny market efficiently, quickly filling her basket with fruits and veggies that were on their way out of season. Summer was still here, yes, weighing down the small space with a touch of humidity. But Juniper was undeniably in flux once again; when she was atop the lighthouse, Mabel could taste the crispness of fall on the air.

A hand reached out to snatch the apple from Mabel's grip, being sure not to brush her skin at all. Her pregnancy, her witchery, or her very being—she wasn't sure what they feared and hated most.

With a sigh, Mabel looked up into the face of Judy Poole, the woman who ran the market alongside her husband. Her little boy, Jackson, watched with rounded eyes from behind the counter. He was no different from the rest of the customers, who did nothing to hide their own gawking at the would-be confrontation, looking at Mabel like she was a stranger, as if she had not been here every single day all her life.

"We don't sell to witches. Or to sluts," Judy spit.

Mabel took an involuntary step back.

She was used to their coldness and their glances and their whispers. But she was not used to such open vitriol, such sharp words pointed directly at her rather than behind her back. She had thought these people couldn't hurt her now that she no longer cared what they thought. She was wrong.

Judy snatched the basket out of Mabel's hand, which reflexively fell to her stomach, guarding her unborn daughter from the world of hate she would be born into simply because of her name.

Mabel glanced around briefly, cheeks heating. Plenty of folks in the market met her eye, but of course no one stepped forth to help her.

Judy took the basket to the corner of the room and began dumping its contents into the trash can. It was a show, certainly, and folks were looking.

It was a message clear as day that Judy was making, and the rest of them were endorsing it. They would rather lose money and livelihood than touch a thing that a Cole woman did.

The hypocrisy almost made Mabel want to laugh. She doubted they'd feel the same way if she managed to flee Juniper, if she left them to the economic ruin and death that they all believed would occur once the angry phantoms in the sea sensed the lack of Cole women safe on shore.

The room was quiet enough that you could hear a pin drop. Or, in this case, the thud of plenty of perfectly fine produce being wasted. Mabel felt tears burn along the edges of her eyes, and she hated herself for it, hated that they could see they had gotten to her. She took a step toward the door, deciding she'd rather starve than let them see her cry. But a gentle hand on her arm stopped her.

Evelyn breezed through the market like a goddess; eyes followed her without contempt. Even the sunlight streaming through the far windows seemed to hug her. She touched Mabel's arm in passing, a brief sign of solidarity, as she made her way over to Judy.

"My, is something wrong with all that food, Judy?" Evelyn smiled. Mabel knew it was her polite one, but sharp too. The smile of a woman who knew she came from the best family on the island, had married into the second best, who was the most beautiful and most revered. Evelyn didn't need to posture like her husband to flex the power she had.

"Well, it's just . . ." Judy paused. Everyone in town knew that Evelyn and Mabel ran the library together. Mabel imagined most of them rationalized that it was an act of charity on Evelyn's behalf, that they praised Evelyn's bravery, or maybe they even thought Mabel had put a spell on her, along the lines of what they had accused her long-ago ancestor of doing.

Judy cleared her throat. "I don't sell to witches. Or unmarried harlots."

Evelyn's prim brows rose. "Hmm." She tilted her head as though in thought. "That's not very Christian of you, Judy. So disappointing to see."

Judy's mouth formed a surprised O, but she did not back down. "It's just, well, I don't think it'd be very Christian to sell to a sinner."

Mabel didn't understand what she was watching as Evelyn's smile grew and she reached out to squeeze the other woman's arm gently. "I really do admire your commitment to our faith, Judy." Judy's cheeks stained pink under the heat of Evelyn's attention.

Then Evelyn landed her most powerful weapon. "But, see, no matter what you may think, Mabel Cole is a friend of mine. And my big brother employs your husband in the summers, does he not? So I suppose, in a sense, it's Bradbury money that keeps you able to run your shop through the hard winters."

Evelyn's smile was gone, those deep-blue eyes hard as flint. The others in the market quickly averted their eyes, continued their shopping. They had taken a stance on the side of Judy Poole, but now they were unwilling to stand by as accomplices if it meant making a stand against Evelyn and the Bradburys.

Judy's neck had turned a deep red beneath her blouse. Only a moment passed before she handed the basket over to Evelyn, replacing the items she had thrown out with fresh ones. Evelyn passed over money for Mabel's groceries, which Mrs. Poole accepted with a tight jaw. Judy scribbled out a receipt with the date and total, slipping it to Evelyn with her eyes cast down.

Evelyn twisted her way back through the shop, Mabel's basket in the crook of her elbow. Without breaking stride, she laid a hand on Mabel's back, guiding the other woman out of the market.

"Thank you," Mabel breathed when they were several feet outside the store, walking toward the lighthouse.

Evelyn turned to Mabel, that true smile on her face. "I like seeing Judy Poole put in her place. It was nothing."

But Mabel knew that was not true. Evelyn had not only gotten Mabel food, but she had given her something far more valuable for the first time in her life: a friend who would stand by her side. Mabel thought maybe she and the little girl in her belly wouldn't be so alone after all.

Eighteen
Rebecca

August 30, 1971

Juniper Island, Isles of Shoals, New Hampshire

The setting sun filtered sideways into the little alcove, casting Cal in a sunlit glow. Rebecca no longer hesitated to touch him. She reached up, tucking a falling strand of hair back atop his head, where it immediately flopped back over his brow. They both laughed lightly, the sound echoing back at them in the safe huddle of the rocky alcove along the lighthouse port.

Cal, still catching his breath, settled down, his tall body stretching along Rebecca's side. He laid his head on his arm, but still she could feel him watching her. She allowed herself a little smile, not bothered if he saw it. They knew each other well enough now that Rebecca no longer swallowed every smile and laugh in order to remain mysterious. It had been weeks of kisses and making love and looking out at the sea, chatting about all the places they wanted to go one day. Rebecca wasn't mysterious; she was *known*. And Cal was no longer Cal Bradbury, figment of her daydreams. He was Cal, the boy with the crooked smile and big blue eyes and bigger dreams of the mainland.

Rebecca rolled over onto her side to face Cal, the blanket beneath them already crumpled, sand sticking to their skin. Cal stroked a finger, light, across her bare shoulder, down to the exposed skin of her chest. Even after they'd just been together, so close, Rebecca's skin tightened with anticipation and want. She didn't bother to cover herself entirely; they were nestled out of sight from the lighthouse in the rocky cove, and no one dared set foot on this port so close to the Coles once the lobster boat was long docked for the day, the season soon coming to an end.

But Rebecca no longer worried that she would see less of Cal now that he would take to the standard fishing boats off the other side of the isle come autumn. No, she knew well enough now that what they had went beyond convenience. This was more.

Rebecca leaned forward, pressing her mouth to Cal's. He returned the kiss eagerly. It was not hungry; it was sated, it was comfortable. It was knowing and being known.

She pulled back, glimpsing her long dark hair weaving over Cal's grown-out gold strands on the pearly backdrop of the sand. So different, but intertwined. Something settled in Rebecca's chest, easing an ache, a flurry, that she had never even noticed until it was gone.

She trailed a finger over Cal's features, skating across his defined cheekbones, the dark swoop of his brows, the narrow set of his full lips. They did not speak. The actions they had just partaken in together spoke for them—the simple, easy way they lay together that went beyond sex, the way they looked at each other, directly in the eye and unflinching.

But suddenly, looking into Cal's eyes, Rebecca realized she had more to say. She was flooded with the feeling. No, she was flooded with the realization of a feeling that had been burrowing into her bones for weeks now, maybe since that first time that Cal Bradbury had settled beside her on her rocks, had made this lonely part of the isle theirs. Since he had made her life *their* life, together.

Rebecca leaned forward again, slotting her nose beside Cal's, giggling as his two eyes became one blue orb. Smiling larger as his face split into a grin in return, happy to be with a Rebecca Cole who was no longer so aloof and cool and mysterious. Rebecca realized that this, too, was who she was.

She realized that she was absolutely, undeniably, falling in love with Cal Bradbury.

She might be more open, cracking herself and her heart wide to him ever so slowly, but still she was not ready to say those words. For a little while longer, she would let that emotion keep her company in her chest. She would move around Juniper, shunned and ignored but no longer lonely. And she knew, soon enough, she wouldn't be shunned much longer. If Cal Bradbury loved Rebecca Cole—and she was sure he must; her feelings could not be so strong one-sided—then the rest of the islanders would come to love her too.

Cal's approval and affection would far outweigh the curse of her blood.

Everything the islanders had ever said about her would be worth it because it had brought her to Cal.

Her life had already changed with Cal, and she knew, inevitably, it was soon to change even more.

Rebecca was spared struggling to swallow her declarations of love as Cal pulled away, sitting upright. She watched him toss his shirt back on, stand up. Her skin flushed cold at the sudden loss, something like embarrassment flooding in. Rebecca quickly righted her dress to cover herself, standing too as Cal bent to put on his shoes.

"I'm meeting some of the guys on the other side."

Rebecca's chest pressed tight, like a vise wrapping around her lungs. She felt him slipping away, and she wasn't ready to say good night yet. But maybe she wouldn't have to. Rebecca's heartbeat kicked up. Maybe, just maybe, Cal wasn't telling her where he was leaving her to go. Maybe he was finally inviting her to come along.

She loved their time together being theirs—private, away from the judging eyes of the islanders. But she didn't want them to be a secret forever. She wanted them to scream their love out to the sea, so proudly even the mainlanders would know that Rebecca Cole loved Cal Bradbury. And that he might just love her right back.

"Oh?"

Cal didn't seem to notice her breathlessness, running a hand across his scalp to smooth the disarray of his hair. It fell back into place perfectly.

"Yeah." He shrugged. "Just for some beers and stuff. The guys will probably bring their girls too." He chuckled and Rebecca laughed along, though she wasn't sure why.

Her mind was too busy racing to try to parse it out. This was it. She was right. This was the moment that would change everything for her. For them.

But then Cal leaned forward, his mouth hungrily finding hers once more before he pulled away. He stepped over her crumpled blanket as he made his retreat, walking backward. He called out to her, "I'll see you later. I'll leave a note in our spot."

Rebecca watched, unable to speak, as Cal and that flirtatious glint in his eye disappeared over the swell of rocks. She stood, alone, watching his shadow until it disappeared to nothing. She waited, alone, with just the waves for company. She swore that in the sound of the whitecaps gushing on the rough sand she could hear whispers, warning her, calling to her to listen. But in her sudden shame all Rebecca could hear was mockery.

And Cal left without looking back, as if she stopped existing when she was out of his sight, as if she were a doll that only came to when he touched her. Sometimes, most times, that felt true.

But, she figured, that was just what love was.

Rebecca pushed a hand down her chest, trying to smother the ache there. It was a useless gesture. She snatched the trampled blanket, holding it tight to her chest as she traversed her way back to the lighthouse, where she would spend another night alone in her room thinking about Cal Bradbury, as if nothing had changed at all.

Nineteen
Mabel

October 15, 1951

Juniper Island, Isles of Shoals, New Hampshire

"Lyn," Mabel sighed, standing from her kitchen table. "Let me help. You shouldn't have to come for dinner at my house *and* cook the meal."

Evelyn turned from where she stood before Mabel's kitchen counter, chopping vegetables with a quick, expert hand. She scoffed before fixing her face into a stern look that was every bit that of a mother whose demands would not be ignored. Richie might be spending the night at his cousin's house, but clearly Evelyn didn't take a night off from being a mother. "Sit, May."

She waved a knife toward the chair Mabel had just vacated. With an aggrieved sigh, Mabel sat back down. "I'm pregnant, not helpless." As she found herself doing often these days, Mabel ran her hand mindlessly over the swell of her stomach, which strained beneath her sweater more each day.

The sharp smell of garlic painted the air as Evelyn mashed a clove with the flat side of the knife. The warmth from the preheating oven surrounded Mabel like a toasty blanket. The record player that sat on a little stool spun soft melodies through the air, the waves crashing as the bass. It was nice. Mabel hadn't realized how lonely she always was in the lighthouse until she had Evelyn in it with her. She hadn't realized how long it had been since she'd been taken care of—since she'd let herself be taken care of—until Evelyn was in her kitchen as though it were her own.

"Oh, I know," Evelyn laughed. "But it's nice to get some rest when you can. I can't help you with lighting the beam"—Mabel chuckled, remembering a few weeks ago when she'd tried to teach the other woman, to no avail; seemed it was a job exclusively for Cole women after all—"but I can help with this. I'm taking care of you and your child."

"Daughter," Mabel corrected immediately, without thought.

"Well, you can't be sure of that, of course."

Mabel laughed without humor. "Of course I can. The curse."

Evelyn paused her work, slowly turning around to face Mabel. She leaned back against the counter, her blue eyes sharp even through the low auburn light of the kitchen. "You really believe in the curse?"

Mabel reared her head back, shocked. "Of course. You *don't*?" Mabel had always just assumed that all the islanders believed in the curse against the Cole women. That that was part of the reason they pushed the Coles away, to the edge of the land. That they all believed that in the sea around the isle, dead Coles swam like sharks, protecting their living descendants and threatening the islanders in the process.

"No. I don't." Evelyn shrugged. When Mabel was still too surprised to respond, the blond woman continued, "You really think some long-ago ancestor of yours was a witch? That she cursed you to be alone, to have daughters, to die?"

Mabel shrugged right back. "Yes." It was as simple as that. It always had been. "I've seen the curse. Look at . . . at my mother. Cole women go to the sea and make more Cole women."

Evelyn crossed her arms, stern. "And why would Goody Cole have doomed you to that?"

Mabel opened her mouth. Closed it. She didn't have words. She didn't know. She'd always been taught—by the lasting hatred of the islanders—that her ancestor had been evil, an outcast, a witch. That she had been so hateful she had cursed her line, as if the very existence of the Coles and their curse would somehow be a punishment to the islanders. But being in the toasty kitchen, watching Evelyn Fuller care for her, Mabel didn't think that was true. In fact, she didn't think it made much sense. She believed in the curse, certainly; she was living it. But maybe it wasn't her ancestor who had cursed her.

The Coles didn't prosper in their curse; they only suffered. Again, Mabel struggled to believe her ancestor would doom her line to that. Even if she was evil, if she was a witch, surely she would look out for her daughter, for her own? Something didn't add up—and she doubted her ancestor was really a *witch*—but who else might have cursed her line? Mabel knew how strong animosity could be, and that hatred was strong enough to make a curse. Stronger than any witchcraft, certainly.

"I don't want it to be true," Mabel said so softly her voice could hardly be heard. "I don't . . . I don't want to die and keep my daughter trapped here."

She put a hand on her stomach. She already loved the little girl inside her so much. She would never, could never, wish hardship and loneliness on the girl. And she couldn't imagine Goody Cole would have either.

Maybe her ancestor had just been the first in the line of ordinary women bearing the Cole name, who had so little power but were punished as if they did, as if they were evil and dangerous. If it was someone else—someone with *real* power, magic or ordinary—who had cursed them, then Mabel understood more than ever why those spirits in the sea would be enraged, would want their descendants to stay where the spirits could guard them. Death in the sea, anger in the blue, was the only way Cole women could see their granddaughters. Could protect them.

"You won't," Evelyn said just as softly. "I know you won't."

Mabel nodded as if she had acquiesced. But she knew the truth, knew how real the curse was. The knowledge was in her blood. The proof was in her womb.

Seemingly satisfied that she had calmed her friend, Evelyn turned, returning to her work. "As I said, just rest a bit, May."

Mabel sipped at the warm herbal tea in her hand. She struggled to find a comfortable seat with her aching back, grateful she didn't have to fuss over the kitchen herself. Without thinking, she said, "You're lucky you have a husband. I'm sure Dean took care of you like this when you were pregnant."

Evelyn stilled, her back still to Mabel. But Mabel could see the tension coiled in every muscle, her perfectly prim posture suddenly appearing rigid. Immediately Mabel regretted her words, picturing that bracelet of bruises she'd spotted on Evelyn.

The silence sat in the air for a long time, the record player crooning over their discomfort. Finally, Evelyn whispered, "No, he didn't."

Mabel wanted to apologize, but she knew this was the one thing they were not supposed to look at. And she found she didn't want to welcome Evelyn's husband into this space that was just the two of them, nestled away in the warm womb of the lighthouse away from the rest of Juniper. So she let it go.

Mabel was down to the last sip of her tea by the time Evelyn loaded the food into the oven, snapping off the worn oven mitts that had been in the kitchen as long as Mabel could remember. They hadn't spoken another word, and Mabel wasn't sure if she'd irreparably damaged whatever was between them, this friendship that had finally stopped feeling tentative.

A clever little piano riff broke the silence of the room. Evelyn sighed, her eyes falling closed, a small smile tilting her lips up as Billie Holiday began to sing. Mabel felt frozen as she watched the softness on Evelyn's face while "I'll Be Seeing You" echoed through the tiny space. Evelyn swayed softly to the crooning beauty of the song, eyes still closed.

Mabel found herself standing, crossing the few feet to where Evelyn stood. The other woman's eyes popped open in surprise as Mabel took her hand, placing her other along Evelyn's waist. But quickly the surprise melted into something softer as Evelyn pulled her close. The two women swayed to the music, moving across the kitchen slow as molasses. As Billie Holiday sang of looking at the moon, the silver orb glowed through the kitchen's window, the only thing from the outside world that felt real.

Mabel had never felt Evelyn so close, had never touched anyone like this, not even Otto. This was not fire and lust. It was warmth. It was comfort. As Mabel Cole swayed to the music her mother had loved, Evelyn Fuller held tight in her arms, the slight swell of her baby protected between them, she thought *This is home.*

Twenty
Mabel

January 3, 1952

Juniper Island, Isles of Shoals, New Hampshire

Mabel's screams split the air.

She was dying, she was certain of it. She would die so her daughter could come into the world. There was simply no way, she thought, that her body could survive this feeling of being torn in two.

"You're okay, you're okay," Evelyn chanted, wiping the sweat from Mabel's brow as she guided her up the stairs, settling her into her bed.

Mabel did not believe her.

Another contraction swept in, her body tightening and twisting like it was attempting to wring itself dry. Evelyn paused her fussing over pillows to squeeze Mabel's hand through the wave of pain. Through the haze, Mabel caught sight of Richie in the doorway, frozen and wide-eyed with alarm, their dinner certainly having taken a different turn than expected.

Over the sound of her labored breathing, Mabel heard Evelyn call back to her son, "Go get Dotty Allan, yeah? Quick as you can, dear!"

Time seemed to morph and twist, slowing achingly with each contraction, then speeding up at double speed in the moments between. It turned dark early in winter, and, distantly, Mabel was thankful that she had turned on the beam before the contractions came on. She was glad, through the red glow of her pain, that her daughter would be born at night, that the first thing she would know of the world was the lighthouse and the beam.

As the sky grew to a deeper navy, the contractions came quicker, Mabel's body matching itself to the beat of the waves on the building's side. She felt much like the rocks, hard and damaged and withering away.

The sound of Richie's quick footsteps up the stairs found them before the boy himself appeared, panting, his blond hair matted to his head beneath his wool hat. "She won't come!" he cried.

Evelyn, who was wiping a cool, damp towel over Mabel's forehead, paused. "What do you mean?"

"Mrs. Allan won't come." Robby shot a nervous glance from his mother to Mabel's writhing form before her. "She said she won't help . . . bring another witch into the world."

The last six words were said in a rush, all in one breath, but they were clear enough all the same.

Mabel heard herself let out a soft cry, panic zapping through her body alongside the pain. She would die. Her daughter would die. This was the world she would bring her girl into—othered and left out in the cold.

Evelyn huffed out a breath. "That no-good, selfish, *ignorant* woman."

She collected herself, coiled her anger tight the way Mabel had seen her do many times. She turned to her son, rattling off a list of instructions, things she would need, before sending the boy to wait in the kitchen.

Then she kneeled back down by Mabel's side, her round face inches away as she smoothed the damp hair from Mabel's brow. “We’ll do this ourselves. We don’t need anybody else. We’re gonna welcome your little girl to the world.”

She squeezed Mabel’s hand tight, resting her forehead on the other woman’s. “I’m here. We’re going to do this together.”

Perhaps hours passed, years, or only minutes of waves of pain, of Evelyn’s calm voice saying, “Push, May, you can do this,” of the other woman’s hand in hers, guiding her with a deftness that still betrayed her nerves.

In the moment, Mabel felt every ache, every rip, every twist of her body as it expelled a new life. But, in memory, all of that seemed hazed over. There was the panic and the pain, yes, but it seemed so distant in hindsight. It was all nothing compared to the sound of her little girl crying out as Evelyn guided her from Mabel’s body. The sound of this little girl, the newest Cole, coming into the world already refusing to be silent, calling out to the sound of the waves and the moon high in the sky.

None of the pain mattered when Evelyn, sweating and beaming, placed the wriggling red baby into Mabel’s arms. “Meet your mama,” Evelyn whispered to the little girl.

Mabel held the baby to her bare chest, looking down at the little face, scrunched and pale as a dumpling, and all of the pain was gone. There was only this, and this was worth it. She was worth it.

The little one already had a tuft of dark hair atop her soft head, her tiny fingers gripping Mabel’s pinkie. The curse was worth it. In that moment it didn’t feel like a curse at all to Mabel, but a blessing.

Rebecca Cole was born to the night sea, named after the most beloved book of the grandmother she would never meet. It would be the girl’s first introduction to the world, and with it the first introduction of what it meant to be a Cole woman.

Twenty-One
Mabel

March 17, 1952

Juniper Island, Isles of Shoals, New Hampshire

Spring on Juniper Island, as always, could never quite be sure if it wanted to be winter still or embrace the new season. Today it certainly had chosen winter. Angry wind burst from the sea, then—just as angry—frothed white against the rocks of the burial ground nearby, rattling the window of the library like a vicious intruder. But in here, nestled between the stacks, they were safe. They were warm.

The library was in full swing, a proper place at last. A dozen bookshelves snaked throughout the cottage like a maze of wonder. Most were already full to bursting with books organized by Mabel's whims, but a few were more sparse, awaiting shipments from the mainland. Around each bend of the labyrinth, a cozy nook awaited.

Mable had been happy enough to stack the books up and let people come, but not Evelyn. She made everywhere a home, made everywhere safe. She wanted the library to be a place people nestled, burrowed, loved, not just a place they visited briefly. So soft rugs were tucked between bookcases, and stuffed chairs that Evelyn had reupholstered by her own hand appeared around corners, covered in thick blankets the women had knit together, Evelyn laughing kindly at Mabel's fumbling fingers. Evelyn had appeared one day with a boxful of Tiffany lamps, which now rested on shelves and side tables, casting the space in a warm glow of red and green and copper.

Within the library, wandering between the stacks, they were nestled and warm, separate from the world, giving themselves up willingly to the world of literature. Patrons had been sparse and hesitant, most only daring to visit because of Evelyn's presence and endorsement. But today, the afternoon sky deep gray outside the window, it was just them.

Mabel stepped away from the desk at the door, the two cups of tea she'd just made held in her hands. She weaved her way between the stacks; with each step the sound of Evelyn's twinkling voice became louder, and Mabel followed the noise like it was the beacon she lit atop the lighthouse each night.

"Sal's a mischievous girl," Evelyn cooed. "I have a feeling you might be just the same, mermaid."

Mabel couldn't help the smile that split her face at the sound of Evelyn speaking so softly, so lovingly, to her daughter. Only two months into life and already Evelyn had coined a nickname for the girl, inspired by Rebecca's joy each and every time she found herself in water. The girl, even for an infant, was somber and serious, holding herself tight, the dark eyes so like her father's looking at the world warily, as though already she knew not to trust it. But each time she was by the water—whether it was the little tub in the kitchen sink for her baths or held in her mother's arms to look out at the pounding waves—the girl seemed to come alive. Only then would a small, satisfied smile pull at her little lips; Mabel could feel, while she held the girl, the way a weight seemed to drop off the little being in those moments, her tiny limbs relaxing for once.

Mabel turned the final corner, the sight she found there arresting her heart. Rebecca was swaddled safely in her wicker bassinet, her doughy face as relaxed as it ever was on dry land, her round eyes looking up. Evelyn sat on the ground beside the bassinet, her blue-green skirt pooling around her as though she were an emerging water nymph, her golden hair resting easily on her shoulders. Her smiling face alternated between gazing at Rebecca and reading from the book in her hand, *Blueberries for Sal*.

Standing there, watching this quiet scene, Mabel felt safe. She felt as though her daughter were safe. They were not alone.

And in that same moment too, hazel eyes roving over the smooth surfaces of Evelyn Fuller, knowing the wit and bravery and endurance and playfulness that resided beneath—Mabel realized that Evelyn was not her friend. No, she could see now, chest tightening almost painfully, that the other woman was much, much more to her.

When Evelyn heard Mabel step out from between the shelves, that smile locked on her. Their eyes held, and in that moment Mabel knew their relationship would never be the same. That she had finally awoken to the truth of that static energy between them, the softness it gave her. She could not believe it had taken her so long to realize all that Evelyn was to her and how much more she wanted the woman to be.

She swallowed down the feeling that flushed, warm, across her body as she passed Evelyn a mug. Mabel nestled down on the ground beside the other woman and Rebecca. Evelyn turned the next page of the picture book, but then she stopped, closing it softly as she saw that little Rebecca's eyes were already fluttering shut, her breath smoothing out in sleep.

Evelyn set the book aside, leaning back against the base of the large stuffed chair behind them. Her shoulder pressed into Mabel's. Though the library around them felt still, suspended in time, Mabel's blood raced. She could hear her heartbeat pounding in her ears, and sipping her steaming chamomile tea did nothing to calm it.

"She loves you," Mabel whispered. Cheeks heating, she cleared her throat, clarified. "Rebecca. She loves you."

Evelyn smiled wider, her true one, the one that Mabel saw more and more, only when it was them alone, in this life they had carved out together.

"I love her too." Evelyn reached over Mabel's body to run a featherlight finger over Rebecca's pinched brow. At the touch, the little one relaxed further into her sleep. "So much."

Mabel knew that Evelyn likely thought nothing of the way her arm brushed against Mabel's chest as she leaned over, or the way her golden hair tickled the other woman's neck, or how her hip pressed into Mabel, or the way it set Mabel absolutely on fire. Her skin suddenly felt too small for her, vibrating with want and affection that surprised her.

Mabel was certain she would die when Evelyn's hand found her knee as she maneuvered her way back toward her seat. Mabel thought she was holding her breath, but she must have gasped. Because, midmotion, Evelyn's chin turned to face Mabel. Like this, in this complicated twist between moments, the women found themselves close, hand on knee, shoulders brushing, faces barely inches apart. The smile slowly faded from Evelyn's face, something deeper and more contemplative replacing the look in her sea-blue eyes. Mabel could not help the way her own eyes dipped down to Evelyn's lips, for just a moment. And Evelyn—clever, sharp, attentive Evelyn—did not miss the flicker, of course.

When she breathed out, her shaky breath skated across Mabel's lips. Unconsciously, Mabel's eyes closed, her face leaning forward just slightly, just testing. She couldn't help it; Evelyn Fuller was her sun. She would always be drawn to her. The fine hairs on Mabel's face stood on end, told her that Evelyn, too, was leaning closer.

And then, faint as a bird's feather, as the prick of the Juniper bush, their lips met.

Mabel wasn't new to affection, to kissing. This was like it had been with Otto, yes, but it was different, too, because this was *Evelyn*. And Mabel realized, as she pressed her mouth harder against the other woman's and was met with the same level of awakened enthusiasm, sureness, that she had never felt anything like this before, nor would she ever.

Juniper Island had never truly felt like Mabel's home; the islanders had made sure of that. But this moment, feeling Evelyn's breath and lips and love—this was coming home for Mabel Cole.

Mabel had never stepped foot in church, but she knew that she probably should think these feelings were wrong, for many reasons. But she did not. Something that felt like this—warm and right—could not be wrong.

They separated, but their faces stayed close, the moment between them suspended. Evelyn's nose was slotted beside Mabel's, her pink lips a breath away, a weighted moment of waiting. Was that kiss a mistake? A fluke? They both seemed to be asking the other in that moment of hesitation.

Then their mouths found each other again, soft and sure. Evelyn's hand rose to rest along Mabel's cheekbone. She held Mabel like she was a precious thing, like she was something that Evelyn was sure of, like Mabel was the best thing Evelyn had ever had, like this thing between them was delicate but not fragile. Like this thing between them was worth it.

It was right, Mabel knew.

As surely as she knew, Evelyn's tongue twisting with hers, fingers threading together, that she would not be the same, not ever.

Twenty-Two
Mabel

October 11, 1953

Juniper Island, Isles of Shoals, New Hampshire

Mabel gripped Richie's little waist, lifting the child above her head. The boy reached out, catching the homemade paper jack-o'-lantern on the hook on the ceiling. He gazed down at her with his little missing-toothed smile.

"I got it, May!"

Mabel gave him a little squish as she lowered him to the ground, eliciting a giggle. "Good job, Richie boy. It looks nice and spooky in here!"

As soon as Richie hit the ground, he took off, running up to the front of the library, out of view, the superhero's cape they'd made out of an old pillowcase billowing behind him. More paper Halloween decorations were draped from the ceiling, jack-o'-lanterns and black cats and waving white ghosts. They still had a few hours before the kids' reading night tonight, but Mabel's stomach was already twisted in knots. It was a new initiative they were trying out; a way to bring more children into the library. But Mabel knew the problem wasn't the children, it was their parents. And though Evelyn had insisted that some cute holiday decorations were a must this time of year, Mabel wasn't sure the other woman was seeing the whole picture. Pumpkins and ghosts and familiars might seem like fun coming from someone like Evelyn Fuller; coming from someone like Mabel Cole, they might seem like a confession or, worse, a threat.

Mabel knew, fully now, that she didn't give one damn what those people thought of her. But she couldn't deny a little nibble that cropped up in her belly sometimes at the idea that Evelyn would suddenly realize what they all thought of Mabel. That she would then think it too.

Those thoughts were interrupted by the woman herself crossing Mabel's path.

Evelyn was bent over, gripping the little hands of Rebecca, who toddled before her, still waffling through her first, supported steps. She beamed at Mabel as she said excitedly, "Look at her go!"

And then, as though it were the easiest thing in the world, Evelyn pressed a fleeting, thoughtless kiss to Mabel's lips before Rebecca's little footsteps brought her around a bend. Outside of these four walls, such behavior was impossible, dangerous. But the library was theirs, and they were safe in their own world here.

As if on cue, the little bell above the front door twinkled. The warmth and safety dissipated in a moment as a gruff voice snapped, "What the hell are you wearing, Rich? Take off that damn dress."

Mabel knew who she would find as she twisted her way through the labyrinth of shelves to the door. Dean Fuller trapped a fistful of the pillowcase tied around his son's neck, ripping it off, not giving one care for the way it pulled the boy's head back before loosening. Richie turned at Mabel's appearance, no longer the giggling little boy he had been a moment ago. He was frozen still, eyes hardened, a soldier in a boy's body. Mabel's chest ached. With sadness for the boy, yes, but with a burning hatred for Dean too. Before she could dare say a word, Evelyn breezed into the space, Rebecca in her arms. Without even sparing Mabel a glance, she passed the baby over to her, gliding over to her husband, as though she only had eyes for him. Her small hands found his shoulders, her face tilted up to him, pressing a soft, appeasing kiss to his mouth. The coiling tension of control around Dean's shoulders just barely relaxed.

"Richie, go read." Evelyn still only had eyes for her husband, and the dismissal was clearly not just for the boy. It was for Mabel too.

Mabel reached for Richie's hand, felt the weight of Dean's gaze, thought better of it. She simply followed the boy into the stacks. Heart thundering, Mabel pasted on a smile, settling the children in the far corner of the library in a plush chair. Then she coiled her way back through the shelves, pausing just out of view of Dean and Evelyn. It was wrong, she knew that. Mabel told herself she was eavesdropping for Evelyn's safety, not out of jealousy. She almost believed herself.

"You'll be home right after this little event you're doing." Dean was not asking a question; he was making a demand. Mabel didn't need to see his face to imagine the tight twist of his brow, hard and unflinching, the way he'd pull his shoulders back, posturing to intimidate his wife.

"I can be," Evelyn crooned back, measured, placid. She sounded nothing like herself, not the woman Mabel had gotten to know. Mabel's heart hiccupped. Evelyn and Richie had planned to come to the lighthouse for dinner after story time. It was meant to be *their* time, but of course Dean was claiming it. And Mabel couldn't even be indignant, because Evelyn was

Dean's wife and he had a right. But Mabel sure was mad. Not at Evelyn, but at Dean, at the world of men that allowed those like Dean so much power. For once, Mabel was glad to be alone on this island, ostracized. "But I thought you deserved a quiet night without me or Richie bothering you. I already made you a casserole, waiting to be heated in the oven. And a fresh bottle of whiskey waiting for you."

Though all she could see was the shelf in front of her, Mabel could practically see Evelyn running her hands down her husband's chest. The allure, the coaxing, was in the sound of her voice.

And Dean Fuller might have thought himself powerful and untouchable, but he was no better than anyone else on this island who couldn't help but fall right in step with Evelyn's whims, her cleverness masked as obedience and politeness, as it must be.

"Good, then," Dean huffed. "But you and the boy better not be spending your nights with no witches."

The word wasn't even spoken to Mabel's face, and yet it stung her with a hot lash like a slap across the cheek. She expected to hear more of Evelyn's gentle, coaxing voice, but when the woman spoke, it was sharper.

"Mabel isn't a witch," she practically hissed. "She's—"

Whatever other defense Evelyn had been building toward was, quite literally, choked off. Evelyn made a sort of stuttering, gasping sound, and Mabel did not decide to step forth from behind the shelves; she simply did. Dean Fuller gripped his wife by the neck, tilting her chin up to him. His eyes cut to Mabel, but he did not stop. He had no need to. He was in charge here. Witch or not, she was still just a woman.

"I just thought you deserved a night, dear," Evelyn said softly around his grip.

Mabel stepped forward, heart thundering in rage, arms outstretched to do who knew what. She could not physically overpower Dean, but she would not simply watch him harm Evelyn. But before she took a step, Dean thrust his wife from him. Evelyn stumbled back a step, catching herself. Without looking, she held out a hand, stopping Mabel's advance. Then she swallowed, straightened her hair, and looked back up at her husband, silent.

There was no more defiance in her face. It broke Mabel's heart.

"Don't be late," Dean barked, stepping back toward the door. With one last disgusted look at Mabel, Dean left, the library door slamming behind him with the force of his anger and that of the ocean's autumn breeze.

Mabel rushed to Evelyn's side, taking the woman in her arms, pushing the golden hair from her face, checking over Evelyn's throat, where red prints were stark against her pale skin. "Lyn, God, Jesus, are you—"

Evelyn stepped from her hold, smoothing her hands down the front of her sweater. She would not look Mabel in the eye.

"You look fine, Lyn," Mabel huffed, watching the woman straighten her skirt, rebutton her blouse. "The problem isn't your appearance, it's your damn husband—"

"Enough, Mabel." Evelyn had never raised her voice at Mabel. Had never spoken harshly to her. But she did then. Mabel felt unmoored, having Evelyn's stubborn, subtle power turned on her instead of in her defense. "You do not understand my life. Do not pretend to."

Mabel's chest almost hurt from the size of her anger, hot and heavy. Not at the way Dean spoke of her—she didn't give a damn anymore—but at the way he had spoken to Evelyn, *Evelyn,* and how he treated her. How he loved feeling powerful, in control, more than he loved this wife. How he was allowed to behave in such a way and it was normal.

Mabel had never felt anger like this. She was surprised by the voracity of it. She wanted Dean Fuller dead.

"You need to leave him," she said.

Evelyn guffawed. She peered around the shelves, making sure the children were still in the far corner, not hearing or seeing the exchange. "My parents told me I would marry Dean Fuller when I turned eighteen. And I did. I am his wife, Mabel. He can do as he pleases."

"That's . . . what . . . so *leave* him."

Evelyn finally looked her full in the face. Her dark brows were pinched tight, jaw taut. But as she looked at Mabel, that tension and anger softened. Mabel realized then that it wasn't her that Evelyn was angry with. It was her husband, of course. Evelyn knew it was wrong. She was as angry as Mabel was, more than. But she also knew her lot, knew that she could not show that anger to her husband. Mabel understood, but it only drained her anger into a deep, gnawing sorrow.

Evelyn stepped forward, taking Mabel's face in her hands, resting their foreheads together. "Please, can we just . . . can we let it be? For now?"

Mabel opened her mouth to rebuke her, but Evelyn continued. "I just need to be with you. We were going to have such a lovely day. Let's not let Dean ruin it."

Mabel desperately, terribly wanted to argue back, but Evelyn kissed her softly and, as always, her mind blotted out. But Mabel knew that Dean Fuller would now always be the shadow cast over her and Evelyn.

Lyn stepped away, settling into the desk chair, pulling her little brown notebook out of a drawer and cracking it open. It was her journal, her diary, one of many that crowded her house, she'd told Mabel. Evelyn had been writing down her thoughts and feelings every day since she was a little girl. The first time Mabel had seen the journal, she'd smirked, coyly asked, "Have you ever written about me?"

But Evelyn's response was not laughter; it was sincere as could be. "You're on every page, May."

Mabel suspected the lines of those pages were the only place Evelyn had entirely to herself. Her heart still a knot in her throat, Mabel left her to it.

Twenty-Three
Mabel

January 3, 1957

Juniper Island, Isles of Shoals, New Hampshire

"Happy birthday, dear Rebecca! Happy birthday to you!" The three of them finished their off-pitch tune with claps and cheers.

Snow gathered on the windowsill, the waves white capped and angry beyond. But in here the world was warm, cast in a soft amber glow.

Richie pushed forward, squeezing Rebecca's shoulders, shouting another round of good wishes that were met with her giggling. Mabel drifted a hand over Rebecca's long, dark hair, placing a kiss on her head. "Happy fifth birthday, baby."

Evelyn was next in line with congratulations. "Happy birthday, mermaid!" She hugged the girl familiarly, and Mabel's heart surged at the sight. Despite all of it, centuries of hatred and ostracization on this island—the curse might have been true enough for her to birth a daughter, but they were not alone. Somehow, she and Rebecca had ended up with a family.

Mabel did her best to forget that the ability to have this family night was only possible because Evelyn's real spouse had taken his skiff over to Appledore for the night, to visit or for a fishing trip or something or other. And Mabel did her best to forget that Evelyn had likely had to coax Dean to take this trip with platitudinal smiles and soft kisses.

The three of them settled into the kitchen table chairs around Rebecca. Mabel had had to get two more chairs for their table, so common it had become for the four of them to sit together. But only when they were able; only when Dean allowed it, even if he didn't know where his wife and son were when he was gone or drunk or doing whatever else he did when he wasn't busy hurting the wife he didn't even deserve.

Rebecca's little face was somber as always as she looked down at the still-lit candles on the cake Evelyn had baked for her—vanilla with cherry frosting, the girl's favorite. Shadows danced over Rebecca's pointed little chin, flashing across the serious look in her dark eyes. They somehow had a family, and yet still Rebecca was so like the line of women she was born from, as though Cole women came into this world knowing they needed to protect themselves, knowing they had only themselves.

"Make a wish, baby," Mabel prompted. The girl just stared into the flames as though she were hoping to control them.

Thank God no one else is here, Mabel thought, *or they'd think us witches beyond a doubt.*

Finally, though, Rebecca's serious little expression began to waver. Her chin dimpled and quaked, and even in the dim light Mabel could see tears gather on her daughter's lashes. Rebecca took a quaking breath in before blowing out the candles. They wobbled before going dark.

The three of them clapped, Mabel and Evelyn exchanging a worried glance over the kids' heads. Richie, not even nine yet himself, was young enough to be oblivious to the other child's near tears.

"What'd ya wish for, Rebecca?" he prompted, reaching out to try to swipe some frosting onto his finger before his mother stopped him with a stern look.

"You're not meant to ask someone what they wished for or it won't come true." Evelyn smiled.

Suddenly, alarmingly, the silence of the lighthouse was split by the echo of Rebecca's sobs. It was as though a dam had burst and the little girl's sorrow spilled out, as powerful as the waves beating on the side of the structure they were nestled in.

Evelyn and Mabel pressed forth to comfort the girl at the same time, but Rebecca leaned away from the comfort of their arms. Already, no matter what Mabel did, her daughter knew the ways of the Cole women. Knew to keep to herself, to take comfort only from herself; that everyone else was temporary.

"It doesn't matter!" the girl huffed. "It already didn't come true! No one came to my birthday." Her words were broken up by wet hiccups. "Nobody here likes me! Every day in school, they won't talk to me. Margaret said her mother told her I'm a . . . a . . . a bastard Jew."

It was clear that Rebecca didn't really know what those words meant, just as Margaret likely didn't either. But the people of Juniper were doing what they'd always done: teach hatred as if it were as inevitable and intrinsic as the waves, coiling down through generations.

Rebecca continued, voice trembling. "No one will sit next to me because they say I'm cursed and a witch." She looked up at Mabel, her big brown eyes so like her father's. "Is that true, Mama?"

Mabel's throat constricted, stuffed full of cotton. She, too, felt like she was choking on her sorrow.

Before she could answer, Evelyn leaned forward. Rebecca let the woman gently wipe the tears from her pink cheeks. "No, mermaid. No. You're not a witch. And you're not cursed."

Mabel gave Evelyn a hard look. The women were different, but still, they rarely disagreed. But on this, they always did. For once, Mabel felt that Evelyn had overstepped with her daughter. She knew Evelyn didn't see it this way, but as far as Mabel was concerned, she had just lied to Rebecca.

Sure, they weren't witches. But they certainly were cursed. And whether Rebecca knew now or in a decade, the curse would still come, the ocean would still call to Mabel, and Rebecca would bear a girl and the cycle would never end. As surely as the tides pulled in.

But then Mabel looked at her daughter and saw the way her tears had stopped, her cheeks fading to their normal olive-toned hue. Her breathing was becoming steadier and deeper.

"I know you're not in the same class, but you still have Richie at school." Evelyn turned to smile at her boy.

The boy looked down at the table, his expression guilty as could be. Evelyn looked back at Rebecca, whose face had gone hard again. She didn't confirm that Richie was kind to her in school—as it was suddenly clear to the adults that he wasn't—but she wouldn't rat out the boy either. The truth was clear enough regardless.

"Richard Fuller." Evelyn turned her full attention to her boy. "Do not tell me you're partaking in bullying Rebecca."

"I'm not, I swear it!" Richie cried.

"He's not," Rebecca said softly.

"I just don't . . ." Richie looked around nervously, but there was no one to help him. "I just don't talk to her. I pretend I don't know her. If I did, they'd be mean to me too, Mom!"

The boy, too, burst into tears.

Evelyn's blue eyes were dark as the winter sea, her lips pursed with displeasure.

"Have I not taught you to be kind to everyone? Especially our . . ." Mabel heard clear as day the word *family*, though

Evelyn caught herself. "And you know what they say about Rebecca isn't true."

But it was, Mabel knew. The girl had been born out of wedlock, yes. And yes, she was a Jew. Much as it might have displeased the islanders, Mabel had gotten stacks upon stacks of books, learned all she could about Otto's heritage so she could teach it to her daughter because it was Rebecca's heritage too—the girl was proof of her people's survival and endurance, and she should know the beauty of her heritage.

It was true—bastard, Jew, cursed, even witch, Mabel supposed. For what was a witch but a name, a death sentence, strapped to a woman by others?

"But Dad says it is." Richie looked at his mother plain as day. And Evelyn was caught, because she knew, and so did Mabel, that she couldn't disagree with Dean's word. It simply wasn't done.

But Mabel had forgotten how brave her sweet Evelyn was.

"Your father is wrong." Richie's eyes widened as his mother continued. "You know better. If you stand up for Rebecca, the other kids will listen, Rich." Mabel knew it was true. *Witch* was a powerful word that the kids were taught to lob at Coles. But the Bradbury and Fuller names were just as powerful, and just as well taught.

Evelyn continued to talk to Richie, her voice softening. It took time, but soon enough both children's tears had dried. The tear tracks on their faces were replaced with smears of frosting as the family of four enjoyed cake and celebrated five beautiful years of Rebecca Cole.

* * *

"Are you sure it's okay if we stay?" Evelyn whispered.

The two of them stood in Mabel's bedroom, the children already sleeping soundly across the hall in Rebecca's room,

Richie nestled under a blanket on the little couch beneath Rebecca's window.

"Of course." Mabel closed her bedroom door behind them with a soft snick. "You can't walk home in this."

She gestured toward the little port window, nearly covered entirely with snowfall. The lights were still dimmed, casting the space in a silver-white glow coming from the snow and the moon. The light fell on Evelyn just right, making her look like a goddess of the moon, her golden hair silvered, her blue eyes turned softer. As Mabel looked at her, that feeling of being too full for her body trembled throughout her.

And Evelyn looked right back.

"Should I sleep down on the couch?" Evelyn whispered.

It was a question for decorum; they both knew the answer.

"I'd like you to sleep here, Lyn. With me." Mabel stepped forward, slotting her nose against Evelyn's. As though it was second nature, her hands found the sides of Evelyn's face, Lyn's own hands resting on her waist.

Evelyn's hands tightened, fisting the fabric of Mabel's top, pulling her close against every line and curve of her body. Mabel could feel every breath the other woman took, the way her breasts and hips pressed against Evelyn's own.

"I'd like to as well."

It had been years since that first kiss, yet every one since still felt like an unbelievable gift that Mabel could not believe she had been given. This time was no exception.

But there was something different in the meeting of their lips and tongues and searching hands now. What started soft quickly became heated, almost frantic. Mabel's body felt on fire. She touched Evelyn's waist, her back, her shoulders; she ghosted a hand across her breast. Evelyn gasped, arching up into the touch.

The two women wandered toward Mabel's bed, softly twisting together atop the covers. It had been years, but they had never done *this*.

But oh, Mabel wanted to.

With the silver moonlight over them, Mabel undid the buttons of Evelyn's blouse with shaking hands until the garment fell onto the floor. Mabel looked down at Evelyn, the points of her bra pressed to Mabel's chest, her gold hair around her like a halo. And Evelyn smiled up at Mabel, soft and nervous and loving.

Time seemed to somehow both speed and slow. In the blink of an eye, their clothes were gathered in a pile on the floor. Evelyn tried to scoot beneath the blankets, covering herself with nervousness. Mabel placed a gentle hand on her arm, stopping her. "I'd like to see you."

Evelyn swallowed. And nodded.

Mabel slid her hand, featherlight, over Evelyn's thighs, tentatively exploring between her legs until Evelyn gasped as Mabel found the warm, soft heat of her. Evelyn, through the haze of her own pleasure, reached down Mabel's body to mirror the movements.

From then on, time slowed. Crawled. Time, the world, none of it existed. It was just them. It was just the feeling of exploring Evelyn's body with hands and lips, the feeling of Evelyn's soft gasps and her warmth around Mabel's fingers. It was the perfect sound of Evelyn's pleasure, the spreading warmth in Mabel's own shaking body as Evelyn took her own time exploring.

It was following the pull of what felt right, and knowing that it *was* right.

It was love, Mabel realized. This was love.

Twenty-Four
Rebecca

September 21, 1971

Juniper Island, Isles of Shoals, New Hampshire

Rebecca felt naked beside Cal. For once, she wasn't, at least not literally. Yes, she knew in part it was because she was wearing her swimsuit, shivering in the stinging sea breeze, even though she was still bone dry; she always seemed better suited to handle the elements from within the water than without. And autumn was quickly settling into the roots of Juniper, the sea growing fangs, the air thinning with the dropping temperatures.

And yes, while Rebecca wrapped her bare arms around her bare legs, Cal sat beside her fully clothed in a long-sleeved T-shirt and salt-worn work pants that hung loose around his shaped waist. But really Rebecca knew she felt naked because of what was inside her. Because the love she felt looking at Cal, sitting beside him, feeling his hands and lips on her body, was so intense she was certain it must be plastered across her face. She was so overwhelmingly in love with Cal Bradbury that it seemed impossible that the man himself did not know, even in her silence. It was the only thing that existed in Rebecca's mind, after all.

Cal saw her goose bumps and chuckled, then pulled her into the warm halo of his strong arms. And Rebecca's mind screamed *You are so caring, I love you.* He talked about his work, how he was sick of the fishing boats already, how he longed to go somewhere else, do something else. She hardly even processed a word because her thoughts echoed with *You are so determined, I love you.*

At some point Cal either ran out of steam or realized that Rebecca was somewhere else, and he leaned in, sweeping her long curtain of dark hair away, running his nose up her neck, smiling as her skin rose in goose bumps for a whole new reason. His hand trailed up her bare thigh, farther, and Rebecca's body and mind sang in chorus *I love you, I love you, I love you.*

She thought it must be obvious, but she wouldn't tell him. Couldn't tell him. Cal was the heart of Rebecca's whole sheltered life, but she knew she still only got a corner of his, their time together his to determine and control. She couldn't tell Cal she loved him first.

And she knew, without a doubt, that he would say it to her. He might not realize he loved her, but he would soon enough. She could be patient.

The rocks they sat on scraped the backs of her thighs as Rebecca arched into Cal's touch. She loved that this rocky spot they'd first met in was their spot, but she wished it had been somewhere a touch softer. But at least here she got to be at the border of her two loves: Cal Bradbury and the sea. Even if Cal himself had no interest in swimming, insisting he already spent enough time on the water to know it couldn't be trusted. But Rebecca had never felt that way. The ocean had always been her friend. Often, her only one. If it was true that her ancestors lingered as shades in the blue, then she supposed she really did love them.

Cal's hand ghosted up her waist, and Rebecca's skin tightened and shivered. His grip kept drifting upward until his palm met the curve of her left breast. The feeling was immediate, hypersensitive, her breasts feeling heavy and almost foreign lately, tender and tentative. Cal chuckled, palming the swell in his grip, not noticing the slight wince Rebecca tried to hide.

"God, Beck," he breathed, voice hoarse. "I don't know what you've been doing, but I swear these things have doubled in size."

He was right, she realized. Her chest had ballooned in recent weeks. In fact, lately her entire body seemed to be shifting beneath her skin like some sort of second puberty, as if Cal's touch and love and lust were changing her DNA.

He continued fondling Rebecca, the afternoon sun glinting off his gold wristwatch, a present from his well-to-do father, a symbol for the prodigal son. The little clock caught Cal's eye, causing the man to suddenly pull back. Instinctually, Rebecca leaned forward, mind and body craving his touch with the loss of it.

"Shit, I've got to go. Richie's new stepbaby has thrown their whole house into chaos, and I'm meant to go over tonight and help."

Before Rebecca could utter a word, he leaned forward, pressing a searing kiss to her lips, then ran up the rocks, back onto the island proper.

Rebecca turned back to the sea, wrapping her arms around her knees to warm herself, to no avail. But she couldn't move back toward the lighthouse. She was frozen there on the rocks, other thoughts suddenly streaming into her mind.

The mention of Cal's cousin Richie always ticked something in Rebecca's mind. Her childhood was mostly a colorless blur of being laughed at and mocked, working in the library with only her mother and the books for company, sitting alone in the lighthouse listening to her records. But there were clear spots in those early swirls too, spots that looked like Richie's face. She couldn't quite grab the memories clearly, couldn't quite parse out why she felt an instinctive comfort around the man, like she would a brother. She couldn't be certain if those hazy memories of napping together, playing in the library, blowing out birthday candles side by side were anything more than desperate dreams of a lonely child. But why Richie? She also remembered, early, early in her life, her mother and Evelyn being friends. But now the two women didn't even enter the same room; any former friendship seemed impossible.

Shaking off her thoughts, Rebecca dove from the rocks beneath the water, pushing out against the waves, farther out to sea. The cold water immediately shocked her skin with needles, but she was used to the sensation. She welcomed it. Her arms and legs strained as she swam out against the current, her muscles waking up and warming her body quickly. The movements that had once felt natural to her were suddenly so much more draining on her body, her chest aching with each upward press of her arms.

As her body settled in with the movements of the sea, unfortunately, Rebecca's mind didn't stop its swirling around Richie Fuller. She didn't know him now, and she probably hadn't back then either. Besides, she and Richie were no longer children anymore. He had just married his mainlander wife, Liza, whose daughter, Julia, was just a few months old. And Rebecca was an adult now, properly. She had Cal. They had a future.

Suddenly, Rebecca's body went as rigid as the rocks, as cold as the water that enveloped her. Thinking of baby Julia Fuller had switched a flip in her mind. Had made all the puzzle pieces slot together.

Treading water, head above the waves, Rebecca's frozen body bobbed and fell with each wave, but she hardly felt the splash of salt water into her eyes and mouth.

No, Rebecca thought. *It's not possible.*

Except, of course, it was. It absolutely was. And Rebecca knew in her bones that it was true. She was pregnant. She and Cal, they had made a *baby.*

Her swelling, tender chest, her roiling stomach, her odd dreams and sensitive nose. Her body had shifted the last few weeks because it was preparing for something new to take a home there.

She faced away from the island, looking out at the open sea, where she was the only living being in her world. Her dark hair, plastered against her forehead, tickled the small of her back where it floated, but she didn't bother to move it.

Rebecca had never thought she'd have a child. She'd been raised on the islanders' vitriol as the "descendant of a witch" and her mother's stories of their curse. She wasn't sure she believed it, not entirely, but Rebecca figured the only way to play it safe was to never have children.

Rebecca supported the right to choose. She had followed the news—though the papers from the mainland arrived so late that Juniper was always weeks behind. But she knew that abortion was a topic on the tongues of America, and though the islanders and their conservative ways might oppose, Rebecca certainly didn't. She knew that she could probably go to the mainland and get an abortion if she wanted to. Keep her entire life from being upended, from changing.

But she was shocked to find she didn't want to.

There, treading water between the past and the future, Rebecca saw that future so clearly. Her and Cal married, raising their little girl on the mainland, going to all the places on her list together. Her daughter would be raised with a father, would never know that the Cole name came with a curse. Rebecca didn't know if the curse was real or not, but she did know that the only thing stronger than it would be her and Cal's love. She would break the curse. *They* would break it.

Heart pounding with excitement now, Rebecca came back to her body. She laughed aloud, the sound melting into the waves. Joyfully, she dove beneath the sea, feet flicking out. But as her lithe body pushed deeper and deeper beneath the waves, Rebecca remembered the curse properly. As she pressed into the depths of the sea where the world went black and icy, Rebecca remembered all the swallowed souls of the Cole women down here. The water seemed to part for and move with her, as if those Cole women haunting its depths were overjoyed for her too.

But their presence, comforting as it was, reminded Rebecca of so much more.

Heart sinking as much as her body, she knew that even though their baby was now just cells, just a seed, this new life meant death too. For there could only ever be two Cole women alive on Juniper, after all. She wasn't sure she believed in the curse, but the deaths dotting her family tree couldn't be denied.

Suddenly, for once, the sea felt too dark, too cold, to comfort Rebecca. She flipped her body, lungs aching, surging back toward the navy surface. Her head broke with a gasp, ankles flicking, surprisingly fearful of what could be lying in wait in the dark water beneath her. Every wave hitting Rebecca's shoulders felt like a threat, a future just as inevitable as the tide. For Rebecca to become a mother, she would lose her own. And soon, it seemed.

Twenty-Five
Mabel

October 24, 1960

Juniper Island, Isles of Shoals, New Hampshire

Distantly, the mainland looked aflame, topped in shades of red and orange. Then Mabel turned, walking to the other side of the gallery, and the world was just rippling black waves and endless, endless navy night. Juniper wasn't hospitable to trees; like so much else, the richness of fall was far away.

As she did most nights, Mabel settled in on the gallery, welcoming the blistering wind that burrowed the scent of salt and brine into her skin. She leaned against the railing, arms crossed, and looked. Her reverie was interrupted by the sound of footsteps clanging up the steps within the bowels of the lighthouse. Rebecca had already long since fallen asleep in her room. Besides, Mabel would have recognized the sound of Evelyn's footsteps anywhere.

She didn't turn as she heard the door open, waiting with a smile on her face for the feeling of Evelyn's arms wrapped around her waist, her chin already tilted to make room for the soft kiss Evelyn always pressed to her neck in greeting. But beats passed in silence, and no touch found Mabel. Brow furrowing, she turned around.

Evelyn stood in the doorway, lost to shadow. Even in the darkness, Mabel could tell something was not right. Evelyn's hair had come free from its usual neat curls. Her shoulders were pressed forward, no sign of her usual pristine, proud posture. And then the beam of the light swept over Evelyn, and Mabel could see the horror illuminated.

Evelyn's face was red, streaked with tear tracks that she had barely been able to conceal. Her pink lipstick was smudged, hasty attempts to clean it up having been to no avail. And there, right over her left eyes, in the hollow, a purple bruise was stamped onto her pale skin.

Mabel gasped. Evelyn met the sound with a trembling breath, on the verge of tears. It was a sound Mabel had never, ever heard from the other woman. Mabel pressed forward, taking Evelyn's hands gently, aware that the woman she cared for was so tender at this moment.

Mabel's instinct was to ask what happened, but she didn't. She knew. Through the veil of her deep, sinking sadness, Mabel's blood whooshed with anger.

"I'm sorry," Evelyn said softly. "I shouldn't have come here. But I didn't know where else . . ."

Mabel's heart broke. She gathered Evelyn in a hug, whispering, "Hush now, this is your home too."

Evelyn shyly stepped out of the embrace, leaning against the railing. Her eyes were cast down, away from the moonlight, as though a bit of shadow were enough to disguise the violence of Dean Fuller. As if she were ashamed to be seen this way.

There was no shame in it. Evelyn was in no way responsible for the actions of a violent man she had been made to trust. Of the world she lived in that gave her so few options for peace or power.

"Is Richie okay?" Mabel looked around, as though she might have missed the sight of the boy.

Evelyn nodded. "He's spending the night at Jackson's, thank God. Dean came home drunk. He saw me, and he just . . . he wanted to be angry. I guess one of the other men had been taunting him, making jokes about his wife spending time with a witch, being a witch myself. He couldn't show them that they'd gotten to him, so I guess he took it out on me."

Mabel's anger made her heart beat in a steady drum, louder than the waves. "We should tell your brother." The only man on this island who had more power than Dean—could have some sway over him—was Jay Bradbury. He owned the fishing company that employed nearly every man in town, the king of Juniper's own empire. He might have called Dean a close friend, might have given his brother-in-law a role of power within Bradbury Fishing and therefore on the island. But still, if Jay knew what Dean was doing to his sister, he would step in. "He can get Dean to stop. Help you get a divorce, even . . ."

Mabel's words trailed off when she saw the look on Evelyn's face. Sympathy. Pity. A small shake of her head. Because, Mabel realized, of course Jay already knew. And clearly, Jay would not do a thing to protect his sister.

Mabel's rage grew claws. Her instinct was to try to calm herself, but she didn't want to this time. *Someone* should be reacting with anger for Evelyn.

"I was pregnant a second time, when Richie was barely two." Evelyn tried to take a steadying breath, but it came out wobbly. Involuntarily, Mabel held hers. "I was only a few months along. Dean can be rough . . . he didn't mean to, I don't think . . . I lost the baby."

Evelyn's body sagged with the expelled words. Mabel felt her stomach sour with rage and deep, deep sorrow. She gathered Evelyn into her arms, brushing away the golden hair that the sea breeze had battered against her bruised face. With a touch light as a feather, Mabel kissed Evelyn's cheeks where the purple was beginning to blossom, replacing a touch born in rage with one steeped in love.

"You do not deserve this." Mabel's voice trembled with the force of her words, her belief in them. "We will sort this out together. He will never touch you again. Together, okay?"

Evelyn nodded within the gentle hold of Mabel's hands. The women met at the lips, both trembling softly. They were still pressed together, sharing air, when the door behind them crashed open.

Before Mabel could turn to see who had entered, Evelyn was ripped from her hands. The beam passed over the three of them in turns. It was a strobe light over the sight of Dean Fuller grabbing Evelyn by the hair, wrenching her backward.

For all her rage, Mabel was frozen.

"You whore," Dean panted, spittle flying. "You witch. You unnatural beast."

Evelyn made a strangled sound, but no words could form. Dean pressed on with his rampage. "This is the devilry my own wife partakes in? I followed you, Evie, but this, this is worse than my nightmares." His large hands wrapped around Evelyn's neck, and even in the dim light it was clear that his grip was tightening.

He continued a spree of calling Evelyn names that were worse than anything Mabel had ever heard. The sound of such horror woke her up.

He's going to kill her. He wants *to kill her.*

Just as Evelyn had been protecting Mabel for years, just as Mabel's hatred of Dean Fuller had brewed just as long, protecting Evelyn was simply Mabel's instinct.

If it was between Dean Fuller's safety or Evelyn's, Mabel would choose Lyn every time.

She didn't think as she burst forward, wrapping her hands like claws over Dean's shoulders. Mabel wasn't sure if it was her momentum or Dean's that sent him stumbling back, releasing Evelyn, who slammed into the far railing, breath heaving. Dean, too, stumbled back into the walk's railing. But his anger and Mabel's had given his movements more force. And he was taller too, the railing hitting him not in the waist as it had Evelyn but below the hips, throwing off his center of balance.

The world teetered for a moment as Dean Fuller did too, his upper body hovering over the railing's edge, his feet scuffling for purchase on the rain-slick walkway. Mabel didn't know if she wanted Dean Fuller dead or if she just wanted to protect Evelyn. But when her hands reached out toward the man, it was not to pull him back.

Dean's scrambling hands tried to grab at Mabel's sleeve, hold anything for purchase. But they slid right off her.

Both women stepped up to look over the railing as Dean tumbled over it, out of sight. Side by side, Mabel and Evelyn watched Dean fall through the air like a doomed bird. Nothing could be heard over the beating of the waves on the rocks, but Mabel still thought she heard a thud as Dean's skull cracked off the rocks below before he tumbled down the rest of the way. Mabel was certain Dean was dead before his body disappeared into the depthless autumn blue of the ocean, soon to be pulled out to sea like he was nothing more than a Cole woman.

Twenty-Six
Mabel

December 2, 1963

Juniper Island, Isles of Shoals, New Hampshire

The county was mourning the death of the president, but Mabel was already years deep in her own mourning. And she was no stranger to the violent deaths of powerful men, that was for sure.

Mabel ran the feather duster along the edge of the window, the library silent and empty at her back. Of course it was empty. This was a day that Mabel Cole worked. People only ever visited on Evelyn Fuller's days.

Maybe Evelyn finally believed that Mabel was cursed after all.

Everybody believed that those dead Cole women in the sea would swallow lives if their living descendants ever stepped foot off Juniper, left the lighthouse alone. Now Mabel and Evelyn both knew that it was deadly—no curse or superstition needed—when a living Cole woman was in the lighthouse too. These days, those ancestors in the blue felt like the only family Mabel had left; the sight of the sea was more comforting to her than it had ever been.

As she dusted the panes, Mabel's eyes found the sight out the window. Just beyond the crooked crosses of the cemetery, an old beaten skiff was tied to the rocks, bobbing in the waves, filling slowly with the snow falling down. Mabel knew no one would come out to move the boat, to keep the wood from wetting and rotting. It had sat there, exposed to the elements, for over three years.

After Dean fell down into the sea, everything had changed.

Dean wasn't the only thing that died that night. Evelyn had looked at Mabel there on the edge of the gallery, breathed her name just once.

Then she had run from the lighthouse.

It was the very last time they had ever spoken.

Two families were torn apart in that one moment.

They didn't need words to divide up their life. It became natural that the even dates were Mabel's at the library, the odds Evelyn's. All business was conducted through scribbled notes left on the desk, and still, years later, Mabel's heart squeezed to see Evelyn's looping script.

For days Mabel had hidden away at home, waiting for the police to knock on her door or the islanders to throw her into the sea as they had her ancestor. But they never came.

Evelyn might not have loved Mabel anymore—maybe she never had—but the woman had still protected them both.

Mabel didn't even realize what Evelyn had done until two weeks later when Dean Fuller's skiff floated up on the island, packed with supplies for a fishing trip, a single shoe. But no Dean. Evelyn guided the island into believing that Dean had been lost to the sea. It wasn't uncommon here on Juniper. And it wasn't untrue.

Of course, deaths in the sea were also the territory of Cole women. But no one could deny that the beam had been lit every night for decades, that Mabel Cole had never stepped foot off Juniper, never given her ghostly ancestors reason to make the sea angry and deadly enough to swallow a man alive.

Nevertheless, the islanders still looked at Mabel with resentment for a long time after. *More* resentment, that is. But in staging a death that could not be tied to Mabel with any hard evidence, Evelyn had saved her.

Evelyn hadn't spoken to Mabel again, but she had kept her from meeting the fate of Goody Cole, accused and killed. Evelyn had traded her love for Mabel for protecting her. Mabel wasn't sure that was a trade she would have wanted, a price she wanted to pay. But it was too late. It was done.

Mabel told herself that Evelyn kept her distance to protect her, to keep their closeness from drawing more eyes and vitriol, from making superstitious glances turn into inquiring minds that might find evidence of a real, committed crime in the lighthouse. She told herself all that, but it broke her heart all the same.

The door of the library closed. Mabel knew it wasn't a customer. She weaved her way to the front to find Rebecca already settling into the desk, laying out her homework. The girl didn't even look up when her mother stepped up before her.

"How was school, baby?"

Rebecca stared down at the papers before her, jaw clenched tight. She didn't need to say anything. Mabel knew what her daughter's stoicism meant. Mabel herself knew what it was like to be the witch of Juniper Island; she knew the cheers and taunts and thrown objects of the schoolchildren here.

So many times over the past three years Mabel had considered gathering herself and Rebecca, hopping on a boat, and leaving this place for good. Making a life on the mainland where everyone had forgotten what being a Cole meant. If the stories were true, then let the sea turn angry with the violence of dead Coles within. Let them rage at their absent descendants, let them make the sea the islanders feared and relied on a dangerous beast.

But, despite the story Evelyn had woven, Mabel had feared such an action would make her look guilty. She was already, always, going to be blamed for things that went wrong on this island, just as every other woman in her line was. And, for once, they'd be right. But still, she did not regret killing Dean Fuller.

Besides, leaving was always a flight of fancy. She knew it wasn't possible.

Mabel's mother had told the story of her own mother when Mabel was a girl, a tale meant as a warning. Mabel's grandma, Dorothy, had tried to leave, gone down to Boston after her own mom died. She met a man and returned pregnant. She had been gone almost a year. Dorothy said the mainland never felt quite right, like she was an alien among a foreign species, unable to ever find her footing, as if she were living on a boat in a storm that could never be quelled.

Mabel's mom told her that Juniper had gotten its hooks into Dorothy's mind, had ripped her back to these shores. And Mabel's mom suspected that was why her own mother was never quite whole; she had dared to leave the island, and even after she returned, the curse would not leave her unpunished. Aches deep in her body, exhaustion in her bones, a sorrow that never broke—the price of daring to defy their curse.

Some days Mabel thought it might be worth it to try it anyway. That any price or torture she had to endure would be worth it to give Rebecca a better life. But in her bones, Mabel knew the curse was real, every facet of it. They could not leave. Juniper always, always called the Cole women home.

She looked at the tremble rocking Rebecca's lips. The girl swiped an angry hand over her tear-stained cheeks, enraged with herself for showing emotion even in front of her own mother. Despite all Mabel had told herself she'd do differently, somehow there was the same distance between her daughter and her that she and her own mother had had.

Mabel had been able to give Rebecca a family once. That time was long gone. She wondered if Rebecca even remembered those nights of dancing with Evelyn in the kitchen, giggling with Richie, being called a mermaid.

Maybe it was for the best if she didn't. It hurt Mabel enough to think about it herself.

"What happened?" Mabel kneeled down beside Rebecca, running a gentle hand over her hair.

Rebecca ducked out of the touch. "What always happens. They all hate us." She looked up at her mother with those big brown eyes, wise beyond her years yet somehow still so innocent. But Cole women, even at only eleven years old, were never allowed to be children. "Why don't they like me?"

Mabel had seen her daughter leaving school, walking alone, eyes looking hopefully at the other children, who met her with mockery and scorn. And still, still Rebecca hoped the people of this island would one day love her back. Mabel had hoped for the same once, before she saw the way they treated Otto, before Rebecca was born. Mabel knew better. She saw the islanders as they were, and she knew she didn't want to be a part of them.

She put her hands on Rebecca's shoulders, turning the girl to face her. She laid a hand on Rebecca's round cheek, guiding the girl to look her right in the eye. Mabel bored her gaze into her daughter's.

"We don't need them, do you hear me? It doesn't matter a wink what they think of us."

Rebecca listened to her mother, but she did not hear her.

Twenty-Seven
Mabel

June 17, 1970

Juniper Island, Isles of Shoals, New Hampshire

Mabel shifted on the hard seat of the folding chair, but no amount of readjustment eased the aches in her hips. She flexed her wrists, softly gasping as the dull pain there turned sharp. She didn't even acknowledge the judging glances of the other islanders seated around her; they would give her those looks no matter what she did.

The aches in Mabel's body had been growing steadily for weeks now. And the work of the morning hadn't helped. She'd sat on the floor of the library for hours, organizing the town's files into the library's system. The new rule, which saw all files over a decade old moved to library accounting, shouldn't have been such a pain. There weren't many people to die, be born, or get married on Juniper, after all. Still, the morning's work had sharpened the aches in Mabel's joints and muscles.

But she couldn't deny the pain had been there before this morning. And that thought made her heart kick up. Mabel couldn't help but think of the story of her grandmother, of her own mother's complaints of aches so strong she could hardly hold a paperback in the last year of her life. Mabel suspected this was the curse beginning to call to her, the first note of its siren song calling her toward death.

All she wanted was to go home to the lighthouse, rest her aching body in bed or a warm bath. But no, that could all wait. Sitting here, on the edge of the island before a makeshift wooden stage—this was the greatest thing Mabel had done.

The graduates stood in a line, waiting to be called across the stage and accept their diplomas. Mabel had settled herself into a front-row seat, not giving a damn about the weight of the steely, unhappy gazes on her back. Every resident on Juniper came out for the high school's yearly graduation ceremony, but this was Mabel's first time attending since her own. And she had every right to be there; her little girl, little no longer, was soon to be called.

Rebecca stepped up beside the stage, her name coming up soon. Her long dark hair fell down her back, a stark contrast to the white dress that beat around her knees in the sea breeze. The girl's eyes cut across the seated crowd. Mabel smiled widely when Rebecca's eyes fell on her, but the girl's gaze simply skated over her mother. Mabel's chest constricted again with that feeling that she wasn't enough for her daughter. That somehow she hadn't given her daughter enough.

"Barbara Allan!" Jay Bradbury's voice boomed. Jay had no ties to the school, but as the most important man on Juniper, it was his pleasure to welcome the young ones into adulthood.

Cheers went up around the crowd as a petite girl with softly curled blond hair stepped onto the stage. The loudest yell of congratulations came from Mabel's left. Even through all the noise, she would always recognize that one sound.

She couldn't help it. She twisted in her seat, looking back over her left shoulder. There was no way to be coy about it. But she didn't care; she acted on instinct, drawn to that voice as she always was.

Evelyn Fuller sat beside her sister-in-law and nephew Cal—Barbara's boyfriend—a wide smile on all their faces. As always, Mabel had eyes only for Evelyn. They might run the library together, but Mabel could count on one hand the times she had been this close to Evelyn in the past decade.

The woman was older now, the first hints of gray blinking out through the gold, caught in the sunlight beaming down. Every line and valley of her face was the same, just as beautiful and perfect as Mabel remembered.

Evelyn looked happy there, surrounded by her family, Richie seated just behind her. But there was still, clearly, a missing member of their family. Guilt lodged in Mabel's belly. She didn't regret seeing Dean Fuller to his death, not for one minute. But sometimes she did regret how it must have left Evelyn and her boy alone. Because Evelyn had not only lost her awful husband, she had given up Mabel that day too. But at least Evelyn had others on the island who shared her blood and love.

All Mabel had was a daughter who always felt adrift and the sense of calm she felt as she watched the beam sweep over dark water, the depths hiding lines of Cole women past.

As if Evelyn still had a direct line to Mabel's thoughts, her eyes suddenly cut over. Mabel held her breath, afraid to move. The sea breeze fell away, the murmurs of the crowd muted, the world stilled as Mabel locked on to those deep-blue eyes. Evelyn's smile faded, her face showing nothing at all. Mabel wasn't sure what could be seen in her own expression.

But there was only one thought in her mind: *This still feels like coming home.*

"Rebecca Cole."

The only person who could have pulled Mabel's attention away was the only other person she had ever truly loved.

She turned to see Rebecca crossing the stage, nervous gaze still stuttering over the crowd. Mabel cheered loudly, not letting the beat of the waves drown her out. She was the only one. The rest of the islanders did not make a single sound. That, more than anything else, felt like the moment Evelyn Fuller truly abandoned them.

Mabel did not have a soul on this island who cared for her anymore. Rebecca did not have a single friend on this soil, no one to smile with or hug at this turning point in life, like the other kids did.

No one really left Juniper; most of the boys graduating would work for Bradbury Fishing. The girls would get married or start teaching. Rebecca would keep working at the library, full-time now, getting a proper paycheck from the town council, even if it was given begrudgingly.

This moment, of nothing but Mabel's lonely cheers and Rebecca's searching eyes, was how things would always be. That, Mabel thought, was really a curse.

Twenty-Eight
Mabel

September 19, 1971

Juniper Island, Isles of Shoals, New Hampshire

Between having another—picky—mouth to feed and cooking an elaborate meal for each Friday Shabbat, Mabel had become a fairly competent cook. She silently patted herself on the back as she moved through the kitchen, putting the final touches on the meal. The air was sweet and yeasty with the smell of the round challah that she placed on the kitchen table. The chicken was finishing up in the oven, lending its warm, savory aroma to the space too. She could hear Rebecca walking around overhead as she sliced two apples, arranging them on a plate around a little dish of fresh honey she'd paid a pretty penny to have brought over from the mainland.

But it was the new year. They deserved all things sweet for a fresh start.

Mabel was just settling the last of the food on the table when Rebecca trotted down the stairs. She didn't even look over at Mabel as she cut through the kitchen, pulling open the front door. A chilly autumn breeze swept in with her.

"Whoa, whoa. Rebecca." The girl finally stopped at the sound of her mother's voice, looking over her shoulder. "Where are you going?"

Rebecca closed the door but kept a hand on the knob as she turned to talk to her mother. *She is so beautiful,* Mabel thought. *She is my greatest gift. What more could I ask for?*

So it made Mabel's heart shed a splinter to see the way her daughter looked at her, face rife with discontent. Mabel knew that teenagers pulled away, stretched their legs toward independence. In many ways, they became strangers to their parents. But Rebecca looked at Mabel like her mother was the stranger. An unpleasant entity clinging to Rebecca's life.

"I'm going out," she said, clipped. Rebecca had been fairly absent recently. Disappearing at night, returning home smelling of salt and kisses. Mabel stayed up each night, stomach clenched in knots. Rebecca had always been a free spirit, floating around in her bell-bottoms and crop tops, twirling her long hair and short dresses. Mabel knew the world had progressed from when she was nineteen years old, but she wasn't sure that the mindsets of Juniper had.

"It's Rosh Hashanah, baby." Mabel gestured at the spread she'd made them on the table.

Rebecca sighed, as though all the effort her mother had taken into preserving the girl's heritage was little more than an inconvenience. She ripped off a piece of the challah, holding up the doughy bread as if to say *Happy now?* Rebecca turned back to the door.

"Just . . . just remember the curse, baby." Mabel's words were whispered, but you'd think they were a shout the way Rebecca spun back around, rage etched into her features.

"God, enough!"

"Do not—"

"I'm not a baby! And fuck the curse!" Rebecca's voice echoed around the small kitchen, knocking Mabel from every side. "All you care about is the fucking curse. And it's not even real. That's stupid. You're just a lonely woman who doesn't even try to be a part of the island. Just like the rest of our ancestors that you're so obsessed with. Maybe if they had all tried a little more to be accepted, they wouldn't have killed themselves!"

Mabel reeled back from the burning anger in her daughter's words, from the harshness of them.

"It doesn't matter if you believe it." Mabel kept her voice measured, though it only seemed to enrage her daughter more. Hearing Rebecca's words, Mabel knew she disagreed, but she was surprised to find that, for once, the curse was a comfort. Certainly more comforting than Rebecca's notions of their ancestors and their own inevitable futures—or lack thereof. Of the idea that Cole women were not cursed and simply lonely women who suffered and killed themselves. "You may not believe in the curse now, but it's still true. You'll realize one day. I just want to keep you safe—"

"You're the curse, Mom. *You're* the curse on my life."

Before Mabel could even digest her daughter's words, Rebecca disappeared into the night.

"Shana tova," Mabel said to no one but herself.

* * *

Mabel welcomed the way the night wind bit at her, freezing the tears that quivered on her lashes. She leaned against the railing on the gallery, overlooking the dark night sky. The swinging beam cast its light off the navy waves.

It had taken Mabel a long time to shake the deep-rooted desire for the islanders to finally accept her. But Rebecca was still in the thick of that senseless longing. And, clearly, she disappeared every night to see someone. Rebecca probably thought she would be different than the rest of the Cole women. Mabel knew she wouldn't. Rebecca, deep down, probably knew that too; it was likely why she hated her mother so much.

Her daughter didn't need her anymore, not really. Resented her, even.

Even the lighthouse didn't need Mabel anymore, since an engineer from the mainland had shown up a few years ago, insisting that the services become automated. Mabel's hard work, burns, and bruises were now replaced by little more than machinery and an on button.

Everyone here could go on without her.

She blinked, leaned back, surprised by the dark shade of her thoughts. God knew Mabel had experienced plenty of sorrow in her forty-odd years, but never quite like this. Never had it been accompanied by a sense of empty, hopeless dread. Never before had the thoughts burrowed so deep, as though the aches she felt were simply the embodiment of her lonely despair.

Now it seemed both body and mind were turning on Mabel.

As she stood on the gallery, as she had every night of her life, the comforting, familiar hum of the night ocean did not soothe her. Because, Mabel realized, she couldn't hear it anymore. Not clearly.

Instead, like a gnat circling her head, Mabel heard a growing chorus of whispers.

Every time the waves capped white on the rocks, instead of a crash of water, Mabel heard a voice. Then another, lapping over another.

Deep-toned rage. The voices of men's anger. The sounds grew louder, a chorus of enraged men.

The beam swept over the rocks, showing Mabel that no group sat below, seething. No, this was not made by humans. The sounds came as though the men were right there on the gallery walk with her, screaming their rage into her ears.

Panic lashed through her, her heart thundering. Mabel's hands flew to cover her ears, but it did nothing. The voices would not be tuned out. As so many men did, they demanded to be heard. Mabel was trapped in the growing swirl of their anger. One voice seemed louder, though perhaps it was just that it was familiar. Dean Fuller had spit rage in life, and now here his voice still was on her gallery, spitting his vitriol at her in death.

Witch. Unnatural. Evil, you Cole women. Witches.

She looked out at the water between the beams of the railing, finding that she had crouched down. But even shrinking herself did not appease the men. The black water kept moving beneath her, steady, familiar. As Mabel looked at it, her body began to calm. The panic was being replaced by another, rising feeling. Mabel felt suddenly certain that only being in the ocean, allowing it to swallow her in its icy, natural embrace, would soothe her. Only giving herself to the comforting touch of her ancestors deep within. They might never have spoken to Mabel in the way these horrible, angry words did, but for the first time, Mabel still heard them. Felt their words in her soul. She felt the overwhelming urge to give herself to the sea.

And it was this that made Mabel realize. The sounds began to fall away until they were gone entirely. Mabel sat trembling on the cold floor of the gallery, her erratic breath making shaky clouds of air. The sea beat steadily against the rocks, familiar as always.

This, Mabel knew, was the curse.

Her time was coming.

And as she sat there, freezing in the autumn air, the sound of those rageful men still echoing in her ears, she wondered again if it was truly men's anger, not witchcraft, that fueled the Cole women's curse.

Twenty-Nine
Rebecca

October 1, 1971

Juniper Island, Isles of Shoals, New Hampshire

She was going to do it. This excitement would stop being just hers and become *theirs.*

Rebecca was going to tell Cal.

She perched on the rocks of their spot, his long-sleeved shirt hanging off her body. It no longer held his scent, but it was the most comforting thing Rebecca owned. She turned the little tube over in her fingers like a baton. It was there, clear as day. A yes. A confirmation of the being that grew inside her. She had managed to slip it from Poole Market without paying, tucking it into her sweater last night. It wasn't that she didn't have the money; it was that she knew how quickly word spread on the island, especially when gossip included the Cole name. For now, this was just hers. Soon, theirs.

She peered around the corner, balancing on the rock's edge, to catch a glimpse of Cal making his way down the stones toward her. Rebecca's entire body lit up at the sight of him, her skin no longer chilled by the early-autumn bite. He warmed her.

She was nearly trembling with the eager excitement to finally, finally tell him.

Cal sank down on the rocks, hands immediately grabbing for Rebecca. She couldn't help the little giggle that escaped her as his lips moved along the sensitive lines of her neck. Cal paused, the small, giddy sound from Rebecca unfamiliar, but quickly continued his heady embrace of her body.

"Cal, Cal." Rebecca grabbed his hands, ducking from beneath his touch. She leaned back, bracketing his face in her hands. His dark brows pulled together in confusion at her stopping them, but she knew, soon enough, a whole new expression would overtake his face.

"I have something to tell you," she whispered, thumbs brushing across his solid, lifted cheekbones.

"Okay." Cal's voice was as hesitant as his eyes. His blue gaze flickered across her face, searching, so unused to seeing such open excitement and joy from the usually measured Rebecca.

She had never let herself express every emotion to him before. But it was time. It was time to call this what it was: love that had created love in return.

"What is it?" Cal asked.

Rebecca swallowed the excited nerves rising up in her throat. With one deep breath of salty brine air, she said, "I'm pregnant."

Cal didn't pull away, which was a brief relief to Rebecca, though she hadn't known to fear it until it didn't occur. But he also didn't joyfully rush her with kisses and hugs and declarations like she had expected. He just stared at her, gaze vacant. As if he hadn't heard her words or maybe just hadn't understood them.

"Cal," she laughed. "I'm pregnant. We're having a baby."

Rebecca leaned forward to press a kiss to his lips and Cal came alive again, rearing away from her. He scrambled back, pushing to his feet, his balance wavering for a moment on the unsteady rocks. He ran a hand through his blond hair, making it stand on end. His jaw was clenched tight.

Confused, heart pounding, Rebecca stood. The slight rise of the rock beneath her made them eye to eye, so she could see every emotion that flitted across his face. Every emotion that she saw there that felt like a little knife to her chest.

None of this was going how she'd thought. None of this was going how it was supposed to.

"What the hell are you talking about?" Cal nearly shouted. Rebecca flinched, hand instinctually coming to rest protectively over her still-flat stomach. Cal's quick, frenzied gaze caught the gesture, and it seemed to enrage and terrify him all the more.

Rebecca dropped her hands to her sides, helpless, watching Cal look out at the sea, shaking his head back and forth.

"Cal," she said, almost a plea, unsure what else to say to him. How to make him understand. Rebecca reached toward his arm, and Cal stepped away, foot slipping on the damp rock before he righted himself, farther away from her.

"No," he said softly, almost to himself. And then, "No, no." This time he finally looked directly at her.

But it was not her Cal she saw there. It was not her Cal with his quick smirk and fire eyes and protective stances. This Cal was a stranger, trembling with rage, seeming to swell to twice his size.

"Cal," Rebecca said again. It seemed the only word her tongue could form was his name. "I love you."

"*No,*" he snapped. Rebecca stepped back in shock, chest aching. He was overwhelmed, he was surprised, he didn't mean any of this.

Cal took a deep breath, looked away from her, steadied himself. When he finally looked back at Rebecca, he was not loving or soft or even angry. He was calm. He was empty. He looked at Rebecca like she was a stranger.

"Look," he said, voice hard and certain. "That has nothing to do with me. I don't know how many guys you bed out here, but it's not mine."

Rebecca's breath turned to cement in her lungs. She couldn't breathe, couldn't see, her vision going white around the edges. Her heartbeat pounded so loudly in her ears she could hardly hear the waves, let alone Cal's sharpened words.

"You hear me? *It's not mine.* This has nothing to do with me."

Rebecca opened her mouth to say something to change his mind somehow, but everything had gone so sideways, so wrong. She had forgotten all words. It was all so broken. Cal was breaking it.

He didn't even look back at her as he stumbled back up the rocks and onto Juniper, leaving Rebecca and their child in his rearview, as if they had nothing at all to do with him.

* * *

The library was so empty Rebecca could hear every unsteady intake of her breath. Her shaky exhale bounced back at her across the dark room. She crossed her sweater tighter around her body, but it did nothing to quell the trembling chill that coated her skin. It wasn't too cold outside just yet, but Rebecca felt frozen.

Cal's words from that morning were hot and molten, slithering across her mind, unescapable.

"He's just surprised," she whispered aloud to herself so that she could forget how alone she felt. So she could attempt to drown out her thoughts. "He'll come around. He loves me. He'll be happy about our baby."

Her heart soothed, the incessant whirring in her mind calming. Cal was a gentleman; he was kind and sweet and sensitive, and so family oriented. He was just young, too, and shocked. His response that morning wasn't his true character. Rebecca knew him. She knew he would come around.

Glancing around the library once more, Rebecca double-checked that all her tasks for the day had been completed before walking around the space, flipping off lamps until she stood in darkness. Her mom had left early today to go light the beam, the sun sinking before the library closed each autumn and winter. Rebecca had never taken comfort from her mother, had never remembered a time when her touch was soothing. But she almost wished her mother were here now, that she actually understood Rebecca, that she would hold her daughter without judgment and tell her that everything would be okay.

But her mother didn't care what a single person on the island thought of her. She never had. Mabel could never, ever understand what Rebecca was going through. Rebecca knew her own father didn't even know she existed; her mother had never had to endure being rebuffed and abandoned.

No, Rebecca scolded herself. *I'm not abandoned. Cal will come back. He will.*

She draped her scarf around her neck, closing the library door behind her as she stepped out into the crisp night air. She was only a few steps onto the main street toward the lighthouse when Rebecca's feet froze at a sound. Her name was so rarely spoken on Juniper that when it was, it was like a lightning strike.

Unable to help herself, she crept closer to Poole Market, where she could hear a group chattering around back, beer bottles clinking.

"Come on," one male voice Rebecca couldn't identify said. "She's a fox. She just is."

"Rebecca Cole?" another guy asked, this voice deeper.

"Yeah," the first voice insisted.

Rebecca held her breath, listening, the rough side of the building scratching at her arms. If anyone so much as peeked out their window, she would need to explain herself, and quick. She knew she looked suspicious, but she couldn't turn away.

"Well, if you're that interested, I heard she keeps her bedroom door open to any man who happens to visit from the mainland. You might as well go try your luck," a third voice said with a cackle that the others quickly joined.

Rebecca's knees gave out beneath her. She had to catch herself with a hand on the rough surface, but her whole body was trembling so fiercely she could hardly stay upright.

That voice, that laugh, she would know anywhere.

But it didn't make sense, that voice saying those words. It was Cal, but he didn't sound like her Cal anymore.

"Just like her mom, then," the first voice laughed.

Stand up for me, Cal. Tell them none of this is true. Tell them you love me, that there is more to me than my beauty, that you've seen it, that you love me, you love me.

But Cal didn't. He let those other boys laugh at her, call her and her mom sluts and witches, like mother like daughter. He let their words burn her down to the core, withering away all that was left of her. That was what was done to witches after all, wasn't it?

Rebecca stumbled away, back up the path, before she could hear any more. Her chest ached with such pain she was certain her heart was actually cracking right down the middle. But no. Cal was scared, he was confused. But she knew him. She knew what they shared. Those words weren't him.

That was not the man who had touched her with loving hands, the man who pressed into her body and breathed into her mouth, who helped make life inside her. *That* Cal would return.

Maybe not now, but that was okay. Rebecca could wait. She knew that once their baby was born, once he saw their daughter, he would run back to her.

After all, she was choosing him, their future, over her own mother, wasn't she? She knew that bringing her daughter into the world spelled her own mother's death, and still Rebecca wanted this child. She was choosing herself and Cal, choosing them over everything.

Thirty
Rebecca

October 10, 1971

Juniper Island, Isles of Shoals, New Hampshire

Rebecca knew, the moment the lighthouse door closed behind her with an echoing finality, that something was wrong. The small hairs along her arm rose, the back of her neck prickling. She had never thought of herself as the witch they all claimed, but there was a feeling deep in her gut, practically a voice in her ear. *Something is wrong.*

She stood still in the unlit kitchen, holding her breath, waiting for a sound. There was only the consistent patter of rain on the worn outer walls of her home. Droplets that had caught in her hair during her walk home from her library shift slithered down her spine, a trail of fire on her hyperaware skin. She didn't dare move, didn't dare breathe, certain that if she held still enough, things would shift back to normal. But she heard no creak of the lighthouse settling beneath someone's feet, no sound of her mother changing into warmer clothes or climbing the stairs to care for the beam, which was already sweeping proudly across the open sea. The light crept in through the kitchen windows, swinging around Rebecca once, twice, three times, before she dared move. She set a hand on the kettle upon the stovetop, certain that it would scald her, the traces of her mother's nightly tea. It was as cold as her own rain-soaked skin. Rebecca still jerked her hand back as if burned.

Something is wrong.

"Mom?" she called out, ignoring the crack in her voice. Only the rain answered.

Rebecca pushed out of the kitchen, peeking her head into the living room. Empty, one lamp still blazing. Her feet tripped her up as she dashed up the stairs. "Mom? Mom!"

Her mother's bedroom was empty, the lights off, the bed still rumpled from her morning, the half-read book still resting on her nightstand. Rebecca bashed open the door to her own bedroom, as empty and half lit as the rest of her home. Her familiar vinyl stacks and strewn clothing were hulking monsters in the gray light. The sweeping beam of the light above her mocked Rebecca, more time passing, no sign of her mother. She dashed up the stairs once more, her own footsteps echoing around her, the swirling sound of her panic.

Her mother not being at home in the evening when she didn't have a library shift was odd, sure. Not necessarily a reason to panic, though typically she'd leave a note for Rebecca. It wasn't the situation itself that drove Rebecca's heart to gallop, her blood to scream in her ears. It was that feeling in her, that certainty. She feared, she knew, that tickle of the curse.

She burst atop the lighthouse, but there was no one and nothing there but herself and that swinging light, illuminating the thunderous rain. It came down harder, booming, the sky and roiling sea an echo of Rebecca's own heart.

No no no no.

She made her way back down to the living room, only holding the railing to slow her pace for the sake of the being growing inside her. Rebecca felt removed from herself, made of nothing but blood and panic and sea salt quivering along her lower lids. The phone in the sitting room trembled in her hand as she lifted it, pressing the wrong buttons twice before the phone finally rang, blessedly still working despite the storm.

There was a brief moment of just her and the dial tone where she worried that Cal would pick up. Maybe hoped it, even. That maybe this would all mean something if only Cal answered, heard her quivering fear and sorrow and realized the mistake he was making, came back to her, started over with—

"Hello?" It was a soft woman's voice that answered the phone. The one Rebecca had been expecting, yes, but still it bottomed out her stomach.

"Evelyn, hi, yeah, it's Rebecca. Rebecca Cole." Evelyn wasn't particularly a friend of her mother's, but then again, her mother had no friends. The other librarian was the only person Rebecca could think of that her mother might have need to communicate with.

"Rebecca?" the woman asked, her voice crackling down the line, fraying amid the rising storm. "Was there an issue closing up the library?"

Evelyn's voice was as measured and polite as ever, the very opposite of the panic laced in Rebecca's own. "No, no, the library is fine. Have you seen my mom?"

There was a long pause, long enough that Rebecca and her jumping heartbeat were certain that the line had finally gone out. Then, so many heartbeats later, Evelyn answered, voice tighter than before, "No. Of course not."

Another beat passed before Evelyn asked, tentatively, "Is she not home?"

Rebecca's heart fell through her stomach, and she wasn't sure she'd ever get it back. "No. She's not."

"I'm sure she's just running some last-minute errands. The storm will bring her home quickly. She'll be fine."

Evelyn sounded like she believed her words. But Rebecca did not. She was a Cole woman. This kind of tragedy lived in the womb and the heart, an unbreakable line of sorrow that ran throughout them.

This was her fate.

This was her fault.

She put the phone down on the receiver, because she could not be bothered to explain the truth to Evelyn. Rebecca sat for a moment, trembling, eyes closed. Then she made her way back through the lighthouse, not harried this time. The dread of what was happening settled on her slowly, weighing her down. She passed back through the cold empty kitchen, out the front door. The jagged rocks pressed into her bare feet, the rain soaking a frozen skin atop her, shoes and coat left forgotten inside the foyer back when she thought the world still spun.

Rebecca made her way down the rocks, balancing and slipping across the slick edge of the island. Just once more, one last hope, she looked over her shoulder at the signs of life behind her, the distance a golden glow of the other families that were not murdered by this place. “Mom?” she called out. No one answered her.

Chest aching, not from the cold, she made her way down to the water, not caring when she hit her knee against the rocks, sure to bruise, or when her hand bloomed in red drops after scratching against a sharp edge. She felt nothing. She was empty.

But that was her problem. She was not. Rebecca stumbled into the shallows of the dark water, the waves lifting and black and angry as they crashed against her shins, droplets reaching up to her knees. Rebecca’s thick, wavy hair was soaked through, weighing her head back upon her neck, sticking to her spine. She looked out at the black water, raging as she broke, and for once she did not see a friend.

When she could not hold herself and her guilt a moment longer, she collapsed, knees bashing against the jagged earth, waves pushing against her shoulders as she held herself firm. She couldn't tell the difference between the rain, the waves, her tears. She was all salt water inside anyway.

Rebecca had always felt the presence of the Coles in the sea, felt comforted by them. She loved the sea and it—they—loved her. So she knew them, knew the sea, well enough to know that it felt more crowded that night. As if a new soul had joined the deep.

Rebecca did not call out when she spoke next. She simply pressed her palms deep into the water and whimpered, "Mommy." One last time. One last name for the mother who was gone. One hand still pressed into the sea bottom, she pressed the other, almost hard enough to hurt, into the hardening patch of her lower stomach. Her mother was gone to the sea, as all Cole women must be. Rebecca was alone. Alone with the being growing inside her that was the reason she had lost everyone and everything.

Thirty-One
Mabel

October 10, 1971

Juniper Island, Isles of Shoals, New Hampshire

She thought about telling Rebecca. Over the past few weeks, Mabel had thought about it a hundred times. Her own mother had never told her; her death had been a surprise, an earthquake in Mabel's life. But, really, what difference would it make to tell Rebecca? The girl was growing up, she was living her own life. Though Mabel knew a woman was never, ever ready to be without her mother. Not really.

But such was the fate of Cole women. Telling Rebecca wouldn't change that. It would just sour the time they had together. So she stayed silent, drinking in every glimpse and smile and waft of honeysuckle perfume she could get from her daughter while she was still here. She spent her evenings perched on the gallery, watching as Rebecca dove and swam beneath the waves. Soon enough, Mabel knew, she would be there too.

Rebecca had always seemed to embrace the feeling of all those dead Coles in the water. She wasn't scared of them. And they seemed to embrace Rebecca right back, Mabel's little mermaid. Mabel could only hope that when her time came—soon, she knew—they would embrace her too.

Every day, she felt closer. Every night the screaming men came for her, unraveling her mind one thread at a time. The sounds burned her skin like fire. And every night the water seemed like the only salve.

Mabel paused before the front door of the lighthouse, turning to look out at the speck of the mainland in the distance. It glowed with the changing leaves, the oranges like a reflection of the sunset sky above them. Over the darkening shades of the ocean, the sky was striped with paint strokes of pink and orange and red. Mabel breathed deep, felt the briny air settle into her lungs. She looked out at the flat expanses of the other isles in the distance. She had never gotten to step foot elsewhere. That was okay. She had lived on Juniper and she would die on its shores, just as every other Cole woman before her. Just as Cole women were meant to do. She entered the lighthouse.

As she crossed the threshold into the kitchen, something crinkled beneath her left foot. Mabel looked down at a small bit of paper, clearly slipped beneath the front door. She picked it up, noting that it was a hastily scribbled receipt from Poole Market.

And when she turned it over, Mabel's heart stopped. One sentence was scratched onto the blank side of the receipt. There, at the very top of the white slip, one line was written with haste, in thick black ink.

I know you killed him

Bile rose in Mabel's throat. She hardly made it to the kitchen sink before she was spewing. It wasn't stomach bile that came up but thick, briny salt water. She wiped a trembling hand across her mouth, looking at the note again, willing it to change. The words did not.

She'd known, in her heart, that eventually someone would find out. Someone would have seen something that night or put the puzzle pieces together. Secrets never stayed buried on Juniper.

This was it. Mabel knew what the islanders did to Cole women. The mainland might have progressed, might have forgotten the alleged crimes of Goody Cole, but Mabel knew full well that the islanders did not. They had accused her ancestor time and again, driven a stake through her heart, abandoned her kin to waste away on an island. The survival of her lineage was due to their own strength, not for lack of the islanders' trying. There were no police, no judges, on Juniper. And island business was island business.

If someone was found guilty of a crime—especially one who had been declared guilty at birth—they would kill her. They would kill Rebecca. There would be no trial. There would be only colonial justice, an excuse to end the line of the Cole women. An excuse they had been waiting for for centuries.

Whoever had left this note meant it as a threat. For whatever reason, they wanted Mabel gone. But she couldn't leave the island. Nor could Rebecca. The island, the lighthouse, never let them stay away long. Even if they did, old logic said that the islanders themselves would pay the price with their lives. But whoever had sent this note didn't seem to care about any of that. They simply wanted to threaten Mabel. To let her know that her death and her daughter's—angry sea phantoms be damned—was imminent. Was in their hands. All the islanders needed was a reason to act, and here, this note, was the perfect one.

The only hope she had of saving her daughter was doing the task before the islanders could. They could rationalize killing Rebecca beside her mother, but Mabel didn't think even they could rationalize killing the girl for the sins of her mother if her mother was already gone. And, God, what if they somehow came for Evelyn too?

There was only one thing to do. At least, now that the curse had come for Mabel, she would give in for a good cause. She would die so her daughter could live.

Perhaps this was what all the Cole women before her had done too.

As if they were a record player turned up, those familiar ragings began to echo in Mabel's mind. This time she did not try to fight them.

Mabel climbed the winding stairs of the lighthouse for the last time, the note trembling in her grip. Each step made her knees and hips sing with pain. She paused at the threshold of Rebecca's room, breathed deep the scent of her daughter's perfume, her skin, her sleep. She stepped into the space, riffling across Rebecca's desk for paper, but came up blank. Finally she settled for grabbing a pen, laying out the note before her.

Beneath that horrible death sentence of a line, Mabel left her daughter one last message. Panic and pain surged in her, making her delirious. Her tears stained the paper as she scribbled out her final words.

Mabel stepped away from the desk, turning to the large bookcase in the corner. It was full of Rebecca's things now, rows of colorful vinyl. But there was one book, cover worn ratty, pages curling and yellowed. Mabel slipped out the old copy of *Rebecca* and nestled her note into its final pages for her own Rebecca to find one day. One day when enough time had passed that her mother's death, her final words, would not feel like such an open wound. The lighthouse would give the note to Rebecca when it was meant to find her.

Silently, Mabel apologized to her daughter, and to her future daughter and so on, for going to join the sea-bound ghosts that would keep them trapped on the isle. Mabel hoped that was at least one inevitable curse she could one day break.

That her spirit, in the deep blue, would not rage and kill when and if her daughter tried to leave. That Mabel would keep the seas calm so Rebecca could leave if she pleased, could live a life of exploration and reunion, like her father.

It was nightfall by the time Mabel made it to the top of the lighthouse. One last time, she turned on the beam. She had always thought that lighting the sea was her great purpose in life. Mabel knew now that it was her daughter. It always had been.

She could hardly hear her own thoughts over the violent wave of the men's screaming, growing louder and louder. She stepped out onto the gallery, looking out at the crashing waves, the endless sea and sky one deep hue. Her skull throbbed with the growing voices, twisting her stomach, making reality feel so far away.

Then the screaming began to fade as another chorus of voices swept in. Not raging, screaming men. Instead, these were the soft voices of women. Dozens of them, saying her name, speaking to her softly, lovingly. Mabel looked down at the sea, heard those gentle tones finding her from the depths of the darkness. One voice was clearer than the others. Her mother's voice. It had been decades since Mabel had heard it, but she would not forget it.

It's time to come home, Mabel.

It's time to make room for the next Cole woman.

It's time to come home to the sea, Mabel.

Mabel felt no panic, no pain, no dread. Her body and mind were awash with calm.

Mabel had always loved the circularity of beginnings and endings, in her books and in her life. She climbed up to the railing's top, balancing on it, seeing the endless blue for the very last time—it felt only right when Mabel stepped off and flew on the ocean breeze.

The sea and everyone within it welcomed her home.

Thirty-Two
Rebecca

January 28, 1972

Juniper Island, Isles of Shoals, New Hampshire

The wind and sea were as angry that day as Rebecca was self-conscious. Her arms ached trying to pull the library door fully closed against the screaming winter sea air. She pulled her open jacket tighter across her front, cursing the slow-growing bump of her stomach that kept it from fully closing. Rebecca kept her chin up as she crossed through the center of the island, resisting the urge to rest her hands protectively against the small swell of her stomach, which was still fairly invisible to the eye of anyone but the mother.

But she knew the people of Juniper could still see it, fully formed as it was in their imaginations. She could feel more than see, through the twitching curtains as she passed, the many faces that peeked out of their homes at her. Most folks were already tucked away for the evening, their homes full of food and family so they could burrow together against the winter chill. And they spent that time glaring out at Rebecca, none daring to say a word to her. She might not be showing her babe yet, but she knew that didn't matter; Cal seemed to have done good groundwork whispering of Rebecca's condition, blaming it on some traveler who'd come to the island just like the one who'd come to her mother, blaming it on Rebecca's own promiscuity. She wanted to hate Cal as the sharp wind bit at her cheeks, her eyes struggling to hold back tears. But she didn't hate him. She couldn't.

She understood his fear. She knew Cal. She knew he would come around. At least, she had told herself as much for the first few months. She hadn't believed it in a while.

If only the curse didn't exist. If only she weren't a Cole. Then everything would be different. Her birthday had come and gone, a new year gained sitting alone in her silent home. She had realized, with horror, that that was to be her future. Inevitable, barreling toward her.

The dimness of the lighthouse's windows as she approached seemed to cement the notion. From the corner of her eye, she caught sight of Alexander, an older man who lived on the mainland and often made deliveries for the library. His little boat was docked on the shore just behind the lighthouse, his wares having been delivered just an hour ago. She raised a silent hand in greeting, and the white-haired man raised one back. He wasn't an islander; he didn't know to hate her.

Rebecca closed the lighthouse door with an echo, the sound reminding her how alone she was within it.

The quiet, the memory of twitching curtains and stony glances, put Rebecca in the mood to poke the bruise. She did as she had too many nights the past few months. Settling onto the cold, lonely surface of her bed, she pulled the pile of scribbled-upon paper scraps onto her lap. The ache in her chest sharpened, choked her, just the way she'd hoped, as she flicked through those little notes Cal had left for her so many moons ago. It felt like another life, another Rebecca, the one she was meant to be. Quick words, soft phrasings, reminders of what she didn't have anymore. Rebecca's fingers trembled so much that at first she couldn't make out the larger piece of paper with the outlying handwriting. She blinked, steadied herself, looking down at her own hand, that list of places she wanted to go one day.

Back then she had been so sure she would. Back then the curse felt like an abstract thing, magic, a problem that couldn't touch her infallible youth. But still, reading that list, deep down Rebecca felt the girl she had been then stirring in her breast. Just like that baby that had fractured her world irreparably, that hopeful girl was still inside Rebecca too.

Rebecca held her breath as an idea landed heavy upon her. And in that moment of stillness, there was nothing around her. No footsteps, no human warmth, no hugs, no Shabbat dinner she reluctantly attended, no scent of spoon-strong black tea, no guaranteed future to look forward to anymore.

That list was meant to be her future with Cal, all those beautiful, foreign places seen by his side. But there was no more Cal and Beck. She was Rebecca, alone.

But, damn it, she did not need to give birth and die on this lonely island. On this little patch of soil amid rough seas, where she was met on every side with stony glares and darkness and bitter cold. Even her beloved ocean had turned against her the moment it swallowed her mother whole. The stories might have said that the ghostly Cole women within felt betrayed and angry when their living ancestors left the island, when they didn't have proof of the safe continuation of their lineage. Well, Rebecca felt mad at them at the very idea of staying here. The sea—*they*—had taken her mother.

If Cal wanted to leave her, fine. But that didn't mean she had to let him take her future with him.

Rebecca hardly thought as she snatched her backpack, stuffing a few sweaters and dresses into it, filling most of the space with her beloved records. The crushed handfuls of all the cash she and her mother had ever saved.

Rebecca packed everything she couldn't live without and found it was very little. She raced down the stairs, her jacket clutched in her fist, flapping behind her like a flag as she burst through the lighthouse door. She didn't even pause to turn on the beam first before dusk set. Damn these people and damn this ocean.

She was done leading them all home when she didn't have one anymore.

Alexander had one foot on his boat when he spotted Rebecca, frantic, racing toward him, kicking up the frozen sand around her. With her wild dark hair flapping in the breeze, her cheeks stung pink, and brown eyes bright with fervor and sorrow, she knew she looked the role of the witch for once.

"Rebecca? You okay?" Alexander looked her over as she came to a stop before him.

"Yes," she said, and for the first time in a long time she thought it just might be true. "Can I come with you? I need to come with you."

Alexander blinked. "What do you mean? I thought you folks tended to stay as you were. You've never left Juniper, have you?"

She looked out across the sea, at the distant flat line of the mainland. The sea had always felt like her home, her place. But it had betrayed her. Her ancestors in the deep had betrayed her. This island and its judgment had betrayed her. She didn't owe any of them anything anymore.

For once, that patch of unknown mainland was her future.

Rebecca hoisted her backpack up higher on her shoulder. Mindlessly, her hand floated to rest over her stomach. "No, but it's about time I do."

Thirty-Three
Rebecca

May 26, 1972

Portsmouth, New Hampshire

"Aren't you lucky, having such a sweet husband?" The cashier smiled wide at Rebecca, her blue eyes darting down to the swell of Rebecca's stomach, which bulged out from beneath the loose fabric of her dress.

Rebecca did not smile back.

In a quick flash of movement, she pulled the cash from her wallet and thrust it into the unready hands of the older cashier. She didn't have to look at Sam by her side to feel his slight frown, his hand already reaching toward his own billfold. His frown was his problem, not hers. Without another word to either of them, Rebecca took the bag of her goods and pushed out into the sunny afternoon. She felt Sam, silent, on her heels as she cut her familiar path across the city streets. Strangers passed by, heads tilted in conversation or lifted to smile up at the sun. A few glances stuck on her belly or on her beauty, but for the most part no one paid any mind to the young woman strolling in their midst. For once, blessedly, Rebecca Cole was anonymous.

Sam caught up to her easily, and without looking she knew that he had swallowed down his earlier disappointment. *Good,* she thought, *he has no right to it.*

"The afternoon should be a bit easier for you now, hmm?" He smiled, hazel eyes flicking down to the grocery bag. Rebecca knew he was resisting the urge to offer to carry for her, knowing she would decline.

"How is a lady meant to survive without a root beer float?" she joked back, rattling the bag, which was heavy with cans of Barq's and a pint of vanilla bean ice cream. Pregnancy cravings had grabbed her by the hair in the last trimester; the bubbly, creamy dessert was her most recurring.

"Exactly," Sam quipped as they waited at a red-lighted crosswalk on Islington. "It'd be inhumane."

Rebecca looked up at him, his curly dark hair backlit by the sun, his round tortoiseshell glasses making his eyes look bigger. There were a few lines starting to bracket his smile, to stretch from his eyes, a sign of the almost decade he had on Rebecca. He was handsome.

And he was interested in her, despite her swelling womb and the mysterious past she swaddled around it. He was interested in her in spite of her beauty, she knew. He liked the flat, sarcastic way she responded, the meticulous way she handled their shared work, the way she lit up organizing the vinyl collection. He was *very* handsome. He was kind. He was here and interested and willing. Even if he didn't know Rebecca Cole, not really, she still knew he was a good prospect. But just the thought tightened her stomach with guilt. She looked away from his eager eyes, hurrying across the street just as the light changed.

They pushed their way into the rectangular, red-bricked library. The smell of aged pages and Ellen's beloved lavender incense enveloped them immediately. The old librarian leaned against the lending counter, smiling up at Rebecca as they entered. She and Sam passed back behind the counter, Rebecca bending around her large stomach to tuck the supplies beneath.

"Oh, come now," Ellen tutted, grabbing the grocery bag from Rebecca. She laid out the supplies amid the records and interlibrary loans, making quick work of preparing a float.

"I thought we weren't supposed to eat in the library." Rebecca smiled, resting a hand beneath her stomach, trying to relieve some of the weight on her lower back.

Ellen rolled her blue eyes to the ceiling, tossing her long white hair over her shoulder. Ellen had been the head librarian of Portsmouth Public Library since the Truman administration; the rules didn't apply to her anymore. With a simple efficiency, she presented the completed float to Rebecca's eager hands. "Drink up, Beck."

Rebecca took one immediate, deep slug, the cold creaminess and riotous bubbles immediately quenching the tight craving inside her.

"Beck and her root beer floats," Sam laughed before passing back outside the desk, disappearing into the stacks behind a returns cart.

Beck. Because it was always meant to be Beck who traveled, Beck and Cal together. Because Rebecca Cole was a name that was cursed, because Beck on the mainland might just be some sort of call to Cal's soul, a siren song finding him across the waves, reminding him of all their plans. There had been a moment where Rebecca contemplated being someone entirely new, stripping herself of *Cole* alongside *Rebecca*. There was so much pain sewn into every syllable of the name.

But, somehow, she hoped that if Cal did search for her, that little thread of her past would help him spot her in the chaos of the mainland and all its people and sounds and sights. And, deeper, Rebecca knew she'd feel a stone of guilt were she to abandon *Cole*. Despite all the pain that name had brought her, she couldn't quite bring herself to turn her back on that line of women from whom she came. But here, on the mainland, *Cole* didn't mean anything anymore. The mainlanders had long forgotten the whispers and tales of Goody Eunice Cole. The name had been stripped of its power. And, as such, Rebecca felt she'd gained a little, for once.

Rebecca sipped her float, tidying up the counter and the last of the day's returns as the lingering patrons filtered out the front door and into the still-bright summer evening. It had all become familiar: the library, the surrounding city, Jackie, Sam, Ellen. It was familiar, sure, but still, sometimes it shocked her. Rebecca could hardly believe this was her life, her world suddenly stretched into so much wide-open space that it often overwhelmed her, this feeling of freedom. This feeling of trying on someone else's life.

Her world had expanded, yet still Rebecca would never dare go to the edge of the city. She avoided the sight of waves, the scent of salt on the air, the pinprick view of the isles, like it was her personal plague. She stayed inland and she told herself, every day, as her body changed and every new encounter made her feel like a newborn herself, that this was her life now and no one could take it away.

She told herself that she didn't care about her ancestral lighthouse sitting empty, the beam unlit. Told herself she didn't care if the rumors were true, if her ancestors had turned the sea angry and violent and dangerous. It wasn't her problem. It wasn't her life. Not anymore.

Rebecca felt a sharp pang in her stomach, low, sharp, and squeezing, for several long seconds before it passed. With a small gasp that echoed around the empty library, she placed a hand on her stomach until it faded as suddenly as it had appeared. She was slightly bent, still catching her breath, when a soft hand appeared on her back.

"You okay?" Jackie's young face was tightened with concern. She, Sam, and Ellen had made their way back behind the counter and were gathering their things to head home.

Rebecca tried to casually sidestep away from Jackie's kind touch. Swallowing the echo of the pain, she smiled at the three concerned faces. "Just fine. Sometimes the bubbles rile up the little one is all."

Jackie, young and unaware, accepted the answer. Sam, too, though still gazing at Rebecca from the corner of his eye, relinquished his concern. But Ellen's gaze didn't waver, sharp on the younger woman. Rebecca held the smile until finally Ellen turned away.

The three librarians headed toward the front door, Rebecca trailing behind them. She walked slower, delicately, afraid that any movement might trigger the pain again. She did her best not to let the others see the fear on her face. She still had never shaken the inherited ways of the lighthouse, the idea that *our pain is ours to bear alone; no matter how kind others may seem, at the end of the day we have no one but ourselves and our women.*

Jackie opened the large library door, letting a rectangle of blue sky and soft yellow light into the dim library. The three of them filtered out, lingering on the cement front steps of the grand library building. Rebecca stayed within, holding the door open. As always, she would be the last to leave, locking up the library behind her. Though there was no *behind* her. When she had arrived months ago, scared, shocked, unaware of the world, a library was the only familiar place she could find. And Ellen, seeing a pregnant young thing with hardly a dime to her name, had not only given Rebecca a job but given her a home in the form of the furnished attic space above the library. Still, the arrangement was quiet; only Ellen and Rebecca knew that she was the last to leave not because it was her shift but because home, for her, was just up the stairs.

Another intense gust of pain gripped Rebecca. She did her best not to heave forward over her belly, to fall into the pain in her middle. Fighting to keep herself upright, she held the door in a death grip, her knuckles blooming white.

"You sure you're okay?" Ellen asked, a hard, knowing look in her eyes.

Rebecca breathed, the sound shaky. "Of course, of course. Good night, now." She stepped back, pushing the door closed on the others' concerned faces. Rebecca leaned against the closed door, holding her breath through the pain until she heard their receding footsteps and mindless chatter fall away on the other side. Then she bent double on herself, her gasp of pain echoing across the empty library.

Rebecca had done her best to forget the being growing inside her. Even as her stomach swelled, her ankles ached, her body changed into something foreign, Rebecca generally could forget that she was not alone, that the girl inside her would come out into the world and change her life irrevocably. Rebecca wasn't even certain when the child was due to come. But it seemed the newest Cole woman was done being forgotten.

As Rebecca bent over herself, a warm gush of moisture burst, trickling down her legs. Rebecca might be a young woman in a new world, but she knew what her body was telling her. It was time for another Cole woman to enter the world.

Thirty-Four
Rebecca

May 26, 1972

Portsmouth, New Hampshire

Rebecca managed to keep her breathing steady as she made her way up to her attic apartment. The small space looked liminal, the golden hour streaming in through the windows, slicing her simple bedding and dresser with the haze of the in-between. The contraction passed, Rebecca releasing an exhale. She was fine. She was okay. She would birth her daughter as Cole women did, by themselves.

But her daughter would be different. She would be born on the mainland, on soil that didn't remember them at all, that wasn't cursed to kill and hate them.

Rebecca sat on the edge of the twin bed, body tensed in fear of the next cresting wave of pain. She knew the ocean well, knew the swells and fades. This was like that, that was all. She could handle it.

Rebecca looked around the space, the little life she had carved for herself in this new world. She had done her best to forget the being inside her, but Rebecca couldn't ignore her anymore. And she could see, so clearly, that this new life of hers made no space for the baby. Rebecca knew that most mothers who sought a new life did it for their child, so they could create a better world for their babe to enter. But Rebecca could not, would not, deny that she had left for herself. The months that child had sat in her had been the most difficult of her life. She knew it wasn't fair, but sometimes it felt as though, as that baby grew in her belly, its growth sucked all the joy and love and companionship from Rebecca's life.

Rebecca was folded double in pain as another contraction crested, her middle feeling like it was being squeezed, stabbed, a werewolf's bone-cracking transformation in the gloaming light. She bit her tongue to keep herself from screaming out. It was only as the contraction began to fade that she realized the tang in her mouth was not the copper sting of blood. No, her mouth swirled with the salty taste of brine, seaweed washing up on shore. Her mouth felt thick, cragged, and as she coughed, it was sand and pearlescent broken shells that she spit into her palm. Rebecca's racing heart kicked up faster to see this piece of Juniper rise up from within her. As though, even on the mainland, the being inside her was made of the Shoals all the way through, brine and salt water already in her veins. Rebecca rinsed her mouth with water, spit it into the little dusty dish on her nightstand. But the taste of the rocky Juniper shores could not be washed away.

She scrubbed a hand across her belly; she wasn't sure if she was trying to soothe her unborn daughter or keep that thing made of Juniper inside her. More pain came on, Rebecca squeezing her eyes closed. But it wasn't the normal black popped with orange behind her lids. No, in the blackness of her closed lids, there was a swinging silver light, highlighting ripples in the darkness, a depth beneath. Rebecca would know the sight anywhere; she had lived beneath the lighthouse's beam all her life, after all.

Rebecca knew this was not in her mind. This was not fear or homesickness or some odd birthing side effect. The proof was there in the broken shells in her dish, in the salt water on her tongue, in the swing of the beam behind her eyes. Juniper Island was inside her, inside this baby. They were Cole women. That was their home.

That was their curse.

And Rebecca knew, as surely as she knew her own name, that if she tried to birth her daughter anywhere but on the soil of Juniper, she and the child would die. The curse killed Cole women, yes, but it also, always, called them home. *Dragged* them home.

With one last look at the space she would never see again and a sob she tried to smoother, Rebecca made her way downstairs to the library. It was slow going, moving in the reprieve between contractions. Hands shaking, she gripped the phone, fingers slipping once, twice, before she managed to call the number she had memorized. It rang four times before a gruff voice answered, "Hello?"

"Alexander?" Rebecca gasped. "It's Rebecca Cole. I need . . ." She paused as she felt her child shift in her belly, restless, the feeling like the ocean waves contained within her womb, an angry sea stirring. "The baby and I, we need—"

"I'll be right there. Hold tight." And with a click, Alexander hung up the phone.

"You'll be home soon," Rebecca whispered to her baby. But Juniper was not Rebecca's own home anymore. She saw now, clearly, that it was her prison.

* * *

The cold evening air stung Rebecca's eyes, salt water rising along her lashes to match that beneath her. She closed her eyes tight, feeling the rush of the boat, the scent of brine heavy on the air as she and Alexander cut through the Atlantic. The angry gales made her dark hair snap against her cheeks, each strand a stinging, stiff lash.

Even with her eyes jammed tight, Rebecca felt the moment Juniper Island came into view. The contractions eased, the swirling, swimming baby inside her soothed. Rebecca's body calmed at the nearness, at the rightness of the curse being assuaged, at being nearly back on Juniper. Even the water beneath them stilled its rocking, the tide suddenly pulling them to the isle.

But her heart ached so tightly Rebecca thought it might kill her. There was no swinging beam of the lighthouse; no one had dared enter her home to tend it in her absence. With an ache, Rebecca realized that the islanders probably would have never realized she was gone without the absence of the light too. Without whatever horrors the betrayed Cole women in the waters had enacted.

"To be honest with you, Rebecca, I wouldn't be daring to make this trip if you weren't in such a state," Alexander called over the sound of the night breeze. "I haven't made it to Juniper in . . . what, six, seven weeks? The water's been too choppy for my little boat. In winter, sure, but spring isn't usually so rough. Heard a fishing boat or two have gone down, the big Bradbury ones. Odd, though; the other isles haven't had any rough currents . . ."

Rebecca tuned the boatsman out, lost in pain and sensation. Alexander might have heard whispers about the curse, but he was still an outsider, despite his frequent visits. He wouldn't know to blame the dead Coles in the sea for the harsh waters, to blame Rebecca for upsetting them by leaving.

"My," Alexander huffed as they got closer to Juniper. "The sea seems soothed at last. Must be happy to have you home."

He joked, but Rebecca knew how true it was. The curse that killed her mother, the angry Coles in the sea—she couldn't deny the truth of them any longer. She had wanted so badly to believe none of it was real. But the truth was in the ocean that raged in her body, in the sea that calmed beneath their boat, in her mother's body long gone beneath the waves.

Eyes still closed, she reached a hand over the edge of the little skiff, letting the cold ocean bite at her fingertips. Still, her heartbeat steadied at the feeling. The sea, the presence of her ancestors, had once been her friend, but now Rebecca wasn't sure she could trust it. Trust them. But she let her fingers be nipped at by the water and tried to feel her mother, many months gone into that blackness. She had never thought she needed her mother, but God, as she was about to become one herself, Rebecca hated the curse more than ever for taking her away.

The patter of the boat quieted, the structure slowing until they came to a scraping stop. With a deep breath, Rebecca opened her eyes and looked up at the looming presence of her lighthouse.

Despite it all, she had ended up back on these shores, the sea on every side her captor.

Despite it all, she was still a Cole woman.

Rebecca pushed herself out of the boat, feet sinking into the sand. She had abandoned all her belongings back in the library attic; let Ellen find them and realize, over time, that Rebecca was not coming back. Those things didn't belong to Rebecca anyway; they were the proof of life of a woman who no longer existed. Who maybe had never existed at all.

"Do you need help—" Alexander started, but Rebecca waved him away.

Without a word, she headed up the beach and rocky edges, her heavy body dragging her, making her feel like a beached animal of the sea. But now that her wet feet were firmly back on Juniper, her body had eased too. She knew that now her daughter was truly coming, ready to be delivered not to the world but to Juniper Island; it was this place that Cole women belonged to, after all.

Thirty-Five
Rebecca

June 12, 1972

Juniper Island, Isles of Shoals, New Hampshire

Those big eyes blinked up at Rebecca from the folds of the blankets in her arms. Rebecca blinked back. There was no sound but the steady lick of the waves against the rocks outside, the soundtrack of Rebecca's life once again. The sea was gentler than it had been when she returned. The summer sun sparkled off calm waters. It seemed the phantom Cole women inside were quelled by her return after all. By the presence of not just one of their descendants, but two.

Simone Cole.

The newest Cole woman.

It seemed too big a name for the little being in Rebecca's arms, who hardly looked living at all. Rebecca had chosen the name because it was serious, it was elegant, it was tough but beautiful. All the things she hoped her daughter would be. All the things she'd need to be to survive the life fate and curses had dealt her.

It was a name that gave big shoes to fill, but the little girl with her doughy hands and pink face and big, unnervingly seeing eyes seemed like she might just grow into it. She certainly seemed to be tough already. The baby had been in the world for a few weeks, and yet she hadn't made a peep. Barely a cry when she was hungry. She was silent, seeing, assessing. Rebecca already felt unnerved under the gaze of the child.

Sunlight cut across the still kitchen, the afternoon outside the lighthouse's gloom glowing bright with summer. Rebecca knew what happened on Juniper on days like that, though she had never partaken. The islanders drifted out of their homes like mussel shells yawning open, set up chairs and beers out front along the main street, chattered away to one another under the warm sunshine.

Rebecca hadn't had the energy to light the beam since she'd been back, though it was little more than pressing buttons; her body still felt as though it had been cleaved in two. No one knew she was back on Juniper, she'd reckon, since she'd arrived by nightfall and shadow. Or maybe they, too, felt the new calm of the sea.

Well, Rebecca figured this was as good a time as any to make her debut. To make Simone's debut.

She wasn't so fussed about seeing most of the islanders, about her little girl being introduced to the many souls who lived on this island but still felt a world away from the Cole women, who were treated as an insidious species. No, there was only one person Rebecca wanted her daughter to meet.

As Rebecca preened her bloated face with makeup, as she shook her shiny hair down her back and slipped on her nicest, flowy dress, she thought of him. She held the baby in her arms and pressed out of the lighthouse into the sunshine, her heart pattering so hard that her daughter vibrated in her arms.

They made their slow walk toward the main part of the island, where chatter already echoed to them across the rocks. It was Simone's first time feeling the cool air on her face, the kiss of sunshine, the gentle sting of brine and sea salt in her nostrils. But Rebecca didn't think about any of her daughter's firsts, about the way the child who had grown from her was meeting the world for the first time.

No, Rebecca thought about Cal Bradbury. She was certain, more so with each step, that once Cal saw them he would change his mind. The baby was too fresh to hold features of either parent, but when Rebecca looked into her little, unformed face, all she saw was Cal Bradbury staring back up at her. And she was certain that Cal would see the same. That between their baby here, in the world and real, and Rebecca's own shimmering beauty viewed up close again, Cal would realize his mistake. That he would return to the lighthouse with the little girl in his arms, Rebecca at his side, and they would begin the life as a family that they were meant to. Rebecca was certain that before autumn swept across the sea, she would be Mrs. Beck Bradbury.

The islanders were just where she'd expected them, strewn across the island in their camp chairs, swigging drinks and chattering away happily. It took a while before they noticed the Cole women in their midst. But once they did, all conversations fell away. Whispered vitriol danced on the breeze.

"Looks like she's finally back."

"We should charge her for how the fish dried up while she was gone. Her fault the sea wouldn't give up its fruit anymore. Her damned ancestors pissed off by her leaving."

"Not like we made her go. No, we didn't. But we paid for it, didn't we?"

"Four lives lost. Four fishermen died out there this spring. We haven't lost a man in five years, then that? Her fault, her and those damned witches that came before her."

"If she had stayed in that lighthouse, none of that would've happened."

"Damn right."

"And now looks like we've got another generation of those witches."

"Always two of them. That's the way."

"Wish it wasn't."

"Fucking witches."

Rebecca tried to ignore the words. It seemed the stories were true; her ancestors were enraged when she wasn't on the island, safe within their sights. They—the sea that contained them—did take it out on the islanders. Stealing lives and emptying fishing nets. She noted a few men who were missing, those fishermen whose lives must have been the price for her absence. Rebecca didn't resent her ancestors their anger. In fact, feeling the vitriol of the islanders lashing against her and her daughter, she almost admired it.

Rebecca had been gone for months, and they hated and feared her just as they had before. *More* than they had before.

But still they watched her. The men especially.

She floated down the street, hair and dress streaming behind her, like the ghostly witch they all feared Cole women to be. Beautiful, undeniably so, the type of beauty that made the wives all the more certain that she was bewitching their husbands' and sons' eyes to light upon her. They didn't understand that, at that moment, Rebecca didn't care about any of their gazes or hatred or desire or jealousy. That day, she was only looking for one set of eyes.

Rebecca saw Cal before he saw her. Her feet were suddenly rooted to the ground, heart cracking and falling away into the soil. She nearly dropped her arms to her sides in shock, forgetting the gentle weight of the baby she held.

Because, in Cal's arms, also sat a baby. A little one, only a few months older than Simone. He smiled down at the baby just the way Rebecca had always imagined. The look of a proud father. As if he could hear her thoughts, Cal confirmed it, rocking the little one and cooing, "How's Daddy's little man?" The baby chirped back happily.

It seemed Rebecca Cole wasn't the only woman on the island to have shared Cal Bradbury's bed. It seemed she wasn't the only one to have given him a child. And a son, too. The one thing a Cole woman could never create.

Barbara Allan sat beside Cal, her full cheek resting on his shoulder, the baby twirling her long blond hair around his meaty little fingers. Their baby. They were the perfect image of a young family. And Rebecca saw then, standing onstage before the entire island, that she was simply the secret, hidden away beneath twilight and the crash of waves.

Cal had never been hers, at least not *only* hers. He had never loved her, never intended to marry her. She was little more than an anomaly, a distraction until his life as a husband and father began. He had never even been hers alone.

The baby in Rebecca's arms suddenly felt too heavy, burned too hot. She tore her eyes away, looking down at the little girl. This stranger who had made Rebecca lose everything, who had ushered in death before she was even really given life. This living proof of Rebecca's naivete and heartbreak.

Rebecca felt the burn of eyes on her scalp. She looked up, immediately finding Cal's gaze, locked on her. Empty. As if she were a stranger. As if she were just a beautiful embodiment of the curse that was upon her and that her lineage was on this island. And, worse, was Barbara at his side, a flash of pity in her eyes before it fell into nothingness.

It was as if Rebecca's grief had screamed through her throat; suddenly they all looked at her. At her daughter. No celebration for new life, simply distance, fear, wariness, for a new generation of witches.

Rebecca backed away, the sun on her shoulders suddenly burning through her. She did her best not to wilt in front of their gazes. All she had wanted was for them to love her, but they looked at her and her child simply with fear. She wasn't Rebecca, her daughter wasn't Simone. They were just witches. When she was here, they hated her. When she was gone, they hated her for what her absence caused. They didn't care that she was a prisoner here, that Cole women were always dragged back to Juniper against their will.

They hated her as their ancestors had hated hers, feared her as they feared those very ancestors in the deep blue.

But Rebecca knew that love and fear weren't so different after all. One could so easily morph into the other; she knew that well. She felt it in that moment.

They did not love Rebecca Cole, who she really was. But maybe they could learn to accept her if she just gave in and became who they expected her to be.

They spoke of a curse; well, Rebecca would curse Cal Bradbury every damn day of her life. She would make him regret that empty look in his eyes as he stared blankly at her and the daughter he would not claim.

If they wanted a witch, she would give them a witch.

Thirty-Six
Simone

January 6, 1998

Juniper Island, Isles of Shoals, New Hampshire

Simone kept her eyes cast down as she stepped onto the ferry, Ezra on her heels. Hiding her face likely wasn't necessary. She didn't recognize the boat's porter and didn't think he would have recognized her, even if they had known each other once upon a time. Simone was a different person than she had been when she last stepped foot on the ferry from Juniper nearly ten years ago. She had shed that scalded, traumatized skin. She was different now.

The woman who leaned against the railing as the ship kicked off from shore, winter air beating her expensive camel-colored wool coat, was not the same as the teenage girl who had built a hard shell to protect herself, who left behind the only person she had let inside it. She had still had her hackles raised when she met Ezra at a Jewish studies lecture her sophomore year. Slowly, by his trusting hand, she had let the walls down, climbed from her protective shell. Now she wasn't alone. She wasn't just weird, different, whispered-about Simone Cole.

She was Simone and Ezra. The Hoffmans. Successful couple, embraced by his loving Jewish family: his parents, his sister, Naomi, and her wife. Ezra and Simone were that couple that all their friends aspired to be, not because of their success but because of how much love and trust ran deep into their solid foundation.

Simone had traded a shell for steady land beneath her feet with Ezra. But now, as the rugged shape of Juniper Island bloomed into sight across the choppy waves, Simone felt that old shell growing back over her skin, a size too small now.

She had told Ezra every single piece of her childhood. She had dripped out the sorrows and the loneliness and the pills and the books and the curses and the names slowly over time as she came to trust that he would not leave when he saw the soft, scarred parts of her. And he had welcomed every piece of her into gentle hands, drip by drip. He knew of the names they'd called her on Juniper, the distance of the mother she had just lost, the first love she had had and walked away from, choosing a new life, choosing herself. He knew every piece of her, and despite his own loving childhood, steeped in Jewish culture that he did not feel he had to prove or earn the way Simone did too often, he empathized.

Simone knew her Judaism through others. She knew it through the sharp glances and the whispered words she hadn't known to be hurt by until she was older and learned their serrated meaning. She knew her Judaism by the way she was othered. Before Ezra and his family, all Simone knew of being Jewish was a title, was being different, was being alone. But he and his family had welcomed her with open arms, taught her the prayers and the high holidays, brought her into their synagogue and community on the Upper West Side that she now thought of as her own. Simone got to know her own lineage, her own family, in joining another.

And join she had. It was only Ezra who knew her past in its entirety, but he had helped her craft a story that was true enough to share with his own family, their friends, coworkers. Enough of the truth for them to know Simone, to have a reason for why her own mother didn't attend her wedding, why her side of the aisle was only occupied by people she had met in her twenties. If people sometimes wondered why Simone referred to New York as "the mainland," why she missed cultural references from a shared generation's childhood, why cities and cars and crowds still awed her—well, no one asked.

Ezra stood by her side, of course, literally and figuratively. His arm was wrapped around her waist, holding her together as the ferry swayed. They didn't say a word as the ship docked briefly on Appledore, a little longer on Smuttynose, quickly at White and Seavey and Duck, before rumbling up along the shore of Juniper. Simone kept her eyes closed until she felt the boat slowing against the water, until the tinny voice announced her destination.

"We're here, babe," Ezra whispered.

But Simone didn't need to see Juniper to recognize it. Every sense of her body was made for this land; she recognized the shape of the waves hitting the rocks below the lighthouse, the stinging smell of salt mingled with the dead juniper bushes, the thickening on the air as she breathed in her past, the ghosts of Cole women scraping against her lungs.

She was never meant to be back. She had never intended to be back. But she was.

Simone and Ezra were the last passengers on the already scarcely ridden ferry, and they were the only ones to exit onto Juniper's shores. Nobody came here that wasn't from here. There was nothing for them here. They wouldn't be welcomed.

Ezra carried their duffel bags in both hands, each full of only enough clothing and toiletries to last a week. When he'd gently asked if maybe they should pack more, Simone had insisted they wouldn't need it; they wouldn't even be here long enough for it to be worth unpacking.

Simone had never stumbled through the rocky sands on Juniper's edge before, but she did then. The heels of her polished black boots sank into the earth like the isle was trying to swallow her, like it was reminding her that fine shoes were not meant for this terrain, for her, that her expensive camel coat was just a mask, not enough to keep her warm against the beating of the ocean air. She and Ezra swayed and lurched across the beach as the ferry retreated, trapping them here for a week.

A small figure crested the rise of the rocky edge, hands flapping uselessly in a show of aid as Ezra and Simone scrambled their way up the rocks. Jimmy Allan stood before the lighthouse, looking just as he had the last time Simone saw him. Small, light haired, nervous. And the lighthouse at his back looked like it always had too, felt like it always had to Simone: worn down, a weight she had inherited, the only place in the world that cradled her and protect her. A reaching figure of binaries.

She tried not to look at the building as she reached a hand out to Jimmy, giving the older man a formal shake and a nod. He was flustered for a beat before taking her hand like this was a foreign gesture. Everyone on Juniper was born knowing each other; there was no one to meet.

"This is Jimmy." Simone introduced him to her husband.

Ezra cut her an odd, confused look. It was only when Jimmy stuck his hand out and said "Jimmaye Allan" that Simone understood her husband's bafflement.

There were all kinds of accents in New England: the open-mouthed tones of Boston, the slight twang spoken by Mainers. Even Ezra, in discussion with his family, often fell into a hybrid of New Yorker and Yiddish, a speech not uncommon to hear in their Upper West Side synagogue. That speech sounded like home to Simone now, so much more so than the one that had just slipped from her own lips.

The accent of the isles was its own unique tongue, exchanging ending *-ys* and *-es* for elongated *-ayes*.

They had hardly stepped foot on the island, and already Simone's tongue has betrayed her. It was as if the salt air had seeped into her lungs, burning her, changing her back from the inside out.

Inescapable.

"Again, I'm so sorry for your loss, Simone," Jimmy said, eyes down on his Bean Boots. Jimmy was nice enough, sure, but Simone knew he wasn't sorry. None of the islanders had ever grieved a Cole woman. She didn't need his pretenses. She was here to sort what she must and then leave. Nothing less, nothing more.

"Right, well . . ." Simone finally looked up to the lighthouse, trying to keep her heart rate down as she subtly dismissed the lawyer. "Thanks for greeting us, Jimmy. I remember the way."

Her play for lightness landed like an anchor, her own voice too tight, Jimmy too nervous. Ezra, at her side, seemed baffled by the interaction as much as the landscape. In her peripheral vision, Simone saw his dark eyes widen, spinning over the endless raging sea, the remote shore, the decrepit lighthouse. He did his best to hide his surprise, but Simone could sense it, knew he must be shocked, a city person through and through. And as much as Simone might have tried to become one herself, the tender underbelly of her truth was exposed to him now. Her knuckles tightened where she gripped her work bag, weighed down with manuscripts waiting to be read and marked up.

The ground was solid beneath their feet up here, ice heaves beneath the soil making the earth mirror the waves of the sea around it. Winter had settled firmly over the isle, burrowing, making its home. Juniper was covered in ice and frost, frozen in more ways than one to Simone's eye.

"It's just that . . . you see . . ." Jimmy waffled. Simone knew the tongue of Juniper well, knew the minds of the islanders. She had grown up fed on their distrust, after all. "Some folks are just wondering how long you'll be sticking around. What you're planning to do with the . . ." He faded off, gesturing up at the lighthouse. "The past few days the sea has been awful rough, real dangerous, we already lost a fishing boat . . ."

Simone had no patience for the invasive islanders, circling her return and her home and her mother's death like the vultures they were. She didn't know what they hoped to feed on here, but she was certain they wanted assurance that the final Cole woman—much as they resented their need for her—would be sticking around. Keeping them safe from the evils and threats they believed her absence loosed.

But Simone didn't believe in the curse or her angry, seaside ancestors, and even if she had, what happened here wasn't her problem. She had no desire to give the islanders any comfort.

"I'll let you know as soon as *I* know. But it won't be long," she said, voice curt. Jimmy just blinked. "Have a good evening, then."

Though he opened his mouth to say more, Simone turned away from him. She stepped past the two men, pressing a palm to the lighthouse's front door. It swung open for her easily, as if the touch of Cole bones and blood and skin was a secret passcode. Simone chided herself for the fantastical thought. *Look what this place is doing to you already.*

They had just never locked the door, that was all. Ezra pressed against her back as he stepped in, bumping into Simone where she paused on the threshold. He scooted around her, placing their bags beneath the coatrack, which was still weighed down with her mother's colorful scarves that would never again adorn her thin neck or her shining dark hair. Simone kept her eyes on her shoes. She couldn't bring herself to look up, to take in her surroundings. As if making eye contact with the rusting kettle on the stove, the old record player perched as always on the stool, the drawer that might still hold those little white pills, would drag her back to being a desperate, angry, neglected seventeen-year-old girl.

She opened her mouth to say something, anything, she didn't know what. Something to speak over the screaming memories. But an echoing sound stole her words. Through the small doorway to the left that led toward the stairs and the living room came a solid thud. Not the creak or crack of the old structure settling on the sinking soil but a hearty, earthen sound. The sound of another living being already in the lighthouse.

Simone's heart jumped as she placed her bag on the kitchen table, silently creeping through the doorway toward the living room. Ezra, eyes wide with worry, followed at her heels.

It was stupid to leave this place unlocked. Anyone could come in, could have already cleaned the place out, though Simone supposed that would save her some work, but this was still hers, still Cole property—

Simone froze in the arched doorway of the living room, unable to digest what her eyes took in. A ghost from her past sat up on the couch and looked directly in her eyes.

Thirty-Seven
Rebecca

September 6, 1978

Juniper Island, Isles of Shoals, New Hampshire

The lighthouse's kitchen had slowly morphed over the years to something more resembling a laboratory than a family gathering space. Or, as Rebecca was sure the islanders saw it, more of a witch's den. That was fine by her; she knew how helpful appearances could be.

Pots boiled atop the small fires of the stove, the scent of herbs and the sea wafting across the small room. Rebecca's elbow ached as she used the oversize pestle and mortar to grind down and integrate the last of her concoction. With a small grunt, she hefted the contraption onto the countertop, scooping the contents into a small glass container. She screwed the lid on top, locking in the sea salt scent of the body scrub.

She turned, setting the jar in front of the customer seated at her table. Liza Fuller and her little girl, Julia, both sat silently at the kitchen table, their matching brown eyes wide with interest—thankfully not with too much trepidation or, worse, hatred. Richie Fuller's new wife—at least new by Juniper standards of newcomers—and stepdaughter were both from the mainland. Liza had met the islander when he spent time over there for some sort of winter fishing detail or other. He had returned for the season with a new bride and daughter, the little one now seven years old. They didn't talk much, but Liza was perhaps Rebecca's favorite customer. She was new enough that she was still learning the prejudice she was meant to practice. Liza got the scrub often enough that Rebecca, thankfully, didn't need to go over the usage and details with the woman. The kitchen could remain silent, save for the quiet crooning of Fleetwood Mac from the old record player in the corner.

Rebecca sat down in the final open chair at the table, between Julia and Simone. Rebecca's daughter was, as always, lost to the world in favor of the book clenched in her little hands. As the girl had grown, she'd come into herself more surely. And, much as Rebecca stared at her daughter, bored her eyes into her, the girl showed nothing of Cal save for her narrow, rose-tinted lips. Her dark eyes, her olive skin, all favored Rebecca herself. And while the deepest brown hue of Simone's hair might come from her mother, the coarse frizz of it was straight from the grandmother she had never known.

Unfortunately, Rebecca had quickly realized, her daughter was a Cole woman through and through.

Liza's strawberry-haired girl was quick to smile, looking at Simone, waiting to bond. Rebecca's daughter didn't even notice. Rebecca felt a pang in her chest at the sight, though she wasn't quite sure why.

She didn't have much time to think on it, as Liza placed some cash on the table, tucking the jar into her coat and grabbing her daughter's hand.

"See you in a few weeks. Have a good one." Liza's Boston accent was still fresh, so at odds with the tongues of Juniper. "Bye, Simone."

Simone looked up, face blank, unspeaking. She nodded once, tight, before returning her gaze to her book. Rebecca didn't reprimand her daughter for her lack of politeness; she knew it didn't matter a lick how they treated these islanders. Nothing would undo centuries of prejudice.

Liza knew enough to leave the lighthouse quietly, staying in shadows. No one wanted to be seen visiting the Coles. Still, it was barely a moment before a new, tentative knock came.

Rebecca opened the door to the furtive, tense-looking face of Donna. The local woman pushed past her, eager to be out of sight from any prying eyes who might be this far out, witnessing her enter the house of the island witch. Rebecca resisted rolling her eyes as she turned to face the blond woman. Donna stood nervously, fingers twisted, chin lifted with false haughtiness.

Every time Rebecca looked at Donna, she thought of that time—it felt so long ago now—when she had heard Donna call Rebecca "pretty enough for a Jew." Rebecca might have forgone all the Judaism her mother had tried too hard to instill in her, but she knew that didn't matter. To those like Donna, she would always be Jewish, always be other. But, well, Rebecca saw the irony in those words now; for now it was that very fearful, legendary beauty that Rebecca capitalized on.

She scooped some of the deep, rosy liquid blush she had made into a container for Donna. It was one of Rebecca's signature creations, made of crushed juniper berries and some of the other deep-hued growths that only bloomed on this side of the island. It gave the cheeks a fresh flush, the bloom of first love on the cheekbones. Rebecca didn't put any spells or magic into her creations; she didn't know any. She simply used natural ingredients from the sea as beauty treatments. And the women from the island flocked to her for them.

She knew they thought of it as witchcraft, but Rebecca knew it was just the closeness to her own beauty and her mysterious, ostracized status that gave the women confidence; they felt better being close to beauty, even better seeing how they and their lives seemed wonderful in comparison to Rebecca's lonely one.

As if to confirm her thoughts, when Rebecca turned, she caught sight of Donna longingly eyeing the long, shining waves of her hair. It was still healthy and full even as it tickled the small of her back. Unconsciously, Donna fingered her own strands, too thin, made dry and brittle by the salty air. Donna might have been born to Juniper too, but she was like so many of the ladies in that the extremes of the weather and climate still didn't agree with their beauty, instead leaching it from them. And then there was Rebecca, whose beauty seemed to align just right with the shores, who seemed to grow and thrive beneath the rough temperatures. The bite of the salt air waved her hair instead of drying it. The dropping temperatures flushed her cheeks instead of chapping them. The rocky coasts exfoliated her to shining instead of making her crack like porcelain.

The Cole women had been the first blood and bone on this soil, and therefore many believed they had an inherent, special connection to the land and sea here. They said the concoctions were extra effective because they were collected and made by a Cole woman, sourced from the dangerous waters inhabited by the rest of the Coles. That no one else could be so connected to this treacherous slice of Atlantic, could take from it. But Rebecca hadn't found family in the ocean since it took her mother. Every outing collecting ingredients felt more like robbery to her, and there was something empowering in that too. All the sea—and those within—had done was trap and take from her. Whatever communication, connection, *magic* she used to feel with the sea had soured.

With a pang, Rebecca remembered diving into the depths of the ocean, finding herself cradled in the seaweed and salt. But she hadn't stepped foot in the Atlantic in years. She didn't know if her creations were made stronger by some true connection in her name and blood or simply by the power of the islanders' belief.

Donna made sure not to touch her fingers to Rebecca's as they traded cash for the little plum-hued jar. Rebecca didn't much care anymore if the women of the island feared or resented her. In fact, she realized how powerful their disdain made her feel, as she took more than just cash from these women. Rebecca's "witching ways," as she knew the islanders called it in whispers, had become much more lucrative than the steady trickle from her work at the library.

Donna scuttled out the door, head down, fading into the growing twilight. In the silence of her absence, the swell of music from the corner came through clearer, the beat of the waves outside a consistent bass beneath it all. Stevie Nicks's voice danced around the kitchen as Rebecca cleaned up. Then she heard more clearly the words she was humming along to, the sorrowful, longing chords of "Silver Springs." There wasn't a song in the world that spoke to Rebecca's heart more. As it always did, the new song made Rebecca think of Cal, brought to mind the few times she had seen him over the years: arm in arm with his beautiful blond wife, playing catch with the son Rebecca could not give him. And as if he were in her kitchen at that very moment, her chest cracked fresh with heartache, and through the cracks her body filled with anger, at him, at his bride, at the happiness he found with a family that had not a thing to do with her. At the way she had been little more than a game to him.

As in the song, Rebecca didn't want to know if Cal thought it all worth it; she feared she knew the answer. And as in the song, Rebecca felt that her heartbreak, years on, must be so powerful that it sank into the soil of this island, as rough and dangerous as the terrain. That it must curse Cal somehow.

She pressed a hand against the ache in her chest, hands suddenly shaking as she fiddled open the farthest kitchen drawer. Much as it had pained Rebecca to visit her rival's father, she had gone to see Chet Allan, the doctor, months ago, desperate for something to help numb the sorrow and mania that gripped her in turns. And, blessedly, he had given her something to help with it all. Rebecca managed to get the top off the bottle, to shake it out into her hand. The moment that little white pill hit her tongue, Rebecca felt her jaw unclench, her shoulders gently fall.

Within a few moments her thoughts had blissfully hazed out into intangible wisps. The world curled at the edges like a dream that Rebecca could float downstream on. She sank into the chair, catching sight of the world outside the window. The sky was deepening like a bruise, night preparing for its arrival. She would get to the beam soon enough, but right now she needed to sink into the calm.

Rebecca did not open her eyes as she said, "Up to your room, Simone." She wasn't sure when the child had last eaten, but she was a resourceful and obedient girl. She heard her daughter wordlessly pack up her book and make her way up the twisting steps. Rebecca settled into the kitchen chair with a glass of wine, waiting for her next guests.

The wives of the island visited Rebecca at the gloaming hour.

The husbands came by nightfall.

Thirty-Eight
Rebecca

February 19, 1987

Juniper Island, Isles of Shoals, New Hampshire

Rebecca was on top of the world. More specifically, she was on top of Hank Poole. The light-haired man finished with a grunt, lids closing over his blue eyes. Rebecca swung her leg over his body, falling to his side on the bed. Her body was still thrumming, mind still running so fast it felt like the rest of her was sprinting to catch up, an impossible target. At least she felt fucking amazing—though, really, that was no thanks to Hank Poole.

Hank, for his part, rolled off the bed and dressed himself without so much as a glance back at Rebecca, her olive skin glowing under the indigo twilight seeping in through the lighthouse windows. It didn't matter much to Rebecca; she was chattering away, her listless words filling the empty space, saying a lot but not much of anything at all.

Hank gave her a tight smile, interrupting to mutter, "I should be off . . ."

Rebecca was already twisting away from him, draping a long, silky dressing gown over her body. As Hank pushed out the door, he gave a soft exclamation of surprise. Through the closed door, Rebecca heard Simone's typically subdued tone saying, "Oh. Hello."

Rebecca couldn't decipher Hank's mumbled response. A moment later came the sound of his footsteps receding down the twisting steps. The front door closed with a final clang.

Rebecca's body felt like a live wire in a way that the sex had done nothing to ease. She felt alive, more alive than Hank could understand. She felt amazing. She *was* amazing.

She made her twisting way down the stairs to the kitchen, her mind carrying on several steps ahead of her.

The beam of the lighthouse swung past the kitchen window, highlighting Simone standing there, arms crossed tightly over her chest. Rebecca caught sight of some gauze wrapped around her daughter's knuckles, an injury she hadn't noticed before, something that must have happened at school. Not that Rebecca saw much of Simone. Even if they were in the same lighthouse, in the same room, Rebecca struggled to see her daughter. To look at her. Each line of her face, each curl of her hair, was the scraping loss of Cal, the still-open wound of her mother's death. Of all that had to die so Simone could live.

Besides, Rebecca knew the curse well by now; she knew her time with her daughter was limited anyway.

"I lit the beam for you," Simone said, her voice as rough and hardened as her face. "Again."

"Well, that's good." Rebecca shrugged into the room, stepping past Simone to fill a glass with water, chug it down, hands shaking.

Even through the haze of yellow joy bouncing around her brain, Rebecca distantly noticed the tight anger in her daughter's voice. It couldn't be with her. Of course not. Rebecca felt invincible. She felt perfect. Why did that make Simone so bitter?

Besides, lighting the beam was hardly much work anymore. Simone didn't need to be so cross about it. The teenager had no idea how much work it used to be, back when Rebecca was a girl. It was easier now. So Rebecca had forgotten about it tonight. So what? Her mind contained the entire world at the moment. How could she be expected to remember something so trivial?

Rebecca filled another glass of water. Slugged it down. Ignored her daughter's glare burning the side of her face.

The mainlanders had started getting involved in Juniper more lately. They even had a doctor from Portsmouth come to the island twice a year, the islanders waiting in a long line all day for the chance to see him. Rebecca had done the same last summer, just a check-in for her sexual health that she knew Dr. Allan would have judged her for. But she wouldn't ever to do so again.

She had mentioned her mood swings to Dr. Milgrave, the way she sometimes felt down in the pits of despair, the world turned black around her, shame choking her, her thoughts turning to how she might as well just walk into the sea now and be done with it. How the moods came on as sudden as a summer storm and then disappeared in a snap after grueling days. Then he had asked her if she had days like today. Days where she was on top of the world, right where she belonged. She'd said yes.

And he'd given her a bullshit diagnosis. Manic depressive.

The memory almost made Rebecca laugh out loud. As if the days like today, where she felt—no, *was*—invincible, were a problem. There was nothing wrong with her. She felt amazing. The good days didn't need to be medicated away. She just needed something to cope with the bad ones. Something to keep her steady. Something to keep the good days high.

Hands jittering, Rebecca reached into the back of the kitchen drawer, shaking out one of her little white pills. She kept her back to Simone until the pill was down her throat. She wasn't ashamed of it. But she knew her daughter wouldn't understand.

The moment the pill hit her tongue, Rebecca felt better. Better than the best.

"Jesus," Simone huffed, laughing in a way that lacked any humor. In a way that made Rebecca's hackles rise, the judgment that always lived in the teen's voice clearer than ever. She knew what her daughter thought of her.

Well, Rebecca couldn't lose herself in her books like her daughter could, couldn't be content to disappear that way from this shitty life they'd been born into. Simone was always so angry, every day. Angry at the islanders who pushed her out, angry at the island itself, angry that her mother wasn't angry.

"I also had to cover your shift at the library today. *Again.*"

Rebecca looked at her daughter, the puff of dark hair around her head casting her into shadow. The light swung over her face for a moment, highlighting her big eyes, her dark brows, her short, stout build.

Why did Simone insist on ripping a good day from her mother's hands?

"Well, I just forgot about it, hon. Besides, you like the books more than I do." Rebecca tried to laugh lightly, to extricate herself from the negativity rolling off her daughter, this stranger that she had birthed from her own body.

"That's not the point." Simone's voice was as deadly flat as her gaze. Rebecca pulled her robe tighter around herself, swished her long hair down her back. She tried to lean against the kitchen counter casually, thankful for the slow, pleasant numbness the pill was already spreading through her body like an oil spill.

"Enough, Simone." Rebecca rubbed between her eyebrows, that spot where Simone's hostility and judgment always hit her.

"No. Jesus, for once, just listen. Give a shit about me for once!" Her calm daughter disappeared. Rebecca had never seen anger that was anything but silent on Simone. But now the girl grew in size with her rage, throwing her arms up in frustration.

Rebecca rebuffed her. "You're not being fair. I do care about you. I'm your mother—"

"Then act like it," Simone snarled, stepping forward. Rebecca still towered over her daughter, but her trembling sense of joy was no match for Simone's swelling annoyance. "I mean, come on, Hank Poole? Yesterday you had Eddie Fuller over, screaming loud enough I'm surprised they couldn't hear you on the mainland. They make our lives miserable, but you're still willing to sleep with them. They have *wives*, but you don't care about anyone but yourself. You certainly don't give a shit about me."

Rebecca knew she was the adult, the mother; she was meant to be the one to reprimand her child for daring to speak to her that way. But God, she felt good. She didn't want to fight. She just wanted Simone to chill out so she could settle into this hazy joy.

But her daughter's words cracked that bubble. Simone didn't understand. She had no idea what Rebecca had been through. She wasn't grateful for a shred of it.

"My private life is mine, Simone. It doesn't have a thing to do with you, and I don't need your judgment on it."

Simone could never understand the brief thrill that came from receiving the desire of the men on the island. Like the women buying her wares gave her a boost of power, seeing that those men would choose her, despite the rumors, despite the curse, made her feel something akin to important. God forbid Rebecca take acceptance from these people the only way they would ever give it. Her daughter didn't even know who her father was; she would never understand that every man who passed the threshold of Rebecca's bedroom was a hope that word would get back to Cal, that jealousy would finally prevail.

"It has everything to do with me!" Simone cried. "Do you think people don't know? They do. You should hear what they say about you. What the kids at school say to me about you. They used to make fun of me for not having a father; now they make fun of me because you open your legs for all of theirs. I know it's not fair that they only judge you, that they don't hold it against their fathers. But that's how it is. And it's constant—they never leave me alone about it."

"The islanders are cruel, they always have been to us, it wouldn't matter what—"

"No," Simone interrupted. "You don't get it. You couldn't. I have to pay for the sins of my parent, every day. They don't let me forget who my mother is, what my mother does. I don't ever get to be anything other than a Cole, than *your* daughter. I wish you would make that mean something better that it does."

Her words like a slap to her mother's face, Simone turned on her heel, pushing out of the lighthouse and into the winter chill. The door slammed behind her. Rebecca shook her head, not letting the words take purchase among the race of her thoughts. No, no, no.

Her shaking hands finagled the drawer open, cracked the top on the bottle. She swallowed another white pill down. She needed it.

Thirty-Nine
Simone

January 6, 1998

Juniper Island, Isles of Shoals, New Hampshire

"Jimmy has been assurin' everyone you were coming back. Everyone's been talkin' about it. But I didn't think it could be true, knowing you."

Simone said nothing. She couldn't find a word.

"I've just been staying here, on the couch, in case some angry old folk or curious teens have mind to come breaking in. Looking for proof, challenging each other to take something belonging to the witches or . . ." A gruff clearing of the throat. "Well, you know the rumors, of course."

Julia Fuller stood up from the couch as she spoke, as if she needed to be on her feet to face Simone Cole after a decade, after how they'd left things. Simone, for her part, felt like her legs wouldn't keep her standing much longer.

The large brown dog lying by Julia's feet got up slowly, his movement labored. He lumbered over to sniff at Simone, and she held her breath until the familiar animal whimpered, rubbing the dome of his head against her hanging arm.

She chuckled, scratching his head, which was now flaked with the white hairs of age. "Hi, Oli."

They were the first words Simone had spoken, and it seemed to unlock her throat. Seemed to remind her who she was. Now.

"Thank you for keeping an eye on the lighthouse." Her voice sounded too firm, and she was unable to look in Julia's dark eyes any more than she had been able to look at the signs of her mother in the kitchen.

"Of course." Julia nodded, looking at Simone hard, daring her to look back.

"You must be Julia." With a gentle hand on Simone's elbow, Ezra stepped forward, reaching a hand out to Julia with a smile. She took it, her grip surer than Jimmy's had been, her strawberry-blond eyebrows rising in surprise that Simone's husband seemed able to recognize her by tension alone.

Julia didn't know that Simone had told Ezra everything. That there was, blessedly, no piece of her that he couldn't look at, no fleshy part that he would hesitate to handle with care.

First the lighthouse and now Julia Fuller. Ezra was being tossed into Simone's past headfirst. He stepped back to Simone's side, subtly rubbing a hand across her back, a comforting gesture, making her shoulders loosen.

She might be surrounded by relics of her past, but she had Ezra by her side to keep her ashore.

"This is Ezra, my husband," Simone said. She looked closely at Julia's face, searching for a flicker of surprise, of hurt. If there was any of either, Julia hid it well; Simone wasn't so skilled at reading the other woman's face anymore, perhaps.

"Lovely to meet you. I heard you got married last year. Congrats to you both." Julia shoved her hands into the pockets of her jeans—faded from use on rough land, not for aesthetics. Her thick blue flannel shirt hung off her body as she leaned down slightly, resting a hand on Oli's head as he settled back at her side. "Sorry, I didn't hear you come in." She gestured back to the lumpy couch where'd she'd been napping. "I thought Oli here would wake me but his hearing isn't what it used to be."

She shrugged.

Looking at age wearing lines into the dog's face made Simone's chest clench. "He's getting up there, huh?"

"Yeah. Almost fifteen now," Julia answered. The women spoke around the elephant in the room, saying anything but the truth to acknowledge how much time had passed, how much had happened while Simone had been on the mainland, how much of her life Julia had heard only through rumors.

Silence stretched. Even Ezra, charismatic and able to make conversation with a tree, knew it was not his words that needed to be said. His hand still circling Simone's back lightly was the only thing keeping her pounding pulse from derailing her.

"Well, I ought to be off, then." Julia nodded. She and Oli pushed past Simone and Ezra into the kitchen, careful not to brush arms. She tossed a heavy, downed L.L.Bean coat on. "Welcome hom—back, Simone. Nice to meet you, Ezra. You can still find me over at the library if you need anything."

She pushed outside, the sound of the waves spilling into the lighthouse until the door closed behind her.

* * *

Ezra had never judged Simone a day in his life, but still she was embarrassed as she led him up the winding stairs that ran up the center of the lighthouse. The railing was rustier than she had remembered, the steps creaking louder than they had in the memories she shoved down late at night. But Ezra truly didn't seem to share her contempt, and if he noticed her embarrassment, he was doing a good job of overriding it. He'd cooed with interest when they'd reached the top of the lighthouse, asked questions about the mechanism as she turned the beam on. Simone answered his questions on autopilot, the movement second nature, as natural to a Cole woman as breathing. All the while she wondered who, if anyone, had lit the light in the absence of her and her mother, how the island continued without Cole women keeping them afloat, thankless and shunned to the shores.

The door to Rebecca's bedroom was closed, which Simone was intensely thankful for. She turned her back on it, keeping her gaze flicking, not landing on anything, as she had been since she arrived. It seemed to be working, keeping her whooshing, panicked thoughts at bay. But she knew it wouldn't last forever; they were here to take the contents of the home apart, after all, to wipe away any trace of the Cole women from the lighthouse. Unfortunately, that would mean looking at her history directly, holding the dusty remnants of it in her hands.

She shouldered open her bedroom door, Ezra following behind with their bags. Their bellies still full from a diner dinner in Portsmouth before the ferry, they silently set about getting ready for bed.

Simone slipped into a matching silk pajama set, the material the rich, shiny color of the sea peeking through the windows. She did not unpack, did not want to see the threads of her past self, the cocoon she had left behind, still filling the drawers.

"I think I'll go for a swim tomorrow," Ezra said casually as he stripped out of his clothing. His skin pimpled and tightened with the cold air. Even inside it was harsher than anything he had ever experienced. Simone, perched on the edge of the bed, had an unreasonable surge of jealousy that her own body had not reacted the same, that it still remembered this climate enough, was still made for it.

"In the ocean?" She sat up straighter.

Ezra smiled over his shoulder. "Yeah, of course."

"You can't." Her response was quick, wrestled from her chest, ripped up her throat. All she could picture in that black ocean was her mother's corpse, her grandmother's, an endless stretching graveyard for Cole women. She could not bear the thought of that darkness touching Ezra's skin.

He must have heard the seriousness, the urgency in her voice. He nodded, stepped toward her, took her face in his hands, kissed her forehead with so much empathy and loving that it made her want to weep. She had never been loved in this house before.

"Okay, baby, I won't."

Simone scooted on the bed, settling herself on the side nestled against the wall. Ezra flipped the covers and crawled in beside her. He leaned over the nightstand on his side, long fingers reaching toward the lamp.

"What's this? A hobby from when you were a kid?"

"What?" Simone sat up, looked over his shoulder, followed his gaze to her windowsill. She had stopped collecting sea glass when she was a child, a hobby of the childhood that had been far too short. But the windowsill was cluttered with sea-smoothed pieces, some dusty with age but others newer, still smelling of the salty sea.

In each shining piece of rock, Simone saw the reflection of her mother, gone. Her stomach clenched, somewhere between loved and confused. Without a word she flipped off the lamp herself, the sight suddenly too painful to bear.

Simone lay back in her childhood bed, her husband curling around her like a protective shell, her body in the now but her mind caught somewhere in a past she was seeing with new eyes.

Forty
Rebecca

October 13, 1987

Juniper Island, Isles of Shoals, New Hampshire

Everyone you love leaves you. You were born to be left. The thoughts were an unending loop in Rebecca's mind, the only sounds she could hear through the empty void of her sorrow.

Everyone you love leaves you. You were born to be left.

Then why go on? She felt trapped in her emotions, hideous, harmful; a malformed spider in the amber of her depthless despair.

Maybe it was the date that caused it, this sudden snap of depression that had bowled her over three days ago. She *thought* it was three days, though who could be certain. She hadn't left her bed, wasn't sure she'd eaten. She'd twisted herself in her covers, hugging her bottle of little white pills like a stuffed bear, only noting the passing of time when the beam of the lighthouse began to sweep over her room and when it parted for the rising sun. Someone else must have lit it, must have taken care of everything but her, the thing that could not be taken care of. The thing that was not worth taking care of.

Rebecca turned over in bed, away from the wall, pushed one of those little white pills down her throat. There was no spread of ease, no oil spill of warmth. Just emptiness, an open field of nothingness before her.

It happened to her sometimes, yes. She had wondered if it was part of the curse. Or maybe it had been the date, that looming presence of October 10. A reminder of her true curse, a reminder of the day she had lost both her mother and the sea, the day she had truly become a mother herself. And sixteen years had passed and still she was alone, still she was cracking and crumbling, still she knew that she was hardly a mother at all in anything but title, yet she couldn't quite find the energy or the desire to change that.

Her personal ghost, the personification of all she had lost and continued to neglect, appeared in the doorway.

Simone crossed the room toward where Rebecca lay prone, a tray in her hands. She wasn't a girl anymore. She was a teen, nearly an adult. When had that happened? Where had Rebecca been for it?

Shame washed over her like the deadliest wave. She could hardly breathe beneath it. She lay still and let it consume her.

Simone set the tray down on the nightstand, traded out one tepid, full cup of tea for a fresh new one.

"Come on." Her face was expressionless as she hefted her mother up into a sitting position, Rebecca's body a lifeless weight. Simone brought the tea to her lips, held her chin, forced Rebecca to swallow. The shame was overwhelming.

This was where her child had gone. Simone was so busy being a caregiver that she'd never gotten a childhood. While Rebecca had been depressed or manic or high, her daughter had been filling the gaps, living outside the range of Rebecca's thoughts. Because Rebecca had never gotten *help*, she had only been given ways to numb herself. Even if she wanted to change, to save her life, save Simone's . . . it felt too late. And that left Simone to light the beam, work in the library, collect the ingredients for Rebecca's potions, feed her mother, keep her mother alive.

Rebecca realized all of that. Yet none of it stuck to her empty mind. All that nestled into her bones was the look of disappointment on Simone's face as she spotted the bottle of pills, nearly empty now. Her daughter's sigh as she wrestled it from Rebecca's grip.

Simone took a deep breath. "I just wish you gave a shit." Rebecca's skin was clammy with days-old sweat mixed with the autumn chill coming through the window that had been opened at some point. Rebecca wished it was closed; she had no desire to hear the traitorous beat of the sea.

Simone's face was nearly trembling with her frustration, a mask to hide the tears that gathered on her lower lashes. But her movements were gentle as she sat her mother up, wrapped a blanket around her, made sure she was settled and comfortable. Simone tended to her mother like a toddler. Rebecca tended to her shame.

"But honestly, who even cares?" Simone spoke to herself. She stepped away, job done. She looked back once from the doorway, her adult face stern as it had always been, those dark eyes holding so many more years than her body. "You won't remember any of this anyway."

Her laugh sounded like heartbreak as she closed the door behind her. Rebecca felt herself sink back into despair and the temporary release of sleep, the body she did not want anymore slumping into slumber.

It was true: Rebecca would not remember anything Simone had done, anything Simone had said.

No, Simone alone would carry the weight of those days, the burden of her life so much heavier than any curse could be.

Forty-One
Simone

January 7, 1998

Juniper Island, Isles of Shoals, New Hampshire

Simone had been speechless the first time she'd seen the mainland. She'd stood in awe beneath the shadow of large, sturdy buildings, free of a rough layer of salt on them. Her eyes had widened at the sight of blinking traffic lights, heart pounding as she dodged racing cars, wonderstruck by the contraptions, by the idea that there were people who used this for travel instead of just their feet, a boat. Amazed that there was more of the world to travel than just one strip of land. She couldn't believe that she could turn in a circle, walk for miles, and not have the sea anywhere in sight. The first day she'd seen New York City, visiting the Hoffmans for the first time, she'd nearly fainted in shock.

Ezra was much the same as he took in Juniper Island as they strolled away from the lighthouse. Juniper had seemed so large when Simone was a child, a suffocating, backward prison as she became a teenager. But now that she was seeing it through Ezra's fresh eyes, she wasn't sure what it was anymore. Familiar, foreign, both and neither.

But, Ezra, for his part, was enchanted by the rural simplicity of Main Street, the sight of rickety boats docked all along the shores, lobster and fishing nets strung over their edges, bobbing. The small, rough wood houses all crammed together. The sharp juniper bushes, dotted with purple bulbous berries even in winter, the isle's trademark oddity. He walked backward for a moment, looking at the lighthouse standing proudly alone on the very edge, the mainland a speck across the water. To him, it was all enchanting, for its novelty, yes, but also because he was finally seeing the space that had made his wife. His tough, hardened wife who had learned to be loved and tenderhearted.

Simone supposed the island could be pretty enough, sure. The people, on the other hand, she knew to be ugly.

Simone felt a quiet shame that she'd dressed in her nicest, most expensive clothes. But it was satisfying when she saw how moneyed and pristine she looked next to the islanders, who were wearing the same flannels and Bean Boots they'd been wearing a decade ago. She looked like an outsider; for the first time it was by her own hand, her choice, for reasons she wanted. She was proud to look like she didn't belong here, her handsome lawyer husband by her side, holding her hand, thoughtlessly proclaiming to the island how casually loved Simone Cole was.

And they were certainly noticing. Eyes locked on the couple, did a double take, realized that these were not just visiting mainlanders. This was Simone Cole. Whispers followed in their wake like an ocean breeze, words those speaking them didn't even try to keep from reaching Simone's ears. *She really came back? She looks like a mainlander now. She does, doesn't she? Didn't know it was possible for a Cole. What with, you know, the curse. The curse. The curse.*

Deep down they were relieved that she had returned, that the angry ocean would ease. But that relief just made them hate her all the more.

"Jeez." Ezra leaned over, whispered in Simone's ear as they passed through the main street, heads poking out of windows into the winter air to catch sight of them. Even the waves beat heavily against the shore, visible in the thin line between homes, as if the sea, too, was desperate to snag a glimpse of the returned Cole woman. "It's like *Children of the Corn*."

The tension in Simone's chest cracked, her defiantly lifted chin falling as she let loose a genuine chuckle. "I know, right? Even the kids." She nodded her chin at a group of young boys, who had frozen, basketball clutched in little hands, to stare.

"Is it me, or are they all checking out your—?" Ezra grimaced.

"No, they are," Simone answered.

The children gaped at them both openly, but the adults, especially the women, cut their eyes to Simone's stomach. She knew they were looking for a swell beneath the buttons of her coat, some indicator that she was with child, a sign that there was a new Cole woman on the way and that was why her mother had been called to the sea. Looking for signs of—

"The curse," she said, deadpan.

"Wow." Ezra looked directly at the staring women, his gaze challenging and protective. "You weren't joking."

But the couple walked on, knowing that the prying eyes would find no sign of an occupied womb. The moment Simone had stepped foot on that ferry a decade ago, she had decided that she would never, ever have children. She was stubborn, stood by this decision, told Ezra of it on their very first date. He had agreed. They were not pregnant now and they never planned to be. Not because she believed in the curse but because she knew how trauma had been handed down her lineage like an heirloom and she meant for it to die with her.

Poole Market had blessedly few customers. Ezra and Simone squeezed through the narrow aisles, filling their basket with pasta, veggies, potatoes, a cut of meat, cheap instant coffee that already made Simone homesick for New York—enough food to fill the lighthouse's fridge and cupboards for the few days they would be there without them needing to return to Main Street.

Ezra set their basket on the counter in front of Mrs. Poole, who looked more weatherworn and frail than Simone remembered her. Simone stood beside Ezra, her left shoulder slightly behind his, brave enough to be seen but still tucked a bit behind his protective form, letting him lead the interaction. Like the rest of the island, Poole Market eschewed modernity, Mrs. Poole entering the price of each item into the click-clacking old-school register.

"That'll be fifty-six fifty," she said, speaking to Simone directly.

Ezra's head reared back, quickly looking over his shoulder at the aisles, little handwritten white slips of paper hung before each item marking their price. He had always been particularly adept at math, and Simone could practically see him searching and adding sums in his mind.

"Are you certain?" he said, straining for politeness. "I think it should be closer to forty dollars."

Mrs. Poole didn't even bother to look around at the listed prices. She didn't even bother to look ashamed. "Nope, fifty-six fifty."

The few other customers slowed their steps, rubbernecking at the sight, waiting to see what the witch and the mainlander would do.

Ezra's shoulders steeled, confusion settling on his handsome features. A strand of his wavy, dark hair swung across his brow, unstyled for a day not spent in the office. He leaned forward slightly, still naive enough to think it must be a mistake, that he could explain the correct sum to the cashier. Simone knew better.

She stepped in front of Ezra, pulling out her wallet. Ezra turned to her, saw her stern-jawed resignation, finally understood that the prices listed did not include the extra fee for being a Cole.

Simone pulled out her credit card, saw Mrs. Poole open her mouth, and quickly stuffed it back in, handing over a few bills instead. Mrs. Poole did not give her change.

The woman's expression was stony, an unhidden glare. Simone knew that Mrs. Poole—and the other customers milling about—thought Simone and her sleek shoes and her credit card were uppity, thought that she considered herself better now that she lived on the mainland. But to them, she was still a Cole. Simone suddenly felt foolish in her fine clothes, a child playing dress-up long after Halloween had passed.

She stuffed their food into the bags they'd brought, her and Ezra each shouldering one. Simone kept her eyes down as she pushed out of the store, turned quickly back toward the lighthouse, feet racing under her. She wasn't sure who she resented more: them, for not allowing her to be a new person, or herself for proving that she wasn't, not really.

Neither Simone nor Ezra spoke until they were well clear of Main Street and the eyes and ears of the islanders. The lighthouse hovered above them, and Simone remembered what it was like to think of the structure as a safe haven because at least her high, sleeping mother didn't look at her like the islanders did. Didn't look at her at all, really.

"I know you said, but I never thought . . ." Ezra's voice trailed off. He brushed a hand through his hair, pushing it away from his eyes. The blistering wind pushed it right back down. "I didn't realize how seriously they took this curse. This witch business."

He pushed the lighthouse door open, letting Simone walk in first. The door closed behind them, muffling the sounds of the island, but their words were still loud in Simone's mind.

"They're all so . . . hostile." Ezra set his grocery bag on the counter, which was stained with decades of coffee and tea and her mother's potions. The kitchen still smelled like algae and rosemary and red wine. "That was more than just superstition. My God."

He turned to Simone, saw her caving shoulders, her fallen face. With gentle hands he removed the bag from her grip, placing it beside the other on the counter. He pulled the jacket from her shoulders, hung it, guided her to sit. Ezra lifted her hands, icy cold, and held them to his mouth, breathing his warm air on them, kissing her knuckles.

"I'm sorry you grew up being treated that way." His eyes were as sincere and soft as his voice. "I'm sorry you had to deal with it alone."

Simone mustered a small smile as she felt her chest unclench, the edges of her walls that had been instinctually rising fall down again. Ezra poured her a glass of red wine from a half-full bottle he found on the counter. She brought the glass to her lips and wondered if her mother, too, appreciated the earthy notes, the dryness on her tongue.

"Just relax, baby. I'll cook you some dinner." Ezra moved around the kitchen with confidence, sometimes searching for a spatula or a pot lid, struggling to cook in a kitchen that her mother had only ever used for her witching ways. Simone finally breathed deeply when the kitchen air was humid and warm, the smell of briny sea air replaced with simmering garlic and vegetables in oil. She let herself settle as, for the very first time in this lighthouse, she felt that someone not only saw her but was taking care of her.

Forty-Two
Rebecca

March 11, 1989

Juniper Island, Isles of Shoals, New Hampshire

The knees of Rebecca's dress were soaked clean through where she kneeled in the soft, damp sand, the waves licking at her kneecaps. She did her best not to flinch from the touch, that of an old lover who'd proven how much their gentle caresses could bruise.

Rebecca grabbed a thick rope of algae before it could be swept back out to sea. With fingers already numbed from the cold, she twisted the seaweed, weaving it into the largest black bottle she had. She corked it tight, sure to keep the phlegmy moisture in the plant. Algae was great for skin treatments, brightening as well as soothing irritation. She tossed the bottle out onto the dry sand, uncorking a new bottle to scoop a serving of salt water. The sea might harm her, but it brought her positives too, her hair treatments and anti-dryness cream being some of her bestsellers to the women of the island.

Spring was always slow to sweep in on Juniper, the air as biting as the sea. But still Rebecca looked as she always did, long, flowing dress, toes peeking out of black Birkenstocks. Her sandals sank into the wet sand as the ground fought against her retreat for drier land. Rebecca was so focused on putting one foot in front of the other that she didn't even notice him at first.

Not by sight, anyway. But, even after all these years, her body was still attuned to his. She felt his presence, her bones aching, her blood blooming the moment his feet landed in the same sand as hers, connected through those millions of little grains.

Rebecca looked up, right into the eyes of Cal Bradbury. He was older now, of course. Though, unlike Rebecca, he looked it. Cal was on the other side of the beach, hauling his little skiff inland. But Rebecca could still see him clearly, as though her eyes were made just for him. His blue gaze was brighter than the sea and sky, but little lines etched the corners. His sunshine hair had dulled ever so slightly with age, the youthful swoop of it replaced with the practical shear of a worker and father. His beauty had been carved out for convenience now, but God, Rebecca found him as beautiful as she ever had.

The little white pill she'd swallowed an hour ago had successfully dulled the edges of her world into a dreamscape, but Cal, as always, was the sun. Bright and unmissable and burning on her skin. Rebecca felt awake after a hundred-year sleep.

As if her sight struck him with a curse, Cal looked up, their eyes locking across the long stretch of beach between them. Rebecca wished she'd had the forethought to lift her chin, calm her shoulders, place her beauty at the forefront. But she could hardly think, let alone act. So she was beautiful, of course, but less calculated as Cal looked at her, dark hair and dress whipping behind her. She was beautiful but she was terrifying, a powerful witch, the sea at her back waiting to do her bidding.

Their eyes stayed as linked as their history for a long moment. Then Cal's eyes cut over Rebecca's shoulder, and his face suddenly changed.

A dozen expressions flitted across his face in rapid time. The lifted brows of shock pinching together into horror, eyes squinting into confusion. The quickest pang of tight-jawed anger. Before, finally, settling into neutrality. Rebecca looked over her shoulder at whatever had captured Cal's gaze, had affected him so much.

If any expression he wore had been the slightest hint of soft, of kind, Rebecca might have been able to forgive him all of it. But Cal Bradbury looked at the sight of his teen daughter cresting the rocks with no expression that could ever hope to morph into love. So Rebecca could not forgive him, much as she wanted him still, much as she achingly loved him still, for some, some reason.

By the time Simone crossed the sand to her mother's side, Cal was gone, swallowed deep into the center of the island, where he was loved, unlike the daughter he'd left to be pushed to the margins.

Simone held a large white envelope in her hands, opened, clearly having just met the irregular mail boat on the far corner. She stared down at the torn envelope in her hand, her usually controlled face open wide with surprise. For reasons she was not yet sure of, Rebecca's heart kicked up, a surge of panic finding her through the haze provided by her pills. She could feel it wearing off, the reality of what Simone gripped in her hand squeezing in through the corners. Rebecca's jaw clenched with a craving for one of the little aids left tucked in the kitchen drawer.

"What do you have there?" she asked her daughter. She didn't want to know, knew that nothing coming in from the mainland was ever good. It only ever meant change that Cole women could not afford to see through. She didn't want to know, but, like a crash happening in slow motion, Rebecca just wished she could rush through the torture, get the pain over with. Whatever the letter contained, her hammering heart told her it would bring pain.

With fingers trembling with more than the chilly spring air, Simone pulled a paper out of the envelope, unfolding it slowly. Rebecca watched the expensive, thick paper come to life, eyes transfixed on this little piece of simple, folded luxury. Her heart pounded so surely against her chest that her ribs ached from keeping it contained. The waves rose up against the sand, crawling higher, licking at her sandaled feet. She couldn't feel a thing beyond the burn of the letter against her dark eyes.

As Simone turned the paper in her hand, Rebecca caught sight of a deep-blue, shining logo. Simone smoothed out the paper with a lover's touch, a small smile crawling up the edges of her lips. An expression that, Rebecca realized with a swoop of sorrow, she had never seen on her withdrawn, controlled daughter.

Simone held out the piece of paper toward her mother. It flapped in the salt breeze for a moment before Rebecca convinced her body to plunge into the cold deep, to rip off the Band-Aid.

The paper was as luxuriously thick in Rebecca's hand as it had looked. She dropped her eyes down to it, scanning rapid-fire across the words.

Congratulations!
Accepted
Class of 1993
Comparative Literature program
Minor in Jewish Studies
Yale University
Yale University
Yale University
Yale University

The words became difficult to read, flapping in the breeze. No, Rebecca realized, flapping from her quaking touch. She shoved the paper back into Simone's hands like it would brand her too, burn her with her own memories of leaving Juniper, of having a life on the mainland, of having a life at all.

When Rebecca was Simone's age, when she was Beck, she'd thought that was possible too. She knew better now.

"Well, that's nice you got in, then." Rebecca's words were as flat as the expression she schooled onto her face.

She stooped to gather her bottles of ingredients in her arms. Even as she moved to collect herself from the beach, Rebecca could feel her daughter's gaze burning into her, the heat of it and the girl's anger growing. After many long, painfully pregnant moments, Simone deadpanned, seething, "That's all you have to say?"

Rebecca could not look at her daughter. She tried to busy herself with other things, sliding her toes into her sandal. Even that part of her trembling.

"I got into *Yale*, and that's all you have to say to me?" Simone's tone was colder than the ocean kissing their feet.

"What else do you want me to say?"

Rebecca only looked up when Simone made something like a sobbing noise, involuntary, echoing. But by the time Rebecca looked at her daughter, Simone had fixed her expression back into nothingness. When had her girl become so good at that? How often did Rebecca get to see beneath that mask?

"I want you to say you're proud of me. That you recognize how fucking huge this is." Simone's words were steady, making the harshness and hurt all the more gutting.

Rebecca shrugged, her body feeling both too heavy and too light, drifting away from her. She felt that familiar ache of despair beginning to echo in her chest, panic alongside it that the switch of her mood would be flipped to darkness. "Yale is on the mainland, right?"

Simone nodded, wordless.

"Well, that's that, then." Rebecca tried to step around Simone, but her daughter reached an arm out, gripping Rebecca's bicep. Simone was short, stout, so much smaller than her mother, but she suddenly seemed tall and powerful. Rebecca saw her child as an adult for the first time. Simone had never really felt like a piece of Rebecca, but now it was undeniable that she was entirely her own person.

"I'm going," Simone declared.

Rebecca's face instinctually melted into pity. Simone visibly bristled at the sight of it. "You're a Cole woman, Simone. The island doesn't let us leave for long. The curse won't let you go just because you've forgotten who you are."

Beyond the impossibility of it, Rebecca's panic grew at the thought of the phrase "Jewish studies," at the idea of Simone openly claiming that heritage that only othered them further. It was all wrong. It was dangerous. Why didn't Simone understand that?

"No, I haven't forgotten. This"—Simone shook the acceptance letter—"is who I am."

If Simone wouldn't understand pity, Rebecca would make her understand with anger. That had always been her daughter's language. Angry, angry Simone. As if rage could undo a curse just because rage had, long ago, started it.

Rebecca laughed, the sound sharp and cruel. Her daughter flinched back. "What? You think you're stronger than the curse? You think it doesn't apply to you?"

"I don't believe in some stupid curse—"

"Yeah, I didn't either," Rebecca interjected. "And yet here I am. Stop being a child, Simone. Grow up. You're a Cole woman. You stay here. It's not just the islanders who suffer if we leave. It is *not possible*. This is all there is for people like you and me. Don't forget yourself."

The childlike shock on Simone's face hardened to stone. "I'm nothing like you. I'll never be anything like you." Simone didn't spit the words in vitriol but whispered them, so self-assured. She stormed away, stamping feet leading her up the rocks and away from the lighthouse, inland.

Maybe Rebecca should have told her daughter about her brief time on the mainland, about the taste of sea in her mouth, the sounds of the shore pounding in her brain. About how she, too, had tried to leave and felt she could have gone mad from it. About how nearly all of the Cole women had tried to leave at some point, yet it was back on these shores that they had all lived and died. Then maybe her daughter would have known her mother as a real person, not just some high, depressed two-dimensional image. Then maybe her daughter would have understood that Rebecca's words, her laughter, came from a place of fear, the closest thing she could get to expressing love for her daughter.

Forty-Three
Rebecca

August 17, 1989

Juniper Island, Isles of Shoals, New Hampshire

"Well, I'm leaving."

Everyone leaves you.

Simone stood expressionless as she waited for Rebecca to respond. A mother should be able to read her daughter, shouldn't she? Rebecca could not.

As she looked at her daughter, blossomed into adulthood, suitcase and duffel bag in hand, Rebecca finally realized that the years that had been smudged with sorrow and mania and pills and aching memories had been Simone's childhood. And now it was over.

And Rebecca had missed the entire thing.

"Get there safe, okay?" Rebecca said.

"Okay." Simone leaned forward as if she wanted her mother to embrace her. But Simone had always been the caretaker of their relationship, because she had had no other choice. Rebecca lost her nerve, simply squeezed her girl's shoulder. That time the disappointment on Simone's face was clear as day. With a tight-lipped smile and a nod, Simone stepped out of the lighthouse for what Rebecca knew the girl hoped was the last time.

The silence in her absence was heavy. The exchange broke the heart that Rebecca had been sure was already long shattered. She wished she had been better for her daughter, could be better now. But all she had known for too long was pain and fear. *Maybe I'll try to be better tomorrow.*

But today Rebecca snatched the bottle from the kitchen drawer and threw the little white pill back.

As the haze seeped in, soothed her aches, Rebecca thought maybe it was a mother's duty to see her girl off properly. Grabbing a scarf, she pushed out into the windy morning, ready to stand on the sandy shore as the boat to the mainland retreated with her daughter on it, the two of them waving to each other until they were too far away to see. But it seemed Simone already had someone to see her off.

Rebecca stepped silently into the shadow of the lighthouse as she watched her daughter embrace someone. The wind whipped frizzy dark curls and glossy strawberry strands together.

Rebecca knew so little of her daughter's life that she didn't realize the girl would have anyone on Juniper who would make saying goodbye difficult. But it was clear, as Simone withdrew from Julia Fuller and put her hands on the girl's cheeks, that she did.

Rebecca might have lived on the outskirts—literally and figuratively—but gossip still came to her from around Juniper: whispered words from the women who came to her for beauty, complaints from the men who occupied her bed. So Rebecca knew Julia's story even if she hadn't given the girl a thought in years. It was well known that both her mother and stepfather, Richie Fuller, had been killed in a car crash on the mainland a decade ago. That the girl had since been raised by her step-grandmother, Evelyn Fuller, a hazy figure on the periphery of Rebecca's own childhood. Evelyn had lost her husband in a mysterious boating accident decades ago that no one seemed to speak about, just to lose her only child too. If there was anyone who could understand sorrow, understand being left, it was Evelyn, who, too, had been left alone to raise a young girl.

But Julia was not a child anymore. She was an adult, tears gathering in her eyes as she looked deep into Simone's gaze. The intimacy between them was clearly not new. It was so potent that Rebecca's cheeks blushed just to be looking at the moment.

The briny wind carried their tender words to Rebecca's ears.

"You were born on the mainland, right? Maybe you could . . . together we could . . ." Simone's voice was pained, trailing away into nothingness after whatever she saw on Julia's face.

Julia's large brown Lab snuffled at the girl's feet, pushing into Simone's knees familiarly.

"My life is here now. My roots are here." Julia smiled, but even from a distance Rebecca could see it was an empty one.

The girls leaned together, foreheads resting against one another, as if it were only their sorrow and affection holding them up. Keeping them from crumbling.

Simone leaned forward, pressing her desperate mouth to Julia's; the two girls kissed in a way that was practiced, fervent, desperate. That was a goodbye.

In that one moment, Simone's face wore more emotions than Rebecca had ever seen on it in the last seventeen years combined. Sometimes, in her cruelest thoughts, Rebecca thought Simone took after her father after all. That she wasn't capable of love.

But there she was on the seashore, all but declaring it for Evelyn's girl.

It wasn't that Simone was unable to love. It was just that she hadn't learned it from her mother, so why would she love Rebecca? She wouldn't, and she didn't. And it was too late to do anything about it.

"Stay with me." The wind carried Julia's whisper, lips moving against Simone's.

"Leave with me," Simone whispered back.

The two girls looked at each other. And that was all there was to it: a fork in the road, two boulders that would not budge. Some things were simply not meant to be.

Simone stepped on the ferry waiting for her on the shore. She never once looked back.

Rebecca held her breath as the boat moved away from the isle, chugging steadily toward the mainland. The waves pushed against it, as if the sea itself were reluctant to let Simone leave. Julia stood on the sandy shore and watched and Rebecca stood beneath the lighthouse and watched, a world between them.

In the days and months that followed, the two women—two inherited librarians—would find themselves sharing a space. Sometimes, in the long hours of dusty books and stacked documents, Julia would sit in the corner strumming a guitar, humming out lyrics to herself. Rebecca wondered how many of the tunes were love songs written for the daughter she'd never known, the woman Julia loved. But the two librarians hardly spoke, and they certainly never spoke of the ghost that connected them.

Rebecca realized, too late, that a mother's job was not just nurturing and holding, in ways she had never been able to without the pain of memories. Sometimes it was also a mother's job to watch a daughter go out to sea and know she would survive the waves and whitecaps and still be able to steer her own ship. And, no thanks to her, Rebecca knew, her daughter just might be able to.

When Simone was young and stubborn, Rebecca would call the girl a nudzh. Now she saw what an asset that was.

No Cole woman had ever managed to pull the curse taut, to stretch their leash, to live on the mainland long-term. But if anyone could do it, it was Rebecca's headstrong girl.

As the boat became a speck between Juniper and Portsmouth, Rebecca prayed to every Cole woman in that water that Simone was right: that she was different from them all.

Forty-Four
Rebecca

April 6, 1997

Juniper Island, Isles of Shoals, New Hampshire

With Simone gone, it fell again to Rebecca to help Evelyn care for the library. Rebecca hadn't realized how much of the burden Simone had shouldered until the weight returned to her. It was too much for a child.

For the past few years, in the shadow of her daughter's absence, Rebecca's shame had become a daily presence. Julia too worked at the library; it must have been how the two girls met. And both Rebecca and Julia carried anxiety and sorrow in the days and months following Simone's departure. It was clear Julia hoped Simone would return but hoped even more that the woman she loved wouldn't have to. Rebecca, too, feared each day that her daughter would be returned, dragged back by the choke hold of the curse. But it seemed Simone had stretched the leash after all, for months became years and the girl stayed on the mainland.

Rebecca had no more love for the library than she ever had. But, like the curse and the lighthouse, this too was her inheritance, and she maintained it. Her own witchy ways had not wavered, but she no longer offered her services to the wives of the island as often; with only herself left, money hardly felt like it mattered anymore. Simone had gotten a scholarship, gotten a degree, gotten a job; she certainly didn't need her mother's money. She didn't need anything from her mother.

Usually only one librarian was needed to maintain the little library, but since it had also become something of a town hall, Julia was often there alongside Rebecca. The younger woman had taken on the task of updating and organizing the many documents they stored: births, deaths, marriages. The history of Juniper was all there in those worn papers passing through Julia's hands.

Now the young woman pulled the door of the library closed behind her, the two librarians stepping out into the chilly spring evening. Julia wrapped her thick blue flannel tighter around her body. Her brown dog nosed around Rebecca's sandaled feet suspiciously as the two women looked at one another awkwardly, never sure how much to say to each other.

"Have a good night, Rebecca." Julia nodded once before stepping away toward her little house that she still shared with Evelyn. She whistled once, high and tight, like a bird's call, and the dog obediently trotted after her in a loping gate.

Rebecca set off idly along the main street. From the corner of her eye, a flash of bright green caught the fading sunlight. Nestled in among the jagged rocks on the island's edge was a piece of true green sea glass, sharp edges worn smooth by licks of the sea. Rebecca bent for the item, tucking it into the pocket of her dress before she continued. She was halfway down the main street when the door to Poole Market swung open, nearly connecting with Rebecca's shoulder.

Suddenly she was face-to-face with Barbara Allan—no, Barbara Bradbury—a bag of groceries in her arms. The two women both froze, eyes locked on each other, only inches away. Two sides of the same coin, light and dark, beloved and othered, loved and forgotten. Rebecca opened her mouth, not at all certain of what words were threatening to push out. But then a young man stepped out from behind Barbara, plucked the bag from her hands familiarly, and the words died on Rebecca's tongue. Barbara's boy, Cal and Barabara's boy, was a man now. He had the golden hair of both his parents, their blue eyes, Cal's strong jaw.

The sight of the boy was a stab to Rebecca's chest, puncturing her lungs, stealing her breath. But to him Rebecca was nothing more than the island's oddity. With tightened brows he led his mother away, a gentle arm on her shoulder. They walked away from Rebecca, and it took her a moment to jump-start her feet and press toward home.

Rebecca did her best not to feel the burning presence of the mainland offshore, her own child lost somewhere in its depths. She was just pulling the lighthouse door closed behind her when the little white telephone in the living room began to ring. Kicking off her sandals by the doorway, Rebecca crossed the space and put the phone to her ear. It was an instinct, and she moved without thought. She would never have answered the line otherwise; no one ever called.

"Hello?"

"Oh. Hi, Mom," Simone's barely familiar voice breathed down the line.

No matter how many years passed, every time Rebecca heard that title, she thought of her own mother. Did we ever stop being girls, ever stop being daughters?

Simone had only ever called twice, both times her voice crackling down the line from the mainland. Once it was to say she had graduated Yale the day before, the news shared when it was too late for Simone to ask her mother to attend a ceremony and to hear her refusal. The second time it was to tell Rebecca that she and her boyfriend—Eddie? Ernie?—had moved in together in New York City, where Simone had gotten a job as a fiction editor for some fancy New York publishing house. That call hadn't been for mother and daughter to reminisce on accomplishments or pastimes or romance; it was merely so Rebecca would have Simone's new landline number. But the unsaid words had been clear to them both, not that Simone expected Rebecca to call her. Not that Rebecca ever did.

"I wasn't sure if you were in," her daughter continued. She sounded surprised Rebecca had answered at all.

"Hi," Rebecca answered on a shivering swallow. "I just got home from the library. Have you been calling many times?"

"No." Simone's answer was immediate.

In that quick answer, Rebecca realized Simone was surprised not because she'd been waiting for the phone to be answered but because she had been hoping it *wouldn't* be. Simone had been expecting to leave a message, never to actually speak to Rebecca. Rebecca was surprised that the realization landed in her chest like a dagger. It wasn't as if she had tried either, she knew.

"How are you? Are you okay?" Rebecca felt like she was reading a script someone else had written. She had never learned how to speak to her only child.

"I'm fine, yeah." But Simone's tone sounded strained, stressed. She rushed the next words out, as if she just needed to get them over with. "Ezra and I are getting married."

Rebecca's first thought, on the surface, was *Ezra, that's right.* Her second thought was deeper, coming from her blood and bones: *Don't do it. He'll only leave you. That is what it means to be a Cole woman.*

But she didn't say those words out loud, because she heard in the tight, awkward strain of her daughter's voice that Simone already anticipated them.

"Congratulations." Rebecca tried to make her voice sound happy, truly congratulatory. Simone's frustrated sigh told her she had failed.

"The wedding is in two months. Here in New York. I would . . ." Simone paused. Took a deep breath. "I was hoping you could come. I would like you to be there." The rest of Simone's words ached with authenticity: a young child asking the parent who had always rejected them to care for them for once.

So it made it all the worse when Rebecca replied the only way she could. "I can't. I'm sorry, Simone. I just . . . I can't. You know that."

She couldn't leave. Maybe Simone could, but Rebecca knew it was temporary. Rebecca had tried to leave before. And she had failed. She was anchored here now, she knew that.

"You can, though. You just don't want to," Simone huffed, clearly fed up. Rebecca heard a man's voice in the background, trying to console her daughter. "You're the only family I have. Don't you get that? It's just me and you. I'm starting a new chapter of my life, a new family. And I want you to be a part of that. For once, just give a shit about me."

Rebecca was nestled into her forties, yet she was still a being with smudged edges, only held together by staying in place. As if the lighthouse and the waves and the hatred held her on every side so she didn't leak out into nothing.

She didn't know how to be someone else, someone on steady land instead of the shores. She couldn't forget the stabbing pain of the curse the night that Simone entered the world. Simple as fact, Rebecca was too afraid to go to the mainland.

Too late, Rebecca realized she loved her daughter. But she didn't know how to love her daughter any more than she knew how to step foot off Juniper. She was certain it was all too far gone to be amended.

"I'm sorry, Simone. I just can't. I can't."

Simone sighed, her disappointment crackling down the line, across the sea. But worse, beneath it Rebecca heard her daughter's relief too. And in that sound Rebecca felt sure of her choice. Still, she knew what her daughter heard in her words: that, as always, Rebecca was choosing the curse over her daughter. Maybe it was true; after all, it was the curse, not motherhood, that had determined the decades of Rebecca's life.

Simone had a new life, one with no room for the memories of Juniper, and her mother was nothing but walking reminiscing. It was better for them both this way, even if mother and daughter both felt an ache in their chests as they hung up without another word.

Only once she'd set the phone gently back in its cradle did Rebecca notice she had been squeezing the sea glass in her pocket until the colorful bit of the ocean had made an angry red indent in her palm. Rebecca was filled with that familiar feeling of hating herself, the one that not even her little pills could soothe. Shame burrowed deep into her bones as she made her way up the winding stairs running up the lighthouse's core.

For years she had left the door to Simone's room only cracked, but now she nudged it open. Everything was as her daughter had left it: empty, impersonal, hardly an item left behind because hardly any items had ever filled it. Simone's time on the island had always been temporary in the girl's mind. Everything in the room was white and gray and abandoned. And Rebecca knew that she hadn't known her daughter any better than this space had.

The only bits of color, of personality, were the little chips of blue and green sea glass on the windowsill. When Simone was still small enough not to resent her, Rebecca had taught the girl how to find the pieces on the shore by their house, to keep them here in her home for good luck. When Simone had left the island years ago, only ten pieces had sat on the chipped white paint. But over the years Rebecca had kept adding to this altar to her daughter's memory. Now she added the triangular green piece from her pocket to the collection, making nearly twenty now.

Even if Rebecca could not tend to her daughter, she could tend to her memory.

Forty-Five
Simone

January 8, 1998

Juniper Island, Isles of Shoals, New Hampshire

"Let's get this over with," Simone said to the closed door of her mother's bedroom.

"There's no rush." Ezra's gentle voice came from behind her. "We can start somewhere else. The living room or . . ."

"No." Simone's voice was steady. Her rocketing heartbeat was anything but. "This is where most of the stuff to clear out is. The sooner we finish this room, the sooner we can leave."

And that was still, as it had been a decade ago, Simone's deepest desire.

She pushed the door open.

Her mother had always blasted through a room, her hair and dresses streaming out behind her, taking up space and declaring it her own. So it shouldn't have been a surprise that, even in death, her bedroom was brimming, stuffed full of *Rebecca Cole*. Flowing dresses tossed over the chair back, vinyl records on every surface: Fleetwood Mac, the Who, Creedence Clearwater Revival.

The messy sheets on the bed still bore the imprint of her body, gone now to the sea forever. Simone swallowed the sob that caught her by surprise.

She bent down, gathered up one of the empty cardboard boxes they'd found collecting dust in a kitchen cupboard, clearly once having held bottles of wine. The sight, the reminder, steadied Simone, sobered her. Ezra, his gentle eyes assessing her face, took the large box from her outstretched hand.

"Can you just pack all those shoes into a box?" *Rebecca's* shoes. Simone paused for a moment. "Actually, a trash bag would be better; we'll just toss them all anyway."

Ezra opened his mouth to question her rash determination, but Simone spoke on. She kept her gaze on the boxes. The rest, the signs of life in this dead room, were too hard to look at. "I'll pack up all the books so we can drop them off at the library."

"You? Getting rid of books?" Ezra's joking tone was worn with effort, but Simone appreciated it nevertheless. "You sure you don't want to keep any?"

"I work in publishing. I already have too many books, if such a thing is possible." Simone's own attempt at a joking tone fell much flatter. Ezra politely pretended to believe her words and tone both.

Time passed easily as they both set to work, Ezra crouching over shoe racks and lone sandals and boots strewn across the room like they were on a scavenger hunt, like it was the space of a teenager. Simone sat on the floor before the bookcase, grateful for the warmth of her matching sweats as the winter cold seeped up. Seasons on Juniper were a stretched gradient, reaching slowly from one to the next. But the island was deep in the heart of winter now, the sea making the already-cold air punishing, even inside the lighthouse.

The bookshelf before Simone was packed with books that she knew must have belonged to Cole women long before her mother, who had never been a reader despite her inheritance. Midcentury romances were stuffed beside classic Gothics and farmer's almanacs. Simone pulled them out stack by stack, setting them in the cardboard boxes without even glancing at the spines. She didn't need to get to know the other Coles through the words they loved. She was here to pack. She had returned to leave.

But she couldn't help but spot one book, a tome, really, the spine pristine and crisp with newness and disuse. Ezra wasn't a big reader, but he was a loyal Stephen King fan. In fact, Simone had had to insist multiple times on their drive that, despite being in New England, Juniper Island wasn't going to look like a Stephen King setting. Though it certainly was creepy in its own way.

She reached out, pulling the book from its spot tightly nestled on the shelves. *It* tipped forward into Simone's palm, but the movement upset the delicate structure of the other books. A thinner, worn paperback slipped free from beside the King, tumbling onto the ground with a thud. And as it fell, splaying out across the air, spine so frequently cracked that it seemed to flutter open with the barest resistance, a small piece of paper fell from between the pages, sliding to land under the bed. Another slip of paper poked out from the top of the book, nestled in the middle of the old worn copy of *Rebecca*. Simone didn't believe in signs or fate or witchcraft, but seeing her mother's name looking up at her, those hidden papers coming to the surface, did make the hairs on her arm stand to attention.

Tossing the King book aside, Simone stretched out, fingers grasping into the shadows under the bed until she felt the thin paper. Curiosity blooming, she slid it out. Plucking a dust bunny from the corner, Simone looked at what she held.

Disappointment landed quickly as she saw that it was nothing more than a handwritten receipt from Poole Market, a few beers bought back in the seventies. She reached out to toss the slip of paper into one of the trash bags dotting the room, but as she moved, the lamplight stretched golden over her arm, and through the thin bit of paper Simone saw other words written on the back. Settling back down onto her knees, she flipped it over.

There was so much writing crammed onto the tiny slip that it took Simone a long moment to make sense of it. But there was a clear delineation: One line sat alone at the top, and below, in an entirely different hand, was a scribbled paragraph. Simone's stomach plummeted as she read that one line that stood stark on its own.

I know you killed him

Heart suddenly thundering, rattling her rib cage, Simone read the other note written beneath.

My sweet Rebecca girl,

I haven't had a long life, but I've lived a lot. I've loved deeper than most Cole women get the chance to and I've done some bad deeds. These islanders have loved to punish us as far back as our Goody Cole. I may deserve punishment, but I won't let them all find out what I've done and hurt you for it, my girl. And they would. These folks don't see any good in a Cole woman. But you can be good, Rebecca, I know it. If it's my time to go that means you must have a little girl coming soon enough. I hope she's happy. I hope you love her as much as I love you, always. I'm sorry to leave you. But I'm not sorry for what I've done.

There was no signature to the note, but it was clear as day to Simone that her grandmother had written it. That—what?—someone had written the threatening line at the top to her grandmother, and she had written that in response. It was clear to Simone what it was: a suicide note. A note she had left before she gave herself to the sea, as all the Cole women had.

That should have been enough to grab Simone's attention. And it was. Moreover, she was suddenly gripped at the throat by the thought that maybe her mother, too, had left a note before walking into the ocean forevermore. Hands shaking, silently scolding herself against her foolish hope, Simone plucked the paper still nestled in the copy of *Rebecca* out.

Beck's Travel Bucket List

Beck? Simone had never heard her mother go by that name, but she recognized her writing instantly. And, she figured, maybe that was a nickname her mother had used; Simone hadn't really known her, after all. How would she know? Little stars and hearts dotted the margins, signs of a young woman perhaps, of a lightness and gaiety that Simone would have never associated with her perpetually grieving mother.

Simone thought of every time her mother's stony face had told her they couldn't go to the mainland, they couldn't travel, they couldn't have a life outside Juniper, the shackles on their ankles binding them here. But Simone had done it. Her mother had not. And these were clearly the dreams of a young Rebecca, back when hope still buoyed her. And that first place on the list, New York City—the place Simone herself now called home—seemed an extra stab to her suddenly and surprisingly tender heart.

But, just like on the other paper, Simone glimpsed writing on the other side. It might just be a journal entry from a teenage Rebecca, another bucket list. But Simone couldn't help but hope that she would get what her mother had: a note written from mother to daughter, telling her that, despite taking her own life, she would always love and live on in her daughter.

The words Simone found on the back side of the paper seemed to be a note, yes. But not like she'd hoped. She chided herself and her stupid heart. She knew her mother. She shouldn't have expected love declarations to her daughter. But, Simone thought, maybe it was because her mother had thought that not even her death would bring Simone back to Juniper, that there was no chance it would be her wayward daughter who would find the note. Simone read Rebecca's note, and a suicide note it, too, clearly was. And just as baffling as the first.

I don't know if we're all cursed. But I know I am. Everything I love, dies. Leaves.

At that, Simone felt a stab to her center. But she read on.

It wasn't a threat of discovery that killed my mother. It was me. My actions, my decisions. My choices led my mother to the sea. It's time I follow her.

And that was all it said. Just a few brief lines that only baffled Simone further. She didn't understand.

"Look at this," she breathed. Choked out.

Ezra leaned over, resting his head on her shoulder. She gripped a note in each hand, and the two of them read them, heads side by side, eyes darting across lines.

"Whoa," Ezra said after a beat. "Is that—"

"That's my mom's handwriting." Simone pointed to the shorter note, on the paper listing the dreams of someone named Beck, some version of her mother Simone had never met.

She read both notes once more, twice. Her grandma had done something—killed someone—and taken her life rather than have that be exposed, thinking she was protecting her daughter. Then Simone's own mother had—what? Found the note? Somehow blamed herself for what her mother had done?

Blamed herself for someone threatening her mother? And then Rebecca had killed herself in that guilt.

None of it made sense to Simone. But that first, deeply grooved, thick-lined threat burned through her gaze over and over. Clearly there was a mystery to uncover here, one realer than some curse caused by a distant ancestor. There was something to unravel, and Simone knew it started with that bold-faced threat.

Forty-Six
Rebecca

January 3, 1998

Juniper Island, Isles of Shoals, New Hampshire

Nothing brought sorrow to Rebecca's doorstep like her birthday. Another year gone, another year on her own. And how was this year different than the last, or the one before that?

Her birthday reminded her of her mother every year, the pain and ache and joy her mother must have gone through to bring her into this world. Rebecca wondered if, on her own birthday, Simone ever thought of her. Maybe it was the despair speaking, but she had a feeling the answer was no.

Perhaps driven by a need to poke her bruised heart, or just because her mother was heavy on her mind, Rebecca spent the afternoon of her birthday on the floor of her bedroom, looking through the books she had long shoved to the back of her shelves. Her vinyls had always taken precedence, but these books had lived before Rebecca and would outlive her too, her mother's most beloved possessions. The tears Rebecca hadn't even realized she was weeping stained the yellow-worn pages, softened the already malleable, diluted paperback covers. Each kiss of worn paper on her fingers was the touch of her mother's hand on her head.

Rebecca felt like a small child again, the world too big for her to understand. She was forty-six but she knew nothing, felt everything, could hardly keep herself afloat or steady. She tossed aside the book in her hand, some old romance. Another thing Rebecca had had and lost. Despair came on slowly, waves to shore, but Rebecca's anger—rare as it was—always came on like a lightning strike. It bubbled up in her almost painfully. It felt better to tear the books from the shelves, throw them onto the floor, than it felt to turn her rage on her own worn, tired skin. She grabbed a red-and-black spine, threw it down onto the floor, that expression of anger doing the barest to soothe the fire in her.

But as the paperback landed on the floor with a thump, not only did Rebecca see a familiar face, but she spotted a thin, aged slip of paper slide from between the pages and glide beneath her bed. For a moment, lingering on her knees, Rebecca stared down at the book's cover, her own name staring back up at her. She leaned down, stretched an arm out into the dark abyss beneath her bed. Her fingers whispered against the lost paper, which was too thin for a notebook—a receipt, she guessed. She pinched it between pointer and ring finger and pulled it out. She stared down at it.

Why in the world would someone save a random receipt from Poole's from the seventies? The edges curled, as if they had been damp before being flattened again within the book's pages for decades. But as she looked closer, Rebecca saw it wasn't just any day in the seventies. It was the date that haunted her as horribly as her own birth. October 10, the day she had lost her mother to the curse, to the sea. And as she looked closer, Rebecca saw, through the thin paper, scribbled letters strewn across its back. She turned it over, heart plummeting into her stomach at the familiar hand.

A few words, written in haste, in sorrow, scratchings of despair that felt so close to Rebecca's own heart. She read those few brief lines. She read them again and again until the words were tattooed on her brain. Rebecca had always felt three steps removed from her mother, too full of resentment to grasp the olive branch her mother kept stretched toward her. And in those brief few words, even if Rebecca had no context for them, she saw the depth of her mother's love. The depth of her mother's protection.

And then, just above, Rebecca got a hint of context. Her mother's words were not the only ones written on the little receipt. Above them was a threat.

A threat that had, on that October night decades ago, backed her mother against a wall, forced her to take her own life to protect herself and her daughter from her past. Rebecca realized exactly why her mother had received those threatening words, why they had come that day, why someone had wanted the Cole women not to die but to flee from Juniper Island, to keep a man's secret.

But the Cole women could not flee this island. So her mother had walked into the sea instead to protect Rebecca, and it had worked. Mabel's actions had protected Rebecca from the fire and brimstone of the islanders, but it had not protected her from their malice, from their ice. It had not protected Rebecca from icing out her own daughter. It had not broken any sort of curse or cycle.

It had strengthened it.

Rebecca's hands shook as she set the note back down on the book. Her blood rushed in her ears, head pounding with the racing of her thoughts. But it wasn't just that that Rebecca heard, loud and demanding in her mind. It was the screams and anger of raging men, decades of them, centuries. But that was not the worst part. The worst part was the guilt.

Because Rebecca saw then, clear as day, that if it were not for her own actions, her mother would not have been threatened. Her mother would still be alive. Maybe there was no curse at all. Maybe Rebecca was the horrible parasite on her mother's life, her daughter's, her own. Guilt and shame squeezed the life out of her chest, and she could not see a way that she could go on living every day of her life with those feelings choking her slowly.

Rebecca decided to give herself what she thought she deserved.

She slid across her bedroom floor, ripping through notebooks until she found a familiar page. She shoved down the stab to her heart as she tore the page out, scrambled for a pen, flipped it to the back, wrote her own message of goodbye. Of confession. She took her slip of paper and the receipt, folded them both, tucked them back in the copy of *Rebecca*, placed it on the bookshelf.

Now that her decision had been made, there was an odd sort of euphoria spreading from Rebecca's center. A sense of rightness, maybe, or just the peace of knowing she wouldn't suffer much longer. With an unnerving calm, she cleaned the mess her rage had made, lining the books perfectly back up on their shelves. Then she closed her door, made her way down the stairs, wrapped a scarf around her neck, and slid her socked feet into her sandals.

There was something she had to do first. Words she had to say that could not be left in a note for someone who would never find them. Though soon enough none of it would even be Rebecca's problem to worry about.

She didn't feel the winter biting at her through her thin, flowing dress as she walked across the island. The evening was just rising, soaking the houses in a pink half-light as Rebecca stopped before the house that had long haunted her. The future she'd thought she might have that had been stolen from her.

Now she saw that it would never, ever have been hers anyway. She had spent her life holding out for a fantasy.

She knocked. She heard footsteps on the other side, blessedly light enough to indicate that it was a woman. Barbara Bradbury pulled open the door, surprise splashing her face to find Rebecca Cole on the other side, a bright mania lighting her dark eyes. Then the shock melted into acceptance.

"Rebecca," Barbara said, flat. It was as if she had been expecting this knock at her door to come one day.

Barbara looked down as Rebecca began to speak, the words hitting her on the crown of her blond head. As though she had long expected them, was tilting her head down to weather the storm she had seen creeping up the shore for two decades.

They were alone on the street; there was no one here to hear their words. Still Rebecca spoke softly; she was not here for revenge, not here to embarrass Barbara. None of that mattered anymore.

"Cal is Simone's father," she said.

Barbara nodded, looking down still. She took a deep, bracing breath. When she finally looked up to Rebecca, there was a bittersweet smile on her face.

"I know, Rebecca." She shrugged. "I've always known. Since the first time I saw her. I never believed the rumors."

Rebecca's odd calm was so profound that nothing could surprise her anymore.

"He was seeing both of us at the same time," Rebecca continued, as if Barbara wasn't understanding.

"I *know.* I've known. Even then." Barbara looked up at Rebecca, the years suddenly visible on her small, angelic face. "I knew the man I married. I knew then that I didn't have all of him. But I still made my choice. I stand by it."

When Rebecca didn't say anything, Barbara continued, "He was never going to be with you, Rebecca. But I'm sorry he hurt you. I'm sorry he hurt you and Simone. Neither of you deserved it."

The words should have hurt, but they glinted off Rebecca's armor, though the sound of her daughter's name still stung. But all she felt was the affirmation, the rightness of her decisions.

"You didn't deserve it either, Barbara."

Rebecca had nothing more to say.

Nobody on this island had anything she needed to hear anymore. She was done. She was ready to be free.

For the last time, Rebecca crossed the island in the sinking evening light, pink and yellow streaking behind the lighthouse. The standing structure that had been her haven and jail both, the distant mainland, and the endless stretch of the sea were painted in watercolor. Rebecca observed the art of her life for the last time.

The wind grew stronger as she got closer to the island's edge. She didn't look up at the lighthouse as she passed beneath its shadow. She didn't scramble down the rocks; she glided down them with sure feet. Her body was made for this terrain, after all.

She kneeled, grabbing the smaller, loose rocks, piling them into her pockets until she was weighed down so heavily it took effort to stand. It was a glimpse into the future she would never have, the ache of old age limiting movement. But this was the closest she would ever get; Cole women did not get old age. They only got the sea.

The closer she got to the water's edge, the growing scent of brine and crashing waves, the louder the sounds in her mind became. The whirl of her thoughts, yes. The scream of angry men who hated Cole women, yes. But other sounds too. Softer voices. Familiar voices, coming from the sea itself. Hearing the voices, for once Rebecca knew she was not alone on her birthday. Over the angry sounds of men was that familiar tone of her mother, of her mother's mother, of all those Cole women waiting to embrace her. The stories were true, their spirits lived in the sea, the Cole women passed were those navy depths and the white frothing breaks.

Rebecca had not touched the waves since the day Simone was born. The sea used to be her very best friend, but for so long she had deprived herself of its touch. It was time to make amends. She stepped off the rocks, the cold bite of the ocean freezing her skin, freeing her in its familiar, long-missed touch. The gentle, affirming touch of a mother, a grandmother. Of women who had loved her and come before her and were a part of her. The salt water soaked through her dress quickly as she swam farther out to sea.

Rebecca Cole was never more herself than in the embrace of the Atlantic. With each stroke of her arms, each pump of her legs, her chin sank lower in the water, the rocks pulling her down. She did not turn around to say goodbye to the soil of Juniper when she finally dove beneath the waves. The rocks pulled, but Rebecca went willingly, down until she couldn't see the pink sky dancing on the water's surface. Until everything was deep navy and icy cold, the place in the world Rebecca had always loved most. The sounds of the Cole women danced in Rebecca's waterlogged ears, the hands of long-gone Coles lovingly grasping her.

The sea hugged its favorite daughter and held her to its bosom.

In the end, stepping into the Atlantic wasn't a punishment or a curse. It was an escape. It was a reunion. Rebecca returned home to the sea.

Forty-Seven
Simone

January 9, 1998

Juniper Island, Isles of Shoals, New Hampshire

Growing up, the library had been Simone's only safe haven. The only piece she had of the grandmother she never knew. It looked as it always had: a rough, worn little shack, apparently fixed up decades ago by her grandmother and Miss Evelyn, Julia's grandma, the librarian who had worked beside the two girls.

Simone had thought that maybe she could go the rest of her trip on Juniper without seeing Julia again. That she and Ezra could hole up in the lighthouse, pack dawn to dusk, and disappear when the ferry returned a week after. Leave the islanders to their misery and their curses.

In the quiet bed that first night, Ezra had said softly, "That's her? Your Julia?"

Simone's chest had ached at the question. *Yes. No. Once upon a time.* No answer was correct. She had shrugged, nodded, a wavering gesture of confirmation. Ezra, sweet, understanding Ezra who had loved Simone and her every scar, no matter what, had not been jealous. He had smiled, unbothered, said simply, "She seems kind. It was really nice of her to stay here. To protect the lighthouse."

Still, Simone had hoped she could avoid Julia and all the memories in the woman's dark eyes. Cowardly, she knew.

Either way, it seemed impossible. Because Simone had two scraps of paper and questions scratching at her mind endlessly. And it was Julia who had spent years collecting and categorizing the documents on Juniper and its history and inhabitants. It was Julia who could help guide her to answers.

Ezra was stuck back at the lighthouse, trying to sort out a work emergency that had sprung up that morning. He had said he could handle it later, that supporting Simone was more important. Those words had healed her a bit, steadied her in how clear it was that Ezra meant them. But she'd kissed him softly and told him she could do it, that she'd see him in a few hours, that if he finished early to meet her at the library.

So Simone was alone when she pushed open the door to the cottage, the old, damp wood swollen with the cold burrowing into it. The door closed behind Simone without a sound.

The library had never been a particularly busy place, so Simone wasn't surprised to find it empty. She could hear Julia somewhere in the stacks, her soft humming echoing around the small space. The single lamp on the desk up front was lit, winter-white afternoon light cutting in through the window.

Simone wasn't sure if she should call out Julia's name, alert the librarian to her presence. Maybe she should search the stacks for Julia, but she didn't want it to be too nostalgic, like old times when Simone would wrap her arms around—

"Whoa!" Julia appeared between two shelves, drawing back in surprise when she saw Simone standing in the doorway, hands twisting anxiously. She quickly righted herself, wiping the dust from her hands onto her thick flannel and weathered jeans. "Did you pay extra for those expensive shoes to make you move without a sound?"

Julia's eyes flashed down to Simone's gleaming leather boots with their thick, sturdy heels. But there was a joking smile on Julia's face, making it clear that the words weren't mocking or judgmental, just teasing. It wasn't surprising. Simone couldn't remember Julia ever saying anything unkindly—at least not to her.

The two women stood across from each other, silently noting the differences in their appearance: Julia's strawberry-blond hair pin straight as always, pulled into a messy ponytail, the faded stains on her torn jeans, the worn out soles of her chunky Bean Boots. The clean lines of Simone's camel coat and black slacks, her thick knit turtleneck. The frizzy waves of her dark bob, bangs curling against her forehead, always resistant to Simone's control, always twisting and tangling in the sea air. In tandem, the women broke into soft laughter at the sight of them, so opposite, yet still sharing so much.

Julia wasn't a teenage girl anymore; she was a woman now, with a life Simone wasn't so familiar with, just as Simone herself was. But their laughs were still the same, echoing and easy, a natural harmony.

"What can I do for you, Simone?" Julia said on one last chuckle.

For a brief moment Simone had forgotten the two notes folded neatly in her jacket pocket. But with that question, reality crushed back down on her. She pulled them out and laid them on the desk. Julia stepped to her side to read the scraps. Simone briefed the other woman on where she had found them, how she suspected the first note was her grandmother's in response to the threat. And the second note, her mother's, recent, maybe, clearly in response to reading her own mother's words.

Julia loosed a long, heavy breath. Simone breathed deep, pushing the scent of old books into her nose, hoping it could calm her.

Seeing her mother's—and presumably her grandmother's—handwriting choked Simone up still. But it was that ominous wording, the threat that must have come first, that was the starkest and most gripping.

I know you killed him

"Shit," Julia said, freeing and then retying her hair, a nervous tic Simone noticed that she still had. "Wicked creepy."

"Yup."

"Okay." Julia stepped away, toward the silver filing cabinets that lined the back wall behind the desk. Fingers flitting over drawers, she eventually squatted down to a drawer marked *Deaths 1970–1980* in her own hand. "So I think the first thing we've gotta to do is make sure that the first note is actually from your grandma. Mabel, right?"

Simone realized she had never heard her mother speak of her grandmother. But Simone had grown up hearing the villagers murmur about her witchy ancestors. All she knew of herself, of her family, had been gleamed from their vengeance. "Yeah. Mabel Cole."

Julia tossed a thin manila folder on the desk, flipping it open. "The receipt on the front is from what date?"

Simone checked again. "October 10, 1971."

"Okay, so let's see if that's around the time Mabel . . . died." Julia's long fingers flicked through the paperwork within, stacks of death certificates issued from the state, on the mainland. "If that creepy threatening note is what made her . . ."

Neither of them wanted to speak the words of what the Cole women did. Of the curse the Simone didn't believe in. They had talked about it as girls, or rather talked around it, Simone whispering that the curse wasn't real, that she would prove it. Julia holding her as she did.

Simone held her breath as Julia checked each page before quickly coming to a stop. She held one of the pages out. Simone took it, stupidly careful not to let their fingers brush.

It was a death certificate for Mabel Cole. Suicide by drowning. Dated October 10, 1971.

"Shit," Simone breathed, echoing Julia's earlier exclamation.

"Shit." The other woman nodded.

Simone felt the heavy tug of grief through her center, mourning for a family member she had never known, had never really had. A family member who she now knew for sure hadn't been taken by some stupid curse but by a threat someone on this island had made against her. A threat that had pushed Mabel to take her own life rather than face it. Simone had always known that it was these islanders and their hatred and their prejudice and their ostracization that was killing Cole women, a slow disease rotting them in exile.

But the date stirred Simone's unease. October 10, 1971, just a few months before Simone was born. She didn't believe in the curse, didn't think this was any confirmation of it. Didn't believe there could only be two Cole women on Juniper, that one always died when one was soon to be born. Nevertheless, goose bumps rose on her arms.

"All right, then." Julia nodded, walking back over to the filing cabinet, opening shelves of death certificates labeled from 1940 to 1971. She plucked out folder after folder, creating an intimidating stack on the desk. "Let's see if we can find anyone on the island that was killed. That . . . you know . . ."

"That Mabel may have killed," Simone said, wearing a firmness on the outside that she didn't feel inside. It was like an instinct, a second skin growing over her since the moment she'd stepped foot back on the isle. "Or that someone, clearly, thought she did."

Though Simone had to admit Mabel's note certainly read like a confession. But, well, Simone knew in her bones there was more to the story than cold-blooded murder. She knew, better than most, maybe, that nothing on Juniper was ever so clear as it might seem, especially where the Cole women were involved. Besides, Simone had been a skeptic from birth, since she had been told that she was a witch descendant and destined to die by these shores. She never took anything at face value.

The sun tilted in the sky as Julia and Simone went through folder after folder in silence. Juniper Island housed only a few families and was not particularly populated, but death was not uncommon out here. It wasn't so taboo on the isle; death was simply what came with living with the sea as a neighbor and benefactor both. Though there were phases where there was an uptick in deaths, one after the other. Though Simone didn't believe in any curses or magic or ghosts, she couldn't help but wonder if those periods corresponded with when Cole women had attempted to leave the island. Those times when superstitious belief said that the dead Coles raged and made dangerous waters.

There were death records crediting drowning—plenty of those—world wars, cancer and illness and old age, boats lost at sea, childbirth, alcoholism. It was a grim portrait of life on Juniper, the same things that ate at generation after generation. The addiction that blazed through the isle, burning down Simone's own childhood. The cruelty of the sea and aversion to mainland medicines.

Simone thought about how Julia, alone, must have had to file her mother's and stepfather's death certificates. She felt suddenly nauseous.

The two women, seated side by side, saw dozens of lives come to a close, paper after paper. As she read through some files from 1968—two deaths, old age and a heart attack—Simone found herself mindlessly rubbing her thumb over her left knuckles, feeling the pink puckered skin of a scar there. Like everything else in this place, it came with a memory. The split knuckles and bruised skin from punching Greg Allan in the jaw when she was fourteen, after he'd called Julia a dyke. The boy's verbal violence had been Julia's punishment for her closeness to Simone. Simone, always cool and aloof, even then, finally lost her control, even after months, years of Greg calling her a heeb, a witch, or worse. But something about his hate being directed toward Julia had spurred Simone on before she could think. She had never, not once, regretted this scar or what she had done to get it. In fact, she was certain she'd do it again. In rubbing that scar on her hand, Simone realized maybe she understood her grandmother a bit, that the words in the woman's final letter rang true in her own memories.

I'm not sorry for what I've done.

Simone had been defending Julia, their closeness, the care they had for one another. What was her grandmother defending in "killing" someone that had come back to her in a threat?

Simone dropped her hands, tucking them beneath her legs.

Afternoon was settling into evening when Julia closed the last folder from 1972.

"Anything?" she asked.

Simone shook her head. "Nothing out of the ordinary. Not even any accidents that could be foul play. Could they mean a time when your grandmother left the island and . . . ?"

And, as always, people died in the Cole women's absence.

"Maybe," Simone acquiesced. But it didn't feel right. The threat felt like more, more specific, more singular. From Mabel's own words, she had *done* something.

Simone's chest felt clenched tight. They had run into a firm brick wall before they had even gathered much information at all. She wiped her sweating palms on her trousers, pushing away from the desk to stand, stepping back from Julia. Simone's lower back panged from where she'd been curled over the papers for hours.

She couldn't look at Julia, knowing the woman would see her disappointment, as she said, "Thanks for trying. For the help. I guess it just . . . is."

Simone began to stuff paperwork back into folders, to recreate the stack as though she were turning back time to hours ago, no more informed than she was then. She swallowed heavily, not letting the burn of her eyes turn to moisture. It didn't matter. Whatever.

She wasn't here to try to solve some old mystery about family she hadn't know and didn't even need. She didn't need them and she didn't need answers. This wasn't her life. She was here to free herself for good, to unshackle herself from the lighthouse.

But Simone did not believe herself, and neither did her stinging eyes.

"Whoa, whoa, whoa, slow down." Julia put a hand on Simone's forearm, stopping her frantic packing. Simone's arms fell to her sides. She blinked back tears, staring past Julia's head at the stacks of books. Julia chewed her lower lip in thought. "We'll need to try something else. Come at this whole mystery from a new point in time, then."

"We?" Simone asked.

"Of course." Julia shrugged, as if there was still friendship between them even years after Simone had crushed their love underfoot in her efforts to flee this place. Julia checked her watched, tutted as she saw the time. "Meet me back here tomorrow morning. I have an idea of where else to look."

Simone nodded, silent, unable to voice her appreciation around the lump in her throat. She felt lighter at the thought that she might be able to untangle the web of her family's past, to solve at least this one mystery. That she was not attempting to do it on her own, that she had Ezra and Julia, too, helping her. Together they would find out what her mother and grandmother thought had happened, what horrible past they both blamed themselves for. They would find out who had threatened the Cole women, ignited a fear and a guilt deep enough to drive two Cole women to the sea, decades apart.

For once, Simone almost wished she believed in the curse. It was easier to swallow magical imaginings than the truth that every Cole woman had chosen to kill herself. Simone only had her mother as a picture of the Cole women before her. There was no curse. There was only hatred and isolation, and in her own mother, at least, that had bred addiction and illness and pushing away her own daughter. Maybe Rebecca had learned that behavior. Simone didn't believe in a curse, but she did believe that her mother had inherited a doomed life on a doomed island full of cruel people that ate away at the heart and the mind and the spirit until the only relief was death.

There was no curse of the sea, only the curse of their past. Of the people who made up this place and their hatred. Simone was determined to find out what all these notes and threats added up to, to trace them home like footsteps sinking in wet sand. She wasn't certain if it was so she could free herself of the curse or so she could try to make someone or something on this island pay for what they'd done to the Cole women, for once.

Forty-Eight
Simone

January 10, 1998

Juniper Island, Isles of Shoals, New Hampshire

"I'm not sure this is the best idea." Simone pushed her weight from foot to foot, her toes frozen in her boots. Both Ezra and Julia clocked the movement as more than just the cold.

How annoying to have the only two people who had ever known her here together, Simone thought. She couldn't hide a thing.

"I mean, yeah, they don't exactly seem like . . ." Ezra's face pinched, and Simone knew he was searching for a way to make his point kindly. "The biggest fans of Simone's family."

Julia shrugged. "No one on this island is." It was factual, but it still stabbed at Simone. "We've gotta try, though, right? The records were no help. This is the only other way I can think to go about cracking this thing."

She looked at Ezra and Simone, waiting for one of them to make another suggestion that they all knew didn't exist.

"Besides, surely they can't be that bad. Not anymore."

Simone's time away must have made Julia forget some of the horrors and cruelties she had witnessed by Simone's side.

Because Julia stepped into Poole Market confidently, but Simone and Ezra were much more hesitant on her heels.

"Hiya, Mrs. Poole," Julia called gently.

"Just going for it then, I guess," Ezra chuckled.

Simone could tell that Ezra liked Julia, was entertained by her loud, brash demeanor, so opposite of Ezra's own gentle, measured nature. Some piece of Simone's inner child was comforted by the sight, by the idea that her past and present could, at least through these two people, get along.

"Julia, how are you?" Mrs. Poole greeted her. But her smile flicked off like a light switch when she spotted Simone over the redhead's shoulder.

Simone resisted the urge to roll her eyes. The islanders might be cruel, but they certainly were predictable in that cruelty.

"What do you want?" This the grocer said to Simone.

Simone thought of Mrs. Poole's husband ducking his head as he stepped out of Rebecca's bedroom many a night. Simone felt sick for both the grocer and herself, despite the woman's hard glare.

The air of the small market hung heavy with the smell of scales and death from the ice-lined shelves where rows of fish rested, their unseeing eyes boring into Simone. Death and the sea; the scent of Juniper. Simone sniffed, no longer so used to the cloying smell.

"You keep logs of all the folks you sell to, yeah?" Julia asked. She stepped up to the counter, blocking the grocer's view of Simone. She leaned down familiarly, propping her down-clad elbows on the counter. "What everyone buys? For inventory and whatnot?"

Julia asked the question, but they already knew the answer. Everyone knew Mrs. Poole was meticulous in her record-keeping. Old-fashioned, still with the clacking manual cash register and the handwritten receipts. But for each receipt given to the customer, Mrs. Poole was known to make a copy, to keep a log of the purchases alongside the buyer's name and maybe some scribbled notes on how they seemed, what they said, what they wore, who they were with.

It wasn't that Mrs. Poole was known to particularly love or thrive in her role as the island's grocer. No, she was known to thrive in her role as the isle's gossip, and those records gave her plenty to whisper over and speculate about with the other wives once the shop closed for the day.

"Why're you asking?" The woman's voice was somewhere between her harshness toward Simone and her friendship toward Julia. Even though Julia might have been born a mainlander, she had been raised nearly her whole life on the isle. Moreover, she had been raised since childhood by Miss Evelyn, a Fuller and a Bradbury. So kindness to Julia was a knee-jerk reaction for most of the older generation around Juniper. It seemed Mrs. Poole was at war with herself over it at present.

Simone fingered a stack of eggplants, surely shipped from the mainland. She felt Mrs. Poole's glare on the side of her face. Simone dropped her arms and drifted away to the other side of the market, facing away but close enough she could still hear. Ezra followed her lead, wandering, detaching himself from Julia.

Simone attempted to appear disinterested in the conversation happening at the counter. She knew the more invested she appeared, the less likely Mrs. Poole would be to help.

"Oh, we're just trying to sort some things out," Julia said casually. "You know, *I* am. For the library records."

Simone swallowed her chuckle. Julia had been a terrible liar when they were teenagers. She clearly hadn't gotten any better in the past decade.

Mrs. Poole seemed to sense it, too, unsurprisingly. "Well, I'm sorry, I'm afraid I can't help you out with that."

Julia was undeterred. "I just need the records from one day. Back in '71, the—"

"*Nineteen seventy-one*?" Mrs. Poole said incredulously. But she was as bad a liar as Julia was. "I don't hold on to receipt copies that long. Good luck with whatever it is you're after. You have a good day now."

It was a clear dismissal. Simone would bet her right arm that Mrs. Poole did, in fact, have records of purchases from 1971 still. But Simone had entered the market expecting the grocer to be obstinate, so she wasn't surprised the situation had gone that way. And if anyone knew a curt dismissal from one of the folks on Juniper Island, it was Simone Cole.

"But—" Julia started, but Simone reappeared at her side, laying a hand on her arm. Ezra was already by the door, either sensing that Mrs. Poole was done with them too or else just sensing the panic rising in Simone's chest, the need to get out of the small space.

"Let's go, Jules."

Julia sighed but followed the Hoffmans back out into the blistery winter air. As they stepped out of the market, Simone's steps were downtrodden, weighed heavy with defeat. She had expected no other outcome, she had thought. She didn't notice the hope until it deflated in her chest. Simone only lifted her sinking head when she felt gazes pressing heavy on her. Across the street, stepping out of their house, covered cake plate in hand, were Cal and Barbara Bradbury. Julia's—what, step-second cousin? Step-great-uncle? Everyone on Juniper was nearly related anyway. Except the Coles, of course.

Cal's blue eyes, bright against the flatness of winter, glanced off Simone for a quick moment. He nodded to Julia behind her, then continued on. But Barbara Bradbury, petite and beautiful in middle age, froze. She looked at Simone as if she were seeing a ghost. Then she seemed to remember herself, falling after her husband, shooting one last glance Simone's way.

Maybe Simone would have dwelled on the oddness if she hadn't been so used to being a spectacle for the people of

Juniper. Life on the mainland, in New York, had made her comfortable with anonymity, but she couldn't easily forget the burning spotlight she had on the isle.

"We can try something else," Ezra said as the three of them gathered into a loose circle outside the market. He tried to sound encouraging, but Simone knew him well enough to hear that he was at a loss.

"It's a dead end," Simone said, trying to hide her disappointment.

"No, no," Julia insisted, arms crossing over her chest. "Ezra's right. Let's think on it for a few days. We'll figure out another way to come at the notes. I mean, come on, there's got to be a way to figure out who threatened Mabel or even *what* they think she did. This place loves its history. There's a trail somewhere, I know it. We just have to find the puzzle pieces so we can put them together and—"

"Look, I'm cold. I'm tired. Thanks for your help, Jules." Simone turned to Ezra, picked up his hand, avoiding his dark-brown eyes, so gentle and sympathetic that she knew she'd crack. She couldn't let him hold her—hold her *together*—until they were alone. She would not let the islanders see what they did to her, not now and not ever. "It is what it is. Let's just go."

Before Ezra or Julia could open their mouths to say another misdirected, emptily encouraging word, Simone turned, pulling Ezra toward the lighthouse.

Let it go, she scolded herself. She was here to pack the lighthouse, to throw out history so she could be free, not dig around in it. The dead end was a blessing in disguise, she tried to convince herself. But really all Simone could think as they crossed the isle was that, as always, the prejudice of the islanders was keeping the Cole women from getting to know their own.

Forty-Nine
Simone

January 11, 1998

Juniper Island, Isles of Shoals, New Hampshire

Simone stared at the words in front of her until they made sense. That moment, frustratingly, did not come.

She had been on page twenty-eight of this manuscript for—she checked her watch, squinted to see it through the dim light of the kitchen—thirty-seven minutes. The red pen in her hand creaked beneath Simone's frustrated, white-knuckled grip. She read the first line again. And by the time she got to the end of the sentence, she realized, again, that she had retained approximately zero of the words. She dropped the pen on the kitchen table with a clatter.

The manuscript was great, the latest from a favorite among her authors, the newest draft of a languid, erudite literary fiction. It wasn't the book's fault. It was Simone's. She had never had trouble focusing her mind on a task, especially when the task was reading. But her mind was everywhere but with her tonight.

She'd taken a break an hour ago when she noticed the afternoon light creeping darker, though it was barely four in the evening. Such was the way of winter, of Juniper. She'd gone up the old stairs that threaded like a spine through the center of the lighthouse. Mindlessly lit the beam up top, not looking around, not thinking about how, even now, the sight of the sinking sun spurred her body into action like a reflex she was born with. She'd come back down to the kitchen. Called to ask Ezra if he wanted a cup of tea. Responded to his negative. Made herself a cup, chamomile she'd found in a cupboard. Smelled the dry, stale tea bags, realized they were likely the same ones she'd left back there a decade ago. Poured hot water over it, cursed when it splashed on her hand. Let the bag steep until it should have been shocking. Took a sip, tasted nothing, couldn't entirely blame the old bag. Sat back at the kitchen table, pulled the manuscript and her red pen toward her. Stared at the words as she heard Ezra packing up the living room through the open doorway.

Time had passed. Plenty of it. And Simone's work was still stuttering and dying in her grasp. She had severed the limb of her past to get to the mainland, get her degree, get this job. And now the phantom ache was keeping her from it.

She sat back, tipped her head back against the chair, closed her eyes. Ezra's steady thuds from the room over found her, the sound of antiques and broken clocks and cracked coasters being packed into boxes. For donation, for the trash, Simone didn't know yet.

Her thought process before arriving hadn't quite gotten that far. She had shoved down grief and shoved down fear and told herself that she would arrive, pack everything up, toss it into the Atlantic for all she cared. That she would sever every tie to the lighthouse on Juniper Island and return to the mainland, free.

But now, hearing that exact situation coming to fruition on the other side of the wall, it didn't feel right. Simone's chest pinched with guilt, like it had when she begged off classes in undergrad, when she told people at her wedding that, no, she had no family, actually.

Packing everything up and running away on the ferry didn't feel right anymore. It felt just like that—running away. Because those two mysterious notes—the last words of her mother and grandmother—burned like bright coals in her pocket. Leaving the lighthouse and Juniper behind for good didn't feel right anymore, because those notes made things feel unresolved for Simone.

She had spent years—her entire childhood, really—convincing herself that she didn't owe a single thing to her mother, to the Cole name and its doomed lineage. And yet, even in marriage, Simone had kept that name. She'd told herself she would change it, yet time passed and she had never quite gotten around to it.

The Cole women had never given her a thing besides a name that ached. It felt wrong to empty the lighthouse with so much unresolved, like wringing a rag dry and tossing it out, making it meaningless, scraps.

Simone had never believed in the curse or witches or the supernatural. But, sitting in this revered and rumored about, yet familiar, lighthouse, she felt haunted. And she feared that even if she left this place and returned to the mainland, that haunting would continue, would seep its poisonous spores into her life and her mind and never let her free. It was clearly already interrupting her ability to work. She didn't feel confident that the horrible ache of guilt at leaving her family's words unresolved would simply fade away with each departing chug of the ferry.

No, Simone knew she could not have herself, her mind, or her life back until she resolved this. Until she dug into this mystery, until she got to the root of it. Simone told herself she would find a new way to crack into the mystery for her own well-being. But she knew, deep down, that she needed to do it, wanted to do it, for the mother and grandmother who'd had their worlds robbed from them.

Fifty
Simone

January 14, 1998

Juniper Island, Isles of Shoals, New Hampshire

Simone and Ezra should have had the lighthouse all packed and scraped clean like an old wound. They should have been preparing to catch the ferry back to the mainland. Instead, they sat in the dim light of the library as a morning storm raged outside, battering the thin structure.

Simone sat at the desk, the wood beneath it invisible beneath the spread of files covering the surface. She rooted through them as she had for hours, any documentation at all on the Cole women.

Ezra, sitting cross-legged on the floor in a sweatshirt, went through the stack of folders by his side one by one, every kind of document on record for the 1960s. Births, deaths, marriages, illnesses, home renovations, standardized tests regulated from the mainland, every visitor that passed through on the ferry, every islander that took a day trip to the mainland. Julia was in the far corner of the library, her animated voice ringing back to them as she helped a young, pigtailed girl find a new chapter book. Her own stack of files, similar to Ezra's but credited for the entirety of the 1950s, also sat, teetering, on the floor.

They had been at it for days. They couldn't think of another way to come at the mystery, to unravel the meaning beneath the Cole women's suicide notes or what the threatening line could be referencing. So they had done all they could with what they had at their disposal, which was, clearly, far too many mundane files. But the only path forward they had was to go through *everything*. And it certainly seemed to be everything.

Simone jotted down a note about her grandmother's birth back in the thirties, her sheet of notes scribbled with dates and events that seemed to add up to not much at all.

Julia and the girl made their way to the front of the library, where Julia stamped a stack of books for the girl while she stared at Simone with the wide-eyed awe of children. Simone smiled awkwardly, feeling like a celebrity garnering attention for some horrible scandal. The child, seeming more frightened by Simone when she smiled, grabbed her books and dashed out the door.

Simone sighed. Julia returned to her stack of files. After another fruitless hour, Simone sighed again, the harsh sound grabbing the attention of Ezra and Julia both. Ezra, seeing his wife's budding frustration, suggested they pause, share their notes with each other, recap anything they might have found. They each shared their—brief—jotted notes in turn, and somehow Simone felt worse than she had before. They had nothing. Less than nothing; they had hope and not a single lead. And Simone's supply of the former was dwindling.

Simone pulled out the two notes, setting them in the center of the crowded desk. They grabbed the attention of all three as if there were a spotlight on them. Julia and Ezra kneeled, all reading the notes one more time as Simone sounded out the words aloud. As if, somehow, this time, they would find a clue waiting within.

Simone had just finished reading Mabel's note when a loud gasp made all three of them nearly jump out of their skin. Ezra scrambled backward, knocking over a stack of documents from the early 1940s. Julia froze. Simone pushed to her feet, spun to find their intruder.

Not an intruder after all; they were in *her* space. Miss Evelyn stood before the closed door. It was the first time Simone had seen the older librarian since she'd returned to Juniper. But a decade of aging hadn't changed Evelyn Fuller much. Julia's grandmother was as fashionable as always, wearing the skirts and sweaters of the 1950s, softened and paled to accommodate the passing of time and trends as well as her age. Her gold hair was woven into a bun at the nape of her neck, some white strands threaded through like the first signs of winter.

Miss Evelyn had always been odd around Simone. Simone had never thought much of it; everyone here was odd around her. And at least Miss Evelyn was never cruel, had always welcomed and guided Simone in her inherited work at the library, though they never really spoke much. Even as a child Simone had been aware of the way the older librarian seemed nervous around her, had trouble looking her in the eye. Evelyn had supported Simone in the safe haven of the library in a removed sort of way. Simone had always assumed that even that tempered kindness was purely due to Simone's closeness to Julia, or even her and Evelyn's shared love of books.

But the look Miss Evelyn gave now was not kind or removed or measured. It was outright shocked. The older woman stood frozen in the doorway as if Simone's gaze were that of Medusa. But her narrow chest rose with quick, staccato breaths.

"What is that?" she finally said, the syllables coming out ground through a clenched jaw and a frozen tongue.

Simone and Julia locked eyes, silent questions flying. Simone's gaze screamed hesitation. Julia's screamed assuredness. Breaking the silence of their exchange, Julia nodded, said in a whisper to Simone, "Gramma Lyn was alive back then. Maybe she knows what the threat is about. Maybe she knows of some odd death or knew Mabel."

At the sound of Mabel's name, Evelyn let out a soft sound somewhere between a gasp and a whimper.

Simone, baffled, still just on the edge of giving up, nodded. What difference did it make who knew now? There was no further to travel down their dead end without a new perspective.

Julia carefully picked up the decades-old receipt. She read the threat aloud and then Mabel's note, explaining anything they knew to her grandmother, which was, admittedly, not much. As Julia read Mabel's words, Evelyn's eyes fell closed. Her features pinched together in pain.

Simone could feel Ezra's confused gaze on the side of her face, but she could not look away from Evelyn. Could not stop looking for clues in her furrowed brows, her tucked chin, the single tear that slipped down her cheek, quivering on her jaw before it fell, a bloom on the shoulder of her sweater.

Julia didn't read Rebecca's letter—yet—clearly also seeing some sort of answers in her grandmother's sudden show of emotion, the drastic shift in her expression. Simone had never seen the older woman look so attainable, so human, so decidedly broken.

"Did you know my grandmother?" Simone whispered, afraid to speak too loudly and break the spell.

Evelyn took a deep breath. Opened her eyes. Looked at Simone. She nodded. "I did, yes. I . . ." Her voice was breathy. She swallowed. "Yes."

Julia had walked over to her grandmother, laid a comforting arm around her shoulders, which were shaking slightly. It burned through Simone to watch that experience, one that she would never have, in large part because of the notes they'd just read aloud.

"Do you know what she might have done? Why someone threatened to expose her for . . . killing someone? And why she seemed to confess to it herself?"

Evelyn swallowed heavily. She nodded again.

Simone's heart took off in a gallop. The older woman shrugged out of Julia's hold. She composed herself in silence, swallowing the lump in her throat, straightening her already pristine sweater. She seemed to be measuring within herself how much to say before her shoulders sagged. Before she decided it was time to finally tell the truth, all of it. She spoke to Simone, blue eyes locking on brown. Hearts thudding in tandem.

"I knew your grandmother. I loved her. I loved Mabel Cole since the first day I found her in this dilapidated cottage." Evelyn's chest deflated, as if she could breathe easier now that a confession that had lived lodged in her breast, silently, for decades, was finally free.

She continued on. "And I've loved her every day of my life since. I loved Mabel the day she killed my husband to save my life. And I loved her when I abandoned her too."

Face heavy with nostalgia and heartbreak, Evelyn sat gracefully in the open chair behind the library desk. And then, for the first time ever, Evelyn Fuller told them everything.

Fifty-One
Simone

January 16, 1998

Juniper Island, Isles of Shoals, New Hampshire

A wooden ladder clattered down from the ceiling, landing on the carpeted hallway with a muffled thud. Ezra wiped the dust off on his pant leg, leaving a faint trail of light gray across the black.

"Thank you, dear." Evelyn placed a gentle, grateful hand on his shoulder. "Sorry about the dust. I'm afraid it'll probably be even worse up there. It's been a decade or two since I've ventured up into the attic."

"No worries," Simone answered quickly. She tried not to be too obvious as she looked around herself, reining in her wide-eyed gaze that wanted to drink in every corner of the house where Julia had grown up, where she and Evelyn and before that Dean and Richie had lived. It wasn't just that that made Simone want to absorb every detail. It was that this was the first time she had ever been in someone else's home on Juniper. Never, not once, had she been invited to cross someone else's threshold. It was a wonder. It was a wonder that it had taken nearly thirty years. "Thank you so much for doing this, Miss Evelyn. Really."

The older woman climbed up the ladder to the attic first, the three younger people reaching out useless hands should she need them. But Miss Evelyn got up the ladder quickly and disappeared into the shadows, tutting at their offers for assistance. Julia went up next, then Simone, followed by Ezra last. The four of them stood shoulder to shoulder, surveying the crowded landscape of the attic. The ceiling was slanted on both sides, making both Ezra and Julia crouch, as they were inches taller than the others.

Miss Evelyn led them on a weaving path toward a stack of boxes with years scribbled on the side in a thick, black masculine hand that looked vaguely familiar to Simone. Ezra hauled the boxes to the ground, laying them out in chronological order.

"My memory isn't quite what it used to be," Miss Evelyn said, leaning over a box marked *1952*. "But I'm hopeful if we look through all my journals, we might find some clue I missed. I wrote—I still do, really—every detail of my life. Maybe we'll find someone who was always hanging around, who was lingering about when Mabel and I spoke, who might have seen us push Dean or me sending out his boat. Something."

Simone could not deny how generous it was that Miss Evelyn was letting them read through her private words. If Simone had had any doubt, it made it clear the woman really cared for her grandmother, that Miss Evelyn was willing to crack open her past and privacy to help Mabel, even in death.

They knew now the murder Mabel had admitted to in her letter, after a stranger had threatened to expose her for it. But still they did not know who had sent Mabel that threatening note or how they knew what she'd done. Or why, when Rebecca found the notes decades later, she somehow felt responsible. Was it just that her mother thought that taking her own life would keep Rebecca safe? Or was there more to it? For all the answers she could provide, Miss Evelyn had no guesses at all as to who could have sent the letter.

She had staged Dean's boat lost at sea, then abandoned Mabel because she thought it was the only way to keep her lover safe, to keep from drawing the town's attention. As far as Miss Evelyn knew, not a soul beyond her and Mabel knew how Dean Fuller was really given to the sea. And Miss Evelyn assured them she hadn't sent the letter herself. She had no reason to want the woman she loved dead or departed, even if she had spent painful decades loving her across the sea and soil of Juniper in harrowing silence. In every word Miss Evelyn spoke, Simone heard the heartbreak and the love and the grief, and she believed her.

All the more so because of what Miss Evelyn was giving them now.

The boxes were stuffed to the brim with perfectly matching brown leather journals, each spine softened and cracked with use and love. They started with the box marked 1951—when Miss Evelyn had met Mabel properly—and the last was labeled 1971, the year Mabel had received the note and stepped into the sea as a result.

"I rearranged the house a bit in '71, as a matter of fact," Miss Evelyn said, crouching toward the last box. "All the journals before the summer of '71 are up here in storage. I don't think we'll need any from later, though?"

Simone shook her head, settling herself down toward the other end of the lineup, by 1951. "I think these are the important years. Thank you, Miss Evelyn. Truly."

"Oh, enough of that." Evelyn waved Simone's gratitude away lightly, as if Simone had ever received gratitude from anyone on Juniper. "I'd do anything for my May."

Miss Evelyn said it softly, with awe and wonder in her voice. As if she was amazed that she could finally say the words aloud, for the first time in decades. Maybe for the first time ever.

There was no doubt that the task before them was daunting. Miss Evelyn was a detailed journalist indeed, a double-edged sword for them. With light coming from an old Tiffany lamp, each of them settled before a different decade's stack, Simone on the first half of the 1950s, Ezra on the second, Julia on the early 1960s, and Miss Evelyn handling the remainder.

Sitting cross-legged on the rough wooden floor—hoping she didn't get a splinter—Simone reached in and plucked out the journal Miss Evelyn said she should start with: March 1951. The month she first truly met Mabel.

Time seemed to stand still as Simone read Evelyn's words. Every bit of longing in the woman's voice now was there too, growing from a bud of interest to a friendship of trust, to comfort, to love. Simone read about Mabel and Evelyn fixing up the library from an old fishing shack, about her own grandfather—her grandfather!—there helping them. About how Evelyn felt envious of the man but convinced herself it was nothing. Of Evelyn helping Mabel realize she was pregnant and vowing to herself that she would do anything to help the other woman, thinking that sometimes it was a blessing to raise a baby without a man in the picture. Almost wishing, guiltily, that that was her own case. Simone read about Evelyn's heart pounding as they slow danced in the kitchen of the lighthouse, of how she felt more at home in the old structure than she did at her own house. How their first kiss changed Evelyn's life, how she would always divide her existence into *before* and *after*. About how Evelyn's world seemed brighter seeing her little boy and Mabel's little girl at the kitchen table together, how right it felt to be like a family.

But in those pages, too, there were mentions of Dean. Of whiskey and beer and bruises. Of Evelyn shielding her child with her own body. Of purple finger marks wrapping around a wrist, making her wear sweaters in the summer. About black eyes that made her miss church and town meetings. Miss Evelyn thinking this was simply how it was, until she met Mabel—really met her—and saw that what she endured in her own house was not love or order. It was abuse, plain and simple.

Dean Fuller haunted these pages like a ghost lingering in the margins, but this was, truly, the story of Mabel Cole.

The love that Miss Evelyn had spoken with the other day was there in her journals tenfold. Mabel and Evelyn's entire love story stretched out before Simone's eyes, and a love story it certainly was. With each word, looking at Mabel through Evelyn's adoring eyes, Simone felt she got to know her grandmother better. She would forever be grateful for that.

Simone nearly forgot what they were there to do until Julia's voice broke through her reading. "Wait, what?"

Simone looked up, saw Julia urgently looking through her stack of journals. Counting, checking, double-checking. "What is it?" Simone asked.

Both Ezra and Miss Evelyn paused to watch Julia's frantic movements.

"Dear?" Miss Evelyn prompted when Julia kept checking through the stack. "What's wrong, Juju?"

"There's a journal missing," Julia answered, holding up two journals, one in each hand. "September 1960." She lifted her left hand. "November 1960." She raised the journal in her right hand.

The three others held their breaths for a long moment. Everyone in the room knew what happened in October 1960, arguably the most important journal for their quest. The month that Mabel Cole pushed Dean Fuller to his death.

"Where's October?" Julia asked the question they were all wondering. "The journal from when Dean was killed is missing."

There was a small gasp. Simone realized it was her own. Simone, Ezra, and Miss Evelyn took turns meticulously counting through the journals from 1960. They searched all the other boxes to see if it had been misplaced. Miss Evelyn and Ezra went downstairs, checked the entire house, every bookshelf and desk drawer.

It was nowhere to be found. Someone had taken the journal where Miss Evelyn had written, explicitly, about how her abusive husband had died at the hands of Mabel Cole. Simone's skin broke out in ripples of goose bumps. It wasn't a far leap to say that whoever had that journal was probably also the one who had sent Mabel the threatening note a decade later, having gained the knowledge of what really happened right there in that journal. But why?

Miss Evelyn stood in the center of the attic, arms wrapped around her middle, face cracked with worry. She looked at all the labeled boxes. Simone watched as her dark eyebrows popped up on her forehead, then pulled together as the older woman went through memories in her mind, putting information together, dissecting it, hoping for a different answer but landing on only one.

"My God," Evelyn finally breathed. She looked up, her eyes finding Simone's immediately. "I know who sent the note to Mabel."

Fifty-Two
Simone

January 16, 1998
Juniper Island, Isles of Shoals, New Hampshire

"It was him." Miss Evelyn spoke so softly the others could hardly hear her. "I wouldn't, but . . . it can't be, I would have . . . it's him."

The drafty attic seemed to have dropped in temperature. Simone's body trembled. All three of them stood in a line before Miss Evelyn, frozen and alert, like schoolchildren waiting to hear a teacher's proclamation. Ezra was shocked, dark eyes and brows wide and lifted, hands hanging uselessly by his sides. Julia was baffled, arms crossed, mouth pinched. And Simone stood with dread. She could see in Miss Evelyn's fracturing face that solving this mystery was going to crack them all open further. Simone was afraid what the cracks would let in.

"Gramma Lyn?" It was Julia who was finally brave enough to speak. "Who is it?"

"I'm so sorry, dear," Miss Evelyn said to Simone, eyes filled with hardened sorrow. "I think it was Cal. It has to be."

Simone blinked. Ezra looked at her, baffled, the name not ringing a bell for him. And it wouldn't. Simone had never mentioned the man, couldn't remember ever sharing two words with him. He'd never visited her mother at the lighthouse; his wife never snuck in for Rebecca's cures. Why in the world would Simone be sad it was Cal more than anyone else on Juniper? It was surprising, maybe, the man being so far down on her radar, but not any sadder than if Miss Evelyn had said any other name.

"Cal Bradbury?" Simone asked, certain she was missing something. "Your nephew?"

Miss Evelyn nodded. "When I said I packed up all the journals and moved them up here in '71? It was Cal that helped me. I couldn't lift it all myself."

Evelyn looked to the boxes. Three heads turned toward the scribbled dates on their sides, and three minds, seeing with fresh clues, immediately saw how the handwriting was a dead match for the threatening note.

I know you killed him
August–December 1971

There were the same deep-bellied *u*'s, top-heavy *e*'s tilting to the left, the same tall, leaning strokes making *l*'s and *t*'s.

"He could've read one of the journals, found out what happened to Dean." Miss Evelyn shrugged, but her eyes were far away, haunted. "And a few months later written that note to Mabel."

"Why would he want to threaten Mabel?" Ezra asked. He looked around like maybe he was the only one missing information, not caught up on enough town lore. But Simone and Julia were both equally stumped.

Simone held her breath as Miss Evelyn looked at her again.

"I'm so sorry, honey." And Evelyn looked it. But it didn't soften the blow of her words. "I think it's because Cal's your dad."

Simone's stomach didn't fall out from under her, bowling her over in shock. But it did clench with horrible affirmation; she was surprised, sure, but she had been waiting her whole life for the other shoe to drop. Simone had asked plenty, but her mother had never once let word slip about Simone's father. And Lord knew the kids at school teased her enough about it; said her mom fucked a fish, some traveler, another Jew on the mainland. Her father could have been anyone. Simone supposed that also included Cal Bradbury.

"Around the summer and autumn of '71, Cal was seeing your mom. Seeing Rebecca." Miss Evelyn's eyes were pinched at the corners, the lined skin there showcasing her heartache as her mind put it all together, as her mouth shared unpleasant truths. "It was hushed, but I noticed. I've suspected maybe Cal was your dad, but everyone on the island insisted it was some visitor. Rebecca briefly went to the mainland for a few months before you were born. Did you know?"

Simone shook her head. She hadn't known. Somehow this, more than the potential truth of her lineage, was shocking. Her mother had feared leaving Juniper so much, refused it so much, that Simone assumed she had never dared. Now Simone wondered instead what had happened out there to bring her mother back.

"Well, she did. Was gone for months, then one day was back, screaming from the lighthouse all that night, then there you were. Folks said she had gone out there to reunite with him, your father, and returned when her lover scorned her. And Rebecca never said a word to the town on the matter. But Cal was over often that summer, helping me out with the house. I spotted him more than once headed out to the lighthouse at night, saw the way Rebecca looked at him. I've suspected for a while. I'm sorry, dear."

"It's okay. My mom never said a word on it," Simone answered. Miss Evelyn had no reason to apologize; the islanders should apologize for their gossip and cruel words. And it seemed, maybe, that Cal Bradbury should apologize for abandoning the woman he got pregnant. "Why would he . . . when . . . ? I was born in May. She probably found out about me around October."

The pieces clicked for Simone alongside Evelyn.

Evelyn nodded. "She likely told him around then. I'd guess Cal was desperate for it not to come out and ruin his reputation, being mixed up with a Cole woman."

Simone's chest ached. But Ezra spoke up first, defensive. "Is it really so bad in this place to love a Cole woman?"

Simone could almost smile to hear the defiance in his voice. Unfortunately, the answer on Juniper was yes.

Miss Evelyn seemed embarrassed, but she nodded. She, too, had loved a Cole woman, but unlike Ezra, she had hidden it. "They'd all say so. And not just that. Cal was already engaged to Barbara around that time, but it was still quiet, if I remember correctly. Their daddies set it all up. Cal was supposed to inherit his father's fishing and lobster business."

Julia and Simone nodded. Cal did, in fact, own that business now. It kept him the most prosperous and powerful man on Juniper.

"If the engagement fell through, if Cal was caught with another woman, especially a Cole he'd gotten pregnant . . . I imagine Jay would have taken away his inheritance." Evelyn paused for a moment in thought.

Julia connected the pieces. "So when Rebecca told him, he turned her down. But he must've been scared she'd say something publicly, eventually. Ruin it all for him. But then a golden nugget fell in his lap." Julia gestured toward the journals, the one that was missing, the one that had given Cal Bradbury ammunition to blackmail a Cole woman.

Evelyn nodded guiltily. “Seems so. I’d guess he saw a way to blackmail May, thinking she and Rebecca would leave Juniper.”

“But they didn’t.” Simone’s voice was deadpan, a foil to her raging thoughts, her rushing blood and pounding heart. “Instead, Mabel killed herself to protect my mom. Even so, Mom never said a word about Cal. Not to me or anyone.”

The rest of the phrase stood unsaid but heavy on the air. *Cal threatened the Cole women for nothing. Mabel killed herself for nothing.*

Simone swallowed an influx of spit, her jawline tingling. She did her best not to be sick in the cramped attic, but it was hard. Her father was the one who had caused generations of heartbreak.

Cal had done this. He might not have killed Mabel by his own hand, but he’d set off a chain of events that he’d never had to pay for, that he likely didn’t acknowledge even to himself. That he hid away from. Once again, as always, the angry, scared men of Juniper killed the Cole women rather than facing themselves and their actions. And men like him would never pay.

Once again, Miss Evelyn’s thoughts seemed to follow Simone’s, as if they, too, were kin. When they made eye contact, the anger and betrayal lancing across Evelyn’s face—the thoughts of how her own nephew had hurt the woman she loved—were replaced by resignation. She said softly, “Cal hasn’t paid for it. He won’t.”

Men like him never do.

“Well, he *should*,” Julia said, indignant.

“Yeah.” Ezra nodded. “We should report him. Blackmail, at least, is illegal.”

“Report him to who?” Julia asked.

“The police.”

Simone, Julia, and Evelyn huffed all as one. "Police don't come out here," Miss Evelyn answered. "The island handles its own business."

"And they'll never punish Cal," Simone said. She knew, maybe better than anyone, the hierarchy of Juniper. She knew, had always known, that she was at the bottom, looking up at folks like Cal. How sick to think that if he had been braver, more honorable, if he had cared for her mother at all, he could have reached down and brought the Cole women up too. But he didn't. He had saved his own skin instead and doomed and damned the Cole women along the way.

"Maybe not. But you should at least confront him!" Julia insisted.

Simone and Miss Evelyn made eye contact. They had both thought of this already, of course, and they both knew the biggest barrier. If Simone wanted to confront Cal, go public with what he had done, the truth of Dean Fuller's death would need to come out. Mabel Cole might be long dead, too far for hatred and village punishment to reach her. But Evelyn was not. She was alive, and she would be seen as guilty too. And they didn't have police out on Juniper because the people were keen to handle punishments themselves. Evelyn Fuller might be from royal Juniper lineage, but she was an old woman, not a man. For that reason, her safety and status could never quite be guaranteed.

Simone wished that she could answer, indignantly, proudly, that she would never risk exposing Evelyn. That revenge or retribution was not more important to her than Miss Evelyn's safety. But she couldn't. And Miss Evelyn saw that in her eyes.

The older woman looked at her with understanding. "Think on it for a few days. Whatever you need to do, I'll understand, Simone. Don't you worry about me."

But such a request was impossible. As Simone and Ezra walked home toward the lighthouse, her steps dragged heavier with the weight of responsibility, balancing revenge on one side and care for Miss Evelyn—for the person her grandmother loved—on the other.

Fifty-Three
Simone

January 19, 1998

Juniper Island, Isles of Shoals, New Hampshire

"Mrs. Rosenberg is always kvetching about something. I wouldn't let it get you, Ma. She'll be on to something new next week." Ezra spoke into the phone, comforting his mother over his parents' meddlesome downstairs neighbor. "Though that might be your problem too."

He laughed. Simone could hear his mother's answering chuckle down the line. Ezra and Simone had gone to dinner at his parents' on Monday nights for years. And now, states away, that tradition was still maintained through the phone line. That's how close the Hoffmans were.

Ezra was nestled into the large, overstuffed chair in the living room that nobody ever used. The one beside the old rotary phone, there purely to make phone calls more comfortable. But neither Simone nor her mother had ever really had any of those.

A pang of guilt ran right through her center, like a lightning strike. Like a puckered scar that still aches when you touch it, years after the accident.

The crackling laughter on the phone faded, replaced by mumbled words that Simone couldn't catch as she passed through the living room, sliding on the slippers resting in the corner. The ones that had been there longer than Simone had. Could they have belonged to Mabel?

Ezra's face turned more serious. He looked over at Simone, ignored the fake, shallow smile she gave him, knowing his mother had asked about her. "She's managing, yeah," he said quietly, somber. As if the volume of his voice needed to respect her complex grief, which was growing more complicated with each passing day.

Simone, feeling some desperate need to reassure others that she was, in fact, fine, leaned down over Ezra. Her face against his, she spoke into the receiver. "Hi, Miriam. Hi, David."

They gave suddenly enthusiastic greetings in return.

Ezra's family had welcomed Simone with open arms. She had felt like a Hoffman nearly from that very first day. But now, standing in her childhood home while they sat in their sun-drenched Upper West Side apartment, Simone felt othered. It wasn't that she wasn't welcome, just that she was different. And, in fact, she was. Simone knew she would always be a jutting addition to the house that was the Hoffman family. Meanwhile, her own family was immortalized in this lighthouse: singular, disconnected, standing alone and crumbling.

With a suddenly tight smile, Simone pulled away, stepping toward the doorway. She answered Ezra's pinched brows by pointing up. Evening was sinking in. She had to go light the beam, of course.

For once, while Simone climbed the creaking metal stairs toward the top of the lighthouse, she didn't try to turn off her mind. She let herself take in the rusted railings, worn in certain spots where generation after generation of Cole women had held them. She stepped out on top, her body going about lighting the beam with a second nature that had never quite transferred to any other activity.

Then she stepped through the little door, leaned against the railing and, for the first time in a decade, properly looked out at the Atlantic. The winter air battered her thin sweater, whipped her dark waves around her, bangs flapping in her peripheral vision. It made her eyes sting, ever so slightly, but it was right.

Simone stared out at the endless black sea. She tried to imagine her mother and grandmother down there in those depths, bones and hair and skin sunken to the bottom, feeding the ocean like all Cole women had. But, despite her gruesome thoughts, it didn't quite look fearful to Simone, even now, even with all she knew. The beam swept over her for a moment, highlighting her white knuckles against black metal, a sliver of roiling waves. Then it moved on, across the water, the long-reaching eyes of the Cole women.

New Hampshire, even the isles, its stretching fingers, boasted the motto *Live Free or Die*. But that didn't apply to the Cole women. It never had, had it? Cole women were never meant to be free. They were only meant to die.

She leaned her elbows on the worn metal railing, wondering if this was the spot that Dean Fuller had leaned against moments before he tipped over into nothing, into death by sea. There was something kind of sickly gratifying about an abusive man, the most powerful man on Juniper, dying like he was just another Cole woman.

This was the scene of a crime, she supposed. But it didn't feel that way. It felt like the glowing hold of the womb, the most comforting place Simone had ever had.

Simone wasn't one of those young queer people who thought queerness had only started with her generation. But she and Julia had always hidden, had always thought that no one on the island had been like them. But now, after hearing Miss Evelyn's story, Simone saw that wasn't true. For a period of her youth, Simone's own mother had basically been raised by a couple of women, and that was probably the most real love this lighthouse had ever seen. It made Simone feel closer to her grandmother, made her think that even with decades between them, they'd probably had pretty similar experiences here, in at least one way.

Simone felt silly for only a moment as she opened her mouth and spoke out at the sea, said a title she had never used before. "Grandma, Mom . . . what would you want me to do?"

She tried to feel them there in the water, but she could only feel herself, her own body. And, Simone supposed, that was them too. They lived on in her blood and bones and her heart too.

Simone had glimpsed Miss Evelyn's diaries, heard her words. She had seen the love pouring through her grandmother's final words to the world. She knew what her grandmother would want. And Simone thought that revenge and punishment wouldn't give anything to her mother either. It would not heal her wounds, the ones that had plagued her in her final moments.

Simone stood on the walkway, surrounded by night, and contemplated how to move forward. Not just for herself but for her grandmother, her mother, her family. If she confronted Cal—if she put Miss Evelyn in danger as a result—did her mother's and grandmother's memories really gain anything?

She wondered what it meant to avenge your ancestors. Was it punishing, an eye for an eye, or was it choosing the future, choosing your own peace in their image?

Simone contemplated it all with the help of the moon, the sea, the lighthouse.

Fifty-Four

Simone

January 21, 1998

Juniper Island, Isles of Shoals, New Hampshire

Simone looked at Ezra over the chipped lip of her mug. She took a sip, swishing the pulpy orange juice along her gums mindlessly before swallowing it down. She hadn't had the juice since she was a child; it was an old favorite, a comfort, tart and brightly colored and thick with pulp. Yet when she'd opened the fridge of the lighthouse upon arriving, there had been a fresh, unopened carton. Her mother had always, vocally, hated the drink. If not for herself, who was Rebecca purchasing it for?

Simone had wondered for days at the oddity. It was only that quiet morning that she'd thought maybe her mother had purchased it before bringing about her own death. That she'd thought Simone might come back to the lighthouse as a result. That her daughter would want the beverage, would open the fridge looking for it. Rebecca Cole had never known her adult daughter; she only knew how to comfort Simone as a child.

That morning, decisions and history weighing on her shoulders for days, the gesture wasn't lost on Simone.

But the drink brought only a flash of comfort. It didn't help her with any decision-making, that was for sure. Ezra and Simone, as a couple, were talkative with one another. Open. It was the norm for them to talk through every little decision, stressor, problem, with each other. But Simone had hardly said a word for three days, though it felt like she was dragging along one of the heaviest choices of her life. Confront Cal, maybe even expose his blackmail, his role as her absentee father . . . but in doing so, also expose Miss Evelyn's hand in a decades-old crime? Expose that a crime had occurred at all, the truth of how a violent man met his end? It would be her mother's revenge, maybe, for Cal to know that he had been caught. But was it really revenge that Simone needed? That Mabel and Rebecca needed? And, God, at the cost of Miss Evelyn?

Simone had no more answers than she'd had two days ago. Ezra sipped deeply from his mug of instant coffee, unconsciously flinching at the taste. Simone couldn't help but laugh, the sound echoing around the curved walls of the lighthouse. It was the first sign of life in days. Ezra smiled at her. She smiled back.

It was as if the sound broke a spell, as if it were the sound of a timer going off. Simone still had no idea what she would do, but she felt it was time to decide. Time to take Miss Evelyn off the eggshells of worry the other woman had surely been stepping around since they'd put together the identity of the blackmailer.

Ezra knew his wife well enough to know what her nod meant. Wordlessly, they both stood, tucking on boots, wrapping themselves in scarves and coats and thick, expensive knit hats. The winter wind whistled when they stepped outside. The white frothing waves beat as angrily as Simone's thoughts, as chaotic and powerful.

Whatever she did next, there was no coming back from. Whatever she did next was on behalf of three generations of Cole women.

Neither of them spoke as they walked toward the center of the island, the soil and pebbles crunching beneath their feet, frozen solid in the winter air. They crossed into the Main Street area, which was fairly empty, with folks tucked away inside their homes, safe from the violence of the season. Only one other person was outdoors. A tall figure, golden blond, stepped out of the Poole Market, so close they nearly collided directly with Simone. They both stumbled back.

Simone looked up into the surprised eyes of her father. In that moment Simone was certain that some higher, universal power existed, because here was Cal Bradbury smack in the center of her indecisive path. If she was ever going to confront him, now was the moment, on the empty, silent street.

Simone's answer only came to her when she looked at his blue eyes, flashing first with shock, then fear, then disinterest. Disinterest. And in that moment Simone knew what she would do. A man like Cal Bradbury would never be sorry; he had never had to be sorry a day in his life. He would always be golden, always be the one who could take with no consequences. Just like he had done to the Cole women, three generations of them.

But in that moment, Simone's body went as cold as the season and she knew that confronting him would not change that. It wasn't a matter of what it would do to Cal Bradbury. It was a matter of what such a confrontation and punishment would give to Simone Cole, to the memories of her mother and grandmother. And she realized that it would give her nothing.

She could see in Cal's eyes, silence heavy on the air, that he knew what he had done. That every time he looked at her, his daughter, he knew what he had done.

Let him live with his past. Let him punish himself, or decide that he was a good man, someone free from punishment. Simone realized, standing there, that she didn't care. She didn't need a thing from Cal Bradbury. She never had.

And she thought maybe the best gift she could give her mother and grandmother had nothing to do with punishing this man and everything to do with choosing her own survival. Maybe the best gift she could give them was to stand on the soil of Juniper Island, look into the eyes of this man, and walk away first.

So she did.

Simone twined her fingers through Ezra's and shouldered past Cal Bradbury as if he were little more than the hazy outline of a ghost in her path. And from that moment on, Simone decided that's all she would allow him to be. Not a father, not a lover, not a blackmailer. Not her past, her history. Not someone who defined the lives and legacies of the Cole women. Just a ghost, just a story that she didn't need to hear told anymore.

Her chest felt lighter than it ever had as she stepped up to Miss Evelyn's door. Simone didn't even bother to look over her shoulders, worrying who would see her arriving at the house. Let them stare, let them whisper. None of it could touch Simone Cole. She was safe in the embrace of her mother and grandmother, of the Cole women.

Miss Evelyn answered the door moments after the first knock. It was clear she had peeked out the window to see Simone's arrival. Her beautiful, aged face was lined with worry.

"Hi, dears." Even through the worry of the power Simone held over her, Miss Evelyn had nothing but smiles for her and Ezra. "Come in, come in."

Miss Evelyn closed the door behind them, locking out the rest of Juniper. Julia wasn't home; over at the library, Simone would guess. Miss Evelyn ushered them into the spacious kitchen, encouraging them to sit at the scratched table. She flitted around the kitchen confidently, making a pot of tea, laying a tray of homemade cookies out on a plate. She placed all the goodies on the table, poured cups, before sitting down herself. She looked Simone directly in the eye, unafraid. Trusting, Simone realized. Miss Evelyn didn't know what Simone would choose to do, but she trusted her either way.

Seeing that trust only cemented the silent decision Simone had already made within herself.

Miss Evelyn opened her mouth to ask about how they were faring at the lighthouse, but Simone cut her off, unable to keep her words in. "I'm not going to do anything."

Evelyn's rosebud mouth opened into a little O before she swallowed down her surprise and confusion. "Oh, well, I . . ."

"I have nothing to say to him. To Cal," Simone continued, each word building a wall, not around her but within her. Keeping her sturdy as the lighthouse. "He doesn't deserve a word from me."

Simone blushed but pushed on. Ezra rested a featherlight hand on her thigh under the table. "You are more important than revenge. More important to me, to my mother when she was a little girl, to my grandmother. You've cared for the Cole women for a long time, Miss Evelyn. Thank you. *That* is our history with the islanders."

Miss Evelyn did not try to cover the pink that rose on her cheeks, the moisture that bloomed along her lash line. She smiled at Simone and Simone smiled back. Evelyn reached a hand across the table, gripping Simone's.

Simone could tell that it wasn't tears of relief for her own safety. No, Miss Evelyn was moved by Simone's words, at hearing that she meant something to the Cole women.

"You are so like her," Evelyn said, voice soft. "Like Mabel. Stubborn and sure and loving, beneath it all."

An ache that had lived in Simone's chest since she was born on this soil began to lessen, a knot slowly loosening through the center of her. Evelyn stood from the table, stepping around to meet Simone, who stood in tandem. The two women embraced. And in that hug, they comforted each other, both women feeling closer to Mabel Cole.

Simone knew she had made the right decision. In letting go of revenge, she was gaining much more.

She had nothing to say to Cal. Men's anger and violence had always cursed the women of her line. Always brought their death. Simone realized the only way to break the curse was to break the power those men had over her family. Holding Evelyn and being held by her, Simone felt that controlling power splintering.

Fifty-Five
Simone

January 23, 1998

Juniper Island, Isles of Shoals, New Hampshire

Simone had never seen so many people in the lighthouse at once. Ezra was back in the living room, packing up and organizing in there, dusting off relics that hadn't been touched since they were pushed into drawers and shelves decades ago. Miss Evelyn was upstairs starting on sorting out the bedrooms. Julia and Simone were in the kitchen.

They weren't doing the task Simone had initially set out to complete when she'd first arrived weeks ago. They weren't sweeping everything into trash bags, clearing the lighthouse to its bones. No, they were organizing the overstuffed home, cataloging the history of the Cole women.

The house echoed with gentle sounds, footsteps and muffled laughter and pages flipping, four bodies breathing in one space. Simone wondered if this was what it was like to have a family, to have a home.

The windows were cracked open, letting out the decades of mustiness and damp accrued in the home. The winter wind sweeping in was biting, but it made Simone feel alive in the house, let the sound of the island nestle into the nooks and crannies of the lighthouse. Julia poured vinegar into the teapot, swirling it around, the sound in the container like the sucking, swishing waves out the window. It was old and had certainly seen better days, but it must have been around since the 1930s and, for once, Simone felt okay with keeping the past around a bit. At a safe distance, still. She was still herself, still carried her own past and its aches.

Most kitchens housed one junk drawer; in the Cole lighthouse, every kitchen drawer was a junk drawer. Simone was making her slow way clearing them out, one by one. She pulled out the highest drawer in the right corner. As she did, its contents rolled out from the back, the little orange pill bottle knocking against the front like it needed to announce its presence. It didn't, that was for sure. Simone could never, ever forget that those pills existed, were always nestled there, Rebecca's most prized possession. Simone had seen the orange flash of that bottle in her mother's palm as much as other children saw their fathers. That little innocuous pill bottle, with its little harmless-looking white pills, was the horror of Simone's upbringing, the thief that stole her mother.

So many times in her youth she had thought about flushing them, making her mother get proper medication that would actually help her brain, her moods. Medication that was meant to help, not those little bullets that shot through a life, through a family, smoothing the edges for a mother while ripping them ragged for a daughter. But she never had. She couldn't bear to hear her mother outright refuse, to choose those pills, that addiction, over her daughter.

Simone didn't realize she had frozen and held her breath until Julia's hand appeared on her shoulder. Simone jumped, immediately embarrassed by her reaction, at being caught off guard. But Julia was gentle. Julia had been there throughout that childhood, heard the anger in Simone's voice, knew why teenage Simone stayed late at the library so she wouldn't be at home, why Simone had fled the island and swore she'd never return. Julia knew all the history held in that bottle, five little pills still rattling in its bottom.

"Come on." Julia plucked up the pill bottle, taking one step left to lean over the worn kitchen sink. With a twist of the wrist and some elbow grit, she removed the top off the bottle. She flicked on the sink, the sound of water pounding into the basin echoing. Simple as could be, Julia turned the bottle upside down, letting the pills fall into the sink. They spun for a moment in the rush of water before falling down the drain, out of sight. Finally, finally, out of sight. As simple as that, they were gone.

Twenty years too late. Simone's face must have been a war of emotions, because Julia put a light hand on her elbow. "You know, I think I've got the kitchen under control." Her voice was gentle, consoling. "Why don't you go help Gramma Lyn up in the bedrooms?"

Simone was surprised, a bit embarrassed, to find that emotion clogged her throat, choking her words. She nodded silently, quickly making her way up the twisting staircase. Both bedroom doors were cracked open on the next floor up, but she could hear gentle thuds and humming from her own room.

"Hi," Simone said, nudging the door open. Miss Evelyn was in the corner, folding up and properly organizing the few sweaters in the dresser drawer from when Simone was twelve at the oldest. "Need help?"

Though it was clear that the barren room was little work for even one person, Miss Evelyn smiled widely. "Please, dear." She put a casual arm over Simone's shoulder as the younger woman stepped up to her side, gave Simone a gentle squeeze in greeting. It was such a simple, automatic motherly touch for Evelyn, but it meant everything to Simone. The sight of the pills down the drain had clogged her throat and that gentle squeeze made her eyes burn, emotion finally cresting in her, some long-barred dam cracking open.

Simone cleared her throat before she spoke. "You know, the real chaos is over here." She stepped to the far side of the room, opening the closet that she had never used in her life, for it was full to the brim with items belonging to Cole women long before her, items shoved out of sight after the women passed. Hidden but not lost.

"Oh my." Miss Evelyn stepped up beside her, shoulders lightly brushing. "Chaos indeed."

Simone gathered some empty boxes so they could sort through the items. The original plan was to sort into what to give and what to keep, but with each unfamiliar item, each with a different scent and clearly belonging to different woman, Simone found she couldn't give them away. Instead they assigned each box to a different Cole woman and did their best to guess who each item had once belonged to. They worked in companionable silence for a while, Simone feeling like she was slowly wading through the shoes and knits and books and jewelry of her past.

After a while of peaceful work, Miss Evelyn let out an alarmed chuckle. She plucked the balled-up piece of knitwear from Simone's hands, shaking it out so it took on the shape of a little cardigan, bright enough yellow that, even aged and dusty, it was a shock to look at.

"I made this little sweater," Evelyn said, eyes and voice wistful. "It must have been . . . Rebecca's third birthday, I think? I let Richie pick out the color, hence the . . ." Evelyn gestured at the eyesore in her hands. Both women laughed. Almost unconsciously, Evelyn held the little sweater to her chest for a moment. Remembering her son, remembering Rebecca, remembering Mabel most of all, Simone knew. Thinking back to a time when they were a little family unit, the four of them.

Simone knew her guess was right when Evelyn spoke again, softly. "After we . . . after Dean, I didn't stay away from Mabel because I was angry with her, or scared of her, or hated her." Evelyn's voice broke on the last phrase. It was impossible to think Evelyn had ever hated Mabel. The love was cascading from every word, from every line and look on her face. "At first, I didn't want to draw attention to us. Make us look suspicious. But then, well . . . Mabel had always been such a loving woman. Stubborn and difficult at times, sure, but so loving. So kind, even when the people on this damn island treated her and her line like dirt. I couldn't bear the thought that Mabel had done something because of *me* that would haunt her. I stayed away because of my own shame and guilt, not over Dean but over what I may have done to Mabel."

Simone barely breathed, watching Evelyn intently, silently. Her words were so passionate Simone could nearly feel the love on the air, palpable and sweet on her tongue. Bitter, too, tinged with loss.

Miss Evelyn took a deep breath, steadied her voice. "I would do anything, *anything*, to see her again. To speak to her. To take it all back, to be by her side every day of our lives. She was the love of my life, my May."

Simone sniffled. Swallowed the crackling emotion in her own throat. Said softly, "You were the love of her life too."

Simone had never known her grandmother, but she knew it was true. Because she could feel the love, the comfort, toward Evelyn in her own chest, and Simone knew it was an inheritance. Evelyn smiled a small smile, private. For herself and for her lost love, Mabel's memory in every stone and knit and book in this lighthouse. Evelyn handed the sweater to Simone, who couldn't help but bring it to her nose, breathe deeply. It smelled of salt and seaweed. Simone had only ever known a mother who feared the water, but from Evelyn's stories as they worked, Simone learned that the ocean was Rebecca's true home.

Evelyn cried soft tears when they pulled out a pair of worn work gloves, Mabel's from when they built the library. As they organized years of items, stories flowed from both women. Stories of Mabel's laugh and Simone's grandfather and a first kiss in the library and birthday parties for two little ones. Stories of Rebecca's adulthood, of ocean cures and Simone's love of books, her now realizing that she'd flipped through the same pages her grandmother had, and her great-grandmother too.

"You know," Evelyn said as the afternoon sank down through the windows. "Rebecca was the love of Mabel's life. She might have believed in that damned curse, let it rot her mind, but she always loved her daughter more than anything. Even when she knew, always, that she would be parted from the girl too soon. That kind of information . . . that's a hard thing to carry. A hard thing to believe. It can get to you. Twist you. But . . . she still loved her daughter. So much. I imagine, in her own way, you were the love of Rebecca's life too."

A week or two ago Simone would have laughed at the prospect. But now the words settled in her chest with an odd sense of certainty. She had never believed in the curse, but her mother sure had. And Evelyn was right . . . maybe it was that, that belief, that really haunted and stalked the Cole women. Simone could only imagine how free, how full of love and life, her family could have been without it.

As they sat together in that room, for once the lighthouse didn't feel like Rapunzel's tower, Simone's own prison. The space felt like having Mabel and Rebecca there in the room, given back to Simone at long last through Evelyn's words, through their closeness. For, after all, isn't it the ones who love us, in life and death, that keep us alive?

The lighthouse had always been a lonely place for Simone, even when her mother was within its walls. But now it meant everything to have three other people in this house with her, caring for her, helping her. Ezra, a part of Simone's new life and unflinching from her past one, seeing her and loving her in all of it. Julia and her forgiveness and patience and gentle understanding, giving Simone room to grow and still welcoming the new person who returned to the island. The love of Simone's life and her first love, both in this place together.

And Miss Evelyn, a silent shadow in Simone's childhood, allowing the library to be the girl's sanctuary, now bringing the sunlight to Simone's life, being there for three generations of Cole women in different ways, even if the older woman wished she had been there more and longer. Evelyn was here now, by Simone's side, mending old wounds, repenting for sins that only she held against herself. Simone thought maybe this was what family felt like.

Miss Evelyn looked down at the items in her hands, these remnants of the past, the only proof that Mabel Cole had lived and loved here. "When it's my time, I'll go to the sea. I want my bones to find hers again. I want to finally rest with my love."

Simone wondered if that was enough to make a woman like Miss Evelyn a Cole: a marriage of hearts, even if not on paper. She wondered if that was enough, if when she left and Juniper was allegedly left to the angry and dangerous sea in her absence, maybe Evelyn remaining would be enough to soothe them. Those aching, angry Coles in the sea. If love, even tinged with regret, was enough to change the tides. To change a curse.

Simone didn't believe in a curse—either of them—but she could feel, as real as an object held in her hand, the weight of Evelyn's love. And if anything could soothe a curse, it was that.

Fifty-Six
Simone

January 27, 1998

Juniper Island, Isles of Shoals, New Hampshire

The ferry was a speck on the horizon, growing larger as the waves pulled it toward the shores of Juniper Island. Simone felt a sense of déjà vu as she and Ezra stood on the rocky shore, their duffel bags and work totes sitting by their feet, waiting to be loaded up onto shoulders and fists, glided across the Atlantic to Portsmouth, tucked into their little car and driven back down 95 to New York. Julia stood on Simone's other side. Both of them looked out at the growing shape of the ferry, knowing time was ticking, waiting to say goodbye, not knowing the right way to form the words.

The moment was like a flashback to a few weeks ago, a flashback to a decade ago. Neither moment was a happy one in Simone's memory. But, she thought, resisting the urge to kick herself for hoping, this moment could be. This moment, at least, didn't feel weighed down.

Simone turned her back on the sea, turning to face Julia and Miss Evelyn, backlit by the rest of Juniper: the distance hoods of houses, the little peak of the library, the rough rocks and the sea that held her ancestors, and the shadow of the lighthouse over all of them. The tall, proud building didn't feel like a beast to Simone anymore. She felt safe in its presence. Its worn edges and weathered stones showed its history, showed that, no matter what, it would still be standing. It would endure. It would wait.

She hadn't emptied the lighthouse after all. When it came down to it, Simone found that she couldn't. She couldn't scrape the building clean, throw the history of the Coles in the trash, and forget that this place had ever touched her. Amazingly, Simone found that that wasn't what she wanted. She didn't suddenly love this island, didn't just embrace the pain of her past. But she found that maybe she could live alongside it, a scar that would heal and smooth over, that wouldn't hurt to the touch anymore. A memory that would live in her skin. All of the Cole women, from Goody Cole to Rebecca, had been misunderstood and mistreated and abandoned. But not by Simone. All of those women lived in her, her blood and bones. The seawater might be in Simone's blood, but she wasn't alone in her skin either. For once, that might just be a comfort.

Julia stepped up to hug Ezra first, the two squeezing each other tight, laughing over some inside joke they'd formed, an easy camaraderie. No competition, no bad blood, just understanding, meeting on the middle ground of having loved the same woman. Still laughing just a bit, Julia and Ezra parted. The woman turned to Simone. Her eyes turned serious.

Simone knew they were both remembering another goodbye in this very spot, remembering begging words whipped on the wind, salty kisses. Now, though, Simone and Julia were able to smile at each other. Able to hug and keep the past safe and alive there in their embrace. To hold each other close and let each other go. Julia was made to stay here and Simone was made to leave, and that was okay now.

Evelyn stepped up to Simone, pulling her in tight. The older woman smelled like lavender and roses and sea air. And only this close did Simone realize it was the scent, too, of the library, of Simone's childhood. Just like it had been the scent of her mother's early childhood, of her grandmother's moonlit nights. One of Evelyn's arms disappeared for a moment, reaching out to pull Julia toward them. The older woman held both Simone and Julia in her arms, keeping them in her embrace.

Simone stiffened, unused to this type of affection, of being touched by anyone but Ezra. If Miss Evelyn and Julia noticed, they didn't indicate it, giving Simone a beat to decide if she was comfortable. And after that first wave of uneasiness, Simone found she was. She found, actually, that it felt quite nice. She softened into Evelyn's embrace.

"My girls," Evelyn whispered against their hair, dark brown and strawberry blond together. And they all knew that when Evelyn said that, she didn't just mean Simone and Julia. She meant Rebecca, she meant Mabel too. Simone's eyes stung from more than the beating sea air. It felt like the briny air could suddenly reach a deeper part of her lungs, some part of her body that she had kept coiled for decades beginning to unravel piece by piece, letting some of the world in. Letting some of Juniper in.

"Come here. You too." Evelyn laughed, reaching out an arm toward Ezra, who stepped into the embrace with an awkward chuckle of his own.

"All right, all right," Simone said after a minute, breaking up the group's embrace. She looked over her shoulder. The ferry had made it to the edge of the island, lingering within the shallows. The captain of the empty vessel leaned a head out toward them, waving.

It was time to leave.

Simone looked back at Julia and Evelyn, standing as sturdy on the rocks of Juniper as people who would never leave. Simone lifted her bags into her arms. They might not have scraped the lighthouse clean so Simone could abandon it and her past behind, but they had sorted through it, discovered its old corners. And Simone, still surprising herself, was taking some of it back to the mainland with her. Her mother's handwritten book of her little witchy ways, her cures for beauty and self-care made from pieces of the island. The old, tattered paperback copy of *Rebecca* that had seen the Cole women through generations, two notes still tucked deep in its pages. And her grandfather's name, scribbled on a piece of paper in her luggage. Simone thought maybe she would try to find him, if he was still alive and in London. Maybe she would try to add some branches to the lonely line of her family tree.

That was all she was leaving with. Everything else would be here, cared for like the lighthouse, waiting for her when she returned. For the very first time, Simone thought that there would be something like love and family awaiting her on Juniper Island, if and when she chose to come back.

"We'll take good care of her for you," Evelyn said, nodding up at the large lighthouse.

Simone had been surprised to find she wasn't ready to let it go yet. But she wasn't willing to be like her foremothers, tie herself to that lighthouse forever. So she had left it with family. Evelyn and Julia would tend to it in her absence, just as they had tended to so many Cole women.

"For whenever you're ready to come back, for a visit or a stay." Evelyn smiled. Simone heard her words, but her body was still built on trauma. She couldn't help her eyes flicking out toward the main street, toward all the people who had long kept their shared island from feeling like Simone's too.

Her worry must have been clear on her face. Julia lifted up a middle finger toward the center of the island, saying, matter-of-factly, "Fuck 'em."

Simone and Ezra laughed. Even Evelyn let out a chuckle as she tutted at her granddaughter. "This is as much your home as it is any of theirs," Evelyn said, her soft face turned stern. "You can always come home. We'll keep the light on for you."

And Simone knew they would. That was what lighthouses were for, after all, to guide those at sea back home.

She knew that it was never a curse that would pull her back, some goddamned curse she had never believed in. It was the possibility of what would, finally, be waiting for her on Juniper. It was knowing that the light would always be there, swinging across the water, helping her find her way home.

Ezra and Simone loaded their things onto the ferry. They stood side by side as the boat rocked and rattled, until finally pushing off from the shore. The boat cut quickly through the Atlantic, headed toward the mainland. But Simone did not stand on the western side, watching the shore of Portsmouth grow larger as they approached. For the first time Simone kept her eyes open, watching the shrinking form of Juniper until it was swallowed by the waves of the sea.

[illegible] through, she thought, was that what lighthouses were meant to guide? Those who were lost here.

She [illegible] if it was [illegible] that would call her back, some gentle [illegible]. She had once believed in the possibility of that world. And yet now, standing on the landing, she was knowing that the light would always be there, swinging across the water, guiding her home, however [illegible].

Kora [illegible] golden [illegible] into the [illegible]. They [illegible] and [illegible] glinting off from the shore and back [illegible] headed toward the [illegible] but [illegible] the [illegible] side [illegible] grew larger as the [illegible] her eyes [illegible] form of [illegible] and [illegible] was swallowed by [illegible] the sea.

Epilogue
Simone

October 10, 1998

New York, New York

Midtown was abustle with the five o'clock foot traffic of suited corporate workers streaming out of skyscrapers, making their steady paths for the packed subways. Simone Cole was just another anonymous face in the crowd headed toward the Fiftieth Street station.

Autumn left the dense city air with a bite that made her nestle further into her light coat. Her mind was elsewhere, on the manuscript she'd left half finished on her desk, on catching the uptown E train, on the friends she and Ezra were meeting for dinner, and whether she actually liked these new boots she was wearing. Her mind was a million different places at once, all of them in New York City.

So she was caught off guard when she felt it.

Simone was about five hours' drive and a ferry trip from Juniper Island, but she would know the feel of the sea breeze on her face from anywhere on earth.

Steps fumbling, she breathed deeply. It wasn't the smell of trash and a million beings that hit her nostrils but the scent of salty air and brine and crushed juniper berries. Simone could see New York City around her, but her body, her soul maybe, was on Juniper.

She felt the air like she was standing on the rocks beneath the lighthouse, smelled the distinct sharp musk of the Atlantic coast. She felt the sharp pricks of sea air, tasted the squelching saltiness of seaweed on her tongue. The air dropped in temperature, pleasant, familiar, that languid pull between seasons on the Shoals. The rush of city traffic in her ears became the steady crash of waves against a rocky coast.

Simone was transported back to Juniper, like she'd never left. Like she never could.

And through those sounds of the island, the waves and the creak of the lighthouse walls and the gulls came another sound. A symphony of sound, soft at first but growing, swallowing the noises of the city.

Frozen there on the sidewalk on Forty-Ninth Street, Simone heard her mother. Rebecca Cole's voice was there, in her daughter's ears, in the city she never got to visit. And Rebecca was not alone. A dozen voices were layered along with hers. And somehow Simone knew who the women in her ears were. Her grandmother and her mother and hers and hers. A line of Cole women, down to Goody Cole at the beginning, all the women who had been swallowed by the sea, reaching all the way out to Simone.

There were no harsh words, no violent tones, no anger. Just a group of women, her women, telling Simone that they loved her and they would wait with her and be with her always. There was only those steady voices of a lineage of women wronged and lost to the sea, sounding at peace. Living on, in, and for Simone.

It wasn't a desperate, frantic, panicked demand to return to the island. It was a reminder of their presence within her. Maybe Miss Evelyn returning to the lighthouse again, being there to light the beam each night, was in fact enough for

Mabel and the other Coles in the sea to be at peace, to be assured that a Cole woman—in some capacity—was still there.

Simone wondered if maybe her mother, and all the mothers before her, were finally telling her that she could go far, she could see the world, and they trusted her to do so. That the Cole women in the Atlantic wanted their daughter to thrive, even if they couldn't see it.

Simone knew she was still standing on a sidewalk in New York City, parting disgruntled traffic around her. But in every other way, her body and mind and heart were back on Juniper. It was all around her, the isle in every sense of her body.

She knew that some version of Simone Cole would always be back in New Hampshire, living another life. And this Simone would be on the mainland, would go near and far and see the world. Everyone had to choose their path, and Simone thought that maybe this one she had chosen now was somewhere in the middle, the reckoning of the two. She gave herself space to grieve for what was and what would never be. A peaceful agreement.

Simone tipped her chin up, eyes closing. She let the phantom salt air kiss her face, heard the sounds of the Cole women and the sea call to her across the Atlantic. Juniper Island was finally calling Simone Cole home, and for once, it didn't hurt. For once, it didn't feel like a curse.

THE END

Author's Note

Like many born and raised on New Hampshire's Seacoast, the story of Goody Cole was a persistent staple of my childhood. We were raised hearing the tale of the witch who lived near our town centuries ago—the ghost stories of how her phantom strolls the shores, the truth that she was so feared and evil that, when she died naturally, a stake was driven through her heart, and it is still not known what happened to her body. It was only in adulthood that I became curious enough about Goody Cole's story to research the history behind the folklore, to see how she was never really a witch or a figure of myth; she was a mistreated and misremembered woman. By creating a story around her fictional lineage in this book, I hoped to help give some power and balance back to the story of Goody Cole.

Much like the themes of negatively represented female figures, misogyny, and ageism that I explored in my previous book, *The Last Witch in Edinburgh*, this story too looks at the way that women have historically been punished for independence and how, in some ways, we still are. Goody Cole, told as being an old, socially defiant woman, in many ways, hints to the figure of the Cailleach that I am so drawn to, and the larger social themes that both women's portrayal represents.

The Isles of Shoals were, to me, the perfect place to explore this story. Not only is Goody Cole truly rumored to have connections to the islands, having potentially been thrown into the sea off-shore after her death, but the isles, too, are a staple of coastal New Hampshire life. Between childhood trips to the isles, their constant, foggy presence beyond the shore, and the commerce that they bring to the area, the Isles of Shoals are as much a looming presence in the area as the story of Goody Cole. And the isles, too, have their fair share of dark folklore known to locals; everything from pirates and treasure to violent murders that left ghosts howling on the shores of White and Smuttynose. Though Juniper Island is a fictional isle, I wanted to set the story here and allow these atmospheric, richly folkloric islands to help tell this story.

Though I have lived outside of New Hampshire for many years, it is a place I still carry within me. While this story is a magical family saga, rife with tension and twists that chart the effects of a crime across decades, it is, at its heart, a love story to New Hampshire's Seacoast and its rich history and stories. It is a story about what it means to come home again, and, even more, how community makes a home.

Marielle Thompson
March 2025

Acknowledgments

Every author says it, but getting a book on the shelves takes a team. So, of course, I have many people to thank;

Jill Marr—I can't believe we're already on book three. I will always be grateful for your keen eye, endless patience, and encouragement for my stories.

Rebecca Nelson—I could not have asked for a better editor and creative partner on this book. You saw the heart of this story from day one, and I could not have brought forth the magic and emotion without your ideas and vision.

The team at Alcove; Dulce Botello, Mikaela Bender, Bethany Pullen, Megan Matti, Stephanie Manova, Matthew Martz, Lexi Baker, Julia Abbott, and Thaisheemarie Fantauzzi Pérez—it has been an absolute joy getting to work with all of you. I cannot state how much I appreciate all the work you have put into this book.

My fellow writers and friends, especially Natalie Kikić—who read a very early and messy draft of this book and provided such helpful feedback, encouragement, and enthusiasm.

Holly—my feline cowriter, who snored on my chest for most of writing this book. Obviously, you deserve the majority of credit for it.

My family—I am lucky to come from a family filled with so many strong, loving women (and the few wonderful boys among us). I love you all dearly. The women of my family that are with us, and Jeannette, Joy, and Betty, whose memories are everywhere in these pages.

My father—you may not be here to read my books, but I felt you on every page, as my characters and I both learned to love the heritage you gave me.

Juniper—My bubbeleh. I promised you I would put your name in a book, so I put it in this one almost three hundred times.

My in laws—your endless support and curiosity and love means more than you know. I could not have asked for a better family to join.

My friends, and especially, always, Claire and Danielle—thank you for still, three books in, being so excited for me and my stories. And for being a soundboard for all of my ideas before they've become anything coherent.

Haley, Darci, Kelly, and Morgan—no matter where I live New Hampshire always feels like home, and that is because you four always feel like home. (Also I added one "gale" just for you)

Readers—It is still unbelievable that there are people out there reading my words. Thank you for picking up my books, for talking about them, for reaching out and telling me what they meant to you. It means the world, *every single time.*

Beau—Again, and always. I promise that I'll write a happy love story one day. In the meantime, I'm glad I get to live one with you.